普通高等教育"十一五"国家级规划教材

美 国 文 学 简 史

（第四版）

A Survey of American Literature
(The 4th Edition)

常耀信　著

南开大學出版社

天　津

图书在版编目(CIP)数据

美国文学简史：英文 / 常耀信著. —4 版. —天津：南开大学出版社,2023.1

ISBN 978-7-310-06374-1

Ⅰ.①美… Ⅱ.①常… Ⅲ.①文学史－美国－英文 Ⅳ.①I712.09

中国版本图书馆 CIP 数据核字(2022)第 252268 号

美国文学简史(第四版)

MEIGUO WENXUE JIANSHI (DI-SI BAN)

南开大学出版社出版发行

出版人:陈　敬

地址:天津市南开区卫津路 94 号　　邮政编码:300071

营销部电话:(022)23508339　营销部传真:(022)23508542

https://nkup.nankai.edu.cn

河北文曲印刷有限公司印刷　全国各地新华书店经销

2023 年 1 月第 4 版　　2023 年 1 月第 1 次印刷

230×170 毫米　16 开本　32 印张　490 千字

定价:98.00 元

如遇图书印装质量问题,请与本社营销部联系调换,电话:(022)23508339

Preface to the 4th Edition

The 4th edition of *A Survey of American Literature* is offered here in response to the readers' requests. This offers a bird's-eye view of American literature from its beginning through the present. It is sketchy, but panoramic, and good for instructors and researchers to get an overview of the field of activity they are to deal with. Hopefully it will be more accessible in classroom teaching and research.

The new edition is not a mere abridgement of the previous one. It is, in many cases, a restructuring, a reshuffling, of its thematic and formal concerns. Although the new edition still follows the original 26-chapter structural scheme, there is involved a good deal of rewriting. In addition, subheadings are added to facilitate comprehension and make it easier to locate priorities.

The abridgement also involves the diction and syntax of the older book. It has removed some difficult words, structures, and modes of expression.

The original edition of the book is still indispensable for researchers such as some English majors, MAs and PhDs, and those who feel the acute need for more detailed information, as the shorter edition may not be quite adequate for them.

It is good to add here that, as with the passage of time, especially since the 1980s, new faces and new works have appeared in great numbers on the literary scene, the present edition has tried to offer a sketchy account of these developments for the benefit of the readers.

Good and wise prioritizing is strongly advised in reading and teaching the book. Time constraint is the guideline which decides whether we should cut off the following in our reading and teaching: (1) some chapters, or a part of them, or (2) some minor authors, or (3) some minor works. In this way focus would be best ensured.

It is good to note that the material deleted from the previous book is not lost; it is available in the "Link: Scanning Terminal Reading" (扫码终端阅读) part that the publisher has carefully provided.

Table of Contents

Chapter 1   Colonial America

The Settlement of North America

The settlement of the North American continent by the English began in the early part of the 17th century. The first settlers who came on board the Mayflower were some of them Puritans. They came to America out of various reasons. For one thing, the Stuarts back in England were so repressive that the Puritans found it hard to worship as they wished. Then the Puritans left home, partly in quest of an ideal of their own. These people were some of them serious, religious people, advocating religious principles. They were determined to find a place where they could worship the way they thought true Christians should.

When they arrived in North America and saw the vast expanse of wilderness that stretched miles around before them, they felt that God must have sent them there for a definite purpose and that, as God's chosen people, they were meant to reestablish a commonwealth based on the teachings of the *Bible*, restore the lost paradise, and build the wilderness into a new Garden of Eden. [1] So they became ruthless toward anyone that they thought might jeopardize their endeavor to build their "City of God on earth." They persecuted dissenting individuals such as Anne Hutchinson (1591-1643), and committed genocidal massacre of the native Indians[2]: In the two centuries that followed, the native American Indian population dropped significantly, and some Indian tribes became totally extinct.

The American Puritans

The American Puritans were said to be "doctrinaire opportunists." On the one hand, they were pious and religious. They accepted the doctrine of predestination, original sin and total depravity, and limited atonement (or the salvation of a selected few) through a special infusion of grace from God, all that John Calvin (1509-1564), the French theologian, had preached. This was the religious belief that they brought with them into the wilderness. There they meant to prove that they were God's chosen people enjoying His blessings on this earth as in heaven.

On the other hand, they were also practical people. In the grim struggle for survival that followed immediately after their arrival in America, the character of the people underwent a significant change. As they moved further and further westward from the eastern seaboard, they became more and more preoccupied with business and profits. The very severity of the frontier conditions taught the American Puritans to be tougher. It is good to add here that the word "frontier" means, in this context, the borderline between the settled areas and those yet to be settled.

Puritan Influence on American Literature

In the beginning, American literature (or Anglo-American literature, to be exact), was essentially a literary expression of the pious idealism of the American Puritan bequest. It is based on a myth, that is, the Biblical myth of the Garden of Eden. The Puritans dreamed of building a new Garden of Eden in America. They were fired with this sense of mission and felt optimistic. All this impacted the making of American literature. So Emerson saw the American as Adam himself reborn, standing simple and sincere before the world, Thoreau portrayed himself as an Adam in his Eden, Whitman felt rapturous at the sight of the Americans bustling with activity as the children of Adam restored to their lost paradise, and Henry James talked, especially early in his career, about the innocence and simplicity of his Americans as so many Newmans. The optimistic Puritan has exerted a great influence on American literature, especially the early part of it.

At this outburst of optimism, Chinese students of American literature should not be unduly surprised. Neither should they experience anything like amazement when they detect a mood of frustration or despair in the works of later periods. For, always at the latter end of weal stands woe. When the dream did not materialize, and when only a "Gilded Age" came instead of the anxiously expected Golden, what else can one feel? Thus in either way Anglo-American literature was from the outset conditioned by the Puritan heritage to which Anglo-American authors have been the most communicative heirs.

Nor is this all. The American Puritan's metaphorical mode of perception produced a distinctly American literary symbolism. To the pious Puritan, the physical world was nothing but a symbol of God, and the world was meaningful only by reason of "God's salient acts." Physical life was simultaneously spiritual; the world was one of multiple significance. If one cares to read the writings of the early settlers such as William Bradford (1590-1657) and Cotton Mather (1663-1728), it is impossible to overlook the very symbolizing process constantly at work in the Puritan minds. This process became, in time, part of the intellectual tradition in which Anglo-American authors such as Jonathan Edwards (1703-1758), Emerson, Hawthorne, Melville, Howells, and many others have been brought up along with their people. For them symbolism has become a common technique.

In the 20th century, the American Puritan tradition was under attack. The Puritans were often abhorred for their excessively simple taste. The fact of the matter may be somewhat different. The Puritans might have lived as other people did, drinking and dressing themselves "in all the hues of the rainbow."[3] History records that they built schools, encouraged learning, and loved reading, making New England and the east seaboard centers of culture comparable somehow to England and Europe. With regard to their writing, the style is fresh, simple and direct; the rhetoric is plain and honest, not without a touch of nobility often traceable to the direct influence of the *Bible*. All this has left a deep imprint on American writing.

The Literary Scene in Colonial America

American literature grew out of humble origins. Diaries, histories, journals, letters, commonplace books, travel books, sermons, in short, personal literature in its various forms, took up a major portion of the literature of the early colonial period. In content these early writings served either God or colonial expansion or both. In form, English literary traditions were faithfully imitated and transplanted. Anne Bradstreet (1612-1672) and Edward Taylor (1642-1729) were two notable authors then.

Now Anne Bradstreet was a Puritan poet who wrote "ponderous verses of interminable, inter-locking poems" on the four elements, the constitutions and ages of man, the seasons of the year, and the chief empires of the ancient world. Her poems made such a stir in England that she became known as the "Tenth Muse" who appeared in America. Today most of her works have fallen into the obscurity, but her gentle "Contemplations" is still anthologized. Some of her shorter and more personal poems such as "To My Dear and Loving Husband" and "In Reference to Her Children" are interesting to read as well.

Edward Taylor was a meditative poet. In his elaborate metaphors he was reminiscent of poets like Richard Crashaw (1613?-1649), and George Herbert (1593-1633). In his splendid, exotic images, Taylor came nearest to the English baroque poets. He was a Puritan poet, concerned about how his images speak for God.

Colonial America did not always write the way Anne Bradstreet and Edward Taylor wrote. Some people wrote for civil and religious freedom, and some others wrote for America shaking off the fetters of the savage and rapacious British colonial rule. These authors called for independence and rang the knell for the colonial era. Names that deserve special mention include Thomas Paine (1737-1809), Philip Freneau (1752-1832), and Charles Brockden Brown (1771-1810).

The life of Thomas Paine was one of continual, unswerving fight for the rights of man. He wrote a number of works that helped to spur and inspire two greatest revolutions that his age witnessed: the American Independence war and the French Revolution. His most famous works are *Common Sense* that attacked British monarchy and inspired North American colonies to rise and fight. He became a major influence in the American Revolution. Later Paine participated in the French Revolution, and wrote *The Rights of Man* and *The Age of Reason*, spreading the ideals of the French Revolution among the people.

Philip Freneau was important in American literary history in a number of ways. Apart from the fact that he used his poetic talents in the service of a nation struggling for independence, writing verses for the righteous cause of his people and exposing British colonial savageries, he was noted for voicing the spirit of dawning nationalism in American literature. Some of his most famous works, with their lyric quality, their sensuous imagery, their fresh perception of nature, and their theme of "noble savagery," are distinctly American. Poems such as "The Wild Honey Suckle" and "The Indian Burying Ground" have been frequently anthologized.

Mention should be made of Charles Brockden Brown and other eminent 18th-century novelists.[4] These included Francis Hopkinson (1737-1791) with his *A Pretty Story* (1774), William Hill Brown with his *The Power of Sympathy; or The Triumph of Nature* (1789), Hugh Henry Brackenridge (1748-1816) with his *Modern Chivalry* (1792-1815), Gilbert Imlay (1754-1828) with his *The Emigrants* (1793), and Mrs. Susanna Haswell Rowson (1762-1824) and her *Charlotte Temple* (1791). These were in a way all writers of transition, who did the spadework for later comers. They wrote about American subjects such as the westward movement and the American Indians and laid the solid foundation for the American novel. But they were imitative, modeling their writings on British authors. This was to affect their permanence in history.

Charles Brockden Brown was the most prominent among these writers. His first novel, *Wieland; or, The Transformation: An American Tale* (1798) has been regarded as the first American novel. Brown wrote four major novels—*Edgar Huntly* (1799), *Ormond* (1799), *Arthur Mervyn* (1800), as well as *Wieland*. Basically, he was an imitator. The Gothic features of his works are a good illustration. But he did a few things for which he has been remembered. One of these was his awareness that his inspiration was rooted in his own land. Another thing of historic significance was his description of his characters' inner world. He influenced later American writing in no small way.

The period of some two centuries from the arrival of the Mayflower through the end of the eighteenth century was, from a literary point of view, one in which the national experience of the American settlers building the wilderness into a habitable place groped and struggled for literary expression. It represents a process in which colonial literature strove for a higher degree of excellence and evolved slowly but steadily toward an indigenous American literature. If the eighteenth-century literary scene looked still barren and bleak, there appeared at least certain figures who exercised something like a seminal influence on the subsequent development of American literature.

Chapter 2 Edwards • Franklin • Crevecoeur

In his *America's Coming of Age* (1915), Van Wyck Brooks attempted a general survey of eighteenth-century America and the American character:

> For three generations the prevailing American character was compact in one type, the man of action who was also the man of God. Not until the eighteenth century did the rift appear …. It appeared in the two philosophers, Jonathan Edwards and Benjamin Franklin, who share the eighteenth century between them …. Strange that at the very outset two men should have arisen so aptly side by side and fixed the poles of our national life! For no one has ever more fully and typically than Jonathan Edwards displayed the infinite inflexibility of the upper levels of the American mind, nor any one more typically than Franklin the infinite flexibility of its lower levels.[1]

This is a good analysis of American Puritanism as a cultural heritage as well. Brooks is trying to say here that American Puritanism is a two-faceted tradition of religious idealism and levelheaded common sense. Jonathan Edwards represents the former aspect, and Franklin the latter. The one was as a good Puritan as the other.

Eighteenth-century American thinking was dominated, by and large, by two basic patterns of thought. Toward the latter part of the 17th century, a completely new view of the universe came into being. With Newton's laws of motion and universal gravitation, the universe became, in the minds of thinking people, something mechanical, like a clock, subject to certain physical and mechanical laws rather than to the close supervision of God. This gave rise to a whole set of new ideas and philosophies, predominant among which was deism. The deists hold that God is indeed the creator of the universe, "the maker of the clock," but He has left it to operate according to natural law. Thus the best way to worship God is to study his handiwork, namely, the natural world and the human world, and to do good things to mankind. Human reason is extolled. The idea of order became the watchword of the day.

All these ideas were very much in the air in America then, and no one represented them better than Benjamin Franklin. With Franklin as its spokesman, eighteen-century America experienced an age of enlightenment, reason, and order like England and Europe.

Constantly in collision with these ideas were the persistent Calvinist beliefs and tenets that man was, since the Fall, basically evil and enslaved by his sense of sin, and that God would in His mercy work for man's salvation, and man should worship the Almighty and hope. This Calvinist position was very much alive, and Jonathan Edwards was probably the last great voice to reassert it.

Jonathan Edwards

Edwards was, probably, at once the first modern American and the country's last medieval man. His writings like "Personal Narrative" and his sermons like "Sinners in the Hands of an Angry God" all try to convince his flock of the almightiness of God. His "Personal Narrative" is actually his spiritual autobiography:

> I felt an ardency of soul to be … emptied and annihilated; to lie in the dust, and to be full of Christ alone; to love him with a holy and pure love; to trust in him; to live upon him; to serve and follow him; and to be perfectly sanctified and made pure, with a divine and heavenly purity.[2]

Edwards believes in the regeneration of man. To see Edwards in proper historical perspective, it is good to quote Van Wyck Brooks once more: "the current of Transcendentalism, originating in the piety of the Puritans, becoming a philosophy in Jonathan Edwards, passing through Emerson, [produced] the … refinement and aloofness of the chief American writers …."[3]

Benjamin Franklin (1706-1790): Dream and Hope

Standing at the other end of the spectrum was Benjamin Franklin, who represents everything that Edwards does not. The two men, between them, represent the whole of the colonial mind of America.

Franklin was a typical self-made man. He came from a very simple Calvinist background. Born in 1706 into a poor candle-maker's family — "poor and obscure" as he says of himself in his *Autobiography*, he had very little formal education. As he was a voracious reader, however, he managed to make up for the deficiency by his own effort. When still very young, he was apprenticed to his older half-brother, a printer, and began at 16 to publish essays under the pseudonym, Silence Dogood, essays commenting on social life in Boston.

At 17 he ran away to Philadelphia to make his own fortune. His was a long success story of an archetypal kind. He made his living as an independent printer and publisher, issued the immensely popular *Poor Richard's Almanac* and retired at 42, as a financially independent person. Then for the next 40-odd years, he did many things for which he is still remembered today, his public career being one pre-eminent among them. He was one of the greatest of men.

Poor Richard's Almanac

Franklin's claim to a place in literature rests chiefly on his *Poor Richard's Almanac* and *The Autobiography*. For almost a quarter of a century, he kept publishing *Poor Richard's Almanac*, expanding its literary part to the intense delight of its readers. Apart from poems and essays, he managed to put in a good many adages and commonsense witticisms which became, very quickly, household words and, for many, mottoes of the most practical kind. He did not always write the maxims himself. His sources are often easily identifiable. But though he borrowed from such writers as Rabelais, Defoe, Swift, and Pope, he made good use of his own wit and wisdom to simplify and enrich their axioms. Thus sayings like "Lost time is never found again," "A penny saved is a penny earned," "God help them that help themselves," "Fish and visitors stink in three days" and "Early to bed, and early to rise, makes a man healthy, wealthy, and wise"—these and many other similar statements filled the almanac, and taught as much as amused. The practical wisdom of Franklin shone forth rays of grandeur from its pages.

The Autobiography

The Autobiography of Benjamin Franklin was probably the first of its kind in literature. It is the simple yet immensely fascinating record of a man rising to wealth and fame from a state of poverty and obscurity into which he was born. It is the faithful account of the colorful career of America's first self-made man.

The book consists of four parts, written at different times. Franklin was sixty-five when he first wrote it. He was then staying with an English family of five daughters, to whom he must have told, in his charmingly humorous way, the tale of the adventures of a runaway boy, and was urged to write it down. He must have thought of his son, William, who was very close to him when the boy was growing up, and must have written his own life story first for his edification since he began it with "My dear son." The question he asked in the account is how a man should live his life, and the book furnishes the best answer he thought his life had been able to offer.

The first part of the little book, about eighty pages, he wrote with extraordinary facility, bringing the story of his life down to 1730. He did not write anything more until 1784 when he added some more pages. The third part was written in 1788, and some months before his death he labored to write a brief, fragmentary fourth part, carrying the story up to his retirement.

The Autobiography is, first of all, a Puritan document. It is Puritan because it is a record of self-examination and self-improvement. The Puritans, as a type, were very much given to self-analysis. Because they believed in predestination, they constantly examined their conscience to ascertain for themselves how much more they should do to ensure salvation. Thus they were most of them great keepers of diaries and journals. *The Autobiography* reveals an old man, serene and cool, casting a backward glance, looking intensely into his past life and, pen in hand, carefully noting down his experience as if, in this way, he could communicate with God. He set a chart of thirteen virtues to combat the tempting vices, to improve his own person. He believed that God help those who help themselves and that every calling is a service to God. All these indicate that Franklin was intensely Puritan. Then, the book also illustrates the Puritan ethic that, in order to get on in the world, one has to be industrious, frugal, and prudent.

The Autobiography also proves that Franklin was spokesman for the new order of eighteenth-century enlightenment, and that he represented all its ideas in America. These include the views that man is basically good and free by nature, endowed by God with certain inalienable rights of liberty and the pursuit of happiness. The typical best virtues of man the book lists include "order," moderation, and temperance.

Then the book tells a success story of self-reliance and celebrates the fulfillment of the American dream. This is evident in the book's major image of a poor boy's rise from rags to riches. Franklin believed that the new world of America was a land of opportunities which might be met through hard work and wise management, and that "one man of tolerable abilities will work great changes and accomplish great affairs among mankind."

Franklin was supremely human. He knew humanity's foibles and deficiencies, but he was convinced, as his *Autobiography* shows, that man is good and capable of becoming better, and that, although men and institutions are often corrupt, they might be improved. Had this belief failed to triumph over the doctrine of people like Jonathan Edwards, the American Revolution would have been impossible.

Now a look at the style of *The Autobiography* will readily reveal that it is the pattern of Puritan simplicity, directness, and concision. The plainness of its style, the homeliness of its imagery, and the simplicity of diction, syntax and expression are some of the salient features that the readers cannot mistake.[4]

When we have talked about the embodiment in Franklin of the American dream and Franklin's sense of optimism, we must not lose sight of another aspect of life in the New World. As we noted in an earlier chapter, the American dream began with the settlement of the American continent. The wilderness looked like the "Promised land" with which God rewarded His chosen people and offered the Puritans the hope of restoring the Garden of Eden. Thus for a long time the hope kept floating before the people, keeping them happy and optimistic about the future.

Hector St. John de Crevecoeur (1735-1813): Hope and Frustration

The note of pessimism made itself first heard and heeded in Mark Twain's *The Gilded Age* (1871), but it began to vibrate in a much earlier book. We mean Hector St. John de Crevecoeur's *Letters from an American Farmer* (1775). Crevecoeur was a French settler. Obviously inflated with the hope that here at last in the New World man would be able to shake off the shackles of the Old and live the way mankind should, he wrote letters back to Europe, explaining the meaning of America to the outside world.

Letters from an American Farmer

Crevecoeur wrote altogether twelve letters. The first eight of these reveal the pride of a man being an American, the "new man," planted in a new world, who left behind him the old world with its oppression and servility, working and getting "rewards of his industry" and acquiring the dignity and self-confidence of a true human being in what he called "the most perfect society now existing in the world." In his letters we hear the note of pride in democratic equality and the abundance of opportunity, a note we are to hear over and again in the writings of later American authors. It is evident that, to Crevecoeur, the American is a new man acting on new principles: He is self-sufficient, self-reliant, and essentially self-made. Crevecoeur saw and spoke of the hope of a new Garden of Eden materializing in America.[5]

However, Crevecoeur, in his lifetime, also saw and spoke of the illusory nature of the dream that he cherished. In fact, starting from his ninth letter, he began to speak with a different voice, the voice of a definitely disillusioned man. There in the same New World, he became aware of the existence of slavery, avarice, violence, famine and disease, and all other forms of evil that he thought the Americans had left behind with their migration to this side of the Atlantic. His picture of an African American slave left in a virgin forest, being pecked to death by birds of prey, is such a grisly sight that the reader can never forget it.

As a matter of fact, a careful reader may have heard echoes of this tragic note in Crevecoeur's earlier letters which describe, often in minute detail, the life-and-death struggles between different species of the animal kingdom, and may have seen a ghastly picture of what Tennyson later portrayed as "nature red in tooth and claw," a picture that foreshadows "man's folly and inhumanity to man." He was truly dismayed at the "civilized society," that is, the white European settlements.

So he looked toward the Indian tribes for comfort and refuge. "There must be in their [the Indians'] social bond something singularly captivating," he thus wrote in one of his letters, "and far superior to anything to be boasted of among us [Europeans] ...." Maybe, he was trying to say, there in the community of the Indians under their primitive wigwams, existed a better, even an ideal social order, with social cohesion and freedom from avarice and rapine and murder.

Thus almost from the very beginning, the New World had, in its texture, the elements of the Old, and the ideal had, as its twin brother, the anti-ideal. This indicates, in a way, that the note of hope will become ever thinner in American literature and that of disillusionment and even despair will dominate more and more subsequent works of some major authors.

Chapter 3   American Romanticism •
Irving • Cooper

American Romanticism

The Romantic period is one of the most important periods in the history of American literature. It stretches from the end of the eighteenth century through the outbreak of the Civil War (1861-1865). Here a rising America was fast burgeoning into a political, economic, and cultural independence it had never known before. Democracy and political equality became the ideals of the new nation. Radical changes came about in the political life of the country. Parties began to squabble and scramble for power, and a new system was in the making. The spread of industrialism, the sudden influx of immigrants, and the "pioneers" (the first settlers) pushing the frontier further west—all these produced something of an economic boom and, with it, a tremendous sense of optimism and hope among the people.

A nation bursting into new life cried for literary expression. The buoyant mood of the nation and the spirit of the times led to the spectacular outburst of romantic feeling in the first half of the nineteenth century. The literary milieu proved fertile and conducive to the imagination as well. Among other things, magazines appeared in ever-increasing numbers, of which *The North American Review*, *The New York Mirror*, *The American Quarterly Review*, *The New England Magazine*, *The Southern Review*, *The Southern Literary Messenger*, *The Atlantic Monthly*, *Harper's Magazine*, and the *Knickerbocker Magazine* played an important role in facilitating literary expansion in the country.[1]

Foreign Influences at Work

Foreign influences helped the romantic feeling in America to grow. The Romantic movement, which had flourished earlier in the century both in England and Europe, proved to be a decisive influence on the rise of American romanticism. Sir Walter Scott, Samuel Taylor Coleridge, William Wordsworth, Byron, Robert Burns, and many other English and European masters of poetry and prose all made a stimulating impact on the different departments of the country's literature. The influence of Sir Walter Scott was particularly powerful and enduring. His border tales and Waverley romances inspired many American authors such as James Fenimore Cooper with irresistible creative impulses. Scott's Waverley novels were models for American historical romances, and his *The Lady of the Lake*, together with Byron's Oriental romances, helped toward the development of American Indian romance. Scott was, in a way, responsible for the romantic description of landscape in American literature. The Gothic tradition and the cult of solitude and of gloom came through interest in the works of writers like Mrs. Radcliffe, E. T. A. Hoffman, James Thomson, and the "graveyard" poets. Robert Burns and Byron both inspired and spurred the American imagination for lyrics of love and passion and despair. The impact of *Lyrical Ballads* of Wordsworth and Coleridge added, to some extent, to the nation's singing strength.[2] Thus American romantic writing was, some of them, modeled on English and European works.

Home Factors at Work

Although foreign influences were strong, American Romanticism exhibited from the very beginning distinct features of its own. It was different from its English and European counterparts because it originated from a combination of factors that were altogether American.

First, American romanticism was in essence the expression of "a real new experience" in the New World and contained "an alien quality" of its own. That was simply because "the spirit of the place" was radically new and alien.[3] For instance, the American national experience of "pioneering" into the west proved to be a rich fund of material for American writers to draw upon. The wilderness with its virgin forests, the sound of the axe cutting its way westward, the exotic landscape with its different sights, smells, and sounds (the robin rather than the nightingale is Emily Dickinson's "criterion of tone," for example), and the quaint, picturesque civilization of a primitive race—all these became sources of inspiration for American authors. The new American sensibility began to take shape and make itself felt.

Then there was American Puritanism as a cultural heritage to consider. Puritan influence over American Romanticism was conspicuously noticeable. One such instance was the tendency to moralize. American romantic authors moralized more than their English and European brothers. Although there are exceptions such as Edgar Allan Poe and John Greenleaf Whittier: Poe fought against "the heresy of the didactic," and Whittier advocated both beauty and goodness, yet the fact remains that many American romantic writings intended to teach rather than entertain. For them there seemed to be areas of life better not to touch, such as sex and love. Hawthorne's *The Scarlet Letter* talks about the effect of adultery on the people rather than about the sin itself, and Whitman was for a long time misunderstood by his own countrymen because his *Leaves of Grass* contains lines and passages not quite palatable to their "genteel" taste.

Thirdly, there was the "newness" of the Americans as a nation. Crevecoeur called the American as "this new man," and some American writers, critics and historians placed emphasis on this "newness." Exaggeration there is, it is true, but there is also some truth in describing the Americans of the period as different from the Europeans. Their ideals of individualism and political equality, and their dream that America was to be a new Garden of Eden for man were distinctly American. The ideals and the dream may be fact or mere talk, but their very existence in any form in the minds of the people did produce a feeling of "newness," a feeling strong enough to inspire the romantic imagination and channel it into a different vein of writing. Hence the sense of mission with which some American romanticists undertook to represent their people in the New World.

As foreign and indigenous factors both at work, American Romanticism showed both imitative and independent features. Writers like Irving and especially the group of New England poets tried to model their works upon English and European masters. Thus although they enjoyed popularity in their own day, they failed to speak to future generations. Even Longfellow is not much read today. This is not to suggest, however, that these people could be ignored. The romantic "Flowering of New England" would have been impossible without their contribution.

At the same time, however, writers like Emerson and Whitman, thought and wrote differently. In the third decade of the 19th century, W. E. Channing's "Remarks on National Literature," Emerson's *Nature*, "The American Scholar" and "The Poet," and Whitman's announcement concerning an American national expression in his preface to the first edition of *Leaves of Grass* began to appear, signifying that a vigorous literary independence was emerging. Calling for an independent American culture and literature, these people represent "the deeper forces of a Romanticism at once indigenous and universal," and "the urge to create a literature distinct from and better than importations." They did what history meant them to do for American literature.[4]

Washington Irving (1783-1859)

 Irving was born into a wealthy New York merchant family. From a very early age he began to read widely and write juvenile poems, essays, and plays. Later, he studied law and led for a time the leisurely life of a gentleman lawyer, but he loved writing more. He became a prolific writer in his time.

Irving's contribution to American literature is unique in more ways than one. He did a number of things that have been regarded as the first of their kind in America. To begin with, he was the first American writer of imaginative literature to gain international fame: when he returned home in 1832, he was acclaimed as the one American author whom people in Europe knew about, and this Americans took as a sign that American literature was emerging as an independent entity. To say that he was father of American literature is not much exaggeration. Then the short story as a genre in American literature probably began with Irving's *The Sketch Book*, a collection of essays, sketches, and tales, of which the most famous and frequently anthologized are "Rip Van Winkle" and "The Legend of Sleepy Hollow."[5] The book touched the American imagination and foreshadowed the coming of Hawthorne, Melville, and Poe, in whose hands the short story attained a degree of perfection as a literary tradition. In addition, *The Sketch Book* also marked the beginning of American Romanticism. The Gothic, the supernatural, and the longing for the good old days which some of its pieces clearly exhibit, are Romantic enough in subject if not exactly in style, as Irving wrote in the neoclassical tradition of Joseph Addison and Oliver Goldsmith.

Irving's career can be roughly divided into two important phases, the first of which span from his first book up to 1832, the other stretching over the remaining years of his life. In the first part of his career, he was obsessed with European ruins and relics. "The Authors Account of Himself," which opens *The Sketch Book*, is a confessional one and authentic as such:

> … Europe held forth the charms of storied and poetical association. There were to be seen the masterpieces of art, the refinements of highly cultivated society, the quaint peculiarities of ancient and local custom. My native country was full of youthful promise: Europe was rich in the accumulated treasures of age. Her very ruins told the history of times gone by, and every moldering stone was

a chronicle. I longed to wander over the scenes of renowned achievement, to tread, as it were, in the footsteps of antiquity, to loiter about the ruined castle, to meditate on the falling tower, to escape, in short, from the commonplace realities of the present and lose myself among the shadowy grandeurs of the past.

He found value in the past and in the traditions of the Old World. America, being young (though promising), did not have what Europe had to offer for a man of imagination. So mostly, he wrote about Europe. Back in America, Irving found a whole new spirit of nationalism in American feeling and art and letters. He awoke to the fact that there was beauty in America, too. He wrote a few books about America, as well.

Irving's style can only be described as beautiful. It is imitative, it is true, but he was a highly skillful writer. Never shocking and a bit sentimental at times, his manner seems more important than his matter. The gentility, urbanity, and pleasantness of the man all seem to have found adequate expression in his style.

There are quite a few striking features which characterize Irving's writings. First, Irving avoids moralizing as much as possible; he wrote to amuse and entertain, which departs to no small extent from the basic principles of his Puritan forebears. Then he was good at enveloping his stories in an atmosphere, the richness of which is often more than compensation for the slimness of the plot. His characters are vivid and true so that they tend to linger in the mind of the reader. Humor builds itself into the very texture of his writings. And he is noted for his musical language and consummate workmanship. There is a good deal of craft and skill in the man. Irving modeled himself on Goldsmith so that he is at times called "the American Goldsmith."

Irving is best known as the author of "Rip Van Winkle" and "The Legend of Sleepy Hollow" on which his reputation rests permanently. Both tales have become part of the American cultural tradition.

"Rip Van Winkle"

For "Rip Van Winkle," Irving took suggestions from a German source. He changed the setting of the original and added conflicts of his own to make it American. It is a fantasy tale about a man who somehow steps outside the main stream of life. Rip Van Winkle is, the story tells us, a simple, good-natured, and hen-pecked man. He takes the world easy and feels happy. But his wife does not leave him in peace ("Rip" may be, incidentally, the telescopic form of "Rest in Peace"), and so he finds refuge in the mountains, with his gun and dog as his companions. One afternoon he stays out late near the top of the mountain, where he meets a group of odd-looking people playing at nine-pins. He drinks their wine and falls asleep. He wakes up to find his dog gone and his gun rusted. Back in his village, he is amazed at the tremendous changes that have taken place in what he thinks is just one night. Old houses have vanished, and so have some of his old friends. In place of the former little inn, there stands the large "Union Hotel," with a flag of stars and stripes fluttering in front of it. He discovers, to his great surprise, that he has slept for twenty years. His wife has died; his son is now a farm hand, and his daughter takes him home to live with her. Having nothing else to do, he begins to live the way he did before.

The story reveals, to some extent, Irving's conservative attitude. Rip goes to sleep before the War of Independence and wakes up after it. The change that has occurred in the twenty years he slept is to him not always for the better. Instead of peace and harmony, there is now scramble for power between parties. The tempo of life has quickened. Rip feels happy with his new life chiefly because he is no longer bothered by his wife. The story seems to show an Irving not quite feeling comfortable with a modern America.

"The Legend of Sleepy Hollow"

Then there is the equally famous "The Legend of Sleepy Hollow." Here in this village two young men try their best to win the hand of a young woman. One of them is the schoolteacher, Ichabod Crane by name, and the other is a country bumpkin, Brom Bones. In the heat of the rivalry, something happens that decides the issue for them once and for all: one night, as Ichabod Crane rides home, a headless horseman rushes up and throws his head at him. After that the village never sees Ichabod Crane again.

Here Irving's creation of archetypes is particularly interesting. Readers of the story should be aware that it is set in the period of 19th-century American westward movement. Here the two young men represent two types of people in this historical period. Ichabod Crane is a kind of commercial city-slicker, shrewd, self-assertive, but credulous and cowardly. He is a somewhat destructive force in village life.[6] So in the end, he is driven away from where he does not belong, and the village retrieves its serenity and happiness. Brom Bones, on the other hand, is a Huck Finn-type of country bumpkin, rough, vigorous, but inwardly good, a frontier type put out there to shift for himself. Thus the rivalry in love between the two, viewed in this way, suddenly assumes the dimensions of two ethical groups locked in a kind of historic contest.

As to the style of the writing, it represents Irving at his best. The association between a certain locale and the inward movement of a character, the emotional loading of almost every line of the story, their effect on the five senses of the reader whose attention is so fully engaged and who feels so much involved in what is happening—all these have placed the story among the best of American short stories.

James Fenimore Cooper (1789-1851)

Cooper was born into a rich land-holding family of New Jersey. He wrote thirty-odd novels, but he was best known in his own day and is still read and remembered today as the author of "the Leatherstocking Tales," which is a series of five novels about the frontier life of early American settlers.

Cooper's claim to greatness in American literature lies in the fact that he created a myth about the formative period of the American nation. If the history of the United States is, in a sense, the process of the American settlers exploring and pushing the American frontier forever westward, then Cooper's "Leatherstocking Tales" effectively approximates the American national experience of adventure into the West.[7] Cooper wrote with increasing awareness of the importance to fiction of the Western frontier where American society may be conceived as passing from one set of principles to another in two directions at once, and Cooper's power lay in his assurance that one direction was morally right and the other practically inevitable.[8] Here lies Cooper's conflict of allegiances. He was at once devoted to the principles of social order and responsive to the idea of nature and freedom in the wilderness: Probably none of his contemporaries felt as deeply "the antithesis between nature and civilization, between freedom and law."[9] His *The Pioneers* is a good illustration.

The Pioneers

This ambivalence can be seen from the conflict between Leatherstocking and Judge Temple in *The Pioneers*. Published in 1823, *The Pioneers, or The Sources of the Susquehanna*, was the first of the Leatherstocking Tales. It is a romantic story of life in upstate New York ten years after the Revolution. Its historical importance lies in the fact that it was probably the first true romance of the frontier in American literature.

The story reveals that two forces were at work on the western frontier. On the one hand, Natty Bumppo, a pioneer, represents the ideal American, living a virtuous and free life in God's world. To him, and to Cooper, the wilderness is good, pure, perfect, where there is freedom not tainted and fettered by any forms of human institutions. Natty Bumppo is an embodiment of human virtues like innocence, simplicity, honesty, and generosity, a man born with a clear sense of good and evil and right and wrong. He finds "civilization" both corrupt and corrupting. "Might often makes right here as well as in the old country," he says to Judge Temple in the opening chapter of *The Pioneers*. What he rejects is in fact what Crevecoeur says in his ninth letter, that the adventure into the new world has not produced an ideal social order, and that the "civilization" the white settlers imposed on the wilderness is poisoned at the root from the very beginning. Repudiating the various forms of civilization (in the five tales), Natty Bumppo (in his various names in the novels such as Hawk-Eye, the Pathfinder, the Deerslayer, or Leatherstocking so named because of his wearing leather leggings in the American Indian fashion) crusades against all its evils that he feels have disgraced his race. Natty Bumppo stands for the morally right aspect of frontier life.

On the other hand, there is Judge Temple, the portrayal of whose character is a good indication of Cooper's ambivalence as a writer of frontier life. The Judge is, to Cooper, also a pioneer as is Natty Bumppo. He represents "the practically inevitable" aspect of frontier life. Whereas Natty Bumppo embodies the idea of brotherhood of man and of nature and freedom, and Judge Temple symbolizes law and civilization. Hence the plural in the title of the book, *The Pioneers*.

Cooper is a mythic writer. When Natty Bumppo first appears, he is a real frontiersman in his crude cabin, a man of flesh and blood in the virgin forests of North America. But as he moves out of *The Pioneers* into the world of *The Last of the Mohicans*, *The Prairie*, *The Pathfinder*, and *The Deerslayer*, he becomes a type, representing a nation struggling to be born. Reading the series in the order of their appearance in print, D. H. Lawrence may come closest to the truth when he says:

> The Leatherstocking novels … go backwards, from old age to golden youth. That is the true myth of America. She starts old, old, wrinkled and, writhing in an old skin. And there is a gradual sloughing of the old skin, towards a new youth: It is the myth of America.[10]

First as transplanted Europeans, the Americans seem to have crept out of the fetters of the traditions of Europe and England and gradually come into their own. The five Cooper tales constitute a mythic reproduction of the whole process: The old and dying Leatherstocking in *The Pioneers* and *The Prairie* relives another phase of middle-age maturity in *The Last of the Mohicans* and *The Pathfinder* and enjoys another lease of youth in *The Deerslayer*. Natty Bumppo as a fictional character is therefore the result of careful literary deliberations.

Cooper's imagination is admirable. He never was in the frontier and never saw American Indians, but he wrote vividly about these for the first time in American literature. But his style is not as good. He has been known as a powerful yet clumsy writer. His style is dreadful, his characterization wooden and lacking in probability, and his language, his use of dialect, is not authentic. Mark Twain's comment on his literary technique is exceptionally harsh: in his opinion, one of the literary offences that Cooper committed was that he did not observe things accurately at all.[11]

Copper on America's Poverty of Materials

Like Irving and Hawthorne, Cooper was troubled by the "poverty of materials" in America. In his first preface to *The Spy*, he complained about the absence of lords or castles in America and about the scarcity of events. In his preface to *Lionel Lincoln*, he says "there is … neither a dark, nor even an obscure, period in the American annals." And in one of his letters on "Literature and the Arts" in *Notions of the Americans*, he says, "There is scarcely an ore which contributes to the wealth of the author …. There are no annals for the historian; no follies … for the satirist; no manners for the dramatist, no obscure fictions for the writer of romance, no gross and hardy offences against decorum for the moralist; nor any of the rich artificial auxiliaries of poetry." In all these writings the idea is both consistent and persistent. And Cooper concluded that it was the business of the American writer to discover new sources of fiction, cut off as he was from so many of those that had nourished European literature. He cast a glance backward in time and turned whatever American history can offer—the West and the frontier as a usable past—to good account and helped to introduce the "Western" tradition into American literature.

Chapter 4   New England
Transcendentalism • Emerson • Thoreau

New England Transcendentalism

In 1836 a little book came out which made a tremendous impact on the intellectual life of America. It was entitled *Nature* by Ralph Waldo Emerson. The New World was thrilled to hear the new voice it uttered. "The Universe is composed of Nature and the Soul," it says, "Spirit is present everywhere." It was apparent that a wind of change was beginning to blow. A whole new way of thinking began to exert its influence on the consciousness of man. *Nature*'s voice pushed American Romanticism into a new phase, the phase of New England Transcendentalism, the summit of American Romanticism.

What is Transcendentalism? The word, "Transcendental," was not native to America. It was a Kantian term denoting, as Emerson puts it, "Whatever belongs to the class of intuitive thought." Emerson defines it further in his essay, "The Transcendentalist," as "idealism; idealism as appears in 1842."

What happened about this time was that some New Englanders, not quite happy about the materialistic-oriented life of their time, formed themselves into an informal club, the Transcendentalist Club, and met to discuss matters of interest to the life of the nation as a whole. They expressed their views, published their journal, *The Dial*, and made their voice heard. The club with a membership of some thirty men and a couple of women included Emerson, Thoreau, Bronson Alcott, and Margaret Fuller, most of them teachers or clergymen. They were all radicals reacting against the faith of Boston businessmen and the cold, rigid rationalism of Unitarianism, and trying to reassert the religious idealism of their

Puritan past and rephrase their thoughts in forms and terms they borrowed from sources like German idealism.

The Three Major Features of New England Transcendentalism

The major features of New England Transcendentalism can be summarized as follows:

First, the Transcendentalists placed emphasis on spirit, or the Oversoul, as the most important thing in the universe. The Oversoul was an all-pervading power for goodness, omnipresent and omnipotent, from which all things came and of which all were a part. It existed in nature and man alike and constituted the chief element of the universe. Now this, obviously, represented a new way of looking at the world. It was apparently a reaction to the 18th-century Newtonian concept of the universe: In the 18th century it was generally held that the world was made up of matter. It was also a reaction against the direction that a mechanized, capitalist America was taking, against the popular tendency to get ahead in world affairs at the expense of spiritual welfare.

Secondly, the Transcendentalists stressed the importance of the individual. To them the individual was the most important element of society. The regeneration of society could only come about through the regeneration of the individual. The perfection of the individual, his self-culture and self-improvement, and not the frenzied effort to get rich, should be the first concern of human life. The ideal type of man was the self-reliant individual whom Emerson never stopped talking about all his life. The Transcendentalists like Emerson and Thoreau offered the idea of Oversoul. They held that there is a grand mind, or the Oversoul, in the universe, and that the individual soul communed with the Oversoul and was therefore divine. Now this new notion of the individual and his importance represented, obviously, a new way of looking at man. It was a reaction against the Calvinist concept that man is totally depraved and sinful, and that man perseveres in sinhood and cannot hope to be saved except through the grace of God. It was also a reaction against the process of dehumanization that came in the wake of developing capitalism. The industrialization of New England was turning men into nonhumans. People were losing their individuality and were becoming uniform. The Transcendentalists saw the process in progress and, by trying to reassert the importance of the individual, emphasized the significance of men regaining their lost personality.

Thirdly, the Transcendentalists offered a fresh perception of nature as symbolic of the Spirit or God. Nature was, to them, not purely matter. It was alive, filled with God's overwhelming presence. It was the garment of the Oversoul. Therefore it could exercise a healthy and restorative influence on the human mind. What the Transcendentalists seemed to be saying was, "Go back to nature, sink yourself back into its influence, and you'll become spiritually whole again." The natural implication of all this was, of course, that things in nature tended to become symbolic, and the physical world was a symbol of the spiritual. This in turn added to the tradition of literary symbolism in American literature.

American Transcendentalism and Puritanism

If we go back to our previous chapter on Jonathan Edwards and Benjamin Franklin, we will notice how much American Transcendentalism was indebted to the dual heritage of American Puritanism. The Edwardian notion of inward communication of the soul with God and divine symbolism of nature all find adequate expression in Emersonian Transcendentalism. Emerson recaptured the Edwardian vision and stated his ideas in terms of transcendental idealism, of Oversoul, and in the language of *Nature*, "Self-Reliance," and "The Divinity School Address." [1]

Then, we also notice that the Transcendentalists' emphasis on the individual was directly traceable to the Puritan principle of self-culture and self-improvement as best exemplified by the success story of America's first self-made man, Benjamin Franklin. Virtue alone, to Franklin, led to success: One had to be self-reliant and improve one's person. There exists a notable resemblance, between Emerson's "the infinitude of the private individual" and Franklin's belief that "the least of men can rise" and "a man of tolerable abilities can work great changes and accomplish great affairs among mankind." Thus there is good reason to state that New England Transcendentalism was, in actuality, Romanticism on the Puritan soil.

New England Transcendentalism was important to American literature. It inspired a whole new generation of famous authors such as Emerson, Thoreau, Hawthorne, Melville, Whitman and Dickinson. Without its impetus America might have been deprived of one of its most prolific literary periods in its history.

Ralph Waldo Emerson (1803-1882)

Emerson was the descendant of a long line of New England clergymen. When at Harvard, he reconsidered his Calvinist belief, rejected its major tenets, and embraced the liberal Christianity of Unitarianism. He became a Unitarian minister to the Second Church of Boston, but not for long. He found the rationality of Unitarianism intolerable and left his job.

He went to Europe, and met and made friends with Coleridge, Carlyle, and Wordsworth, and brought back with him the influence of European Romanticism. With people of like minds such as Thoreau, Bronson Alcott, and Margaret Fuller, he formed an informal Transcendentalists' club, something like Dr. Johnson's circle. He became the most eloquent spokesman of New England Transcendentalism. He helped to found, and edit for a time, the Transcendentalist journal, *The Dial*, to explain their ideas. For a while ideas like Emerson's were up in the air and regarded by some people as "crazy." The epithet "Transcendentalist" was rather derogatory when it was first used, meaning one whose feet did not touch ground.

Although he left his ministry, Emerson never stopped "preaching," though now in the lecture-room. He traveled far and wide in the United States, and

Canada and England, taught and spread his Transcendentalist doctrine. During his lifetime he was considered one of the two or three best writers in America, and certainly the most influential among his contemporaries. The prophet of his age, he was likened to a cow from which all had milk though not all liked the taste. Thoreau, Whitman, Emily Dickinson, and many others were indebted to him in varying degrees; Hawthorne and Melville, reacting to his doctrine of optimism, benefited in their ways from his thought. His influence extended beyond his own century. Robert Frost and Wallace Stevens were among the authors of the 20th century responsive to his philosophy.

Talking about Emerson, there are two things that merit attention—New England Transcendentalism and his call for American Cultural Independence.

Emerson and New England Transcendentalism

New England Transcendentalism was in fact Emerson's creation. As Emerson's major ideas constituted its major theses, the following discussion and the previous introduction of New England Transcendentalism may overlap one another a little, with this difference that the discussion here focuses more on some details of Emerson's thought.

First of all, there is Emerson's firm belief in the transcendence of the "Oversoul." His emphasis on the spirit runs through virtually all his writings, especially his most famous work, *Nature*, which is generally regarded as the Bible of New England Transcendentalism. He made very impressive statements there. "Philosophically considered, the universe is composed of Nature and the Soul." He sees the world as phenomenal, and emphasizes the need for idealism; he feels that idealism sees the world in God. He regards nature as the purest, the most sanctifying moral influence on man, and advocated a direct intuition of a spiritual and immanent God in nature. He tells about his emotional experiences, moments of "ecstasy":

Standing on the bare ground, my head bathed by the blithe air and uplifted into infinite space, all mean egotism vanishes. I become a transparent eyeball; I am nothing; I see all; the currents of the Universal Being circulate through me; I am part or particle of God.

Here is a good illustration of the Oversoul at work. It is "the currents of the Universal Being," of which the individual soul transcends the limits of individuality to become a part. Emerson sees spirit pervading everywhere, not only in the soul of man, but behind nature, throughout nature. Emerson's doctrine of the Oversoul is graphically illustrated in such famous statements: "Each mind lives in the Grand mind," "There is one mind common to all individual men," and "Man is conscious of a universal soul within or behind his individual life." In his opinion, man is made in the image of God and is just a little less than Him.[2] This is as much as to say that man is divine. The divinity of man became a favorite subject in his lectures and essays.

This naturally led to his emphasis on self-reliance.[3] This was a subject he never stopped talking about all his life. Emerson states that each man should feel the world as his, and the world exists for him alone. Man should determine his own existence. Everyone should understand that he makes himself by making his world, and that he makes the world by making himself. "Know then that the world exists for you …" he says. "Build therefore your own world." "Trust thy self!" and "Make thyself!" Trust your own discretion and the world is yours. Emerson is noted for his notion of "the infinitude of man." He sees man as he could be or could become;[4] he was optimistic about human perfectibility. The regeneration of the individual leads to the regeneration of society. Hence his famous remark, "I ask for the individuals, not the nation." The possible negative effect of Emerson's self-reliance on his time might have been that it provided a good explanation for the conduct and activities of an expanding capitalist society. His essays such as "Power," "Wealth," and "Napoleon" (in his *The Representative Men*) reveal his ambivalence toward aggressiveness and self-seeking.[5]

Thirdly, Emerson is noted for his symbolic mode of perception. To his Transcendentalist eyes, the physical world, or nature, was vital and symbolic of God. "Nature is the vehicle of thought," and "particular natural facts are symbols of particular spiritual facts." "Nature is the symbol of spirit." That is probably why he called his first philosophical work *Nature*. The sensual man, Emerson feels, conforms thoughts to things, and man's power to connect his thought with its proper symbol depends upon the simplicity and purity of his character: "The lover of nature is he ... who has retained the spirit of infancy even into the era of manhood." To him nature is a wholesome moral influence on man and his character. A natural implication of Emerson's view on nature is that the world around is symbolic. A flowing river indicates the ceaseless motion of the universe. The seasons correspond to the life span of man. The ant, the little drudge, with a small body and a mighty heart, is the sublime image of man himself.

This mode of perception had a significant effect on Emerson's aesthetics, the basis of which is contained in his *Nature*, "The Poet," "The American Scholar," and some other essays. Emerson's poet is no ordinary person. He is a complete man, an eternal man, one whose birth is the principal event in history. He should be able to see into the deeps of infinite time, comprehend the path of things and the divine unity of the Universe by intuition, and communicate the feelings of contact with nature to his fellowmen. True poetry and true art should be ennobling. It should serve as a moral purification and a passage toward organic unity and higher reality. It is evident that the Romantic organic principle was the governing factor in Emerson's aesthetics.[6]

Emerson Calls for American Cultural Independence

Emerson called upon American authors to celebrate America which was to him a long poem in itself, to celebrate the life of today, "the factory village and the railway." He lamented bitterly the fact that there had yet been no genius in America, ruthlessly ignoring the New England celebrities of his time. Emerson's aesthetics brought about a revolution in American literature in general and in American poetry in particular. It marked the birth of true American poetry and true American poets such as Walt Whitman and Emily Dickinson.

Emerson's influence on American literature and culture cannot be exaggerated. His call for an independent culture in his works such as *Nature* and "The American Scholar" played a very important part in the intellectual history of the United States. In fact, "The American Scholar" has been regarded (first by Oliver Wendell Holmes) as "America's Declaration of Intellectual Independence." What Emerson was trying to say was actually this, that the Americans should write about here and now instead of imitating and importing from other lands. "The sun shines today also …. There are new lands, new men, new thoughts. Let us demand our own works and laws and worship," he says. "Our long apprenticeship to the learning of other lands draws to a close. The millions that around us are rushing into life cannot always be fed on the sere remains of foreign harvests." He called on American writers to write about America in a way peculiarly American. Everything here, common and low as they may be, is worth writing about, for we are great in our own way—that seems to be the sum total of what Emerson was trying to get across to his countrymen. Emerson's importance in the intellectual history of America lies in the fact that he embodied a new nation's desire and struggle to assert its own identity in its formative period.

Emerson's Reputation

Emerson's reputation fell somewhat in the 20th century. It might have to do with his seemingly unqualified acceptance of life and his cheerful optimism that stemmed from that acceptance. To him Good is a good doctor, but Bad is sometimes a better. It is not that he did not see the disease and deformity of his age. In fact, he shared with many thinking minds of his day the sad conviction of universal decay and the decline of true Christianity. But it was his belief that moral deformity is good passion out of place. In modern times Emerson is sometimes dismissed as having no sense of evil, and his optimistic philosophy as so much Transcendentalist folly. Major American authors like Nathaniel Hawthorne, Herman Melville, and Henry James, and major modern and contemporary critics such as F. O. Matthiessen and Yvor Winters all agree that there is truth in the allegation.[7] However, Emerson's permanence in American culture and literature is well ensured.

Henry David Thoreau (1817-1862)

Another renowned New Englander of the time was Henry David Thoreau, author of the famous book, *Walden*. Thoreau's father was an unsuccessful storekeeper and a maker of lead pencils, but his mother was an aspiring woman, determined to send her son to college. So she did. Thoreau went to Harvard, but did not like the life and the curriculum of the college much. On graduation he stayed with his family, first helping his father make pencils and then, for a time, running a private school.

Thoreau was an active Transcendentalist. He made friends with Emerson, used his library, and embraced his ideas. He helped Emerson to edit the Transcendentalist journal, *The Dial* and was susceptible to Oriental influences such as Hinduism and Confucianism. By no means an "escapist" or a recluse, he was intensely involved in the life of his day. He did not like the way a materialistic America was developing and was vehemently outspoken on the point. He hated the human injustice as represented by the slavery system and was known to have helped at least one African American slave to get free. His firm stance on the execution of John Brown was most explicit in his "A Plea for John Brown."[8]

Thoreau loved nature. As a young man he took a more than usual interest in the natural world. Like Emerson, but more than him, he saw nature as a genuine restorative, healthy influence on man's spiritual well-being, and regarded it as a symbol of the spirit. He tried to seek a way to unlock the secrets of the spirit. He was never tired of staying alone in nature; he was ever seen lost in contemplation of the world around.

Thoreau thought in images.[9] He believed that "natural objects and phenomena are the original symbols or types which express our thoughts and feelings." In fact, *Walden* is a faithful record of his reflections when he was in solitary communion with nature. He embraced and went beyond Emerson's Transcendentalist philosophy to illustrate the pantheistic quality of nature. *Walden* tells us that he finds woodchucks, moose, and pine trees are as immortal

as he is, that he believes that it is possible to find godhead in the nearby woods.[10] Thoreau's idea came very close to being heathenish and nature-worship, a pantheism which tended to destroy the "transcendence" of God.

Thoreau on the Walden Pond

In 1845 something happened that proved to be important both to him and to American literature in more than one way. With the permission of Emerson, Thoreau went to build a cabin on a piece of Emerson's property on Walden Pond, and moved in on July 4 to live there in a very simple manner for a little over two years. The idea was to move away from the rush and bustle of American social life which was, to him, getting more and more sadly materialistic-oriented.

There on the Pond, he tried to be self-sufficient in everything, spending, as he told us, about six weeks a year, planting beans etc. and working to eke out a scanty yet decent livelihood, but writing and enjoying nature most of the time for the rest of the year. A skilled woodsman with acute senses, Thoreau was in his element in the virgin forest, entirely, as it were, in communion with nature. During his stay in Walden, he went back occasionally to his village, and on one of these visits he was detained for a night in jail for refusing to pay a poll-tax of

$ 2.00 to a government he thought unjust. The event was insignificant enough—
he was, in fact, soon set free after his aunt paid the sum for him, but it inspired
him to write his famous essay, "Civil Disobedience" which, advocating passive
resistance to unjust laws of society, influenced people such as Mahatma Gandhi.
At the end of two years and two months, Thoreau moved back to Concord,
feeling that he had lived one of the lives he was born to live in the world, and
wrote about his experience in the famous book, *Walden*.

Walden

Walden can be many things and can be read on more than one level. But it
is, first and foremost, a book on self-culture and human perfectibility, out in print
against modern civilization and its dehumanization. It is a book about man, what
he is, and what he should be and must be.[11] Thoreau has faith in the inner virtue
and the inward, spiritual grace of man. He holds that the most important thing
for men to do with their lives is to be self-sufficient and strive to achieve personal
spiritual perfection.

Thoreau felt that modern civilization had degraded and enslaved man.
"Civilized man is the slave of matter," he said on one occasion. He felt that, by
trying to amass material possessions, man is not really living; he is digging his
own grave. He was impatient with his fellowmen who took such an enormous
amount of interest in the developments of the outside world like the railroad, the
telegraph, and the French Revolution, and yet did not want to spend so little as a
single moment on the improvement of his own person.

The book is full of ideas expressed to jostle his neighbors out of their smug
complacency. He recorded how he tried to minimize his own needs on Walden
Pond. "A man is rich in proportion to the number of things which he can afford
to let alone," he says in one context. "An honest man has hardly need to count
more than ten fingers, or in extreme cases he may add his ten toes and lump the
rest." And he goes on to prescribe a panacea for the fatal modern craze for

monetary success that came in the wake of mechanization and commercialization of life: "Simplicity, simplicity, simplicity! ... simplify, simplify!" Spiritual richness is real wealth. It is worth trying to live a life in which one needs to work only for six weeks to be free for the rest of the year. One's soul might not help one to get ahead in the world, but it will help make real "progress" in self-improvement.[12]

Thoreau was very critical of and sorely disgusted with "the inundations of the dirty institutions of men's odd-fellow society" with its "life without principle." Through his writings and his behavior he declared war with the state in his quiet way.[13] He went to the woods to experiment with a new way of life for himself and for his fellowmen, and felt that he came out of it a better man, reborn and reinvigorated. Thus regeneration became a major thematic concern of the book. It also decided its structural scheme.

Walden reveals Thoreau's calm trust in the future and sincere belief in the new generation of men. For instance, after relating the impressive story of a strong and beautiful bug coming out to life from an egg deposited many years earlier and pointing to a similar possible prospect of a beautiful and winged life for man, the book concludes on a clear note of optimism and hope:

> The light which puts out our eyes is darkness to us. Only that day
> dawns to which we are awake. There is more day to dawn. The sun is
> but a morning star.

Here may be a place as good as any to note that, in his eagerness to prove his point, he found a fellow spirit in Confucius, the basic tenets of whose doctrine concern self-culture. Thoreau quoted ten times from the *Four Books* to support his thesis.[14]

Thoreau's was not a solitary voice even in his time. He wished to be a chanticleer to wake his fellowmen up from their spiritual slumbers and help make them into a new generation of men. Hence the book is full of people waking up:

as a matter of fact, he woke up several times himself in the book. He might not be aware that his message is of value not merely for his generation, but for all time.

Thoreau's Place in History

Thoreau's reputation as an author is interesting to talk about. In his own time he was considered an eccentric and a loafer. He wrote two books, *A Week on the Concord and Merrimack Rivers* and *Walden*, and a lot of journals and essays, but he had few or no readers. The miserable failure of his first book, *A Week*, intimidated the publishers so that his masterwork, *Walden*, when finished, was destined to wait for a few years before it appeared in print. If the final publication of the book brought its author anything, it was infamy. It proved to be another failure and was regarded as "wicked and heathenish" and anti-social, thus earning him the name of "nullifier of civilization." Emerson's speech at Thoreau's funeral was ambivalent enough: he talked about Thoreau's virtues, but he also expressed the opinion that Thoreau did not do justice to his own talent, which is rather another way of saying that he wasted his life. Here Emerson was not being just.

For half a century after his death, Thoreau remained in obscurity. But his reputation rose steadily, and the 20th century found him charming and great. His works were edited, published, and reverently and profusely commented upon. He became one of the three great American authors of the 19th century who had no contemporary readers and yet became great in the 20th century, the other two being Herman Melville and Emily Dickinson. And his became a major voice for 19th-century America, now better heard perhaps than Emerson's. His influence has gone way beyond his own country. His statue was placed in the Hall of Fame in New York in 1969 alongside those of other great Americans.

Chapter 5   Hawthorne • Melville

Nathaniel Hawthorne (1804-1864)

With the publication of *The Scarlet Letter* in 1850, Nathaniel Hawthorne became famous as the greatest writer living then in the United States (as indeed some critics put it) and his reputation as a major American author has been on the increase ever since. Over the years a good number of biographical and critical studies have been written, and almost all aspects of his life and work have been treated with meticulous care. He is also becoming more and more popular with the Chinese readers. Since Shi Heng's Chinese translation of *The Scarlet Letter* appeared in the 1950s, scholars and readers in this country have shown an ever-increasing interest in his works, which offers another testimony of Hawthorne's power and permanence.

 Hawthorne was born on the fourth of July, 1804 in Salem, Massachusetts. In 1821 he went to Bowdoin College. From 1825 to 1837 he lived in solitude and seclusion. He read widely, became further acquainted with local history, and began to practice writing. The year of 1837 saw the publication of his *Twice-Told Tales*, a collection of short stories. He became well known and well off when *The Scarlet Letter* came out in print. *The House of the Seven Gables* followed in 1851, then *The Blithedale Romance* in 1852 and *The Marble Faun* in 1860.

Hawthorne's Aesthetics

Hawthorne's aesthetics is clearly enunciated in the prefaces to his larger fictions, particularly those to *The Scarlet Letter, The House of the Seven Gables,* and *The Marble Faun*. Like Washington Irving, James Fenimore Cooper, and Henry James after him, Hawthorne repeatedly complained about "the poverty of materials" in a land where "there is no shadow, no antiquity, no mystery, no picturesque and gloomy wrong, nor anything but a commonplace prosperity, in broad and simple daylight" ("Preface to *The Marble Faun*") and where "there has never been" "the genial atmosphere which a literary man requires in order to ripen the best harvest of his mind" ("The Custom House: Introductory to *The Scarlet Letter*"). A man with any literary ambition would have to resort to the help of his imagination, "to recall what was valuable in the past," and "to raise up from dry bones" a treasure of even as small an interest as a rag of scarlet cloth ("The Custom House"). He would have to try "to connect a bygone time with the very Present," "to relate a legend, prolonging itself, from an epoch now gray in distance, down into our own broad daylight" ("Preface to *The House of the Seven Gables*"). In this way he may be able to create "a neutral territory, somewhere between the real world and fairy-land where the Actual and the Imaginary may meet, and each imbue itself with the nature of the other" ("The Custom House"). Thus Hawthorne took a great interest in history and antiquity. To him these furnish the soil on which his mind grows to fruition. "Romance and poetry, like ivy, lichen, and wall flowers, need Ruin to make them grow" ("Preface to *The Marble Faun*"). With their mist brooding over the real world and turning it into a "cloud-land," antiquity and history enable him to "dream strange things, and make them look like truth."

Hawthorne was convinced that romance was the predestined form of American narrative. It is not only "the poverty of materials" in America that led him, as he says in his prefaces, to write romances rather than novels; there is also his Puritan prudence to consider—romance allowing him to treat the physical passions obliquely, to avoid violating the human heart, and not to offend the Puritan taste. Hawthorne knew well that, in becoming a writer of the first rank, he had also become "a citizen of somewhere else."

Hawthorne's Blackness of Vision

All his life, Hawthorne seemed to be haunted by his sense of sin and evil in life. Reading his tales and romances, one cannot but be overwhelmed by the "black" vision which these works reveal. Evil exists in the human heart as is evident, for instance, in the short story, "Earth's Holocaust"; everyone possesses some evil secret as tales like "Young Goodman Brown" set out to prove; everyone seems to cover up his innermost "evil" ("The Minister's Black Veil"); evil seems to be man's birthmark ("The Birthmark"). Hawthorne is at his best when writing about evil. Most of his works deal with evil one way or another. The blackness of vision has become his trade mark.[1]

This may have to do with the influence that the Calvinist doctrine of "original sin" and "total depravity" had upon his mind. In addition, and more importantly, there is Hawthorne's family history to consider as well. Some of his ancestors were men of prominence in the Puritan theocracy of 17th-century New England. One of them was a colonial magistrate, notorious for his part in the persecution of the Quakers, and another was a judge at the Salem Witchcraft Trial in 1692. Gradually the family fortune declined. His father, a sea captain, died in Dutch Guiana, leaving the widow and the child behind to shift for themselves. Young Hawthorne was intensely aware of the misdeeds of his Puritan ancestors, and this awareness led to his understanding of evil being at the core of human life, to "that blackness in Hawthorne," as Herman Melville put it. There is a certain amount of truth in the statement that Hawthorne wrote some of his works like *The House of the Seven Gables* and "Young Goodman Brown" as an attempt at expiating the sin of his ancestors.

Hawthorne's vision of life may, in a sense, explain his aloofness from Emersonian Transcendentalist optimism and his skepticism about it.

Here is a brief analysis of Hawthorne's two novels—*The House of the Seven Gables* and *The Scarlet Letter*, and one famous short story, "Young Goodman

Brown."

The House of the Seven Gables

To Hawthorne sin will get punished, one way or another. As a matter of fact he was said to be often troubled by the thought that the decline of his family's fortunes had to do with the sins of his ancestors. *The House of the Seven Gables* is an appalling fictional version of Hawthorne's belief that "the wrong-doing of one generation lives into the successive ones," and that evil will come out of evil though it may take many generations to happen.

As the story goes, Colonel Pyncheon takes by force the land of Matthew Maule, and condemns him as a wizard. He builds a house on the land while Matthew Maule is sent to the scaffold. Before he dies, the "wizard" curses the colonel, saying "God will give him blood to drink." Retribution does come. The house seems to be haunted. The descendants of the colonel wither and die out, and eventually the descendant of the persecuted wizard gets the upper hand. So the curse, in time, materializes. It is true that the book concludes on a happy note, and that good triumphs over evil, and love and reconciliation end an enmity, but one feels somehow that the tragic part of the story impresses more.

What Hawthorne tries to say here and elsewhere (as in his novel, *The Marble Faun*), may be this, that the tragic rise can be born of the fortunate fall only when evil is engaged and dealt with.[2]

The Scarlet Letter

The Scarlet Letter is Hawthorne's masterwork in which all the elements of Hawthorne's thinking and aesthetics find an adequate expression.

The story is simple but very moving. An aging English scholar sends his beautiful young wife, Hester Prynne by name, to make their new home in New England. When he comes over two years later, he is bewildered to see his wife in pillory, wearing a scarlet letter A on her breast, holding her illicit child in her arms. Determined to find out who her lover is, the old scholar disguises himself as a physician and changes his name to Roger Chillingworth. Gradually he discovers that the "villain" is no other than the much-admired brilliant young clergyman, Arthur Dimmesdale. He begins to torment the clergyman's conscience ruthlessly. At one time Hester plans to leave America with Dimmesdale, but he refuses her help. He dies in the end in her arms while confessing his sin at a public gathering. Chillingworth withers. Pearl, Hester's child, grows up to be married into a noble family of Europe.

The Focus of the Story

The story focuses on the attitude of the three major characters toward the sin of the adultery. Young Hester Prynne is a dark-haired sensual Oriental type of beauty. Her luxuriant head of black silky hair seems to reveal that her drive is sexual. But when the self-righteous community outlaws her, her response to the scarlet letter A is a positive one. She does not panic and run. Instead, she manages to move ever closer to her villagers. Though living on the fringe of the community, she does her best to reestablish her fellowship with her neighbors on a new, honest basis, and tries to keep her hold on the painful "magic chain of humanity." She helps her fellow creatures as a sister of mercy or as a skilled embroiderer in an unobtrusive and undemanding manner, and eventually wins their love and admiration. Symbolic of her moral development is the gradual, imperceptible change which the scarlet letter undergoes in meaning. At first it is a token of shame, "Adultery," but then the genuine sympathy and help Hester offers to her fellow villagers change it to "Able." Later in the story, the letter A appears in the sky, signifying "Angel." Hester has chances to go and live with her daughter in Europe, but she keeps coming back to live in the village which has at one time wronged her.

Dimmesdale, on the other hand, banishes himself from society and torments himself ruthlessly for his sin. Deeply preoccupied with himself, he lives a stranger among his admirers. The result is that, whereas Hester is able to reconstruct her life and win a moral victory, Dimmesdale shrinks away and experiences a tragic physical and spiritual disintegration. He dies, an honest man, but in a way, suicidal.

The real villain of the story is Roger Chillingworth. He is a scholar, the embodiment of pure intellect, who commits "the Unpardonable Sin" (as Hawthorne calls it)—the violation of the human heart. Refusing to forgive a wrong, he keeps preying on Dimmesdale's conscience until the poor wretch is tormented to death. The end of Chillingworth, when it comes, is also tragic enough. Dimmesdale declares God's judgment on him before he breathes his last: "Thou, too, hast deeply sinned!" And Chillingworth simply shrivels. The last time he is seen, he is kneeling down beside Dimmesdale "with a blank, dull countenance, out of which the life seemed to have departed."

The Didacticism of the Story

The Scarlet Letter is didactic. It means to teach people to be good together. It places emphasis on the importance of the community. Hawthorne was mainly concerned with the moral, emotional, and psychological effect of the sin on the people in general and those complicated in it in particular. *The Scarlet Letter* is not a story of a Hester Prynne sinning, but a praise of the moral growth of the woman when sinned against. In the strong character of Hester Prynne the readers see the tension between society and solitude which lies near the center of all Hawthorne's art. The success story of Hester's re-entry into the main social stream affirms the human need for social ties and human fellowship.

"Young Goodman Brown"

Another good example is his famous short story, "Young Goodman Brown." It tells about a young man's trip into the dark forest at night to meet someone who would become his guide and show him what he need see as a young human. What he sees disgusts him and leads him to realize that everyone, including his wife, has a pact with the devil. He comes back to his village and to his wife and family, and despises all and loves no one anymore. Eventually he dies in gloom.

The story can be seen as a symbol of the growing-up experience of the young. Brown's trip to the forest can be seen as the journey of life. The young man leaving his wife despite her repeated pleadings not to go off into the night is, in one sense, symbolic of the inner urge of the young to grow up and get initiated into the adult world. He must go; it is decided by his human nature: it is a phase to go through. He must lose his innocence to discover about the evil that exists in life as well as in himself in order to reach maturity.

The time of the day at which the journey is undertaken, at night, assumes some symbolic significance. The murkiness of night engenders a sense of uncertainty and fear, and signifies an unknown territory stretching in front and the possibility of losing one's sense of direction: all these indicate the archetypal growing-up situation for inexperienced youth. Thus the story relates a general human experience. Young Goodman Brown is not an isolated individual. He is, and probably meant to be, an Everyman. His name is suggestive of this notion: he is a young farmer (Goodman could mean "farmer" at one time in New England), and Brown is a common name. The only thing that tells him apart from humanity in general is that he fails to see evil in himself and that leads to his tragedy.

It is necessary to add here that the story can be read on many levels and in more than one sense. It can be seen as an illustration of original sin, evil inherent in everyone's heart, the need for fellowship and community life, the author's feeling of contrition regarding his ancestors' evil deeds and of repulsion for the self-righteousness of the 17th-century New England theocracy. Any work of art that inspires more than one interpretation is great and permanent. "Young Goodman Brown" is of this category.

Hawthorne's Art

Hawthorne's art is cumulative. Many of his earlier stories had treated themes that led to *The Scarlet Letter*. Puritan severity toward sex and its tendency to suppress bright color and true feeling are revealed in "The Maypole of Merry Mount," and the stern Puritan punitive measure of making an adulteress wear a scarlet A on her occurs in the story of "Endicott and the Red Cross." [3] In all these and *The Scarlet Letter* Hawthorne drew heavily from the New England past.

Hawthorne is at his best when dealing with sin, the supernatural, and New England past.[4] *The Scarlet Letter* is set in the 17th century. It tells about a fact of the life of the Puritan past. In "The Custom House," the first section of the book, Hawthorne tells us how he found a small package which contained a piece of fine red cloth in the shape of a capital letter A. Placing it by accident on his own chest, Hawthorne says that he felt he experienced a sensation, not altogether physical, as of burning heat. There was a small roll of dingy paper, which explained its history. This is a clever artistic fabrication of Hawthorne's in his attempt to give his tale a sense of historical reality and an air of authenticity.

Here Hawthorne's use of the supernatural is evident. In addition, Pearl's response to the scarlet letter A on her mother's breast is descried so that a mystic influence is felt. The appearance of the symbol A in the sky is another good example of Hawthorne's use of the supernatural.

The use of the supernatural can be seen as a hallmark of Hawthorne's art. The voice of the dead "wizard" heard on the death of Colonel Pyncheon in *The House of the Seven Gables*, the contact with the spiritual world in "Howe's Masquerade," the denial of a natural law in "Dr. Heidegger's Experiment," the supernatural allegory in "The Bosom Serpent" and "The Minister's Black Veil," and such vivid studies of the supernatural as "The Birthmark," "The Artist of the Beautiful," "Rappaccini's Daughter," and "The Snow Image"—all these and more are enough to demonstrate Hawthorne's flair for the supernatural.[5]

Another major feature of his art is his symbolism, which merits particular mention. Hawthorne's eyes were symbolic eyes; his mind worked with the help of signs and symbols. Take *The Scarlet Letter* again for instance. In addition to the symbolic significance of the scarlet letter, the names of its characters,

Dimmesdale and Chillingworth, are symbolic, too, as are the flower at the prison door, little Pearl, the wilderness on the verge of which stands the Puritan community. *The House of the Seven Gables* abounds in symbols of various kinds, the house and the rise and fall of its fortunes, the chickens and their dwindling in size, the love between the two young people, etc. Hawthorne's short stories are mostly symbolic.

One other salient feature of Hawthorne's art is his ambiguity, as is illustrated in the technique of multiple view. This is employed in the last part of *The Scarlet Letter*. Here in the "Conclusion," people are offered different views concerning the sign of the letter A on the dead minister's chest. The author's refusal to commit himself gives his work a richness which would otherwise have been impossible to achieve.

Hawthorne's Influence

Hawthorne's influence has been great. He changed Herman Melville's original writing scheme for his *Moby Dick*. He received due recognition in his contemporary James Russell Lowell's *A Fable for Critics*. The Jamesian psychological realism may have taken its cue from his soul-searching works. Other realists like William Dean Howells learned to use Hawthorne's fiction as the benchmark for their novel-writing practice. In the 20th century, William Faulkner and some Gothic novelists clearly show their indebtedness to him. Hawthorne's reputation is still rising. As Henry James put it, "[Hawthorne's] work will remain …. Among the men of imagination he will always have his niche."[6]

Herman Melville (1819-1891)

Melville's childhood was happy until he was eleven when his father died in debt. He had little education and began to work early at various jobs. At about twenty he went to sea, and became a whaler. As such he underwent one of the most brutalizing experiences for a man. His experiences and adventures on the sea, however, furnished him with abundant material for fiction.

The married life of Melville was interesting to talk about. He married the daughter of a wealthy judge and had to write for money to support her and their growing family. He stopped worrying about money only when he was quite old.

Meeting Hawthorne

During the summer of 1850, Melville and Hawthorne met. This was significant for Melville because it brought about a change in his outlook on life. Against the background of New England Transcendentalist optimism concerning man and his world, Melville saw in Hawthorne the one American who was expressively aware of the evil at the core of American life. He found Hawthorne's understanding of evil, that blackness of vision, unusually fascinating. A significant change came about in the original design of *Moby Dick*, about one third of which he had completed when the two men met. The book, which would otherwise have been another of Melville's exotic whaling tales, was now rewritten into the world classic that we read today. It was dedicated to Hawthorne. Between the two, they represented a position of tragic humanism in their time.

Melville was a voracious reader. His discovery of Shakespeare stirred him to the depths of his being. Carlyle and Hawthorne's symbolism fascinated him. For Emerson Melville had mixed feelings of respect and repulsion.

Melville's Career as an Author

For a period of some eight years after his return from the sea, Melville was at his most prolific. Books poured forth like a torrent. *Typee* came out first in 1846, to be followed in close succession by *Omoo* (1847), *Mardi* (1849),

Redburn (1849), *White Jacket* (1850), *Moby Dick* (1851) and *Pierre* (1852). The first three drew from his adventures among the people of the South Pacific islands; *Redburn* is an account of his voyage to England; *White Jacket* relates his life on a United States man-of-war. He was thus known for some time as a popular writer of exotic tales.

The cool response of the public to his *Moby Dick* disgusted him so that he almost left off novel writing in his late forties. Later in life he wrote some other books like *The Confidence Man* (1857), and *Billy Budd* which he left in manuscript at the time of his death, and some famous short stories such as "Bartleby" and "Benito Cereno." He wrote poetry as well, and his long poem *Clarel* (1876), said to be his spiritual autobiography, is a good read. In most of these Melville seemed to continue to deal in black and white and not in the gray of a Hawthorne reconciled with the world of man.

For the last twenty years of his life Melville worked in the Custom House in New York, going off in the morning and coming home later in the day. Even while he was still living he was almost forgotten as an author.

Moby Dick

Melville is best known as the author of one book, *Moby Dick* which is, critics have agreed, one of the world's greatest masterpieces. To get to know the 19th-century American mind and America itself, one has to read this book. It is an encyclopedia of everything, history, philosophy, religion, etc. in addition to a detailed account of the operations of the whaling industry. It is, all in all, a sprawling colossus into which the author kept dumping everything he saw as necessary to prove his point. But it is good to remember that it is, first and foremost, a Shakespearean tragedy of man fighting against overwhelming odds in an indifferent and even hostile universe. As the author had indicated in *Mardi*, we should get to know the extent of evil in life and the human soul to help make life and man better. As he puts it, "The way to heaven is through hell."

The story goes roughly as follows. Ishmael, feeling depressed, seeks escape by going out to sea on the whaling ship, Pequod. The captain is Ahab, the man with one leg. Moby Dick, the white whale, has sheared off his leg on a previous voyage, and Ahab resolves to hunt and kill him. He hangs a doubloon on the mast as a reward for anyone who sights the whale first. The Pequod goes out to sea and makes a good catch of whales, but Ahab refuses to turn back until he has killed his enemy. Eventually the white whale appears, and the Pequod begins its doomed fight with it. On the first day the whale overturns a boat; on the second it swamps another. When the third day comes, Ahab and his crew manage to plunge a harpoon into it, but the whale carries the Pequod along with it to its doom. All on board the whaler get drowned, except one, Ishmael, who survives to tell the tale.

Moby Dick may not be a perfect novel as a novel should be, but it is decidedly a book on man and his world that a serious reader should read and explore. Critics seem to agree that it represents the sum total of Melville's bleak view of his world. It is Godless and purposeless. Man in this universe lives a meaningless and futile life, meaningless because futile. As some critics note, man can observe and even manipulate in a prudent way, but he cannot influence and overcome nature at its source. He must, ultimately, place himself at the mercy of nature. Once he attempts to seek power over it, he is doomed. The idea that man can make the world for himself is nothing but a Transcendentalist folly. It is like the world of *The Confidence Man* which reveals "the absurdity of man's attempts to attribute meaning and value to a world in which these can have no ground or status."[7]

These are all valid comments though they may represent merely one side of Melville's mind. The deeps of Melville's consciousness requires careful excavation. While he successfully draws the portrait of Captain Ahab, he has also spent quality time sketching Ishmael, the narrator. He may have done so intentionally to reveal the ambiguity of his outlook on life. This may explain the appearance of *Billy Budd* toward the conclusion of his career as a true artist.

So, two major characters stand out in the book, Ahab and Ishmael, each representing one side of the coin that is the whole of Melville's outlook on life.

Ahab: the Everlasting Nay

One of the major themes in Melville is alienation, which he sensed existing in the life of his time on different levels, between man and man, man and society, and man and nature. All on board the Pequod suffers from this, and Captain Ahab is the best illustration of it all. He is a typical Melvillean "isolato," and a typical Bartleby whose lips are set ever for an "I prefer not to." Ahab cuts himself off from his wife and kid, and stays away most of the time from his crew. After Moby Dick takes away one of his legs and wounded his pride, he holds God responsible for the presence of evil in the universe. Thus his anger assumes the proportions of a cosmic nature.

Ahab is a Shakespearean tragic hero. His tragedy is his own undoing. Obdurate and bent on avenging himself upon an embodiment of casual nature, he must die. Moreover, as a result of his egocentric obsession and his loss of sanity and humanity, he becomes a devilish creature and knows clearly of all that he is taking with him all his crew in his headlong rush toward doom. D. H. Lawrence sees in him the extreme transitions of the isolated, far-driven soul, without any real human contact.[8] So in a sense Ahab embodies all of the evil he once consigned to Moby Dick.[9]

Ahab may have been Melville's negative portrait of an Emersonian self-reliant individual. Ahab is too much of that kind to be a good human being. He stands alone on his own one leg among the millions of the peopled earth. For him the only law is his own will. To him the world exists for his sake. His selfhood must be asserted at the expense of all else: lives may be sacrificed, and nature may have to be vanquished in order that he may do what he wills. He never stops to think—and he never bothers about it—that, in asserting his private personality, he denies ruthlessly the humanity and individuality of his fellowmen. Ahab is no Odysseus, and his crew seems to be a ship of fools too much under the captain's evil spell to exercise their discretion. Their tragedy becomes a foregone conclusion. Critic Richard Chase is right when he says that the idea Melville conveys in *Moby Dick* is "death—spiritual, emotional, physical," which is the price of self-reliance when it is pushed to the point of solipsism.[10] Ahab is, to be more exact, a victim of solipsism, his tragedy stemming in the main from extreme individualism, selfish will, a spirit too much withdrawn to itself to warrant salvation.[11] By criticizing Emerson's Transcendental self-reliance and rejecting it, *Moby Dick* reveals 19th-century American loneliness and suicidal individualism.

Ishmael: An Affirmative Yes

Just as Ahab's doom is sealed, so Ishmael survives. These characters represent the two opposite poles of Melville's response to human existence. One is determined to say no to it, and the other learns to say yes. Ishmael resembles his namesake in the *Bible* in that he is a wanderer. He starts out feeling bad, hoping to find a place where he can live a happy and ideal life. Up to the time he goes on board the Pequod and midway through the book, he is an escapist, but with a faint hope to find the truth. Gradually he comes to see the folly of Ahab picking a quarrel with God and seeking to conquer nature, and he begins to feel the significance of love and companionship. In his life on the Pequod, he makes friends and learns to accept, an attitude which alone ensures his and humanity's survival. Voyaging for Ishmael has become a journey in quest of knowledge and values with which to survive.

Melville Resolved His Quarrel with God

Melville refused to be pacified until *Billy Budd* came out in print when he seemed to win through years of pain and suffering to a final serenity of mind, an acceptance of the fact that one must live by the rules of this world. It is true that it is a world in which God offers impossible standards, a world which Melville defines as a paradox; but as it is a paradox of existence by no means for men to resolve, Melville decided to quit his quest and reconcile himself with fate. So in *Billy Budd* the young sailor accepts his verdict unquestioningly and dies in peace and humility. Thus *Billy Budd* has been widely regarded as its author's testament of acceptance, a sign that he had resolved his quarrel with God.

The Symbolism of the Book

This, then, leads to the symbolism of the book. The voyage itself is a metaphor for "search and discovery, the search for the ultimate truth of experience."[12] The Pequod is, to D. H. Lawrence, the ship of the American soul, and the endeavor of its crew represents "the maniacal fanaticism of our white mental consciousness."[13] By far the most conspicuous symbol in the book is, of course, Moby Dick. The white whale is capable of many interpretations. It is a symbol of evil to some, one of goodness to others, and of both to still others. He is "paradoxically benign and malevolent, nourishing and destructive," "massive, brutal, monolithic, but at the same time protean, erotically beautiful, infinitely variable."[14] Its whiteness is a paradoxical color, too, signifying as it does death and corruption as well as purity, innocence, and youth. It represents the final mystery of the universe which man will do well to desist from pursuing, as critic Howard P. Vincent observes. As Ahab and his crew do not leave it alone, it is only natural that they get drowned.

The Pequod as a Miniature of Humanity

Melville's design for *Moby Dick* was ambitious. He meant the situation that the novel represents to be a symbol of a universally applicable human condition. Thus the crew on board the Pequod is a meaningful mix, not any crowd that is haphazardly picked and placed together. In addition to the Caucasians such as Captain Ahab, the first mate Starbuck, and Ishmael, a common sailor, there are Tashtego, the American Indian, Daggoo, the African American giant, Queequeg, the Polynesian pagan harpooner, a New Zealand prince, Pippin, a young black man, the Asiatic and Oriental Fedallah, also called the Parsee, in a word, men of all faiths and superstitions, all nationalities, all occupations, and from all walks of life.

Melville's Reputation

Melville was a devoted literary artist. The problem with him, if it is one at all, lies in the fact that he was unwilling to sacrifice his insights and artistic standards to cater to popular feeling and demand. He often began a book with something happy and optimistic, but ended it with a Shakespearean tragedy. No one saw his dilemma more accurately than Hawthorne who, after their last meeting, wrote, in his *English Notebooks*: "He will never rest until he gets hold of a definite belief. It is strange how he persists …. He can neither believe, nor be comfortable in his disbelief; and he is too honest and courageous not to try to do one or the other … he has a very high and noble nature."

Melville spoke ahead of his time. He knew that he was doomed to write a book like *Moby Dick* in his day, but he just could not help himself because he was dedicated to art. There was, as it were, a good deal of Ahab in him. "I have written a wicked book," he said after finishing *Moby Dick*, and the public felt outraged. The result was his tragic fall into the oblivion, from which it took decades and the persistent effort of a man called G. M. Weaver, a Columbia scholar, to resurrect him. The loss of faith and the sense of futility and meaninglessness which characterized the life of the early 20th-century West were expressed in Melville's work so well that the 20th century found it both fascinating and great. In the 1920s G. M. Weaver did solid spadework in reviving him, and Melville has been on the pedestal ever since. His permanence has been ensured in American literary history.

Chapter 6　Whitman • Dickinson

Both Walt Whitman (1819-1892) and Emily Dickinson (1830-1886) were American poets in theme and technique. Thematically, both extolled, in their different ways, an emergent America, its expansion, its individualism, and its Americanness, their poetry being part of what critic F. O. Matthiessen terms "American Renaissance." In technical terms, both added to the literary independence of the new nation by breaking free of the convention of the iambic pentameter and exhibiting a freedom in form unknown before: they were pioneers in American poetry pointing to Ezra Pound and the Imagists, and to William Carlos Williams and Wallace Stevens and other traditions in modern American poetry. In fact, a handy way of seeing modern American poetry is to find its sources in the two founts, Walt Whitman and Emily Dickinson.

Walt Whitman (1819-1892)

 Whitman was brought up in a working-class background on Long Island, New York. He had five years of schooling, a good deal of "loafing" and reading, and tried at a variety of jobs. He wrote some lurid tales, a tear-jerking novel, and some traditionally metrical rimed verse. In 1848 he traveled to New Orleans and saw very much of the Mississippi heartlands. This experience with the people and the country furnished both the material and the guiding spirit for his epic, *Leaves of Grass*. Its first edition came out in print in 1855 which contained the basic strengths of Whitman's art. [1]

During the Civil War, Whitman worked as a volunteer nurse, a "wound-dresser" in military hospitals, an experience which further enriched his knowledge of life and the world. In the meantime he continued to revise and expand his *Leaves of Grass*.

Whitman was susceptible to many influences.[2] The Enlightenment and its ideals, Quakerism, Transcendentalism, German philosophy, especially Hegel's "doctrine of a cosmic consciousness," science, pantheism, the idea of progress, and American western frontier spirit, Jacksonian laissez-faire individualism, general mysticism and anti-rationalism, the theory of "the Great Chain of Being," in a word, the fundamental ideas prevalent in America at the time pervade all Whitman's poems.[3] Nor was this all. Whitman's relationship to Orientalism has been well established by modern and recent criticism.

Emerson's Influence

Special mention should be made of Emerson's influence over Whitman. In his career as a poet, Whitman drew most heavily from Emerson's works. "I was simmering, simmering, simmering," he said in 1860, "Emerson brought me to a boil." Emerson's support came just at the moment when it was most needed. Amid the angry responses at the first edition of *Leaves of Grass*, Emerson sent his famous letter which called *Leaves of Grass* "the most extraordinary piece of wit and wisdom that an American has yet contributed."

Whitman was more indebted to Emerson than any other 19th-century American author. The preface to the 1855 edition of *Leaves of Grass* is an elaboration of Emerson's essay "The Poet." Echoing Emerson's "America is a poem in our eyes," Whitman declares that "The Americans of all nations at any time upon the earth have probably the fullest poetic nature. The United States themselves are essentially the greatest poem." In response to the Emersonian concept of the American poet as the universal man, Whitman states that the greatest poet breathes into the world the grandeur and life of the universe. "He is a seer," he says, "he is individual … he is complete in himself." Both Whitman and Emerson felt that the poet were doing the job of a minister, a clergyman, the Church.

In addition, both Whitman and Emerson wrote on the organic principle. To them, art should be based organically on nature; the poet's work grows out of nature and cosmic processes and derives its form from within. No wonder that the appearance of the first edition of *Leaves of Grass* filled Emerson with such joy that he seemed to see the coming of the American poet on the horizon at last.

Whitman's Poetry: His Thematic and Formal Concerns

Whitman wrote over four hundred poems in his life which he put into one book, *Leaves of Grass*, "a book," as he says, "I have made, / The words of my book nothing, the drift of it everything, / A book separate, not link'd with the rest nor felt by the intellect, / But you yet untold latencies will thrill to every page."

Whitman is not easy to read. His poems contain what he called "untold latencies." This means that his poetry suggests, rather than tells. The whole book is "a passageway [as he says of it himself] to something rather than a thing in itself concluded." It is good to take a close look at some of his poems just for an experience of his poetry.

Whitman's Thematic Concerns

Three things stand out in bold relief regarding Whitman's themes, or his thought.

First, Whitman extols the ideals of equality and democracy and celebrates the dignity, the self-reliant spirit, and the joy of the common man. "Song of Myself" reveals a world of equality, without rank and hierarchy. The prostitute draggling her shawl, the President holding a cabinet council, the stately and friendly matrons on the piazza walk, the Missourian crossing the plains and an infinite number of other things and people find their way into his poem and juxtapose with one another, illustrating the principle of democracy and equality. The poet, walking around, hears America singing. The mother is singing while setting food on the table. The carpenter is singing, planing his boards. And the day is singing "What belongs to the day." Long catalogs of different people and different occupations indicate that here the new children of Adam are being restored to the Garden of Eden, developing their potentiality to the fullest extent possible. In a general sense *Leaves of Grass* is an Adamic song, and its author an Adamic singer.[4]

Then, Whitman responds enthusiastically to the expansion of America. The new bustling and progressive republic, with its dynamic creative fertility and its indomitable energy, finds a willing and refreshing voice in Whitman. Read again "Song of Myself" and poems like "There Was a Child Went Forth," and we see the spirit of an emerging America at its most aggressive and daring. The process of becoming is most clearly seen in the lines that suggest the daily growth of the child who is capable of absorbing everything and goes forth doing so every day "for many years or stretching cycles of years." In "Crossing Brooklyn Ferry," the poet sees everything in the universe as "glories strung like beads on my smallest sights and hearings." It is a universe in constant motion and flux, one in which it is a pride to thrive, expand and live for all time. Whitman's voice echoes the sound of America singing and foretells the future union of the nations and the world and the cosmos.

Thirdly, Whitman embraces idealism. He relies on insight and intuition. His poetry communicates his views on the cosmos and on man. Unity, unreality of time and space, evil as only an appearance emerging into good, the equal potential divinity of everything from grass to mankind, the immanence of God in all creation, plentitude, continuity and gradation, the multiplicity of nature, and the need for a poetry commensurate with it — all these find adequate expression in his poems. His "Song of Myself" is a repertory of his thought. From a blade of "curling grass" the poet sees into the mystery of death and birth and concludes that "the smallest sprout shows there is really no death," and that "all goes onward and outward, nothing collapses." The "I," present everywhere in life, leaves one with the impression of a divine omniscience beholding nature and man alike. It is only natural that "I am deathless," "I exist as I am," and "One world is aware … and that is myself," and that the whole poem ends on an extremely transcendental note: "I am large, I contain multitudes."

Whitman was a transitional figure from Romanticism and Transcendentalism to realism. In later years Whitman came to see the failure of democracy and the social and moral corruption in America ("Democratic Vistas"), but he thought these curable by the self-reform of the individual. Material gains are fruitless without personal morality; individualism without brotherhood is suicide. Thus "Passage to India" extols "the marriage of continents" and different races, and "Proud Music of the Storm" envisages unity of "all the tongues of nations." The emphasis is clearly on brotherhood and social solidarity.

Whitman's Formal Concerns

Whitman was a daring experimentalist who, in the words of Ezra Pound, "broke the new wood." His early poems are in conventional rime and meter, but apparently he found the restrictions disappointing. He began to experiment about 1847 which led to a complete break with traditional poetics. A few features of Whitman's technique merit attention.

One major principle of Whitman's technique is parallelism or a rhythm of thought in which, as critic Bliss Perry observes, the line is the rhythmical unit, as in the poetry of the English *Bible*. Another main principle of Whitman's versification is phonetic recurrence, i.e., the systematic repetition of words and phrases at the beginning of the line, in the middle or at the end. These two principles coordinate with and reinforce each other. They operate also in conventional poetry, but not as about the only rhythmical principles as in Whitman's poetry. Whitman broke free from the traditional iambic pentameter and wrote "free verse." His long "catalogs" of lines gave free rein to his imagination in his life-long attempt to celebrate life in the new world.

Now a close look at some of his poems is in order.

"Out of the Cradle Endlessly Rocking"

"Out of the Cradle Endlessly Rocking" is a reminiscence of a childhood experience. The incident described here is simple enough though its "drift" is profound as we shall illustrate. Once a long time ago a little boy was wandering on a bright "Fifth-month" day on the seashore when, all of a sudden, he heard two mocking-birds, a male and a female, happily singing together. "Shine! shine! shine! / Pour down your warmth, great sun! / While we bask, we two together / Singing all time, minding no time, / While we two together." But they did not stay long together: one day the she-bird disappeared, leaving her mate behind, disconsolate and "solitary." The he-bird, the lone singer, sat there calling out on land for his mate to return and shaking out carols of "lonesome love": "O past! O happy life! O songs of joy! / In the air, in the woods, over fields, / Loved! loved! loved! loved! / But my mate no more, no more with me! / We two together no more." But there was no response: there was only the waning moon, the whispering sea, and the enveloping darkness that was night. The boy was moved. Thrown into raptures and in a moment of inspiration, he became aware of the mission for which he was born: "Now in a moment I know what I am for, I awake / A thousand warbling echoes have started to life within me, never to die." He became restless, thirsting to know "the destiny of me," and seeking "the clew" from the waves. On the seashore where "liquid rims" and "wet sands" met, he heard the sea singing "Death, death, death, death." It was, he realized, the word of "the sweetest song and all songs." He became a mature poet.

As critic J. E. Miller points out, the poem can be split into three subsections. The first of these sings of ideal love and bliss, the second of bereavement and lonesome love, and the third of death as the spiritual fulfillment of lonesome love. A careful reading will reveal that there are two sets of symbols, the sun and the moon, day and night, land and sea, which between them indicate the duality of nature and life. The sun, day, and land suggest life and the physical, while the moon, night, and sea represent death and the spiritual. On the seashore where the sea and land meet and merge, the cycle of nature in its rhythmical evolution ends only to renew itself, with death as the beginning of new life. When the boy became aware of these "meanings which I of all men know," he had progressed to maturity and become a "chanter of pains and joys, uniter of here and hereafter," and a singer of the endless cycle. It is no wonder that the poem begins with the cradle rocking and ends with "some old crone rocking the cradle," carefully encasing itself in an artistically hermetic whole.

"When Lilacs Last in the Dooryard Bloom'd"

"When Lilacs Last in the Dooryard Bloom'd" is, both in theme and form, a tour de force of Whitman's. Thematically, it deals with the typical Whitmanesque love-and-death motif. It was written in memory of President Lincoln, though the name of Lincoln never appears in it. Lincoln was assassinated and the whole nation was in mourning. Read the second section every line of which begins with an "O," a sign of the mouth of a person weeping, and we get to know the intensity of the grief with which the nation, the poet included, was stricken. For over half the length of the poem, the poet is seen writhing in the grip of physical loss. The coffin is seen passing, the great cloud darkening the land, the cities draped in black, the sea of faces silent and solemn, and the mournful voices of dirges strongly rising. Joining, the poet chants a song for the "sane and sacred death." He looks up and sees the western fallen star. "O the black murk that hides the star!" he thus laments. When he looks around he spots the lilac bush blossoming in the dooryard and feels its physical appeal strongly.

Then he becomes conscious of a shy and hidden thrush warbling forth "Death's outlet song of life." The lilac bush, with its rich colors and scent, represents physical life, while the hermit thrush bodies forth spiritual life. And the poet finds himself attracted to both. It is apparent that he has got to progress from the one to the other, namely, to reconcile a love of life, to quote James E. Miller again, with a love of death, death as representing rebirth onto spiritual life. Thus gradually we see the poet recovering from his deep grief over mortality and becoming aware of the spiritual existence of Lincoln and his immortality. The song of the bird, which he is beginning to appreciate, induces in him "a mystical state" from which come mystical visions: "To the tally of my soul, / Loud and strong kept up the gray-brown bird /... While my sight that was bound in my eyes unclosed, / As to long panoramas of visions." In this way, "Lilac and star and bird twined with the chant of my soul."

Reading the poem we perceive the stages through which the mind of the poet goes through. The poetic process is highly symbolic: The star is associated with the thought of death, the lilac with a token of life for the dead, and the bird with insight and knowledge of death not as the end but as the beginning of new life. Whitman was a mystic. He detests talking of the beginning and the end as, for him, "All goes onward and outward, nothing collapses" ("Song of Myself"). "When Lilacs Last in the Dooryard Bloom'd" is one of the best poems which embody his visions.

Whitman's Influence

Whitman's influence over modern poetry is great in the world as well as in America. His best work has become part of the common property of Western culture. Many poets in England, France, Italy and Latin America are in his debt. Modern American poets like T. S. Eliot and Ezra Pound would not have been what they were without Whitman. Pound, who called him a "pigheaded father," recognized him nonetheless as a father figure who led the break from the past, and became a kind of poet-prophet himself in the early 20th century.[5] Hart Crane's *Bridge* derives its incentive and inspiration in part from Whitman. Carl Sandburg was probably the only great poet who carried, in his Chicago poems, the Whitmanesque tradition into the 20th century in a whole-hearted way.

In the 20th century, Whitman's excessive optimism led to a decline of his reputation, but not for long. All schools or forms of modern and contemporary American poetry bear witness to his influence. Whitman has been compared to a mountain in American literary history. You may go around him if you like, but you cannot pretend that he is not there. For his innovations in diction and versification, his frankness about sex, his inclusion of the commonplace and the ugly and his censure of the weaknesses of the American democratic practice—these have paved his way to a share of immortality in American literature.

Emily Dickinson (1830-1886)

Dickinson differs from Whitman in a variety of ways. For one thing, Whitman seems to keep his eye on society at large; Dickinson explores the inner life of the individual. Whereas Whitman is "national" in his outlook, Dickinson is "regional" ("because I see New-Englandly"). In formal terms the two poets are vastly different: Whitman's endless, all-inclusive catalogs contrast with the concise, direct, and simple diction and syntax which characterize Dickinson's poetry.[6] Dickinson denied having read Whitman.

Dickinson was born in 1830 into a Calvinist family of Amherst, Massachusetts. Her father, an old Puritan, influenced her. Emily enjoyed a normal and vivacious girlhood, and had love from her family, though not always understanding. She was shy, sensitive, individualistic, and rebellious.

After school at Amherst Academy and Mount Holyoke College, Dickinson lived a normal New England village life at home. She stayed almost all her life in the same house, and found passionate joy in merely being alive ("I find ecstasy in living," she told a friend on one occasion, "the mere sense of living is joy enough").[7] She read the *Bible*, Shakespeare, and Keats, among others, and lived a simple and independent life (as indicated in her poem "The Soul selects her own Society"). Gradually, she became a recluse. She saw few people later in life, but always befriended her neighbors and all in distress. Her two passions were her garden and her poetry.

The Rediscovery of Her Poetry

During her twenties she began writing poetry seriously. She wrote,

altogether, the well-established 1,775 poems (the new discoveries excluded), of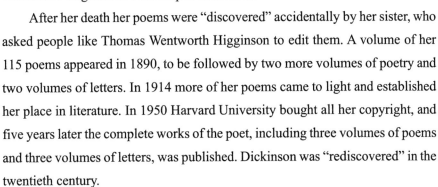
which only seven appeared in print in her lifetime. The "surgery" that the editors
like Thomas Wentworth Higginson and Samuel Bowles did to her published
work appalled her so that she decided to withdraw from a world which was not
ready for her.[8] She trusted to the future ("If fame belonged to me," she wrote, "I
could not escape her"). She kept on writing at a regular pace. At one time, what
could be called "her frenzied poetic creativity" occurred, and that happened in
1862. It has been conjectured that an emotional involvement with a Charles
Wadsworth might have been responsible for it.

After her death her poems were "discovered" accidentally by her sister, who
asked people like Thomas Wentworth Higginson to edit them. A volume of her
115 poems appeared in 1890, to be followed by two more volumes of poetry and
two volumes of letters. In 1914 more of her poems came to light and established
her place in literature. In 1950 Harvard University bought all her copyright, and
five years later the complete works of the poet, including three volumes of poems
and three volumes of letters, was published. Dickinson was "rediscovered" in the
twentieth century.

The Tragic Tone of Her Poetry

The basic tone of Dickinson's poetry is tragic. That has to do with the
pressure of Calvinist pessimism on her mind. She expresses in her work a
passionate yearning for religious certitude, God's help, and the good life ("At
last to pray is left"). But the God of the *Bible* is not always real to her; she does
not always believe in God's plan for an after-life; she cannot bring herself to
reconcile a belief in "our" Father permitting evil to exist. Her poetry shows that
the loss of faith, the religious uncertainty, assailed her thinking. She failed to
confess herself Christian, so in an act of self-recognition, she embraced poetic
life. She affirmed her individuality in her poetry as she realized that poetic
interpretation of life conflicted with religious dogma. She emerged as a mature

poet.[9]

Reading Dickinson, we may find three themes stand out in bold relief: death, love, and nature.

On Death and Immortality

By far the largest portion of Dickinson's poetry concerns death and immortality, themes which lie at the center of her world: about one third of her poems dwell on these subjects. Dickinson's many friends died before her, and the fact that death seemed to occur often in the Amherst of the time added to her gloomy meditation. Her poem, "My life closed twice before its close" portrays the poet as ever-ready for the assault of death:

> My life closed twice before its close;
> It yet remains to see
> If immortality unveil
> A third event to me,
>
> So huge, so hopeless to conceive
> As these that twice fell.
> Parting is all we know of heaven,
> And all we need of hell.

For Dickinson death leads to immortality, as is illustrated in poems like "Because I could not stop for Death." Death comes as imperceptibly as grief and marks the beginning of a higher life ("As imperceptibly as Grief"). So deeply engrossed was the poet in her macabre deliberations that she began to conceive of the process of dying in poems such as "I heard a fly buzz when I died." But she was skeptical and ambivalent about the possibility of achieving immortality. Dickinson believes that man is aided in his struggle by a resolute faith in immortality, as her "Death is a Dialogue between" demonstrates.

On Love

Dickinson wrote about love as well. She was original in her manner of writing. "Mine—by the Right of the White Election" expresses a passionate and eternal love in an elegiac tone. "Wild Nights—Wild Nights" is in more than one respect a peculiar work on love:

> Wild Nights—Wild Nights!
> Were I with thee
> Wild Nights should be
> Our Luxury!
>
> Futile—the Winds—
> To a Heart in port
> Done with the Compass—
> Done with the chart!
>
> Rowing in Eden—
> Ah, the Sea!
> Might I but moor
> Tonight—In thee!

The erotic image is self-evident. Love is expressed in an unabashed manner. The boat and the sea as symbols of male and female lovers coalesce in wild consummated love-making.

On Nature

Dickinson's nature poems are great in number and rich in matter. Natural phenomena, changes of seasons, heavenly bodies, animals, birds and insects, flowers of various kinds—all these and many other subjects related to nature find their way into her poetry. The grandeur of a sunrise ("I'll tell you how the sun rose"), the mixed feelings of joy and grief at the coming of spring and autumn ("New feet within my garden go" and "These are the days when birds come back"), the sense of momentary transitoriness ("A Route of Evanescence"), and the power and majesty of a summer storm are among the themes Dickinson handled beautifully.

Whereas she sees nature as benevolent, she is also aware of its cold indifference. Her poems indicate that she shares in part Tennyson's sense of an evolutionary nature— "red in tooth and claw with raven." "Apparently with no surprise" tells of an accidental murder to which the sun is apathetic and of which God approves: frost kills a happy flower at its play and goes unmolested while both the sun and God look on. A bird that comes down the walk may serve as a symbol of nature itself with which the poet (man) tries to establish a form of connection and understanding, but all in vain: alienation exists in between.

On Transcendentalism, etc.

Emerson was, in a sense, a formative influence over Dickinson. She read Emerson appreciatively and wrote to test the Transcendentalist ethic in its application to the inner life. Her best poetry portrays the psychological tension within the individual. She emphasizes free will and human responsibility and sees the "Renunciation" of anything low or hostile to man's spiritual heritage and self-respect as the highest duty of the individual. Lines like "To fight aloud is very brave, / But gallanter, know, / Who charge within the bosom, / The cavalry of woe" are a clear indication of the poet's preoccupation with self-improvement. With regard to the soul, her conviction of its sovereignty is absolute. "The Brain is wider than the Sky" and "I know that He exists" are but two of many good illustrations. Like the Transcendentalists, Dickinson attacks over-emphasis on materialism and commercialism ("I took my power in my hand / And went against the world").

Her response to the expansion of America was a warm one. Her poem, "I like to see it lap the Miles," offers the impressive and striking image of a galloping horse as a symbol of both the railroad and the developing America. Her sympathy for the poor and the weak appears in poems such as "The beggar lad dies early," and "If I can stop one heart from breaking." She also wrote a few poignant war elegies such as "When I was small a woman died."

Dickenson's Aesthetics

Like Emerson, Dickinson holds that beauty, truth and goodness are ultimately one. In "I died for Beauty—but was scarce," discussing beauty and truth, she concludes that the two are one. In "I reckon when I count at all," she considers "First Poets—then the sun—then summer—then the Heaven of God" (goodness), but concludes that the true poet can "comprehend the whole."

Dickinson delights in "[telling] all the Truth but tell it slant—". She is good at catching the charm of something but dropping the thing itself. A good example is her poem, "A narrow Fellow in the Grass." It talks about the snake all the while, but the word "snake" never appears. This may have made Dickinson obscure and inscrutable sometimes.

Like Whitman she was a courageous experimentalist. "I have no monarch in my life," she declared. Indeed, little that she wrote seemed conventional: her choice of words, her verbal constructions, even her spelling. And, then, there are her images. To her poetry is "a bodying forth by means of concrete images" of an inspired thought. Her poetry abounds in telling images. In the best of her poems every word is a picture seen. A salient feature of her technique is her severe economy of expression. Her poetic idiom is noted for its laconic brevity, directness, and plainest words. All these characteristics of her poetry were to become popular through Stephen Crane (1871-1900) and the Imagists such as

Ezra Pound and Amy Lowell in the 20th century. She became, with Stephen Crane, the precursor of the Imagist movement.

Dickinson lived to write a "letter to the world" that would express her ideas of the world and paint what Henry James called "the landscape of the soul."[10] If the cultivated taste of her own day failed to appreciate her genius, the long day has passed, and she has won the fame that "belonged" to her.

Chapter 7   Edgar Allan Poe

Poe's Life

Poe's childhood was a miserable one. He lost both of his parents when still very small, and was taken care of by John Allan, a wealthy merchant of Virginia. The Allans failed to offer the orphan a normal home. At 17 Poe entered the University of Virginia but did not finish. He went to West Point as a cadet but was dismissed because of misbehavior.

Poe worked as editor most of his short life and wrote a good number of reviews which reveal his insight and originality as a critic. He was poor all his life. At 27 he married his thirteen-year-old cousin, whose death in 1847 left him inconsolable and bitterer with life than ever. He died, in mysterious circumstances, in October, 1849.

Poe began his career as an author in 1827 when his first book of poetry appeared. His second came out in 1829, to be followed by his third in 1831. Five of his tales came out in 1832. His best tales include such as "The Fall of the House of Usher," "Ligeia," "The Tell-Tale Heart," "MS. Found in a Bottle," and "The Murders in the Rue Morgue." His one full-length novel, *The Narrative of Arthur Gordon Pym* was out in print in 1838, and his *Tales of the Grotesque and Arabesque* in 1839. His poem, "The Raven" (1844), was an immediate success and has remained one of his most enduring works. Poe's literary output, some seventy short stories and a dozen poems, is small, but it is immensely interesting and influential as a literary inheritance.

Poe's achievement as a critic, a poet, and a short-story writer has been highly evaluated.

Poe as a Critic

Poe was a literary genius. George Bernard Shaw spoke highly of him on the centenary of his birth. Poe was, Shaw said, "the greatest journalistic critic of his time"; his poetry is "exquisitely refined"; and his tales are "complete works of art."

As a critic, Poe was good at generalizing. He tried to cash in on his own literary practice to rationalize about literary creations. His poetic theories are remarkable in their clarity even if they lack what critic Joseph Wood Krutch terms "intellectual detachment" and "catholicity of taste."[1] His theories are best elucidated in his "The Philosophy of Composition" and "The Poetic Principle." As he was outspoken when commenting on other writers' works, he might have offended some of his famous contemporaries such as Emerson and the New England poets.

Poe as a Poet

As a poet, Poe is opposed to "the heresy of the didactic" and calls for "pure" poetry. In his opinion, art does not lie in its message; poetry does not have to inculcate a moral; it has only to be; the artistry of the poem lies not so much in what is being said as in the way it says it. He stresses rhythm, defines true poetry as "the rhythmical creation of beauty," and declares that "music is the perfection of the soul, or idea, of poetry." Poe was unabashed to offer his own poem "The Raven" as an illustration of his point.[2]

Poe's poetic theories are a rationalizing of his own writing practice. The poem, he says, should be short, readable at one sitting (or as long as "The Raven"). Its chief aim is to create beauty, namely, to produce a feeling of beauty in the reader. Beauty aims at "an elevating excitement of the soul," and "beauty of whatever kind, in its supreme development, invariably excites the sensitive soul to tears. Thus melancholy is the most legitimate of all the poetic tones." And he concludes that "the death of a beautiful woman is, unquestionably, the most poetical topic in the world."

Here his poem, "The Raven," fits in perfectly well. It is about 100 lines (108 in fact), perfectly readable at one sitting. A sense of melancholy over the death of a beloved beautiful young woman pervades the whole poem: the portrayal of a young man grieving for his lost Lenore, his grief being turned to madness under the steady one-word repetition of the talking bird introduced right at the beginning of the poem. After he sees the bird, its response—or its imagined one—"nevermore"—keeps breaking upon the young man's psychic wound ruthlessly and ceaselessly as do the waves on the sea shore until his depression reaches its breaking point:

> And the Raven, never flitting, still is sitting, *still* is sitting,
> On the pallid bust of Pallas just above my chamber door;
> And his eyes have all the seeming of a demon's that is dreaming,
> And the lamp-light o'er him streaming throws his shadow on the
> floor;
> And my soul from out that shadow that lies floating on the floor
> Shall be lifted—nevermore!

The young man, a neurotic on the brink of a mental collapse, outpours his sorrow in his semi-sleep on the appearance of the bird. The tragic effect of the bereavement is well expressed by the phantom of the talking bird.

"The Raven" is heavily tinted in a dreamy, hallucinatory color with its narrator in a state of semi-stupor. This is a major feature of Poe's poems, like "Annabel Lee" which contains lines, "… the moon never beams without bringing me dreams/ Of the beautiful Annabel Lee"; or "The Sleeper" in which the poet, standing beneath the mystic moon at midnight in the month of June, smells an opiate vapor, finds the universe wrapped up in a fog, and half dreams of the dead beauty sleeping peacefully in her grave; or "A Dream Within a Dream," wherein the poet realizes that all his days have been a dream and that, with hope gone, all is dream within a dream.

"To Helen," one of the most famous of Poe's lyrics, was written, as Poe recalls, "in my passionate boyhood, to the first, purely ideal love of my soul." It was inspired by the beauty of the mother of a schoolmate of Poe's in Richmond, Virginia. The poem is famous for a number of things, for example, its rhyme scheme, its varied line lengths, its metaphor of a travel on the sea, and its oft-quoted lines, "To the Glory that was Greece / And the grandeur that was Rome."

In "Sonnet—To Science," the poet is talking to an abstraction, science, which is personified and treated as a villain. Animalized as a vulture, science has relieved the world of a lot of its myth and, with it, the room for poetic imagination: The romance of Diana, Hamadryad, Naiad, and the Elfin is broken, and so is the poet's "summer dream beneath the tamarind tree." The poet is hindered in his aspirations. The tension between science on the one hand and art and imagination on the other endows the poem with a unique power and significance. "Sonnet—To Science" is a good indication that Poe was in essence a Renaissance man. He derived in part from Plato the notion that the universe was endowed with myth, and tried to restore it to the primordial unity which the cosmos once possessed.

The same idea finds adequate expression in another of his best poems, "Israfel." Israfel is a perfect poet, singing "wildly well" in Heaven with his lute of heart-strings. Here is an ideal world in the upper air of which this world is but an inadequate approximation (this is Plato again). This world longs to sing the same songs as does Israfel, and the poet longs for the same kind of poetic ability of Israfel's.

Poe's Poetic Style

Poe insists on an even metrical flow in versification. "The Raven" is a marvel of regularity: W. L. Werner records that, of its 719 complete feet, 705 are perfect trochees, ten doubtful trochees, and only four clearly dactyls.

Emerson called Poe "a jingle man." It probably had to do with the metrical flow in Poe's poetry, which does not say much but sounds well with an elaborate display of pure technique. "The Bells" is a good example. All sounds, vowels and diphthongs for example, and all poetic devices such as alliteration, assonance, and consonance are brought into full play for the "rhythmical creation of beauty," in this ingenious work of sounds, which has little or no substance. This was probably one of the reasons why Poe was and has been regarded as one of the first aesthetes in literary history.

Poe's style is traditional. It is much too rational, too ordinary to reflect the peculiarity of his theme. Somehow he failed to carry the newness of his idea into his style to echo his new theme. Poe is not easy to read. His choice of words and his syntax may have been responsible for his difficult prose. Occasionally one feels his mannerism hindering a smooth and pleasurable reading.

Poe as a Short Story Writer

As a short story writer, Poe is noted for two things. One of these is that he took delight in delving into the deeps of the mind, and the other is that he was the precursor of the genre of the detective story.

First, Poe anticipated 20th-century literature in his treatment of the disintegration of the self in a world of T. S. Eliot's "waste land" and Hemingway's "nada (nothingness)." Poe explored man's mental and moral disease, and opened up for literature a new order of experience that seemed to have been hitherto effectively sealed off.

In his tales, Poe places the subconscious condition of the mind under investigation and probes beneath the surface of normal existence. What interests him most is the deep abyss of the unconscious and subconscious mental activity of the people, and the subterranean recesses of the mind at work.

Poe's tales mostly turn on the central theme of the workings of the mind. For instance, "Black Cat" is an incisive inquiry into the capacity of the human mind to originate its own destruction; "The Imp of the Perverse," more allegory than a tale, illustrates Poe's rationale that "to indulge alone in any attempted thought is inevitably lost." Poe reveals the process with alarming accuracy.

He assumes that every mind is half mad or capable of slipping into insanity. He seems to feel that the human mind would be healthy and alive if it were incapable of thought, but since it is a mind and does possess the power of introspection and self-knowledge, then that very power and knowledge will inevitably spell its death. In other words, thought is the constituent of the mind, but the act of thinking can be its undoing.

So his fictional characters are mostly neurotics. He was the first author in American literature to make the neurotic the protagonist in his stories. His major characters can be a criminal who attempts to establish his sense of identity by the crime that he commits, which is essentially the situation we find in "The Tell-Tale Heart." Or a major character can be a bereaved lover, such as is the case with "Ligeia," and "The Fall of the House of Usher." Some of them are like Melville's "isolatoes," with no sense of identity, no name even, no place nor parentage dislocated, alienated from society, wandering from place to place like William Wilson, or a man desultorily following the crowd ("The Man of the Crowd") because he does not know where to belong.

Poe's most enduring tales are those of horror. The horror comes from the workings of an irrational or criminal mind. The mind is driven to evil or insanity by a perverse, irrational force which, to Poe, is an elementary impulse in man. A number of Poe's tales treat a number of different people who, going mad, are all along aware that they are going mad, thus exhibiting the believable stages of mental disintegration. It is good to remember that Poe has clear theories to offer for writing the short story. His principles are best illustrated in his review of Hawthorne's *Twice-Told Tales*. These indicate that Poe is concerned with the form of the short story. He may not be aware that the significance of his tales lies miles away elsewhere. We mean the theme of his works.

Poe's most famous tale is "The Fall of the House of Usher." Here in this decaying house live a brother and sister. The sister is so ill that the brother buries her alive and puts the coffin away in one secluded part of the house. Then on a stormy night, the sister breaks out of her coffin and dies in the embrace of her brother, who then also dies. The house collapses into the lake on the shore of which it has stood.

Roderick Usher, the brother, is very much a Poe character. He knows every turn of his own disintegrating mind. What drives him crazy is not immediately clear. He tries to destroy his twin sister with whom he may have committed incest. Her removal might free him from his emotional and physical stress as well as his life, for he knows that, as soon as she dies, he dies, too. The destructive, incestuous joining may be responsible for the tragedy of the mind. The collapse of the house is symbolic of the ultimate annihilation of the being that was Usher.[3] Poe places Usher's school friend beside him, watching and then coming back to retell about the appalling process of the dissolution. That device adds to the horror of the story.

Another horror story is "The Tell-Tale Heart." The tale can be read and understood differently. One way of reading it is to see it as a tale of murder that presents the internal disintegration of a mind in an exterior way. The narrator-murderer is obviously a schizophrenic, to whom the eyes of the victim prove to be intolerable. So the murderer commits the crime. However, his neurotic mind cannot resist the temptation, the neurotic joy, of revealing his criminal secret. Here Poe makes a neurotic and a criminal his narrator. Another interesting interpretation of the tale is to see it as representing the love-and-hate relationship between the anxiously overseeing parents and the rebellious urge of the young to remove the parental supervision. Both readings reveal a narrator whose reliability is in question.

Poe's excavation of the human mind is one of the reasons why he is a lot more interesting as a writer now than he was in his own century. In the 20th century Freud, Jung, and their associates and disciples pushed research into the deepest recesses of the human mind, and thus influenced modern life and literature in a profound way. Poe's greatness lies in the fact that he anticipated these developments as no one else had done.

Another thing to mention about Poe is that he wrote half a dozen stories which may fall in the genre of the detective. "The Murders in the Rue Morgue," "The Purloined Letter," "The Gold Bug," and "The Mystery of Marie Roget" are the best of this category. Poe was fascinated with the intuitive faculty, the power to enter intuitively into the mind of another person as a source of technique in solving a crime. Take "The Purloined Letter" for example. Dupin is endowed with the miraculous faculty to place himself in the mind of the criminal. With this power of inductive reasoning, he manages to solve a problem without even having to leave his room. Before he takes the final action to retrieve the critical letter about the Queen, he envisions, and accurately, the place where Minister D would hide it: the criminal would be clever enough to leave the letter where most people of mediocre intelligence would fail to notice—the most visible yet the least attention-grabbing card-rack. Poe exhibits a rare combination of imagination with "a keen analytical mind and mathematical powers of a high order" in proving that the assassin in "The Murders in the Rue Morgue" is not human. Here the pattern which the story follows is immensely fascinating. It is a locked-room puzzle. One opens the door, finds not only no murderer and no weapon, but no trace of any human being having ever moved about in the room. Poe obviously delights in such analytical feats of the mind. He has now been regarded as precursor of the detective genre of writing.

Poe's Reputation

For a long time after his death, Poe remained probably the most controversial and most misunderstood literary figure in the history of American literature. American literary criticism generally failed to give a satisfactory account of his undeniable permanence and power" (P. F. Quinn). Eminent literary figures like Emerson, Mark Twain, Henry James, and T. S. Eliot did not have much good to say of him. And his literary executor, Rufus Griswold, spared no pains, after his death, to sully his reputation and painted him as a Bohemian, depraved, and demonic, a villain with no virtue at all.

It was in Europe that Poe enjoyed respect and welcome. Swinburne, Bernard Shaw, D. H. Lawrence, and W. H. Auden all admired and spoke highly of him. Poe's influence was considerable in Spain and Spanish America, in Italy, in Germany where writers such as R. M. Rilke were indebted to him, and in Russia where the works of Dostoevsky, among others, bear a visible imprint of Poe's influence.

Poe became famous first in France. Charles Baudelaire (1821-1867) first took note of the psychological content of Poe's tales and regarded Poe as "a writer of nerves." He was determined that "Edgar Poe, who isn't much in America, must become a great man in France," and he spent the best part of his mature life translating Poe. It was he who elevated Poe to the status of a literary deity. Other famous French writers such as Stephane Mallarme and Paul A. Valery all paid their homage to the American poet. Naturally enough, the first most exhaustive critical studies of Poe's work were written in France.

Poe's greatness has been well recognized in the world today, and his influence is world-wide in modern literature. His aesthetics and conscious craftsmanship, his attack on "the heresy of the didactic," and his call for "the rhythmical creation of beauty" have influenced French symbolists and the devotees of "art for art's sake." Poe was father of many things, one of which is psychoanalytic criticism, the other being the detective story. Some of his tales left a visible imprint on such major English authors as H. G. Wells and American authors like T. S. Eliot and William Faulkner. His popularity has been on the increase in the last half-century.

Poe's relationship to Chinese literature is not insignificant. A recent study has revealed an interesting fact, that modern Chinese masters like Lu Xun and

Guo Mo-ruo all felt his presence on the Chinese literary scene of the early decades of the 20th century: They read and commented upon his works.[4] It is obvious that further research need be done in this field.

Chapter 8   *The Age of Realism • Howells • James*

Realism: Social Background

Political and social events influence writers in both theme and technique. We are now dealing with the post-bellum period in American history. The Civil War, which was a very important influence on American literature, changed America in a significant way. The industrialized Hamiltonian North fought the agrarian Jeffersonian South like two separate countries for supremacy. The factory defeated the farm, and the United States headed toward capitalism. In a way the surrender at Appomattox marked the beginnings of a course which America has followed to this day. The war led many to question the assumptions shared by the Transcendentalists such as natural goodness, the optimistic view of nature and man, and benevolent God. It taught men that life was not so good, man was not, and God was not. The war marked a change, in the words of critic Lionel Trilling, in the quality of American life, a deterioration, in fact, of American moral values.

In post-bellum America, commerce took the lead in the national economy. Railroads tripled in 15 years and were multiplied five times in 25, and petroleum was discovered in sizeable quantities. By 1880 half the population in the east lived in towns, and movement away from the farm became obvious. Increasing industrialization and mechanization of the country, now in full swing after the war, soon produced extremes of wealth and poverty. Wealth and power were more and more concentrated in the hands of the few "captains of industry" or "robber barons" such as John D. Rockefeller, Andrew Carnegie, and J. P. Morgan. These people had most of them as young men avoided service during the war and made fantastic profits in the booming war-time economy. Now they became dominant in the social and economic life of the nation. The spirit of self-reliance that Emerson had preached became perverted into admiration for driving ambition, a lust for money and power. Preachers shouted it from the pulpits; children were brought up on the Horatio Alger success stories which said that a person with ambition could make his own world. When John D. Rockefeller claimed in all seriousness that his money had been given him by God, nobody laughed. Too few people recognized the chicanery and graft going on around them. In the meantime, life for the millions was fast becoming a veritable struggle for survival.

Added to this was the fact that the frontier was closing.[1] The frontier had been a factor of great importance in American life. As long as the frontier was there, people could always pack up and go, and hope to escape troubles over the next hill and have a better life ahead. Now that the frontier was about to close and the safety valve was ceasing to operate, a reexamination of life began. The worth of the American dream, the idealized, romantic view of man and his life in the New World, began to lose its hold on the imagination of the people. Beneath the glittering surface of prosperity, there lay suffering and unhappiness. Disillusionment and frustration were widely felt. What had been expected to be a "Golden Age" turned out to be a "Gilded" one.

By the 1870s New England Renaissance had waned. Hawthorne and Thoreau were dead. Emerson, Longfellow, and other New England celebrities, though still writing, were old and feeble. Melville had ceased to publish. Dickinson had not been brought to light. Of the older generation Whitman alone remained active, a solitary singer in the field with his *Leaves of Grass*. The age of Romanticism and Transcendentalism was by and large over. Boston and New England ceased to be the cultural center of the country. Meanwhile, younger writers appeared on the scene. William Dean Howells, Henry James, and Mark Twain were becoming established as novelists of no small talent. "Local colorists" like Bret Harte and Edward Eggleston were making their voices heard.

And a good number of other writers such as Loiusa May Alcott (with her *Little Women* [1868-1869]) were beginning to publish. The age of realism had arrived.

Realism: Theme and Style

As a literary movement realism came in the latter half of the 19th century as a reaction against "the lie" of romanticism and sentimentalism.[2] Thematically, it expressed concern for the world of experience, of the commonplace, and for the familiar and the low. William Dean Howells, the champion of the new school, felt that he must write what he observed and knew ("He ... can only write of what his fleshly eyes have seen," as Henry James says of him). The main theme of Henry James' "The Art of Fiction" reveals his literary credo that representation of life should be the main object of the novel. And Mark Twain had, as his aim of writing, the soul, the life, and the speech of the people in mind. In matters of style, there was contrast between the genteel and graceful prose on the one hand, and the vernacular diction and the rough and ready frontier humor on the other. Twain serves as an example of a man who made the bridge, beginning as a frontier humorist and working his way into polite society, while not forgetting where he came from.

The American authors lumped together as "realists" seem to have some features in common: "verisimilitude of detail derived from observation," the effort to approach the norm of experience—a reliance on the representative in plot, setting, and character, and to offer an objective rather than an idealized view of human nature and experience.[3] With Howells, James, and Mark Twain active on the scene, realism became a major trend in the 1870s and 1880s.

William Dean Howells (1837-1920)

Howells was born in a small town in Ohio and brought up in the humble surroundings of the rough-and-ready American Midwest. He had little formal education but was widely read. He became a reporter, and wrote a successful campaign biography of Lincoln to help him win the Presidency. He was appointed American consul in Venice (1861-1865). At the end of the civil war, he moved to Boston and became, first, assistant editor and, then, editor-in-chief of the country's most influential journal, *The Atlantic Monthly* (1871-1881). He made friends with Lowell, Longfellow and Holmes, and married into an eminent New England family.

Howells was a prolific writer. He wrote volumes of novels, drama, and poetry, in addition to criticism, travelogues, and an autobiography. His major novels include such as *The Minister's Charge, A Modern Instance, A World of Chance, Annie Kilburn, A Hazard of New Fortunes,* and *The Rise of Silas Lapham.*

As a critic of eminent standing and a prolific writer, Howells helped to mold public taste and became the champion of literary realism in America. It is estimated that he wrote, in addition to the good number of social novels, eight critical books and about 1700 book reviews to spread the credo of realism. As editor and critic, Howells was generous in constructive and sympathetic reviews, helping younger and more radical writers to get a hearing. Writers such as Hamlin Garland, Stephen Crane, Frank Norris, Edith Wharton, Henry James, and Mark Twain all enjoyed his friendly advice and assistance in times of need. Thus he was, for several decades, the "dean" of his country's literature (the words are H. L. Mencken's) and became, naturally, the first president of the American Academy of Arts and Letters. Yale, Princeton, Columbia, and Oxford all conferred honorary degrees upon him.

 Howells' Literary-Aesthetic Ideas

Howells defines realism as "fidelity to experience and probability of motive," as a quest of the average and the habitual rather than the exceptional or the uniquely high or low. He preferred to "talk of some ordinary traits of

American life," not to look upon man in his "heroic or occasional phases," but "to seek him in his habitual moods of vacancy and tiresomeness." Thus man in his natural and unaffected dullness was the object of Howells' fictional representation. To him realism is not mere photographic pictures of externals but includes a central concern with "motives" and psychological conflicts. Characters should be real.

As Howells sees it, realism interprets sympathetically the "common feelings of commonplace people," and is best suited as a technique to express the spirit of America. The test of a civilization is the principle of the greatest happiness for the greatest number, the good of all.

The Rise of Silas Lapham

Howells' masterwork is *The Rise of Silas Lapham*. This is the novel in which Howells' qualities as a novelist are shown at their best. The book relates the story of an upstart in mid-19th-century Boston. Silas Lapham is a self-made man. He starts his paint business from scratch and becomes a millionaire. That is his material rise in the world. Aspiring to conquer Boston polite society, he spends a lot of money on building a gorgeous house in a "respectable" area of the town. His daughters both fall in love with a young man of an upper class family—the "genteel poor" Coreys. Then competition becomes keener. Silas is in danger. Some English syndicate comes along to offer a handsome sum of money for some of his property, which he knows the railroad needs and would force anyone out at a ruinous price. Silas is in a dilemma. Cheating, he would survive; being honest would be his undoing. He decides to be honest. As he does not sell and fails to find the money he badly needs to save his business, his company goes bankrupt. He falls and suffers, but manages to keep more people from suffering. Falling, he achieves his moral and ethical "rise."

The Rise of Silas Lapham is a fine specimen of American realistic writing. The world of Silas Lapham is that of the late 19th-century commonplace

Bostonian. Here is an average American happy with his family, and proud with his success in the world. He is seen on his trotter going down the streets of Boston where there is a ceaseless stream of cutters coming and going, a burly policeman silently directing traffic amid the rush and bustle of men. We hear Silas talk with his wife and kids, his wife addressing him "Si" when things go well and "Silas Lapham" when she is about to read him a lecture. The Coreys and others are all in their "habitual moods." There is nothing heroic, dramatic or extraordinary. Howells is here so devoted to the small, the trivial, and the commonplace that he was even mocked on occasion for building "in the stones of the street when he might have built in more durable and beautiful material."

Howells' emphasis has always been on ethics. He stresses the need for sympathy and moral integrity, and the need for harmony for different social classes. Thus we see the Laphams and the Coreys trying to overcome their prejudices and reach out to one another. In Tom Corey, Howells attempted to spread a new concept of the gentleman as self-independent, considerate of others, and scornful of class distinctions.

Howells did not approve of competitive economic individualism. He was convinced that laissez-faire competition was evil. Silas Lapham has handled his partner Rogers roughly and is in turn treated in more or less the same way by his own rivals. What Howells tried to recommend as a pattern of virtue was a Lapham acting on the utilitarian principle of the greatest happiness for the greatest number.[4]

In formal terms, there are a couple of things worthy of notice. One is the house that Lapham spends a fortune to build, only to be burned down in the end.[5] It means more than one thing. To Lapham it is a symbol of success, but Mrs. Lapham sees it as a sign of her husband's selfish individualism. The burning down of the house represents the victory of Howells' idealized view of man and society: he would like to see his country become a more humane and morally higher place.

The other is the love subplot which serves as a foil to the main one. The "economy of pain" formula evolved in the subplot, where "one suffers instead of three," prepares Silas Lapham for the self-sacrifice he is to make. Tom Corey falls in love with Penelope, Silas' older daughter. He is not aware that Irene, the younger daughter, has a crush on him. The selfless Penelope decides to withdraw from the triangle. As a result, all three suffer. In the end, the advice of a clergyman helps address the problem. Mr. Sewell suggests that Irene drop out of the game and suffer so that the other two would achieve happiness. This is the "economy of pain" formula to ensure "the greatest happiness for the greatest number." It echoes the main plot in which Lapham decides to suffer alone to avoid the possible suffering of many other people.

Howells' Reputation

Though Howells wrote about "this happy continent" and referred to its "smiling aspects," he was not always happy with an America which he felt was going in the wrong direction. He was disillusioned in the end: "I suppose I love America less because it won't let me love it more," he thus wrote to Mark Twain later in life: "After fifty years of optimistic content with civilization and its ability to come out all right in the end, I now abhor it, and feel that it is coming out all wrong in the end ...."

Howells' reputation fell drastically at the turn of the 20th century, when naturalism appeared on the scene and replaced his "smiling" brand of realism. In addition, he was found wanting in depth. "Much of his realism was external characters and events viewed from without. His works rarely achieved, or sought to achieve 'psychological depth.'"[6] He became a "dead cult." But his contribution will not be forgotten. Now his works have been reprinted, and he is now considered as a major figure in American literary history.

Henry James (1843-1916)

Henry James was born into a wealthy cultured family of New England. He was exposed to the cultural influence of Europe at a very early age. Later he met and developed a life-long friendship with William Dean Howells, who became his "moral police."[7] At Harvard Law School, he read famous novelists and critics such as Balzac, George Sand, George Eliot, and Hawthorne. He toured Europe and met writers such as Flaubert and Turgenev. Not happy with America's lack of culture and sophistication, he settled down in London in 1876 and became a naturalized British citizen in 1915.

James was influenced by some English, European and American writers.[8] He found in George Eliot his ideal of the philosophical novelist, and in Turgenev an "adorable" novelist and a guide. Turgenev's portraits of women proved to be an inspiration to him. Flaubert's *Madame Bovary* and Hawthorne's insight into the human psyche both impressed him deeply.

Henry James was a voluminous writer. His whole life was a long career of continual fertile productivity. The quantity of work he produced filled up a good many volumes—novels, travel papers, critical essays, literary portraits, plays, autobiographies, and a series of critical prefaces on the art of fiction. In addition, he was a copious letter writer and left a good number of notebooks.

The creative life of Henry James can be divided into three distinctive periods. In the first period (1865-1882) he produced a number of novels, among which the most important include *The American*, *Daisy Miller* which won him international fame and reveals his fascination with his "international theme," and *The Portrait of a Lady*, one of the greatest books that James ever wrote. These are James' most readable and most read works.

In the second period (1882-1895), James dropped the "international theme," and wrote tales of subtle studies of inter-personal relationships, which were not well received. Then he turned to play-writing (1890-1895), which failed, too, but endowed him with a better knowledge of literary techniques.

In the third and final phase of his creativity (1895-1900), he wrote a few novellas and tales dealing with childhood and adolescence in a corrupted world. The most famous of these are *The Turn of the Screw* and *What Maisie Knew*. The *Turn of the Screw* turns out to be a good read in its enigmatic way.

In the first four years of the 20th century, James wrote in quick succession, three novels, *The Ambassadors*, *The Wings of the Dove*, and *The Golden Bowl*. *The Ambassadors*, dealing again with "the international theme," has become one of James' most popular works. In the last years of his life, he wrote some American impressions and some autobiographical matter, and left two novels, *The Ivory Tower* and *The Sense of the Past* unfinished.

James' International Theme

During his lifetime James' fame rested largely upon his handling of his major fictional theme, "the international theme." It means American innocence in face of European sophistication. Or it is the meeting of America and Europe, American innocence in contact and contrast with European decadence and duplicity. For the American it was a process of progression from inexperience to experience, from innocence to knowledge and maturity.[9] James presented, through his fiction, the superiority of at least some of the values of the New World over those of the Old.

James' fictional American heroes and heroines, confronting European sophistication, either triumphed over it or were overwhelmed. Christopher Newman (in *The American*) feels frustrated by the evil of French aristocratic selfishness. Daisy Miller (in *Daisy Miller*) withers and dies in Rome. *The Portrait of a Lady* tells about the fate of one of the splendid Jamesian American girls, Isabel Archer, arriving in Europe, full of hope, and with a will to live a free and noble life. But falling prey to the sinister designs of two vulgar, unscrupulous expatriates, Madam Merle and Gilbert Osmond, her dreams and expectations evaporate: her unawareness of evil around her and her money combine to work her undoing.

James was not indifferent to Europe's cultural strengths. *The Ambassadors*, which James considered his "most perfect" work of art, illustrates his stance well. The novel is a comedy of American and European manners. Lambert Strether, the middle-aged American, is sent to Paris to bring back a young man too fascinated with Europe to return home, but is eventually convinced that Paris is the place both for the young man and for himself. James stresses mutual understanding and sympathy between European traditionalism and American individualism, and the harmonious combination of the best of both.

James' Contribution to Literary Criticism

James' contribution to literary criticism is immense. Himself a dedicated artist, he wrote for half a century to help perfect the art of writing. His criticism is both concerned with form and devoted to human values. James defines the novel as primarily having a "large, free character of an immense and exquisite correspondence with life." To him "art without life is a poor affair," "the province of art is all life, all feeling, all observation, all vision." Art must be related to life; it must be life transformed and changed so that the art form would give the truthful impression of actuality. In fact the main theme of his famous essay, "The Art of Fiction," is that the aim of the novel is to represent life. "The only reason for the existence of a novel is that it does attempt to represent life," he says in one context. "The air of reality (solidity of specification) seems to me to be the supreme virtue of a novel," he states in another. The production of the illusion of life, he feels, forms "the beginning and the end of the art of the novelist and is his inspiration, his despair, his reward, his torment, his delight." He advocates an immense increase of freedom in novel-writing and argues for inclusion of the disagreeable, the ugly, and the commonplace. Thus he was one of the three staunch advocates of 19th-century American realism, the other two being

Howells and Mark Twain.

On art in relation to life, James feels that art is important in its own way. Art makes life, makes interest, makes importance. Actual life is "all inclusion and confusion," but art is "all discrimination and selection" of what is centrally revelatory and "typical."

James made a tremendous contribution to modern critical concepts and idiom. "Point of view" is at the center of James' aesthetic of the novel. It concerns the narrator, or the way a story is told. He does not approve of "artificial omniscience" (his way of referring to the author) to intervene much in the telling of a story. Very early in his career, James discovered the trick of making his characters reveal themselves with minimal intervention of the author.[10]

In this way of narration, events and people filter through the consciousness of his characters. In *The Portrait of a Lady*, for instance, James placed the center of the subject in the consciousness of the heroine, Isabel Archer, so that the reader sees and thinks the way she does. The result is interesting: Though told by a third person, the story sounds like a first-person narrative.

James' novella, *The Turn of the Screw*, is interesting because the story is related by a narrator whose point of view is unreliable. The governess, in her narration, misleads the readers and causes confusion in their understanding. Here appears the unreliable narrator.

James was also the creator of what is now well-known as the innocent narrator. The story of his *What Maisie Knew* is a good example. It is told by Maisie, a child, who tells it but does not know its significance. Maisie becomes, probably, the first innocent narrator in American literary history.

James emphasized the inner awareness and inward movements of his characters in face of outside occurrences, rather than merely delineating their environment in detail. In this way, he became the first of the modern psychological analysts in the novel and anticipated the modern stream-of-consciousness technique of modern literature. His consistent conscious attention to the art of the novel earned him the respect of the critical circles, so that toward the latter part of his life there grew "the legend of the Master" around him.

In later years James felt a sense of homelessness and defeat. He admired Howells for staying all his life on his own land, and advised Edith Wharton (1862-1937) to stay on her native soil. All his life, James wrote little about England. A number of his writings are so insubstantial and they provide matter enough only for novellas. James knew what he had paid for expatriation.

The Reputation of Henry James

James was not widely read at his death. His over-elaborate style and the psychological complexities of his novels were (and still are) intimidating. In the first years of the 20th century, however, the importance of his literary theories and practice was well recognized. He has been moved out of his "incorruptible silence of Fame."[11] He is, today, a renowned literary figure in the history of Western literature.

Chapter 9   *Local Colorism • Mark Twain*

Local Colorism

The vogue of local color fiction was, as critic Claude M. Simpson puts it, the logical culmination of a long, progressive development. It was the outgrowth of historical and aesthetic forces that had been gathering energy since the early 19th century.

In his *Crumbling Idols* Hamlin Garland defined local colorism as having "such quality of texture and background that it could not have been written in any other place or by anyone else than a native." Garland's "texture" refers to the elements which characterize a local culture, elements such as speech, customs, and mores peculiar to one particular place. And his "background" covers physical setting and those distinctive qualities of landscape which condition human thought and behavior. The ultimate aim of the local colorists is, as Garland indicates, to create the illusion of an indigenous little world with qualities that tell it apart from the world outside.

The social and intellectual climate of the country provided a stimulating milieu for the growth of local color fiction. The United States, still expanding westward, had not had time to solidify itself into a cohesive cultural whole. Marked differences existed between different parts of the country, with the East assuming the superior "aristocratic" posture. The rest of the country keenly felt the psychological need to assert their cultural identity, seeking understanding and recognition by showing their local character. Intellectually, the frontier humorists, who had flourished several decades before the Civil War, had prepared the literary ground for local colorism.[1] In the humorous "tall tales" of these writers, there was an obvious emphasis on the peculiarities of local speech, dress and habits of thought and the presentation of native character types, which continued, to some extent, into local color fiction. The earlier humorists influenced local color writers so much that one of the latter group, Bret Harte, even declared that local color derived directly from the frontier tall-tale tradition. In addition, a good number of periodicals appeared after the Civil War, unusually willing to accept and pay well for local color short stories: *Harper's Monthly*, *Harper's Weekly*, *The Galaxy*, and *Scribner's Magazine*—to name just a few— all were ready to spread local color.

Local colorism as a trend first made its presence felt in the late 1860s and early seventies. The appearance of Bret Harte's "The Luck of Roaring Camp" in 1868 marked a significant development in the brief history of local color fiction. Bret Harte's stories managed to draw the attention of the nation to the new genre of writing and make editors and readers more responsive to the mushroom growths of similar, regional literature in different sections of the country. The voice of Bret Harte was echoed and made more resonant by those of such local colorists as Harriet Beecher Stowe with her *Oldtown Folks*, Sam Lawson's *Fireside Stories*, and Edward Eggleston's *The Hoosier Schoolmaster*. By the early 1870s William Dean Howells noticed that the whole varied field of American life had come into view in American fiction. Magazines were filled with local sketches and stories. The next decade saw a spectacular growth of regional literature. The writers of different localities rose to join the race to paint their own section of the country in the best colors available. The movement was so widespread that it became as contagious as whooping-cough. Not until the turn of the 20th century did local colorism cease to be a dominant fashion.

Local colorists concerned themselves with presenting and interpreting the local character of their regions. They tended to idealize and glorify, but they never forgot to keep an eye on the truthful color of local life. Bret Harte's *The Luck of Roaring Camp and Other Stories* contains, in his own words, "bits of local color that are truthful" and characters that had "a real human being as a suggesting and starting point." Mrs. Stowe's object was "to interpret to the world New England life and character in that particular time of its history which may be called the seminal period," and her studies for this object "have been taken from real characters, real scenes, and real incidents." And Hamlin Garland, in writing about the region which he knew best, and dealing explicitly with the local environment, coined the word "veritism" for his particular brand of realism. His *Main-Traveled Roads*, a truthful record of the commonplace farm life of the West, Howells saw as a creation out of the burning dust of the truth about human experience on the American soil.

The list of names of the local colorists is a long one. In addition to those mentioned above, there are, among others, Constance Fenimore Woolson's *Castle Nowhere: Lake-Country Sketches*, Sarah Orne Jewett's *Deephaven*, a collection about coastal Maine, Kate Chopin writing of Louisiana Cajun-life in her *Bayou Folk, A Night in Acadie* and *The Awakening* (1899), Gertrude Atherion of Spanish California, Owen Wister of Wyoming cowboy life, and C. B. Fernald of San Francisco's Chinatown. There were also Mary H. Catherwood in the middle West, Mary Hallock Foote in the far West, and Mary N. Murfree, G. W. Cable, J. Chandler Harris and Thomas Nelson Page in the South. For over three decades, there raged such a sweeping vogue of local color that virtually no corner of the country was left untouched.

The local colorist writing formed an important part of American realism. Their truthful depiction of the common people in their commonplace lives added strength to the fight for realism which Howells championed with James and Mark Twain. Although it lost its momentum toward the end of the 19th century, its local spirit continued to inspire and fertilize the imagination of authors such as Willa Cather, John Steinbeck and William Faulkner, who ultimately managed, by rooting their work in their places, to reach the plane of universal meaning.

Mark Twain (1835-1910)

Mark Twain, pseudonym of Samuel Langhorne Clemens, was brought up in the small town of Hannibal, Missouri, on the Mississippi River. He was twelve when his father died and he had to leave school. He was successively a printer's apprentice, a tramp printer, a silver miner, a steamboat pilot on the Mississippi, and a frontier journalist in Nevada and California. This knocking about gave him a wide knowledge of humanity.

With the publication of his frontier tale, "The Celebrated Jumping Frog of Calaveras County," Twain became nationally famous. In 1866 he went east, where he met Howells and married Olivia Langdon of Elmira, New York, both symbols of gentility that combined to tame this "wild humorist of the Pacific Slope."[2] His first novel, *The Gilded Age* (1873), written in collaboration with Charles Dudley Warner, was an artistic failure, but it gave its name to the America of the post-bellum period which it attempts to satirize. His boyhood experience, so happily remembered later in his *Autobiography*, furnished him with ample material for "fiction." *The Adventures of Tom Sawyer* (1876) was an immediate success as "a boy's book"; its sequel, *The Adventures of Huckleberry Finn* (1884) which Mark Twain wrote some years later, became his masterwork. Mark Twain's three years' life on the Mississippi left such a fond memory with him that he returned to the theme more than once in his writing career. *Life on the Mississippi* (1883), another masterpiece of his, relates it in a vivid, moving way.

Mark Twain was essentially an affirmative writer. But toward the latter part of his life, he became increasingly violent in his censure of man and his society. In his later works the change from an optimist and humorist to an almost despairing determinist is unmistakable. *A Connecticut Yankee in King Arthur's Court* (1889), *The Man That Corrupted Hadleyburg* (1900), *The Mysterious Stranger* (1916), and his *Autobiography* (1924) all contain bitter attacks on the human race. Some critics link this change with the tragic events of his later life, the failure of his investments, his fatiguing travels and lectures in order to pay off his debts, and added to this, the death of his wife and two daughters which left him absolutely inconsolable. There is certainly a good deal of truth in this, though the basic reason is to be sought in the darkening social life, as in the case of William Dean Howells.[3]

Twain's Major Subjects

Mark Twain preferred to represent social life through portraits of local places which he knew best. Indeed, he started off as a teller of tall tales and a local colorist. He felt that a novelist must not try to generalize about a nation. "No," he says, "[The novelist] lays before you the ways and speech and life of a few people grouped in a certain place—his own place—and that is one book. In time, he and his brethren will report to you the life and the people of the whole nation." He goes on to state that "When a thousand able novels have been written, there you have the soul of the people, the life of the people, the speech of the people, and not anywhere else can these be had." Here he clearly defined the place and function of local colorism, and foresaw the coming in sections of the "great American novel" to which he did his best to contribute his share.

Twain as a Personal Writer

Mark Twain drew heavily from his own rich fund of knowledge of people and places. He confined himself to the life with which he was familiar, convinced, as he states in a letter of 1890, that "the most valuable capital, or culture or education usable in the building of novels is personal experience." And certainly he was at his best when, in the words of critic Everett Carter, transmuting the ore of his personal experience into "the gold of reminiscence, autobiography and autobiographical fiction."[4] In a way Mark Twain was his own biographer, and the central drama of his mature literary life was his discovery of his "usable past" which took him the rest of his life to transform imaginatively into literature.[5] His usable past was mostly related to the Mississippi and the West which became his major theme. *Life on the Mississippi* was such a truthful description that Howells felt that he could taste "the mud" in it; Tom Sawyer walked out of Twain's pages directly from his fresh memory of his boyhood in the West. By quoting from his own experience, Mark Twain managed to transform into art the freedom and humor, in short, the finest elements of western culture.[6]

The Adventures of Huckleberry Finn

Mark Twain's best work is *The Adventures of Huckleberry Finn*. The writing of the book was evidently not easy for him, for he wrote some of it, then put it away and worked on other things, then later wrote some more of it—he kept this up for a number of years.[7] As Sherwood Anderson observes, here for once, the real Mark Twain became again "the half savage, tender, god-worshipping, believing boy" that he had once been.[8] The book was a success from its first publication in 1884 and has always been regarded as one of the great books of Western literature and Western civilization. It is the one book from which, as Ernest Hemingway noted, "all modern American literature comes."

The Adventures of Huckleberry Finn tells a story about the United States before the Civil War, around 1850, when the great Mississippi Valley was still being settled. Here lies an America, with its great national faults, full of violence and even cruelty, yet still retaining the virtues of "some simplicity, some innocence, some peace."[9] Here is a "hymn" to that ante-bellum America, the moral values of which vanished with the war. The machine and the worship of money were on their way in, but the river-god, with its "sunlight, space, uncrowded time, stillness, and danger," had not been forgotten.

The story takes place along the Mississippi River, on both sides of which there was unpopulated wilderness and a dense forest. Along this river floats a small raft, with two people on it: One is an ignorant, uneducated Black slave named Jim and the other is a little uneducated outcast white boy of about the age of thirteen, called Huckleberry Finn, or Huck Finn. The book relates the story of the escape of Jim from slavery and, more important, how Huck Finn, floating along with him and helping him as best he could, changed his mind, his prejudice, about Black people, and came to accept Jim as a man and as a close friend as well.

The Theme of the Book

Now Huck Finn comes from the very lowest level of society. His father is the poor town drunkard who would willingly commit any crime just for the pure pleasure of it. Huck Finn is an outcast, with no mother, no home, sleeping in barrels, eating scraps and leavings, and dressed in rags. All of his virtues come from his good heart and his sense of humanity, for most of the things he was taught turned out to be wrong. For example, he was taught that slavery was good and right, and that runaway slaves should be reported. So what Huck has got to do is to cut through social prejudices and social discriminations to find truth for himself.

Huck starts by believing that Blacks are by nature lower than whites—inferior animals of sorts in fact. A good illustration is the conversation between him and Aunt Sally after the explosion on the river. Aunt Sally is asking whether anybody had been hurt. "No'm. Killed a nigger" is Huck's reply. And much of the book is concerned with Huck's inner struggle between this attitude (hence his sense of guilt in helping Jim to escape) and his profound conviction that Jim is a human being—one of the best, in point of fact, that he had ever known. At first he cannot see Jim as a proper human being, and less as his equal. Through their escape down the river, he gets to know Jim better and becomes more and more convinced that Jim is not only a man, but also a good man. Thus he ends up by accepting him not merely as a human being but also as a loyal friend.

Huck Finn is a veritable recreation of living models. Huck, his father, Jim, the swindlers (the Duke and the Dauphin), Colonel Sherburn and the drunkard Boggs—all these characters had prototypes in real life. The portrayal of individual incidents and characters achieved intense verisimilitude of detail. Serious problems are being discussed through the narration of a little illiterate boy. The fact of the wilderness juxtaposed with civilization, the people half wild and half civilized, many of whom are coarse, vulgar, and brutal, such as the loafers of the town of Brickville, amusing themselves by torturing animals— pouring kerosene on dogs and setting them on fire, democratic citizens quickly changed into violent mobs, ready to take the law into their own hands and lynch people, or to seize people and pour hot tar over them and ride them out of town on a rail, and the fact of brutal slavery and of human beings—the Blacks—being sold in the market places like animals, the Shepherdson-Grangerford feud shown in all its senseless, sickening perversion of a code of "honor," the poignant portrayal of swindlers which was a common sight in the South then—all these and many other incidents are depicted in true-to-life detail as the background against which Huck Finn's awareness of good and evil develops.[10] Though a local and particular book, it touches upon the human situation in a general, indeed "universal," way: Humanism ultimately triumphs.

The Colloquial Style

Another feature of the book which helps to make it famous is its language. The book is written in the colloquial style, in the general standard speech of uneducated Americans. Mark Twain's introductory note on accents is an indication of his conscious attempt to achieve accurate detail. "In this book," he says, "a number of dialects are used, to wit: the Missouri negro dialect; the extremest forms of the backwoods Southwestern dialect; the ordinary 'Pike County' dialect; and four modified varieties of this last. The shadings have not been done in a haphazard fashion, or by guesswork; but painstakingly, and with the trustworthy guidance and support of personal familiarity with these several forms of speech." He used words which are mostly Anglo-Saxon in origin, short, concrete and direct in effect. Sentence structures are most of them simple or compound. Mark Twain depended solely on the concrete object and action for the body and movement of his prose.[11] What is more, there is an ungrammatical element which gives the final finish to his style.

Mark Twain made colloquial speech an accepted, respectable literary medium in the literary history of the country. The style has impacted American literature and made books before *Huck Finn* and after it quite different. Its influence has been clearly visible in later American literature. It has been continued in both prose and poetry. Sherwood Anderson, T. S. Eliot, E. A. Robinson, Robert Frost, Carl Sandburg, William Carlos Williams, E. E. Cummings, Ernest Hemingway, William Faulkner, J. D. Salinger and more are all indebted to him in this regard.

Mark Twain the Social Critic

All his life Mark Twain took his role as a social critic seriously. "From the beginning, he took the side of the defenseless or oppressed, and fought corruption, privilege and abuse wherever he found them with a fierce humor."[12] His writings, novels, letters, notebooks and pamphlets, and all included, touch upon almost every issue of his time such as politics, religion, capital and labor, slavery, U.S. imperialism abroad, and the persecution of the Chinese and the Jews.

The Gilded Age made legislative corruption, industrial free-enterprise, and speculation the butt of his biting satire, and one of its characters, Colonel Sellers, has become memorable as the gullible man of hope. In some of his works such as *Pudd'nhead Wilson* and *Huck Finn*, Mark Twain made his stance on anti-slavery and anti-lynching unequivocally clear. Mark Twain was fiercely critical of U. S. imperialism in the Spanish-American War, in the Philippines, South Africa, and China.

Mark Twain was a friend of the Chinese. He was not indifferent to the Chinese immigrants persecuted in America or to a China suffering at the hands of imperialist powers. His works such as "Disgraceful Persecution of a Boy," "Goldsmith's Friend Abroad Again," "The Treaty with China" and "To the Person Sitting in Darkness" are all lucid illustrations. On August 12, 1900, a day before foreign troops entered Peking (now Beijing), Mark Twain wrote, "It is all China now, and my sympathies are with the Chinese. They have been villainously dealt with by the sceptered thieves of Europe, and I hope they will drive all

foreigners out and keep them out for good."[13]

Twain's social criticism ranks with that of Milton, Swift, Defoe, and Bernard Shaw, and that it is an important part of Twain's bequest.[14]

Chapter 10   American Naturalism •
Crane • Norris • Dreiser • Robinson

American Naturalism

The post-bellum decades witnessed the emergence of "Modern America." Industrialism and science and the new philosophy of life based upon science were among the important factors which helped to create the economic, social, and cultural transformations of the country. Industrialism produced financial giants, but at the same time created an industrial proletariat entirely at the mercy of the external forces beyond their control. Slums appeared in great numbers where conditions became steadily worse, and the city poor lived a life of insecurity, suffering, and violence. One of the worst slum areas was the New York Bowery which Stephen Crane wrote about in some of his stories. The westward expansion continued to push the frontier nearer the Pacific coast, and the settlers found themselves subject to the ruthless manipulation of forces including the railroad, which charged heavy freight rates and drove farmers to bankruptcy, as can be seen in Frank Norris' wheat novels. Howells' "happy continent" became now "odious" to this once smiling American.

New ideas about man and man's place in the universe began to take root in America.[1] Living in a cold, indifferent, and essentially Godless world, man was no longer free and was thrown upon himself for survival. The world in which God was warm and caring enough to redress the wrong of Hawthorne's condemned wizard was gone not to return, and the comfortable belief that man could hope to fall back on divine help and guidance was exploded and irretrievably lost. Life became a struggle for survival. The Darwinian concepts such as "the survival of the fittest" and "the human beast" became popular catchwords and standards of moral reference in an amoral world. Darwin's ideas of evolution and especially those of Herbert Spencer and his vogue in America helped to change the outlook of many rising authors and intellectuals. All these produced an attitude of gloom and despair which characterize American literature of this period.

The literary climate of the country was also changing. To some young writers just emerging, Howells' kind of realism was now too restrained and genteel in tone to tell the truth of the harsh realities of American life. In the 1890s, French naturalism, with its new mode of perception and new ways of writing, appealed to the imagination of the younger generation like Crane, Norris, and Theodore Dreiser. American literary naturalism now came on the scene.

The young writers tore the mask of gentility to pieces and wrote about the helplessness of man, his insignificance in a cold world, and his lack of dignity in face of the crushing forces of environment and heredity. They reported truthfully and objectively, with a passion for scientific accuracy and an overwhelming accumulation of factual detail.[2] They painted life as it was lived in the slums, and were accused of telling just about the hideous side of it. Also, the naturalist bent of writing received an impetus from other foreign influences like Tolstoi and Turgenev.[3]

A casual look at the major works of Crane, Norris, and Dreiser reveals a bitter and wretched world where human beings such as Maggie, McTeague, and Sister Carrie battle hopelessly against overwhelming odds in a cold, harsh, and at best apathetic environment, driven as "a wisp of wind," with their lives very much determined by forces they have no means whatever of manipulating.[4] The whole picture is somber and dark; and the general tone is one of hopelessness and even despair.

However, the reader also finds humanistic values in these naturalistic works. Here is a desire to assert one's human identity, to define oneself against the social and natural forces one confronts. Though gloomy, pessimistic, and often bitter, American naturalists could not accept the deterministic attitude of the complete helplessness of man and the view of an amoral and predatory universe; they could not adopt a thoroughgoing scientific attitude in the portrayal of the American scene.[5] Here lies the strength and influence of writers like Crane and Dreiser in modern 20th-century literature. Readers should take note of this feature of American literary naturalism in the study of its writings.

Stephen Crane (1871-1900)

Stephen Crane was born in New Jersey. He attended a military prep school, Lafayette College, and Syracuse University where he stayed for less than a year. Then he moved into New York to earn his living as a free-lance journalist. First-hand knowledge of New York slum areas furnished him with material for his *Maggie: A Girl of the Streets* (1893). In 1895 Crane published his first book of poems, *The Black Riders*, and his novel, *The Red Badge of Courage*, which won the admiration of such writers as William Dean Howells, Joseph Conrad and Henry James. His experience as a correspondent in Cuba and his shipwreck on the way there provided the background for his most famous short story, "The Open Boat." His other short stories include "The Blue Hotel" and "An Experiment in Misery."

Crane as a Pioneer

Crane was a pioneer writing in the naturalistic tradition. His writings all reinforced the naturalist motif of environment and heredity overwhelming man, and gave the whole esthetic movement of the 1890s "a sudden direction and a fresh impulse." *Maggie* is a naked representation of slum life, and *The Red Badge of Courage* began the modern tradition of debunking war.

Crane was also a pioneer in the field of modern poetry. His early poems, brief, quotable, with their unrhymed, unorthodox conciseness, and impressionistic imagery, exerted a significant influence on modern poetry: he is now recognized as one of the two precursors of Imagist poetry, the other being Emily Dickinson.

The World of Stephen Crane

Talking about *Maggie,* Crane observed in a letter that "it tries to show that environment is a tremendous thing in the world and frequently shapes lives regardless." Crane's fictional world is a naturalistic one in which man is deprived of free will and subject to the pressures of environment and heredity. It is a world in which "God is cold." His poem, "A Man Said to the Universe," is revealing enough:

> A Man said to the universe:
> 'Sir, I exist!'
> 'However,' replied the universe,
> 'The fact has not created in me
> A sense of obligation.'

So is his poem "A Man Adrift on a Slim Spar":

> The puff of a coat imprisoning:
> A face kissing the water-death
> A weary slow sway of a lost hand
> And the sea, the moving sea, the sea.
>   God is cold.

The universe does not care about man, who is submerged by forces like environment and heredity. Such is the world in which Maggie finds herself.

Maggie: A Girl of the Streets

Maggie: A Girl of the Streets was the first uncompromising naturalistic novel in America. It painted an unabashed picture of the bitter life of the slum-dwellers, and was therefore rejected by all editors and publishers.

The novel relates the story of a good girl's destruction in a slum environment. Maggie grows up in a typical naturalistic home background where mere existence became a battle and where men behave like animals. Maggie is not resigned to her fate. She has her own aspirations. When old enough, she goes to work in a factory where the conditions of life turn human beings into machines. Her home proves also suffocating so that Maggie tries to leave her beastly mother and brother. She places hope and trust in Pete who, himself a product of the hopeless slum, fails to come to her rescue after he has seduced her. In despair she is forced to walk the streets and eventually to plunge herself into the river. Maggie has been a rose in a mud-puddle. All her short life, she has been struggling to escape her mud-puddle prison, but all in vain. As Crane says, environment is a "tremendous" thing for an insignificant human being to battle against.

The Red Badge of Courage

The Red Badge of Courage is a story set in the period of the American Civil War. A boy-soldier, Henry by name, is enlisted and dispatched with his untried regiment to the front. In face of danger, he is seized with panic and runs away. Ashamed of his cowardice, he tries to return to the battlefield later. He gets wounded accidentally by a wounded fellow soldier. For a while the wound becomes, to his fellow soldiers, his "red badge of courage." But Henry still feels guilty. In another battle, he becomes the standard bearer and helps win a victory. Henry feels good and hopeful.

The Red Badge of Courage starts a new way of writing about war. On the one hand, the book is debunking war. Against the romantic view of war as a symbol of courage and heroism, Crane talks about war in alarming honesty. He sees war as a slaughter-house, men fighting are so many helpless animals, and the natural instinct of man is to run from danger and death. War moves men ruthlessly and blindly as pawns on a chess-board. There is no valor, no heroism, no glory and no free will, but corpses of the dead rotting where they are left.

Here Crane is looking into man's primitive emotions and trying to tell the elemental truth about human life.[6] The basic theme of the animal man in a cold, manipulating world runs through the whole book.

Crane's book has a singularly modern touch about it. He initiated the modern tradition of telling the truth at all costs about the elemental human situation, and writing about war as a real human experience. Now this was an event of a revolutionary nature both in theme and technique, which has had a far-reaching influence on later writers such as Hemingway, Dos Passes, Norman Mailer, Kurt Vonnegut, Joseph Heller, and Thomas Pynchon.

On the other hand, it is good to note that the book also paints a once-runaway soldier in a positive light. Henry feels ashamed of his cowardly act and tries to regain his sense of honor as a man, a heroic man. This assertion of human dignity indicates Crane's true understanding of man and his actions.

Crane anticipated the major developments of American literature in the first few decades of the 20th century.

Frank Norris (1870-1902)

Frank Norris studied art briefly in Paris, and entered the University of California at Berkeley in 1890.

During a year at Harvard (1894-1895) he began to write novels, one of which was *McTeague*. Before his death (from peritonitis) he was writing a trilogy on the production, distribution, and consumption of wheat, the first of which, *The*

Octopus (1901), proves to be his best work. It is a long and complex book based upon an actual clash in 1880 between farmers in the San Joaquin valley and the South Pacific Railroad, the octopus of the title. The second of the trilogy, *The Pit*, which appeared posthumously in 1903, concentrates on the distribution of wheat. The third book was never written. Norris' essays of literary criticism have been collected in *The Responsibilities of the Novelist* (1903). Representing a sharp break with the genteel tradition in American literature, Norris exercised a general influence on the writers of the 1920s and 1930s such as William Faulkner and John Steinbeck.

McTeague

McTeague has been called "the first full-bodied naturalistic American novel" and "a consciously naturalistic manifesto." It is a classic case study of the inevitable effect of environment and heredity on human lives, very much like a textbook for naturalistic fiction

McTeague is a fine specimen of the "human beast," with his primitive, atavistic behavior, and wild desires. The elemental forces of his wild birthplace and the hereditary elements of his alcoholic father worked havoc with his civilized life and combined to dehumanize his person. The "beast" in him got the upper hand and drove him to evil and murder.

The story added strength to the American naturalistic writing. Dreiser saw it as a somber and yet true presentation of reality as had been "conceived by any writer in any land."

The Octopus

In *The Octopus* Norris illustrates how social and economic conditions ruin the lives of innocent, powerless people. The railroad reaches out its millions of tentacles, coiling round the throats of the farmers who have to choose between

leaving their crops to rot and carting them out through the railroad at a criminally high freight rate. In either case they end up in bankruptcy and destruction. What is worse, the railroad raises the price of the land it has rented to the people so that all the farmers and the poor in general face stark destitution and ruin.

A typical case is Dyke. He has been a good engine driver but is forced to raise hop in hard times. To finance the project, he mortgages his crop and homestead. He works hard and has a good crop. But the railroad raises the freight rate which ruins him altogether. His life is thus thoroughly wrecked. Dyke becomes a drunkard, does highway robbery, and ends up in life imprisonment. The degradation of the man is complete. Nor is he the only victim. A whole group of the farmers of the San Joaquin valley collapse with him. Some meet an untimely death like Annixter, Harran Derrick, Hooven, Osterman and Broderson. Others are demented like Magnus Derrick. All are crushed under the wheels of the railroad.

It is interesting to note that the novel offers a determinist view of the tragedies.

It says that the railroad officials are not to blame; the conditions, natural forces, are responsible for what happened.[7] The laws of nature could ruin a financial superman like Jadwin as well (in *The Pit*). Jadwin challenges the laws of nature, and so meets a ruin no less cruel than that of others.

Frank Norris is not much read now, but his influence is visible. He may occasionally fail to handle his material well, but the richness and exuberance of his material is appealing. His vibrant and fresh imagery, his ability to etch situations indelibly on the readers' mind, his poetic mode of fiction, as in the choice of words for their precise and exact effect and even his mysticism, were all part of the literary legacy of the period under discussion.

Theodore Dreiser (1871-1945)

Dreiser was born in Indiana, of German-speaking parents. His childhood was spent in extreme poverty. He spent some months at Indiana University, and then became a reporter. His first novel, *Sister Carrie*, was rejected because of its relentless honesty in presenting the true nature of American life. He felt depressed and seriously contemplated suicide. But he held out long, and survived to lead the rebellion of the 1920s. Dreiser was left-oriented in his views. He visited Russia and wrote *Dreiser Looks at Russia* (1928) and *Tragic America* (1931) to express his new faith. He retained a strong sympathy for communism and, shortly before his death, joined the Communist Party.

Dreiser read widely. Balzac, Zola, Mark Twain, and Herbert Spencer had a determining effect on his outlook. He embraced social Darwinism. He learned to regard man as merely an animal driven by greed and lust in a struggle for existence in which only the "fittest," the most ruthless, survive. Life is predatory, a jungle struggle in which man, being a waif and a wisp in the wind of social forces, a mere pawn in the general scheme of things. No one is ethically free; everything is determined by a complex of internal chemism and by the forces of social pressure.[8] Dreiser was critical of his country: "The moral and social codes of his America misrepresent the truth of human nature, and so does conventional fiction."[9] Dreiser intended to report "the coarse and the vulgar and the cruel and the terrible" in life. Dreiser had a warm heart. His sympathies were always with the oppressed and the weak. Even his famous determinism is essentially sentimental at root.[10] Dreiser's writings reveal a tremendous vital lust for life with a conviction that man is the end and measure of all things in a world which is devoid of purpose and standards.[11]

Dreiser's novels are powerful portrayals of American life. It is in his works that American naturalism is said to have come of age. His works include such as *Sister Carrie* (1900), *Jennie Gerhardt* (1911), and two volumes of his Cowperwood trilogy—*The Financier* (1912) and *The Titan* (1914), the third, the posthumously published *The Stoic, The Genius* (l915), *An American Tragedy* (1925), and *The Bulwark* (1946). In these writings, he showed a new way of presenting reality and inspired the writers of the 1920s with courage and insight.

The revival of naturalism in the 1930s enthroned Dreiser as the guide and pioneer for the latter-day naturalists such as James T. Farrell, John O'Hara, and John Dos Passes.

Sister Carrie

Sister Carrie is Dreiser's best known work. It tells about life in an amoral world. The amorality of Dreiser's world is best illustrated at the beginning of *The Financier*. Here stands young Frank Cowperwood before the fish market's tank and watching the life-and-death struggle between a squid and a lobster ending on the side of the stronger. For Cowperwood this represents the sum total of the world's amorality.[12] "Might is right," and the powerful and the ruthless alone survive. This is a Godless world in which man is thrown upon himself to keep alive as best he can against the overwhelming odds of the cold, indifferent environment. It is in such an amoral world that Carrie Meeber finds herself.

On *Sister Carrie* Dreiser wrote, "It is not intended as a piece of literary craftsmanship, but as a picture of conditions done as simply and effectively as the English language will permit." A country girl, Sister Carrie, comes to Chicago to look for a better life. She first stays with her sister whose working-class home is, however, too poor to keep her. Winter is coming and she is seriously ill. A traveling salesman, Druet by name, comes to her rescue and takes her home as his mistress. Sister Carrie's beauty appeals to Druet's friend, Hurstwood, so that the respectable manager deserts his comfortable home and family and forces her to elope with him. They run first to Canada and then settle down in New York. For some time they experience dire poverty. Sister Carrie goes out to find work on the stage, but Hurstwood proves himself to be utterly unfit to survive. He cannot find work, and begs for and receives some occasional support from Sister Carrie. His downfall is complete when he commits suicide one cold winter night. Sister Carrie manages to move up in her career, and Druet comes back to renew some connection with her, but is rejected. At the end of the book Sister Carrie is seen sitting in her rocking-chair, still rocking.

Dreiser portrays three different worlds in which Sister Carrie moves and which between them offer a panoramic view of the crude and savage aspects of social life at the turn of the 20th century. These include her sister's working-class existence, her life with Druet in Chicago, and with Hurstwood in New York. Every detail is related with an amazing dispassionate exactitude and so assumes a sense of importance.[13] Clothes, furniture, how much one owes the grocer, and exactly how much one earns and spends, the contents of a meal—all these indicate the plight of the heroine and her desire for a better life. The world is cold and harsh to her. Alone and helpless, she moves along like a mechanism driven by desire and catches blindly at any opportunities for a better existence, such opportunities as offered first by Druet and then by Hurstwood. A feather in the wind, she is totally at the mercy of forces she cannot comprehend, still less to say control. She does not seem to possess what may be called a moral fiber in her.

Then there is the tragedy of Hurstwood. Here Spencer's influence is seen at its most powerful. Hurstwood cannot help himself in his relationship with Sister Carrie. No respectable job, no handsome income, no "genteel" family, nothing, could overcome his biological need and stop him from returning to savage, atavistic unreason. Dreiser's portrait is an authentic one of the impotent modern man unfit to survive. "His innate instincts dulled by too near an approach to free will, his free will not sufficiently developed to replace his instincts and afford him perfect guidance," he thus hovers between being a man and a beast in his behavior. He must die. And die he does.

Dreiser's style has been a point of heated discussion.[14] Some critics feel that his novels are formless at times, his characterization is deficient and his prose dull, yet his stories are solid and intensely interesting with their simple but highly moving characters. In addition, his journalistic method of reiteration, his taste for word-pictures, and movement in outline—all these have helped make Dreiser one of America's foremost novelists.

Other Authors of the Period

Before we move into the 1920s, the decade in which modern American literature is said to begin, there are a few other writers whom we mention briefly here only because of space constraint. They were once writers of some stature in their own day and have since become minor figures for the simple reason that time beheads reputations.

We begin with **Edwin Arlington Robinson** (1860-1935) who started writing poetry in the closing years of the 19th century, achieved recognition in the first decade of the 20th, and was generally regarded as America's greatest living poet in the 1920s. Robinson's world is naturalistic in nature. Here God is no longer caring, men suffer from frustrations and want of mutual understanding, and life is in general futile and meaningless. These reveal Robinson as a modern poet, capable of a tragic vision in step with the modern spirit, trying to suggest a despairing courage to seek out the meaning of life. Robinson's poems, "Man Against the Sky," "Richard Cory," "Miniver Cheevy" and "Flammonde" are all memorable pieces. Take "Richard Cory" for example. Richard Cory is a gentleman, rich, human, and graceful, the way he is dressed, walks downtown, speaks to people, "In fine, we thought that he was everything / To make us wish that we were in his place." But, all of a sudden, we hear of his suicide: "And Richard Cory, one calm summer night, / Went home and put a bullet through his head." The poem does not tell the readers why Richard Cory dies the way he does: it is anybody's guess. The poem is thus also an illustration of Robinson's fascination with "psychological enigmas," enigmas that were the product of modern life.

Jack London (1876-1916)

Jack London was a popular author in the first years of the 20th century. His rise to fame was in a way meteoric. He came from the bottom of society, read Marx, Charles Darwin, and Nietzsche, among others, and was well self-educated in natural law and determinism. He wrote in quick succession and sold well. Among his best works are *The Call of the Wild*, an all-time bestseller, *White Fang*, *The Sea Wolf*, and *Martin Eden*. Through hard work and will power, he made his way up to the summit of the social hierarchy. But when he became a millionaire, he found fashionable society life empty and distasteful. He died, exhausted and in despair.

His masterwork, *Martin Eden*, somewhat autobiographical, is an interesting book. Martin Eden, the protagonist, is a sailor who works and reads hard so as to break into polite society. His perseverance leads to final success. He reaches the top, only to find that his dream has not been worth realizing at all. A death wish gets hold of him. He drowns himself when out at sea.

Jack London was highly critical of America of his time. But It is critical to note here that he was one of the worst racists ever seen in American literature as well. This is clearly illustrated in his writings such as the "Yellow Peril" (1904) and "The Unparalleled Invasion" (1910).

The "Yellow Peril"

Jack London first coined the term "Yellow Peril" in an article intending to instigate and spread the malice which some vicious people still incite against China even today. Although he spearheaded his attack toward the Japanese as well, his fear of the "awakening" of the "four hundred million Chinese" is more apparent. His is clearly a racist and rapacious mind:

> There is such a thing as race egotism as well as creature egotism, and a very good thing it is. In the first place, the Western world will not permit the rise of the yellow peril. It is firmly convinced that it will not permit the yellow and the brown to wax strong and menace its peace and comfort.

And he shamelessly defends Western invasion and plunder as a glorious undertaking:

> No matter how dark in error and deed, ours has been a history of spiritual struggle and endeavour. We are pre-eminently a religious race, which is another way of saying that we are a right-seeking race.

"The Unparalleled Invasion"

In addition, he wrote six stories related to China and the Chinese, one of which, "The Unparalleled Invasion" (1910), is vehemently vicious toward China and the Chinese. The full title of the story is "The Strength of the Strong: The Unparalleled Invasion."

The story foretells that China would rise and overwhelm the world with its vast population:

> The real danger lay in the fecundity of her loins, and it was in 1970 that the first cry of alarm was raised. ... [n]ow it suddenly came home to the world that China's population was 500,000,000. She had increased by a hundred millions since her awakening. ... [T]here were more Chinese in existence than white-skinned people ... and the world shivered.

Jack London began to make stories about China's possible conquest and expansion. China would overrun Indo-China, Siam, Malay peninsula, Siberia, all Central Asia .... There were two Chinese for every white-skinned human in the world.

Jack London must have been full of fear and hatred when he suggested in his story what the West should do: to start a bacterial warfare, using American-invented bacteria, germs, microbes, bacilli, and virulent germ, cultured in the laboratories of the West, to cause countless plagues all over China.

Jack London must be very happy with the end of the story he designed: the US and its European allies acted upon his idea, and exterminated the Chinese race from the face of the earth. The vast empty land of China was resettled according to "the democratic American program" in 1982. After that the US and its European allies agreed that never again would anyone be allowed to war like this again.

The ghost of Jack London is still walking around today.

O. Henry (1862-1910)

O. Henry (pseudonym of William Sidney Porter) was one of the most prolific writers in the history of American literature. A smart short-story writer, he actually began his career when serving a three-year prison term. There he learned about "gentle grafters" and noble-minded burglars. Later, in New York as he got to know life better and became sympathetic to the socially low, he wrote fascinating stories about them. O. Henry tended to repeat the motifs of his stories and fall into melodrama and sentimentality, but his best stories are free from these weaknesses and remain intensely readable today. "The Gift of the Magi" is one of these. This is an extremely moving story of a young couple who sell their best possessions—Delia her hair and Jim his grandfather's watch—in order to get money for a Christmas present for each other.

At his death O. Henry was regarded as a great master of the art of fiction. His reputation fell after the 1920s because he stayed in heart and in technique a man of the 19th century.

Upton Sinclair (1878-1968)

Upton Sinclair wrote with incredible facility all his long life: his manuscripts is said to weigh eight tons. At the turn of the 20th century Sinclair, with his relentless criticism of American life, became an important part of the famous "Muckraking Movement," the aim of which was to expose corruption, chicanery, and evil existing in American social, economic, and political life. *The*

Jungle, revealing, as it does, the inhumanity and total absence of hygiene in Chicago's Packingtown, made quite a stir both in America and the world outside.

Edward Bellamy (1850-1898)

Bellamy was a preeminent author. He was widely read in many fields such as history, philosophy, military science, and mathematics. Rich in imagination and full of passion, he had the courage to explore what the future would have in store for humanity. His works are noted for their impressive moral idealism.

Bellamy's masterwork, *Looking Backward, 2000-1887* (1888), is a Utopian, science-fiction, and highly Romantic kind of work. Its main character, Julian, having slept for one whole century, wakes up to find himself living in the 21st century. The old competitive capitalist system is gone, and a society of great harmony has taken its place. The book lashes at the private ownership and the extremes of wealth and poverty which the mechanical civilization produced, and extols the socialist system that ensures even distribution of wealth and the happiness of all. The new system would help humanity build a morally higher family life. Material wealth brings joy in marriage and love, satisfaction in education, knowledge and arts, and the elevation of the spiritual condition of man. The book offers a superb contrast between two social systems.

The publication of the book made quite a stir on the literary scene then.

Placed in proper historical perspective, the naturalistic enterprise of the 1890s was not, as some critics thought it was, "an aborted movement." It is true that writers like Crane, Norris and Dreiser had to take risks and were all of them rejected for some time by the genteel magazines and publishers. But they held out and, in so doing, cleared the way for the next generation, the "lost generation" of the 1920s. In theme they represented the life of the lower classes truthfully and broke into such forbidden regions as violence, death, and sex; in technique their works exhibited honest skills and artistry. Thus they prepared the way for the smooth acceptance of the younger writers like Hemingway and Faulkner.

Chapter 11   The 1920s • Imagism • Pound

The 1920s: An Introduction

The social scene in the decade of the 1920s was one of special interest in more ways than one. There were at least two important factors that made the decade different from the periods both preceding and following it: the First World War, and the sense of life being dislocated and fragmented which was more keenly felt in the first years of the 20th century.

First, the war was the biggest event that had a profound impact on the period. The people went into the war with an unusual amount of enthusiasm, inspired by the ideal of making the world safe for democracy. It proved, also, tremendously profitable: the United States made a great deal of money in the war and became a lot richer, so that there appeared an economic boom, a deceptive affluence, when the war was over. There was a feeling that there was money everywhere, and no one could or bothered to foresee the crash that would befall the country in 1929. People became aware of a sudden jump in technology. All of a sudden automobiles and radios appeared, which helped to widen the horizon of the people and increase their knowledge. The movie revolution and the music, notably Jazz, now becoming available to everybody, enriched and impacted the way of popular thinking. The country became urban in those years; a new type of industrial economy developed. Mass production, mass consumption, and mass leisure became essential to economic and cultural life and were soon to dominate the nation's culture and institutions. The wind of vital change began to blow. A social revolution was going on. Old moral codes were breaking down. Old modes of perception were questioned.

One important development related to what had been known as "the second sex" (meaning "women"). Now new women appeared on the scene, demanding the same social freedom as men enjoyed and affecting life significantly. Traditions regarding courtship and marriage, rearing of children, dress length, etc., everything that involved women, underwent a rapid, palpable change. New industries emerged to cater to their needs, such as cosmetics, and new institutions were established to appeal to their taste such as beauty contests. Whereas women were covered down to the ankles only a few years earlier, for example, girls now appeared on the scene in short skirts, wearing bobbed hair, smoking and drinking, and dancing wildly; they were "flappers" (as Fitzgerald calls them in one of his books) of the "Jazz Age." Conservative people blamed all this on the war, but the change had probably more to do with the urbanism that emerged in the wake of industrialism.

After the war there was a tremendous letdown because nothing had changed. The idealism that had spurred droves of young men into the war evaporated in face of its disastrous effects. The heroism, patriotism, and the zeal for democracy that the romantic notion of war had inspired now proved to be false and tasteless to a generation who had once had faith in them. Excitement and enthusiasm subsided to make way for disillusionment. The debunking of war that first began with Stephen Crane's *The Red Badge of Courage* became the paradigm for the war novel in the decade of the 1920s. It was as if the party was over and an anti-climax of discontentment, restlessness, and disgust followed, as well expressed in Hemingway's *A Farewell to Arms* or Dos Passos' *U. S. A.*

On the social scene, there was a high degree of intolerance in American society as a whole. All forms of radicalism and all assertions of social and religious rights other than those known as WASP (White Anglo-Saxon Protestant) values were treated with least tolerance. Pre-war socialist reform movements were ruthlessly suppressed during the war and in the "Red Hunt" after it, very much in the manner that McCarthy was to do following World War II. Minorities, African Americans and newer immigrant people were discriminated against. The Chicago Race Riot of the summer of 1919 resulted in destruction, death, hatred, and bigotry. The Ku Klux Klan redoubled its effort at racial persecution.

In the meantime there was in the south an attempt to conserve the southern lifestyle and southern values which were in the main agrarian as against the industrial north. For some intellectually thinking people like William Faulkner, the American south, with its rise and fall, became the subject for scrutiny and evaluation.

One more thing to note about the 1920s was that it was an era, also, of great popular contempt for the law. The Prohibition of alcohol outraged popular taste; bootleggers moved in to reap huge profits from illegal sales. At the same time there was a general feeling among many who were living through it, like Fitzgerald, that this was a sad period; the dream had failed, and the country was building up economic troubles all along and heading direct toward disaster.

In addition, the loss of faith, which began noticeably with Darwin's theories of evolution and was intensified by the development of modern science, continued with greater intensity into the 20th century. By the end of the first decade of the 20th century, all forces seemed to be pulling apart. There appeared a reality with no mythical center, with God expelled from the universe. Modern science destroyed man's ability to believe unquestioningly.[1] Without faith, man could no longer keep his feeling and thought whole; hence the sense of life being fragmented, chaotic, and disjunctive. And without faith, man no longer felt secure and happy and hopeful in his world; hence the feeling of gloom and despair. In short, people found themselves living in a spiritual wasteland, as T. S. Eliot's epochal poem, *The Waste Land*, suggests, where life was meaningless and futile, and man felt homeless, estranged, and haunted by a sense of doom.

One of the influential philosophers at the beginning of the 20th century, Bertrand Russell (1872-1970), was most eloquent commenting on the spirit of the period. In his "A Free Man's Worship" (1918), he observes to the effect that the universe had become purposeless and indifferent to human wishes. Man must not expect any help from a beneficent God. The idea of a world order that smiles on man's desires is an illusion. Man must recognize that he is of no importance in such a world, and he would do well to adapt himself to it on the basis of that recognition, however disturbing it may be. Nothing can preserve an individual life beyond the grave. Death will doom all human endeavors and achievements to ultimate extinction. All human effort is thus futile and leads only to despair. Man's life is brief and powerless, and the slow, sure doom will pitilessly fall on all his race. Russell advises man to believe in himself, to face life with "a despairing courage." This is the kind of courage with which Hemingway endowed his heroes.

Now the literary scene of the 1920s was no less interesting. The new, varied experience of the new period demanded a new varied literary expression. But the poetic scene of the first years of the 20th century was dismal and uninspired. With Whitman and Dickinson dead, the field was strewn with pieces of poetry extremely moralistic, sentimental, and imitative of what had gone before. This was the situation that prevailed in 1900-1910. There was obvious disaffection widely felt. Thinking minds in the field of art and literature began to feel that the old forms of representation were no longer adequate enough to represent reality and that newer ways must be found. Hence the passion widely felt among the younger generation for experimentation of various kinds. Europe was simmering with the innovative zeal. Paris emerged as the center of experimental art and literature to which ambitious, struggling artists and writers flocked. Impressionism appeared along with Dadaism and expressionism. Symbolism and surrealism became stylish and popular.

Meanwhile, some events of comparable significance took place in music, ballet, drama, and the fine arts, which shocked the audience into a pained recognition of the fact that old standards were beside the point and change became inevitable. The years 1912-1914 witnessed the appearance of all kinds of innovations. In addition to the Imagist movement that will be discussed later on, there was a book by Arthur Symons, an English critic, *The Symbolist*

Movement in Literature (1899), which was exerting a profound influence on T. S. Eliot, Ezra Pound, and practically everybody else who was interested in new voices in poetry. In 1912 Harriet Monroe started publishing a very small volume of verse, called *Poetry*, a magazine of verse, with the declared intention to print new poetic voices in it. A few years later Margaret Anderson published her *Little Review*, another magazine devoted to new verse by people like Pound, Eliot, Sandburg, and Williams.

The indications were evident that a new poetic revolution was taking place, comparable in scope and significance to (if not greater than) the one Whitman represented in 1855. The new poets wrote a poetry that defied most of the accepted rules, and dealt with subjects which had not been dealt with except, perhaps, by Whitman, thus pushing the boundaries of poetry further back. And they wrote in new ways and techniques.

While older writers such as William Butler Yeats, Edwin Arlington Robinson and Theodore Dreiser were still writing to keep step with the changing times, High Modernism began to dominate the world of literature and art. Modernist masters were busy at work, and works of permanent power and appeal came out in print in quick succession. James Joyce's *Ulysses*, Virginia Woolf's *Mrs. Dalloway* and *To the Lighthouse*, Thomas Mann's *The Magic Mountain*, and Marcel Proust's *Remembrance of Things Past* were out there to shine forth the splendor of the new era.

In American literature a whole new generation of younger writers, "the Lost Generation," surfaced with their new voices. The most active, presiding spirit was Ezra Pound whose sense of urgency about revolutionizing literature led him from one movement to another, lending support to people who struggled to add to the newness of the era. By far the most seminal influence of the time was T. S. Eliot and his poem *The Waste Land*, the man soon becoming a leader figure of the generation and the poem a watershed, "spawning" a whole group of "waste-land painters." These include, here to offer just a short list, Hemingway, Fitzgerald and Faulkner in fiction, Cummings, Frost, Sandburg, and Hart Crane in poetry, and Eugene O'Neill, Elmer Rice and Susan Glaspell in drama. Although William Carlos Williams and Wallace Stevens differed from Eliot and Pound in some aspects, they were definitely part and parcel of the group working to represent the *Zeitgeist*, or spirit, of the time. There were also lesser lights to consider. Sherwood Anderson and Gertrude Stein both tried to come up with something unique and help others in need at the same time. Cather Willa, one old-timer at the threshold of a changing world, was creating major minor classics. Sinclair Lewis, though "Edwardian" in form, wrote to pave his way for the first Nobel Prize in literature that an American ever won.

In the meantime the distant rumblings of a different thunderous voice were first heard in Harlem, New York City. Long pent-up emotional lava, stirred up by a new intellectual energy, now found an outlet and erupted into what has come to be known as the Harlem Renaissance. This outburst of African American creative energy was historically important because it marked the further awakening, literary as well as racial, of the African American people. It also heralded an era of multiethnic and multiracial literary expression in America. That would eventually result in possible redefining of American literary history and re-canonizing of American literature.

All these people were in effect creating a poetic revolution in America, and also a very large American poetry reading audience. This audience was in large part a very fragmented one, because modern life was fragmented and dislocated. The West was now, philosophically and religiously, a fragmented civilization. It had no longer a unified set of beliefs which had characterized the world of Dante's *Divine Comedy*, Chaucer's *Canterbury Tales*, Spenser's *Faerie Queene* or the world of Shakespeare, Milton, and Alexander Pope. The new verse was responsive to the fragmentized nature of modern life. Within a little over two decades, it scored a complete triumph over old poetry.

Thus the 1920s was a peculiar period in which the postwar economic boom and the sense of spiritual disorientation combined to produce the peculiar mood of the age. The greatness of the literature of the decade lies in the fact that it managed to capture that mood and keep it on record for posterity. The few chapters that follow are designed to offer a sketchy account of the bustling American literary activity during this famous stretch of ten years.

"The Coming of the Image"

The new age demanded proper literary expression. Between 1912 and 1922 there came a great poetry boom in which about 1,000 poets published over 1,000 volumes of poetry.[2] Quite a few literary movements appeared to express the modern spirit, of which Imagism was the most renowned. It came, it is true, as a reaction to the traditional English poetics with its iambic pentameter, its verbosity, and extra-poetic padding; but it served, first and foremost, to meet the need of expressing the temper of the age.

A small group of English and American poets came together in the first years of the 20th century to work out some new way of writing poetry. Nobody propounded the point more convincingly than the first Imagist theorist, the English writer T. E. Hulme (1883-1917). Hulme suggests that modern art deals with expression and communication of momentary phases in the poet's mind.[3] Poetic techniques should become subtle enough to record exactly the momentary impressions. The most effective means to express these momentary impressions is through the use of one dominant image. "Each word must be an image seen." The image is a representation of a physical object, and the reader is made to react to it as such. "Each sentence should be a lump; a piece of clay, a vision seen." Hulme advises the poet to seek the hard, personal word for expression. These became the basic principles on which the Imagist movement was launched.[4]

The movement underwent three phases in its brief and yet immensely important history. It first began in the years 1908-1909 when T. E. Hulme founded a Poets' Club in London. The club met in Soho every Wednesday to dine and discuss poetry. Hulme, as the presiding spirit of the crowd, theorized a lot on poetic technique, as mentioned earlier on. Ezra Pound was present at some of the meetings; there was a lot of talking but not as much writing. Hulme died in the First World War.

The second phase of the movement was the period of some three years (1912-1914) when Ezra Pound took over and championed the new poetry. Something like an Imagist manifesto of three poetic principles came out in 1912: (1) Direct treatment of the "thing," whether subjective or objective; (2) To use absolutely no word that does not contribute to the presentation; and (3) As regarding rhythm, to compose in the sequence of the musical phrase, not in the sequence of a metronome. The first principle, with its emphasis on direct treatment, indicates a desire to make the expression resemble the "object" as closely as art can make it. By "direct," Pound means no fuss, frill, or ornament. The second stresses economy of expression, a reaction to the 19th-century tendency of philosophical "padding" of extra-poetic matter, or "emotional slither." To Ezra Pound any unnecessary word represents a loss of precision and a moral and artistic defection.

The third concerns a breaking away from conventional prosody and the use of free verse, and the interrelationship between music and verse. Pound did not mean to sponsor "free verse" as the only verse form to use: he advocated freedom in verse. "Free verse" means form, not formlessness. It is not "free"; as T. S. Eliot once said, "No *vers* is *libre* for the man who wants to do a good job." Neither was it new with the Imagists. Free verse went as far back as Milton. But it was with the Imagists that it became a legitimate poetic form. Free verse is a poetic mode closely allied to music; hence the third principle relates to verse form and music at the same time.

In 1914, Pound edited the first anthology of Imagist poems, entitled *Des Imagistes*, which included poets such as Hilda Doolittle, Richard Aldington, F. S. Flint, Amy Lowell, William Carlos Williams, and Ezra Pound.

In the third phase of the movement (1914-1917), Amy Lowell (1874-1925) took over from Pound. Pound left to devote his attention to new movements like "Vorticism," and the Imagist movement gradually lost its momentum. The most concise of the Imagists, H. D. (Hilda Doolittle), became wordier, and the six principles that Amy Lowell and other Imagists worked out were in essence an expansion and an adulteration of the first Imagist manifesto of 1912. In this period three anthologies came out respectively in 1915, 1916, and 1917, edited by Amy Lowell, all entitled *Some Imagist Poets*. After 1917 Imagism ceased to be a movement.

What is the image as the Imagists saw it? Images exist in all poetry, but the image of the Imagists has something new to offer. T. E. Hulme said that the image must enable one "to dwell and linger upon a point of excitement, to achieve the impossible and convert a point into a line."[5] Pound defined an image as that which presents an intellectual and emotional complex in an instant of time, and later he extended this definition when he stated that an image was "a vortex or cluster of fused ideas" "endowed with energy."

An Imagistic presentation is hard, clear, un-blurred, done by means of the chosen "exact word." And the exact word, according to Richard Aldington, another of the first Imagists, must bring the effect of the object before the reader as it had presented itself to the poet's mind at the time of writing.[6] An Imagist poem enables the reader to see the physical thing rather than put him through an abstract process. Lucid logical exposition is no good poetry. The best poetic effect is visual and concrete. Thus an Imagist's image represents a moment of revealed truth, truth revealed by a physical object presented and seen as such. An Imagist poem, therefore, often contains a single dominant image, or a quick succession of related images. Its effect is meant to be instantaneous.

Let us look at some Imagist poems. "In a Station of the Metro," by Ezra Pound, has been regarded as a classic specimen of Imagist poetry:

> The apparition of these faces in the crowd;
> Petals on a wet, black bough.

Pound was once in a Paris subway station and was struck by the sight of the faces of a few pretty women and children in a crowd hurrying out of the dim, damp, and somber station. So impressed was he by the spectacle that he resolved to bring it out in poetic language. The result is, of course, the poem. "The object" to be treated is the faces in that dim and damp context. The impression is brought out most vividly by the single, dominant image of flower petals on a wet, black bough, which serves as the most concise, direct, and definite metaphor for the "faces in the crowd."

H. D.'s "Oread" is another classic example:

Whirl up, sea—

Whirl your pointed pines,

splash your great pines

on our rocks

hurl your green over us,

cover us with your pools of fir.

This is Pound's favorite poem. It presents a vivid picture of the billowing sea. It was H. D. who first provided Ezra Pound with the inspiration for the new school of "Imagists." She brought five of her poems to Ezra Pound in 1912, and Pound was so impressed by her clarity, her intensity, her "hardness"—directness, and absolute economy of expression—that he later even declared that Imagism had been founded in order to get her poems publicized.

William Carlos Williams' "The Red Wheelbarrow" is an oft-quoted and anthologized Imagist poem:

So much depends

upon

a red wheel

barrow

glazed with rain

water

beside the white

chickens.

As critic Frederick J. Hoffman observes, "Here the material facts are reduced almost to the level of plain factual statement."[7] Short as it is, the poem is rich in meaning and is capable of more than one interpretation.

In the history of American poetry, Imagism was only a transient phase of no longer than a decade. Its limitations are apparent. A single dominant image can supply energy for a two-line poem of Pound's or a 16-word one of Williams', but it is hardly capable of sustaining a longer poetic effort. Thus no great poetry came out of the movement. Its own aesthetics stunted its growth into something more ambitious and eternal. But the movement was important in a number of ways in the development of modern poetry. It was a rebellion against the traditional poetics which failed to reflect the new life of the new century. It offered a new way of writing, valid not only for the Imagist poets but for modern poetry as a whole. The movement was in a sense a training school in which many great poets learned their first lessons in the poetic art. Almost all major modern poets were in one way or another associated with it and benefited from it in a significant way. Apart from Ezra Pound and William Carlos Williams, there are Wallace Stevens, T. S. Eliot, Carl Sandburg, and Marianne Moore, to mention just a few American names. Its literary theories and poetic forms have continued to exercise their influence on modern and contemporary poetry. The movement helped to open the first pages of modern English and American poetry.

Ezra Pound (1885-1972)

Ezra Pound was born in Idaho and brought up in Pennsylvania. He studied

Romance languages at Hamilton College and the University of Pennsylvania where he met William Carlos Williams and H. D.

In the first years of the 20th century, the West presented a panorama of a wasteland. It was a world in which Pound saw pervasive gloom, chaos, and barbarism. To him life was sordid personal crushing oppression, and culture produced nothing but "intangible bondage."[8] He considered it his mission to save a tottering civilization. As a sensitive, rebellious spirit, he tried to derive standards from the cultures of the past and resurrect lost principles of order. From Greek, Provencal, Latin, Chinese, Anglo-Saxon, French, and Spanish traditions, he drew and borrowed to "make it new." Pound owed heavily to Homer, Provencal troubadours such as Arnaut Daniel, and Dante.

Not satisfied with the Victorian poetic bequest and convinced that poetry was in a bad way, Pound felt keenly the need to revise the status of the arts and to redefine the artists' responsibilities. So he took it upon himself to purify the arts.

In 1908 he sailed to Europe and published his first book of poetry, *A Lume Spento*, in Venice. Then arriving in London, he came in contact with T. E. Hulme and his Poets' Club, and later founded Imagism together with H. D. and Richard Aldington. In 1912 he appointed himself foreign editor of *Poetry* (Chicago). In this capacity, he moved about in literary circles, discovered and spurred talents to action.

After he published *Homage to Sextus Propertius* (1917) and *Hugh Selwyn Mauberley* (1920), he moved first to Paris where he assisted young American writers like Hemingway, and then settled in Rapallo, Italy, to work on his *Cantos*. Among those who acknowledged their debt to him were T. S. Eliot, Robert Frost, William Carlos Williams, and Marianne Moore. Pound's innovative zeal impressed William Butler Yeats and helped him move into a new period of his career. Pound, as a seminal figure, made a unique contribution to the modern poetry.

Pound's War Crime

The First World War woke Pound up from his preoccupation with poetry, and led him to take an interest in economics. During the Second Would War, he supported Mussolini's fascist regime and broadcast over Radio Rome against the Allies. At the end of the war he was arrested to stand trial for treason. Later he was declared insane, and was sent to St. Elizabeth's Hospital in Washington, D. C. There he completed the Pisan sequence, the *Rock Drill Cantos* and his translation of a Chinese classic, *The Classic Anthology Defined by Confucius*. In 1958, the concerted effort of such eminent personalities as T. S. Eliot, Robert Frost, and Hemingway helped secure his release. He returned to Italy to live with his daughter, and died there in 1972 at 87.

Pound's Connection with Chinese Culture

In 1913 Pound became the literary executor of Ernest Fenollosa (1853-1908), the noted American Orientalist, and began his earnest study of the Chinese language and ancient Chinese culture. Around 1915 he finished his volume of Chinese translations, *Cathay*, and began to work on his *Cantos*, which in time grew into a semblance of an epic.

The greatest cultural influence over Pound came perhaps from ancient China. In a way, it was Pound's intention to celebrate Chinese civilization. He began his career with a "grand abnegation."[9] He saw no effective cure in Christianity for the disease of his times,[10] and even lost faith in Greek culture and Greek thought.[11] Thus when he looked about and turned east, he found in Confucius' teachings the "one lantern" "under the cabin roof" (canto 49). Confucius, Pound believed, can enlighten and "civilize" the barbarous Occident.[12] Pound saw in the forty six characters of the "Text of Confucius" (*Ta Hio* [*Da Xue* or *The Great Learning*]) the notion of order and tranquility, from which light shines forth. Order and tranquility come from enlightened rule, and a salient feature of Confucian enlightened rule is even distribution of wealth and light taxation. These constitute the thematic concerns of the China cantos, and in a sense underlie the *Cantos* as a whole. In addition, Pound found in the ideogramic and pictographic Chinese characters an ideal medium for poetry.

Now a brief analysis of Pound's two well-known works, *Hugh Selwyn Mauberley* and the *Cantos*, is offered here.

Hugh Selwyn Mauberley

The best poem that Pound ever wrote is probably his 400-line two-part *Hugh Selwyn Mauberley*. It is a record of Pound's growth as a poet from his refusal to write "socially useful," "engaged" poetry in his *Homage to Sextus Propertius* to his final realization that aestheticism will not work in the modern world.[13] Many elements of the poem are apparently autobiographical.

There are altogether 18 poems in the two parts, 13 in the first part and 5 in the second. For the sake of easy reference, here is offered a list of the brief accounts of the poems; the serial numbers and the sign of 【 】 are added:

【The 1st part】   Life and Contacts

【I】 "E.P. Ode pour l'Election de Son Sepulchre": an account of narrator-Pound's dilemma and frustration;

【II】 critical of the conservative forces to forestall artists' effort to realize their ideals;

【III】 critical of commercialization of art, of money, publishers' catering to popular taste, etc.

【IV】 critical of the first world war,

【V】 lashing at the war taking young lives for the sake of a hopeless civilization,

【VI】 Yeux Glauques: the Gladstone period hostile to beauty,

【VII】 "Siena Mi Fe; Disfecemi Maremma": the artists of the 1890s harshly repressed,

【VIII】 "Brennbaum": a Jew catering to social demand at the expense of his faith,

【IX】 "Mr. Nixon": a novelist stooping to publishers,

【X】 a stylist holding on in poverty,

【XI】 an educated woman ignorant of the tradition she has inherited,

【XII】 narrator-Pound aware of his insignificance in the literary circles,

【XIII】 "Envoi (1919)": narrator-Pound making a graceful exit.

【The 2nd part】   **Mauberley 1919**

【I】 Mauberley loves beauty and complains about modern inability to create beauty,

【II】Mauberley's belated awareness of his failure to grab at the opportunities life has offered him to get to know about beauty and represent it,

【III】 "The Age Demanded": Mauberley unable to go with the flow,

【IV】 Mauberley leaving for tropical islands,

【V】 "Medallion."

The first part of the poem focuses on the narrator-poet's (or narrator-Pound's) complaints about the commercialization and debasement of art, and about his feeling of frustration and failure in face of the conservative philistinism of the world he is in. He feels disgusted and hopeless, and decides to quit.

The second part of poem introduces Mauberley, a literary figure, who can be viewed on more than one plane of significance. One perspective can be to see him as a foil of a kind to the narrator-poet. As such he is in many ways a psychological reflection of the narrator-poet, caring about art's status, wishing to be of use in its innovation, and feeling bitterly frustrated with the world's indifference to classic beauty. So there may appear to be some overlapping in the delineation of the two characters' basic personalities.

But the two figures differ widely. Mauberley is dull and effete and has not the kind of insight and courage that the narrator-poet possesses to deal with his dilemma. Although both fall in the "slough of despond" (for a while for the poet-narrator), they end up differently. One manages wisely to get out and leaves to continue his endeavor, while the other dies in self-exile, unredeemed.

Thus the whole poem is a mature poet-narrator looking backward and inward. It celebrates his success in "running away," reaffirms his faith in beauty, and foretells his new beginning in his endeavor.

The *Cantos*

The *Cantos* has been called Pound's "intellectual diary since 1915." Containing a total of over 120 poems, it is social history, an amalgam of heterogeneous cultures and languages, a poet's attempt to impose, through art, order and meaning upon a chaotic and meaningless world. It is a diversity in theme and form.

The *Cantos* depicts a cheerless and somber world. There are the Hades of the dead (canto 1), the Spanish hero Ruy Diaz being persecuted, and the murder in a decayed mansion (canto 3), a vast unfruitful world (cantos 4 and 5), a society of phantoms and ghosts (canto 7), the misfortunes of the renaissance Malatesta family (canto 11), and a scene of perversion and "darkness unconscious" on all conceivable levels of life (cantos 14-15). Even in canto 16, which offers a glimpse of an earthly paradise, the readers see a Europe very much ruined and destroyed.

Pound hates usury. He saw it as a beast with a hundred legs, blasting light, life, and love out of existence. Cantos 12, 30, 34, 37, 45, 46, and 51 and more all lash at usury and denounce the malpractices of US and England banks. The first fifty cantos paint a picture of "the complete and utter inferno of the past century."[14]

Pound sees in Chinese history and the doctrine of Confucius a source of strength and wisdom with which to counterpoint Western gloom and confusion.

Canto 13 emphasizes the Confucian ideal of harmony and order. Canto 49 illumines the dim, repulsive world of cantos 45 and 51. Canto 52, based on the Confucian classic, *Li Ji*, throws the idea of order into relief, and introduces the China cantos sequence (cantos 53-61). Here Pound surveys Chinese history from the far-off mythical period to the middle of the 18th century in his simplistic and idealistic way. The Confucian notion, that a good prince keeps down taxes and ensures order and happiness, becomes the yardstick for Pound to evaluate history. The Adams cantos (62-71) are related to the Chinese sequence because there is, to Pound, something in Western thought that conforms to Confucius',[15] and the career of John Adams and other early American leaders embodied for Pound the finest virtues of the national period.[16]

In a sense the *Rock Drill* (cantos 85-95) and the *Thrones* (cantos 96-109) sequences are a continuation of the theme treated in the China cantos. The first of these may dwell more on usury, and the second may devote more to the eulogy of virtuous rulers (or sage kings), but neither deviates much from the general thematic pattern as set in the China cantos. Canto 85 is a liberal rendering of the Confucian classic, *The Book of History*. The theme of usury is again prominent in Canto 87, and in the next two cantos, the American banking system is under fire as a form of usury against the people. As Pound himself points out, the *Thrones* concerns the states of mind of the people responsible for something more than their personal conduct.[17] Cantos 98 and 99 recount the royal edicts of the Qing emperors Kang Xi and Yong Zheng, stressing basic Confucian virtues.

Pound believed that humanity deserved better than it got.[18] He felt that Confucian philosophy could help save the West. Thus the ethos of the *Cantos* is essentially Confucian.[19] If, toward the end of his *Cantos*, his earthly paradise is still in the making, he has at least tried for "the little light and harmony" (canto 113, *Drafts and Fragments*). It is somewhat pathetic to hear him uttering in plain desperation these lines: "I lost my center / fighting the world. / The dreams clash / and are shattered" (canto 117).

Pound's Reputation

Pound's early poems are fresh and lyrical. His Chinese translations are uneven. The *Cantos* is not easily approachable, and is seen by many as a monumental failure.

Yet Pound's influence has been on the increase. In the postwar period when tastes and values began to change and the influence of T. S. Eliot and the New Criticism started to wane, Pound, along with William Carlos Williams, offered a sense of direction to the writing of new poetry. His *Cantos*, especially his *Pisan Cantos*, became the new model for contemporary poets with its features such as its autobiographical and personal tone, and its open, spontaneous, and sometimes agrammatical style. He became a father figure for post-war poets.

His letters, literary essays and selected prose, for a long time out of print, have been reissued along with most of his pre-war writings including *The Spirit of Romance* (1909), *ABC of Reading* (1934), *Guide to Kulchur* (1938), and his Chinese and Japanese translations. With the passage of time, people seem to be forgetting his wartime misbehavior and beginning to evaluate his achievement as a poet, and have realized that he has helped, through theory and practice, to chart out the course of modern poetry in the West. He will be remembered as such.

Chapter 12   *T. S. Eliot • Stevens • Williams*

T. S. Eliot (1888-1965)

In the verse revolution of the 1920s, Eliot made his presence felt and became, around 1925, the acknowledged leader of the new verse and criticism both in America and Great Britain.[1]

T. S. Eliot was born in St. Louis, Missouri where his grandfather had helped to found the University of Washington. He attended Harvard and received a good education in classic literature and neo-humanism. He also studied in Paris and Oxford. He read Dante and Jules Laforgue, explored the poetry of the 17th-century Metaphysical poets like John Donne, and acknowledged his indebtedness to them. In 1915 he settled down in England, teaching, working as a bank clerk, writing book reviews for publishers, suffering intensely from an unhappy marriage, and all the while composing poetry.

Eliot as a Poet

Eliot's poetry was noted for its fresh visual imagery, its flexible tone, and highly expressive rhythm. "Gerontion" came out in 1920, and *The Waste Land* in 1922 which established his position as the leader, not only of new American poetry, but of a whole generation of writers later to be identified as "Waste Land Painters" like Hemingway and Faulkner.[2] "Hollow Man" appeared in print in 1925, exhibiting a pessimism no less depressing than *The Waste Land*. For two years (1917-1919) Eliot was editor of *The Egoist*, founded *The Criterion* in 1922, and was its editor until 1939.

In 1927 he announced that he was a royalist in politics, a classicist in literature, and an Anglo-Catholic in religion. This meant that he had turned conservative. The publication of his poems *Ash Wednesday* (1930) and *Four Quartets* (1943) made his stance more than evident. The change angered many of his followers like Hemingway. Eliot was also a playwright. He won the Nobel Prize for Literature in 1948. The postwar period witnessed the enormous growth of his reputation.

Now let us take a look at *The Love Song of J. Alfred Prufrock* and *The Waste Land*, for an experience of Eliot's poetry.

The Love Song of J. Alfred Prufrock

In 1911 Eliot finished *The Love Song of J. Alfred Prufrock,* a poem with a notable modern emotional coloring. The poem depicts a timid middle-aged man going (or thinking of going) to propose marriage to a lady but hesitating all the way there. It takes the form of a soliloquy, an interior monologue like that of Browning's. Whether the man actually leaves his spot at all remains a question. Most probably he stays where he is all the while, allowing his imagination to run wild.

Prufrock is the image of an ineffectual, sorrowful, and tragic 20th-century Western man, possibly the modern intellectual, who is divided between passion and timidity, between desire and impotence. His tragic flaw is timidity; his "curse" is his idealism.[3] Knowing everything, but able to do nothing, he lives in an area of life and death; and caught between the two worlds, he belongs to neither. He craves love but has no courage to declare himself. He despairs of life. He discovers its emptiness and yet has found nothing to replace it. Thus the poem develops a theme of frustration and emotional conflict.

The title of the poem is ironic in that the "Love Song" is in fact about the absence of love. The name of Prufrock is that of a furniture dealer in St. Louis. The initial "J" sounds tony and classy, giving one a sense of the upper class to which he belongs. The epigraph, taken from Dante's *Inferno*, is in fact a confessional, a kind of "I'll tell you all." The first line, "Let us go then, you and I," suggests that what follows is a dramatic monologue without an audience. It reminds us of Browning's "My Last Duchess" where there is the impregnated line, "Nay, we'll go / Together down, sir."[4]

Prufrock is a middle-aged dandy, well-dressed, self-conscious, and harassed with self-doubt. He cannot well handle his obsession and is afraid of rejection in regard to his marriage proposal. Most probably sexually inadequate, he represents the spiritual impotence of archetypal modern man. What is redeeming is probably his self-perception: he sees his own absurdity.

The poem is interesting also for its method of presentation. It does not move in a sequential fashion. With its surreal vividness, elliptical structures, strange juxtapositions, and the absence of bridges, the whole seems broken; nothing is explained in a logical manner. The poet jumps from one scene to another and from one idea to another. But the association of images establishes the general feeling. Nothing is discordant, irrelevant, or abrupt, and all falls in place when the overall mood of the poem is perceived. We see more of this method in *The Waste Land*.

The Waste Land

T. S. Eliot composed *The Waste Land* in the autumn of 1921, while taking a vacation at Lausanne, western Switzerland. Before returning to London, he visited Pound at Paris and left the draft with him. Pound blue-penciled it and reduced its length which was nearly twice as long as its present form. Impressed by this editorial feat, T. S. Eliot dedicated the poem to him: "For Ezra Pound il miglior fabbro [the better craftsman]," which is a quotation from Dante's *Purgatorio* xxvi, line 117. In October, 1922 *The Waste Land* was first published in the English *Criterion* and in November in the American *Dial*; and in the same year by the New York publishers, Boni and Liveright.

Though the poem has been read differently, the critical consensus reached so far has been that it reveals the spiritual crisis of postwar Europe and has been seen as the manifesto of the "Lost Generation." It has been considered the best work of all to come out of the 1920s to represent the popular state of mind of the time, i.e. the spiritual poverty that stems from a fragmented, disorderly, and meaningless existence.

Commenting on James Joyce, T. S. Eliot remarked once that the only way the modern writer has of "giving shape and significance to the immense panorama of futility and anarchy which is contemporaneous history" is by indicating or "manipulating a continuous parallel between contemporaneity and antiquity." Now out of this famous statement three things come out immediately that merit careful analysis. The first is the feeling that the modern world presents an "immense panorama of futility and anarchy." Secondly, there is the keenly felt need, especially on the part of the artist, to "[give] shape and significance" to the meaningless, futile, and chaotic experience of modern man. Thirdly, the poet should use the "antiquity," the past; a poet can perfectly legitimately draw from traditions of various kinds. So, as *The Waste Land* indicates, Eliot relies, in part, on past literatures and cultures which fuse in his mind with his own personal and private agonies into something rich and strange, something universal and imper-sonal.[5]

The title, *The Waste Land*, draws its significance from the Fisher King legend, as related in the book, *From Ritual to Romance* (1922) by Jessie L. Western. The Fisher King sins against God, who then punishes him by making him sexually impotent. The disability of the King is reflected on his land, so that his kingdom becomes a waste land. Hence the title. Thus one major feature of the poem is that sexual failure connotes spiritual debilitation.

The epigraph of the poem tells about the suffering of a mythical prophetess, Sibyl of Cumae (in Italy), who is shut up in a cage to wither forever, so she wants to die. Thus the epigraph expresses a death-wish and a struggle for salvation,[6] which constitutes the overall emotional gloom of the poem. The Fisher King legend involves a quest to help the king and his land recover.[7]

The Waste Land presents a mélange of fragmentary experiences, incidents and episodes, shifting without much notice from one to the other, in order for the reader to feel the fragmentation of modern life. [8] The poem is subdivided into five sections, not formally connected, but all subsumed into a thematic whole. The five parts of the poem, "The Burial of the Dead," "A Game of Chess," "The Fire Sermon," "Death by Water," and "What the Thunder Said" do not have sufficient formal connection between them. Things stop and begin without explicable shift: the unreal city of London, the lady sitting in splendor, the scene in a pub, the anxiety of a promiscuous wife of a returning soldier, Phlebas the Phoenician sailor, a fortnight dead, and a host of other nightmarish imagery, the reminders, of the waste land—the change is abrupt and jerky, with no hint of logical order and causal relationship. This radical disconnectedness is true even of the transitions between the different sections within any one part of the poem, and between the different ideas within any one section. Through gaps, absence of connective tissues, and discordant juxtapositions, the poet intends the reader to see and feel the fragmentary nature of life.

The Waste Land reveals Eliot's strong historical sense. To Eliot the past is important to writers. In his famous essay, "Tradition and the Individual Talent," he states that a writer should have the historical sense. The past should be altered by the present as much as the present is directed by the past. Eliot was well acquainted with the whole of the literature of Europe from Homer and the whole of the literature of his own country. He wrote with an acute consciousness of the past, trying to contrast the negative qualities of the present with the positive ones of the past, and shock the reader into a recognition of the dismal truth about modern life. For instance, the legendary Tristram-Iseult tragic love contrasts sharply with the modern perfunctory typist, the ancient Cleopatra-Marks loyal tie presents a poignant comparison to the modern lady (or lover)'s precarious connection with her man. In addition there is the anxious promiscuous wife of a returning soldier, remotely relating to the ancient Elisabeth-Leicester devotion.

This is just to mention a few instances.

As eloquent social criticism, *The Waste Land* was the poem of despair for the 1920s and 1930s. But it is not all pessimism. Part five tries to offer a hope of regeneration. It shows an underlying desire to help create order and sense as the thunder shows the way to salvation: "Give, Sympathize, Control," which is another way of saying self-surrender, consideration for others, and submission to God's control. So the poem ends on a somewhat hopeful note.

Eliot as a Critic

Eliot was also a distinguished literary critic. He was "a giver of laws and the arbiter of taste" in the new poetry and criticism. His criticism possessed an air of authority. His critical theory became something like a law for English and American poets for over two decades from the mid-1920s through the 1950s.

One basic theme of his criticism concerns the relationship between tradition and individual talent. Eliot emphasizes the relation of a poem to the poems by other authors and suggests "the conception of poetry as a living whole of all the poetry that has ever been written." It explains the importance of tradition and the past.

Another thing that Eliot is noted for is his "impersonal theory." This concerns the relation of the poem to its author. To him, poetry is not a turning loose of emotion, but an escape from it; it is not the expression of personality, but an escape from it. In this way universal applicability can be achieved. In such poetry, authorial presence is effaced as much as possible. As it is difficult for such poems to be autobiographical and meditative, the theory provoked the Postmodernist poets' strong reaction in the 1950s and 1960s.

Related to this impersonal theory is his famous principle of "objective correlative" as he states in his essay "Hamlet and His Problems":

The only way of expressing emotion in the form of art is by

finding an "objective correlative"; in other words, a set of objects, a situation, a chain of events which shall be the formula of that particular emotion; such that when the external facts, which must terminate in sensory experience, are given, the emotion is immediately evoked.

A good illustration of the principle is Eliot's poem, "The Winter Evening Settles Down." Here a voice, not that of the author's, is speaking. His manner of communication is indirection: he piles up a heap of images, visual, auditory, olfactory, and more for the readers to figure out what is being said. It is necessary to note here that the "objective correlative" principle is based on Eliot's misreading of *Hamlet*; he declared that *Hamlet* is not Shakespeare's best work.

Collections of Eliot's critical essays include *The Sacred Wood, Essays on Style and Order, Elizabethan Essays, Essays Ancient and Modern, The Use of Poetry and the Use of Criticism* and *After Strange Gods.*

Eliot's Reputation

Eliot's search for salvation for the West continued in his *Ash Wednesday* and *Four Quartets*; he hoped to find it in religious belief and self-repentance. *Four Quartets* is the best work of the later phase of his career, and some critics claim that it is one of best long poems (if not the best) to come out of the 20th century. The four quartets are "Burnt Norton," "East Coker," "The Dry Salvages," and "Little Gidding." The first of these was written as a separate work in the mid-1930s, and the rest were composed between 1940 and 1942. Later Eliot put these together as *Four Quartets.*

If *The Waste Land* is a representative work of the High Modernism of the 1920s, impersonal, discontinuous with its fragments, full of literary allusions and ancient myths, measuring modern life against the historical past and finding it wanting in many ways, then *Four Quartets* is quite different in many aspects such as speech, mood, and tone, so much so that it sounds like a Postmodernist poem in some of its passages. In certain parts of the long poem, the speech is personal, the mood is reflective, the presentation is continuous and discursive and less allusive, and the emphasis on the significance of the past is toned down so much that there is little social critique in evidence in the poem. Just as Virginia Woolf sensed the need for a change in style in her later writings such as *Between the Acts* and *The Years* (which indicates her inclination toward Postmodernism), so Eliot felt the inevitable Postmodernist impulse. *Four Quartets* is easier to read. The personal and autobiographical nature of some of its passages and their meditative style have endeared the author to his readers. Personal memories appear, such as those of the rose garden in "Burnt Norton," of his visit to East Coker, of his childhood in St. Louis and boyhood experience in Massachusetts.

However, that the impact of Eliot's change was not comparable to that of Pound's *Cantos*, especially the *Pisan Cantos*, and to William Carlos Williams' *Paterson*. Both of these made their impressive presence felt in the late 1940s and became the harbingers of the new phase of American poetry—that of Postmodernism—in the postwar period. It was Pound and Williams who would become the prophet figures of the new period, and not Eliot whose decline in influence, along with that of the New Criticism, was to become a matter of course. All this is seen in retrospect, and all is now history.

The mist of time has cleared up, and Eliot has remained probably the best poet of his generation and his century.

Wallace Stevens (1879-1955)[9]

Wallace Stevens was an unusual poet in modern American literary history. He was late in starting; his first major volume of poetry was not published until he was 44 years old. And he was successful in two fields of activity which did not seem compatible with one another: he was a very successful business man, rising to the position of vice-president in a Connecticut insurance company, while at the same time writing poetry of a kind which was to make him a father-figure among contemporary poets. He was in his early career influenced by the Imagist movement and the verse revolution of the time. His *Harmonium* bears a visible imprint of Pound's 1912 statement of the Imagist "manifesto." But the style in the final phase of his career (from the 1940s through his death in 1955) underwent a significant change. He became diffuse and reflective. His poems were composed in the meditative mood and were filled with paradoxical generalizations and quasi-philosophical deliberations (to quote critic David Perkins' comments on him). So he became, along with Pound and Williams, a major influence on postwar and contemporary American poetry.

Stevens' Aesthetics

Wallace Stevens was absolutely committed to the notion that a poet lives in two worlds—the world of reality and the world of imagination—and builds bridges between them. So obsessed was he with the interrelationship between reality and art that a key to understanding his poetry and criticism lies in realizing that this is a very basic theme for him. Stevens' poetry is all of one piece, an elaboration or amplification, as some critics say, of Coleridge's famous poem entitled "Dejection: An Ode." What Coleridge talks about is the making of poetry, how to invent joy in poetry in the absence of anything in this world that gives certainty. Speaking in an age of shaky faith, Coleridge saw very few certainties in this world and felt that the job of the poet was at least in part to create through art things that give life meaning and pleasure in the absence of consoling belief.

Like Coleridge, Stevens deals repeatedly in his poetry with the role of the power of imagination. He sees the role of the poet as "Picnicking in the ruins that we live," which is another way of saying that a poet should find beauty, pleasure, excitement and meaning in the sordidness of reality. So we find, in Stevens, the poet as the imaginative man, a heroic type, heroic because capable of imagination. We find poetry as a major modern form of revelation. It reveals, among other things, the heroism of modern man who, even though recognizing the nothingness of modern existence, yet brings order and meaning to its chaos and meaninglessness. The poet operates in the two spheres of the real world and the imagined world and anchors his poetry solidly in the world of the here and now. Or in the words of Keats, one of Stevens' favorite poets, the poet reaches "upward from the world." It is good to note here that, for Stevens, the structured reality as present in a poem, or the "supreme fiction" (in his words), might not be the ultimate truth. Hence his ceaseless search and pondering over the true nature of reality, which is to him not quite knowable.

For Stevens, a poem is capable of more than one interpretation. He was opposed to telling people what his poems meant. He said at one time that things that have their origin in imagination or emotion very often take on a form that is ambiguous and uncertain, and that it is not possible to attach a single rational meaning to such things without destroying the imaginative, emotional ambiguity and uncertainty inherent in them.

Stevens as a Poet

Stevens is, like Keats, a very sensual poet. He delights in depicting the world as revealed to the senses, hoping to relieve the monotony and grimness of everyday existence by finding pleasures in the senses. Colors, sounds, and exotic images appeal to Stevens. There are, in his poems, many references to colors. Blue, the color of heaven, tends to be symbolic of the imagination. Green is symbolic of nature's vitality, and so is red, which also indicates virility. Of all the senses, Stevens values that of sight most. His visual imagery very often builds around the sense of the eyes.

In his later poetry Stevens became increasingly more meditative and even obscure in style, and more difficult to appreciate. But he always kept pace with the spirit of his time.

Stevens' was a long career of conscientious creation. His major works include *Harmonium* (1923), *Ideas of Order* (1927), *The Man with the Blue Guitar* (1937), *Parts of a World* (1942), *Transport to Summer* (1947), *The Auroras of Autumn* (1950), *Collected Poems* (1954), and *Opus Posthumous* (1957) which includes his uncollected works. His prose writings appeared in the collection, *The Necessary Angel*, in 1951.

Let us take a look at some of his poems.

"Anecdote of the Jar"

"Anecdote of the Jar" is a strange poem in some ways, not very easy to interpret. Here lies the wild—and chaotic and formless—rural Tennessee, which we could assume is a symbol of the world of nature. Then the "I" of the poem places a tall, round jar in it. What happens is almost a miracle: it controls the whole disorderly landscape, so that "The wilderness rose up to it, /And sprawled around, no longer wild."

The poem seems to be talking about the relationship between art and nature. The world of nature, shapeless and slovenly, takes shape and order from the presence of the jar, a man-made object, suggestive of art and imagination. The world of art and imagination gives form and meaning to that of nature and reality. Stevens insinuates that any society without art is one without order, man makes the order he perceives, and the world he inhabits is one he half creates.

Stevens firmly believes that the poet is the archetype of creative power on which all human understanding depends. To him, poet is "the necessary angel of the earth," in whose sight man sees the earth and life whole again.

So to Stevens poetry creates an aesthetic order and converts what is evil to something amenable. Read his poems such as "The Comedian with the Letter C") and "Paltry Nude," and the point will become clearer.

"The Idea of Order at Key West"

Here is this girl, facing a chaotic world of nature with its "meaningless plungings of water and wind," walks and sings all the while. What happens is that, at her singing, the world seems to stop being chaotic and becomes orderly. The glassy lights in the fishing boats master the night and portion out the sea, fix the colored zones and fiery poles, and make the night orderly and enchanting. The girl is the maker of the world that was never there until she made it.

Here the girl is presented as "the single artificer," trying to make an orderly world through her artistic endeavor. The effect of her art signifies the universal passion for order. The role of the artist is elevated almost to that of a creator. The poem and Stevens' other works such as "The World as Meditation" all illustrate the poet's exaltation of the role of imagination and art.

 On the other hand, Stevens manages to keep a balance between art and life in his creative work. He knows well that the world of reality determines the limits of art, and that imagination can construct only on the basis of the world of nature. Take "Anecdote of the Jar" again. The two concluding lines, "It did not give of bird or bush, / Like nothing else in Tennessee," indicates that the jar is dependent on the physical world as its "central reference."

"The Emperor of Ice-Cream"

The poem is capable of more than one interpretation. One popular way of reading it is to see the line, "Let be be finale of seem," as its crux. Seen this way, the poem seems to say, let reality show up and accept the real world for what it is—the woman is dead and is lying cold and dumb there, and there is nothing art or imagination or piety could do about it except accept it as a fact of life. It is good to note, however, that this interpretation may not be able to offer an adequate enough explanation for the title and the line, "The only emperor is the emperor of ice-cream."

Another way of reading is to see the poem as a hailing of some attitude like hedonism. This is manifest in the title and the repetition of the line "The only emperor is the emperor of ice-cream." The word "ice-cream" is a homonym for "I scream," a thing which people do when highly excited. "The emperor of ice-cream" should be a person who enjoys life to the utmost. Read this way, the poem seems to suggest that, since no one can avoid death, it is good to enjoy life as much as possible.

"Sunday Morning"

One important idea that gets well expressed in this poem is the poet's meditation on earth and his insistence on accepting earth as against paradise. Here exists a vivid contrast between Christian beliefs on the one hand and, on the other, pagan views and attitudes which exhibit a kind of worship for nature and the sun. The poem possesses a dimension of complexity unique to itself.

This eight-section poem, one of Stevens' major works, portrays a woman lost in thought on a Sunday morning. It records what she sees, hears, smells, feels, and thinks, and at the same time also registers the poet-speaker's comments about these sensual experiences of hers. The two things often merge with and into each other to produce a subtle artistic effect. What the poem tries to convey is man's desire for harmony with his environment, his here and now, and his self, and also his need to experience the harmony between man and nature, the interdependence between man and his environment, and the faith in eternity achievable only through the understanding of absolute values.

The first section of the poem begins with the woman breakfasting on this bright Sunday morning in the sunny courtyard. In the quiet abundance of nature, she thinks of death ("that old catastrophe"), of the crucified Jesus Christ of Palestine, "Dominion of blood and sepulcher." The second section depicts the woman wishing for timeless beauty in paradise and feeling troubled by the encroachment of the notion of mortality. She realizes that divinity exists right in the beauty of nature and in herself, thus accepting this world as the frame of reference for her life and soul.

The sections that follow elaborate on the theme further. Section three portrays her stream of thought moving first to Zeus, the God of gods in ancient mythology, who, though a god, never severs his connection with the human world, and then moving further on to a possible world where man and god would mingle as one. Section four follows up on the idea and insinuates that paradise is here and now. Section five dwells on her desire for immortality: "She says, 'But in contentment I still feel/ The need of some imperishable bliss.'" The poet-speaker comments on this, saying that death is the source of beauty because death opens onward to rebirth. Section six, which reads like both her flow of consciousness and the poet-speaker's comments, exclaims at the amazing resemblance between heaven and earth. The idea is picked up in section seven, which suggests a secular "religion": heaven is "like our perishing earth," and earth is in fact paradise. The section ends by reiterating the idea that death is the beginning of renewal. In the last section of the poem, the woman hears a voice, becomes aware that Jesus himself was mortal as anyone else on earth and that, despite her thirst for eternal joy, she must accept the fact of mortality, without which there would be no renewal. There is almost sadness in the notion of the coming of evening, but then pigeons do come down with a touch of nobility:

> And, in the isolation of the sky,
> At evening, casual flocks of pigeons make
> Ambiguous undulations as they sink,
> Downward to darkness, on extended wings.

"Ambiguous" is loaded. It could mean that the descent is not absolute but relative in the cycle of life. "Extended wings" connote a composure, a peace of mind, in face of the inevitable descent, but not without a resignation that builds itself into the texture of life in its various forms.

William Carlos Williams (1883-1963)

There were, in modern American literary history, two major literary figures for whom poetry was only an avocation. One of them was William Carlos Williams, and the other was Wallace Stevens. Two factors in the life of William Carlos Williams had a determining effect on his literary aesthetics and practice: he worked all his life as a physician in America except for two brief visits to Europe, and he sees America as the place where he should root his poetry. Williams loves and remains faithful to the world of reality and things, which he tries to offer a poetic expression.

Williams' Aesthetics

Williams was independent in his literary judgments. He had his own distinct views concerning the nature of poetry, the function of the poet, and the poetic process, very much unlike T. S. Eliot's. He wrote poetry not because he had to but because he wanted to, and what is more, he did not feel the need to be accepted by the gods of poetry like the Eliots, the Pounds, and the Yeatses. One of the notable features of modern poetry is the absence of any unified concept of poetry. If T. S. Eliot represents a particular attitude toward poetry, then Williams definitely stands at the other end of the line, representing quite a different one. As a matter of fact, Williams was anti-Eliot all his life, spending a lot of time railing at people like Eliot. He was bitterly opposed to those "who know all the Latin and some of the Sanskrit names." His antagonism to T. S. Eliot dated from the publication of *The Waste Land* which, he says in his *Autobiography*, still feeling hurt and enraged beyond consolation, "[giving] the poem back to the academics," and "[returning] us to the schoolroom," was "a great catastrophe to our letters." He had some grudge against Pound as well. Although the two were friends, he resented Pound's broken multi-cultural style; he saw Pound as living among the splendor of ancient human artifacts and thus as "the best enemy the United States verse has."

Williams strongly disapproves of the Pound-Eliot bookish, "internationalist," and intellectual brand of poetry. He believes that "localism alone can lead to culture." One cannot have an imagination which is not rooted in the real world. And American poetry must be rooted in America as its fount of inspiration and its source of information and subject matter. It is *the* place for American poets. "We live only in one place at a time," he states, "but far from being bounded by it, only through it do we realize our freedom." What he wanted to achieve is to reach the universal plane of meaning through the representation of the local, in very much the same way Robert Frost was silently doing all his long life.

Williams was obsessed with discovering "a primary impetus, the elementary principle of all art in our local conditions." His major prose work, *In the American Grain*, though dealing with people and events, is in fact a search for "the impact of the bare soul upon the very twist of the fact which is our world around us." It is "a descent to the ground" of his desires, a "going back to the beginning."[10] Williams liked Daniel Boone who "lived to enjoy the ecstasy through his single devotion to the wilderness with which he was surrounded." He liked Edgar Allan Poe whose greatness was "in that he turned his back and faced inland" and in whose works America as a *place* and a *new locality* first burst into expression. Williams was committed to reproducing the life, the soul, and the music of America in poetry. His long poem *Paterson* is, along with his short works, a poetic embodiment of his devotion.

The Basic Features of Williams' Poetry

William Carlos Williams' poetic power stems from his clear vision of the real world. Clarity of imagery constitutes the essential element of his work. He is very devoted to the phrasing of speech and is anxious to use its numerous rhythms. He is also faithful to his own unformulated thoughts. Williams has been recognized as a forefather of open verse.

A careful reading of Williams' poetry reveals some basic principles of his composition. For instance, he values the peculiarity of an object, and tries to allow it to reveal its true character. He hates to see an object stereotyped by association or sentimentality and lose its true value. Through the use of fancy, Williams gives everyday objects the charm of uniqueness and guides the mind's eye to the loveliness and wonders of the world before us. Williams also takes meticulous care to bring a new sense or meaning to an object and make it vivid and beautiful by creating a clear image of it or attaching a sensory experience to it. Reading Williams, we can sense him always carefully watching human experiences and trying to recapture evocative moments from them. To him there is poetry in everyday life that careless eyes and ears may miss: there is poetry in the words spoken by the people, in the life being lived, in eyes widened or shut, in smiles or grimaces, in the postures of the bodies or in the sights around. Thus his poetry represents the exceptional truth of ordinary life and the beauty of the commonplace. In addition, Williams feels that a poem represents a moment of the mind and that it delineates the shape of life not always planned ahead but often discovered later. The poet should keep taking the world to a new dimension and give it new imaginative validity.

So Williams feels strongly that poetry must be grounded in everyday experience and in the speech of the common people. It must use the common meters of living speech. It must rid itself of all encrustation and ornamentation. Williams is not interested in philosophical and metaphysical speculation which, in his opinion, has absolutely no place in poetry. The most important line he ever wrote is perhaps the line in Book I, *Paterson*, "Say it! No ideas but in things." What he is trying to say is this: Don't philosophize; simply say it in terms of some kind of concretization; and visualize in terms of what is physical and particular. He holds that the poet's business is not to talk in vague categories, but to write particularly, specifically, as a physician works upon a patient, to discover the universal in the particular, the relationship between the actual world and the mental, the relationship between the here and now and the then and there, and to see something for the first time and say it in ways of one's own.

For Williams life as it is lived is the beginning and the end of the poet's endeavor. Life with its sundry concrete details and its rhythms, when closely observed and well appreciated, is in itself poetry simple and pure. Poetry will be defeating its own purpose if it goes, not to life and the actual world, but to books and the past, for inspiration. He is convinced that, if he ever deviates from his faith in life, he is sure to find his "despair." So Williams is noted for his fidelity to the facts of life. Art inheres in carefully observed life.

Earlier on, we cited his famous "The Red Wheelbarrow" as an illustration of the Imagist credo which Williams shared as part of his literary theory. The poem appeals to the imagination because it forces it to visualize and derive an aesthetic pleasure from the contemplation which is the reading of the poem. Placed in strategic positions separately in their lines, words as simple as "upon," "barrow," "water," and "chickens" assume immediately significance of a kind which they would otherwise not have possessed by any other means. With the animate juxtaposed with the inanimate, and the white color in contrast with the red, here we have in our minds' eye meaningful textures and clear, delightful colors. We become aware that it is important to perceive them to make life fuller, and that so much depends on how we perceive them both in our life and in our writing of poetry. Read his "Queen-Ann's-Lace," which is all concrete details well observed and specified, and we understand the relationship of poetry to life and how the physical world is delineated and graphically explained in a common language. Indeed, to Williams, everything in actual life, including even the eating of "the plums/ that were in the icebox," "so sweet/ and so cold" ("This Is Just to Say"), is emblematic of some deeper level of human significance, and is therefore poetic in the very sense of the term.

"Spring and All"

Then there is the well-known "Spring and All" which is almost all perception and observation. Williams wrote this poem to catch that moment in time when winter is on its way out but still lingering, and spring is coming in, though not yet quite sure of its entrance. Here there are no clichés which poets of a mediocre caliber frequently resort to. What is offered is all line after line of visual images giving one that wonderful sense of "spring is here," that captivating effect of the moment in time in between winter and spring. The setting is by the road to the contagious hospital (that smacks of sickness and death). The first two stanzas picture a very much dead landscape, with the cold wind, dried weeds, and the scattering of the trees. From the third and fourth stanzas, which are transitional in nature, we are enabled to perceive life germinating out of death, life juxtaposing itself with death. Though still dead and lifeless in appearance, colors of purple and red appear in an otherwise universal gray, and bushes begin to put forth twigs. Spring is just awakening ("dazed"), from sleep and hibernation. It is not really that growth has started and a new cycle of nature has begun. But life has made its hesitating appearance on the scene (stanzas 5-6): Spring quickens and gives evidence of life. The last stanza indicates that the whole cycle of nature, of which spring is only a part, has begun. The concluding lines, "... rooted, they / grip down and begin to awaken," illustrate the poet's keen perception of nature around him. The poem excels in the visual impression it creates on the reader, and has been seen as an eloquent proof of Williams' supreme competence in handling the objective in poetry.

Paterson

In 1946, the first book of the five-volume *Paterson* came out. Williams first planned to write four books to record "all that any one man may achieve in a lifetime."[11] But he did not stop writing until his death in 1963. By then he had begun volume six.

Paterson is a lucid statement of Williams' aesthetics. "For the poet," he writes of *Paterson* in his *Autobiography,* "there are no ideas, but in things …. The poet does not … permit himself to go beyond the thought to be discovered in the context of that with which he is dealing: no ideas but in things."

In writing *Paterson* Williams tries to find an image large enough to embody the whole knowable world about him. "The longer I lived in my place, among the details of my life, I realized that these isolated observations and experiences needed pulling together to gain 'profundity.'"

A famous line occurs in Book II of *Paterson*: "Why should I move from this place / Where I was born?" This reveals the committed attitude of the poet toward his native place. Another equally famous line, which concludes Book IV, visualizes a man "[heading] inland," which is a distant poetic echo of his chapter on Edgar Allan Poe in his *In the American Grain*, and also a confirmation of the poet's resolve to turn his back on the sea (which is symbolic of a pull outward from the source) and keep his eyes and ears open only on his America. Robert Lowell said in 1962 that nobody, except Williams, has seen America or heard its music.[12]

Williams' description of the pastoral Paterson of early days is a lyrical display of his intense love for his homeland with its vivid concrete particulars:

> In a deep-set valley between hills, almost hid by dense foliage lay
> the little village. Dominated by the Falls the surrounding country was
> a beautiful wilderness where mountain pink and wood violet throve: a
> place inhabited only by straggling trappers and wandering Indians.

Here he sees the river—farms and the simple but pastoral life of the people, wearing homespun clothes, raising their own stock, with rude furniture on sanded floors, primitive in a sense but quiet and hearty. Here he discovers the source for art, for poetry.

Paterson is innovative in technique. It faithfully reproduces the quiet, serene rhythm of life itself in its natural flow, now in prose, now in verse, with interpolations of monologues, conversations, and letters in between the unhurried narrative. The form of the poem is highly flexible to accommodate the variety of themes which keep coming into it. Williams never stopped his experimentation in free verse and accentual verse. He succeeded in lifting the material conditions and appearances of his environment to a universal plane of significance.

Williams' Reputation

Williams lived long in the shadow of T. S. Eliot. Not until the 1950s and 1960s did Eliot's influence begin to wane and Williams' poetry begin to receive its long-overdue recognition. By then Williams had labored in the poetic field for almost four decades.

Now that his position as a major voice in modern American poetry was established, his poems began to exercise their influence on the general course of development of contemporary poetry. *Paterson* came out at a time when a whole new way of writing appeared. The postwar generation needed new models and new paradigms for their creative endeavors. *Paterson*, bodying forth its author's emphasis on American locality and speech, his fresh moral vision, and his "always beginning anew" mode of writing, became attractive to the younger poets, along with Pound's *Pisan Cantos*. Williams became a prophet figure of the new age. In contemporary poetry Williams is a stronger influence, perhaps, than anybody else's. All major schools of poetry, such as the Confessional, the Black Mountain, and the New York school, acknowledge their indebtedness to Williams' literary theories and practice. One contemporary poet, Charles Olson, went as far as calling his generation "sons of Pound and Williams."

Chapter 13   Frost • The Chicago Renaissance • Sandburg • Cummings • Hart Crane • Moore

Robert Frost (1874-1963)

 Robert Frost is popular as a lyrical poet, an authentic painter of local landscape, and a poet whose poetry it is always a delightful experience to read. Few are willing to admit that Robert Frost's universe can be terrifying.[1]

Robert Frost's way to recognition was a long one. It was not until he was forty that his first important volume, *North of Boston*, came out in England. He had gone there in 1912 and met, among others, Ezra Pound, who then tried to get him published because he heard a fresh voice in Frost. In 1915 Frost came back to the United States which recognized him as its bard. Thereafter his road to fame and popularity was smooth. He won prizes and commendations, and received honors from forty-four institutions. He became the nation's unofficial Poet Laureate when invited to read his poem at President Kennedy's inauguration in 1961.

Frost as a Poet of Wisdom

The poetry of Robert Frost is as pleasant as it is edifying. Reading his poetry can be a highly ennobling and relaxing experience. Here readers find wit and wisdom, peace and harmony, that serve for them as "a momentary stay against confusion." "The Road Not Taken" and "Mending Wall" are just two illustrations out of many.

"The Road Not Taken"

The poem presents an archetypal human situation of making choices. In one sense, Frost—or the speaker of his poem—seems to suggest that the choice one makes would "[make] all the difference"; but the poet is too deep and too wise to be so absolute about life and people. There is a visible amount of skepticism, a disclaimer of a kind, about the difference the choice could make: "Then I took the other, *just as fair*, / And having perhaps the better claim, / Because it was grassy and wanted wear; / Though as for that the passing there / had worn them *really about the same*" (italics mine). What the speaker is saying is probably this, that ultimately life would come full circle and the roads or choices make no difference after all. And if we stop to think a little further, we may find, embedded in the texture of the poem, a kind of complaint, even a tragic view, that life does not allow humans any options at all.

"Mending Wall"

One possible reading of the poem could be that it is about the sense of alienation inherent in life and human nature. There is truth in that, but the poem says a lot more.

It could be, for one thing, about understanding life and human nature. The "I" in the poem feels that he is wiser as he no longer lives in the "darkness" in which his neighbor, probably much older and much more experienced with life and people, is still moving. Actually the poem hints that the neighbor is the wiser because his experience has taught him the paradox of life and human nature, that distance makes for close relationships. People need to stay apart in order to be close. Here we recall Benjamin Franklin's almanac adage: "Fish and visitors stink in three days."

It is good to add here that Frost has been linked with the tradition of nature poetry. He wrote a lot in the tradition that Wordsworth and Emerson followed. Nature appears as an explicator and a mediator for man and serves as the center of reference for his behavior. It stands as a kind of perfection against confusion. In "Mowing" there is a momentary awareness of one's relationship to nature. In "Birches," the image of the boy swinging offers a moment of fullness and harmony achievable only in the healthy influence of nature.

Frost as a Modern Poet

But Frost was, at the bottom of his heart, a modern man, keeping in step with the spirit of his time. He recognized "the vast chaos of all I have lived through." All his life he was concerned with constructing, through poetry, "a momentary stay against confusion."

Viewed in this spirit, the poems of Frost assume a sudden, somewhat different dimension. Although Frost depicts mostly New England landscape, those scenes of rural life often reflect the fragmentization and the horror of modern experience. Frost is keenly aware of this and portrays and interprets it in his poetry. The great number of abnormal people his poems talk about is a good illustration. These people suffer no less than the grotesques of Sherwood Anderson's *Winesburg, Ohio*. Read just his *North of Boston* to feel the horror that exists in life. The mother in "Home Burial" about to crack up with grief over her child's death, the common-law wife in "The Fear" with her desires disguised as obsessions, the lunatic in "A Servant to Servants" who makes life bitter and hideous for all as well as for himself—all these indicate Frost's awareness that something has gone wrong with the land and its way of life. Poems like "The Black Cottage" and "The Generations of Men" all describe the feeling of alienation among modern men.

It is good to note this of Frost that, though at moments he is very close to the "slough of despond," he nearly always manages to draw back. For him, no place is better than this world, after all.

"Birches"

A fresh look at "Birches" and "The Wood Pile" reveals Frost's concern for order. In the "Birches," the poet admits that when he feels that life is becoming too tough for him, he would like to get away from the earth for a while, going back to be a swinger, and wishes that fate would willfully misunderstand him and snatch him away not to return. But Frost is committed to life on earth, "Earth's the right place for love: / I don't know where it's likely to go better." What he craves for is a momentary relief from the disorder of earthly life.

"The Wood Pile"

"The Wood Pile" is likewise a metaphor for order. It begins with the narrator far from home and deep in snow in an alien world, full of fear like the bird in the woods and uncertain where to turn in this cold universe. Then he sees a well-made woodpile: "It was a cord of maple, cut and split / And piled—and measured four by four by eight." Against a background of unpredictability and confusion, here is something that generates a sense of order, giving form and meaning to the shapeless and meaningless world around it. He feels good, but the fact that the man has left his woodpile behind suggests to him that a man-created order is transient.

"Design"

The world of Frost can appall and terrify. The short poem, "Design," can overwhelm one with a great sense of uncertainty and fear. The spectacle of the white spider holding a white moth on a white flower enables one to glimpse at the "design of darkness" that governs the world and reflect on the impotence of its inhabitants, including, by extension, man. If we compare Frost's poem with Edward Taylor's work on the spider catching a fly, we will readily see Frost's modern outlook on life: whereas Taylor sees the spider as a symbol of Hell opposed to God's will, Frost associates it with a grand scheme which might be part of God's own design.

"Stopping by Woods on a Snowy Evening"

The poem is poet's most famous and oft-anthologized work. It tells about a man riding on a snowing evening out of a village to go home at another village. He stops in the woods, which stand in between the two human communities, to enjoy the beauty of nature. Probably tired of the troubles that he has to deal with in the human world, he falls in love with "The darkest evening of the year" and the "dark and deep" woods. But he does not lie down there as he might have thought he would do. A brief stay in nature recharges him well enough to remember that he has "promises to keep" and "miles" yet to go.

Here a couple of things merit attention. For one thing, this world can be "too much with us." Then nature can restore. Thirdly, the earth is the best place for people. So we see a clear map that Frost draws for life: village (hassles)—nature (mediation)—village (hassles). An enlarged vision of this map could be the universal pattern that all humans follow as they live through life: participation—escape—participation again. Frost complains but he does not budge in face of trouble.

Frost's Poetics

Robert Frost is often deceptively simple. His poems can be read very often on many levels. He did write, for instance, about his remote and primitive New England, but what he did was to juxtapose the regional with the cosmopolitan, and the human with the natural, rooting his poetry in New England to reach the plane of universal meaning. He was good at exploring the complexity of human existence through treating seemingly trivial subjects, and had always in view in writing the ultimate aim of making life "whole again beyond confusion": "Back out of all this now too much for us," he writes in "Directive," "Your destination and your destiny's / A brook that was the water of the house ..." and "Here are your waters and your watering place / Drink and be whole again beyond confusion."

In one sense at least, Robert Frost stood consciously aside from the Modernist endeavor of his time. He retained his faith in the traditional forms of poetry. For him form is as important as sense; the ordering of sound and theme is one major concern of his poetic career. For him a poem is a joining of meaning, feeling, and metrics. He tends to use the formal stanza pattern and may have taken an enormous delight in the fact that his meaning manages to strike across his rigid meters. Thus he did not attempt to break the back of traditional modes of poetry such as the iambic pentameter, as Williams and Pound did.

The Chicago Renaissance

At about the same time Robinson and Robert Frost were writing and publishing in the east, the Chicago poets Vachel Lindsay (1879-1931), Edgar Lee Masters (1869-1950) and Carl Sandburg (1878-1967) were making their voice heard in the Mid-west. This has been known as the Chicago Renaissance. These poets, along with other writers and artists there, made Chicago a center of literature and arts, and in the field of poetry, added to the momentum of the new verse fighting the dominant genteel tradition of the time.

Vachel Lindsay had close contact with the lower strata of society. He was a poet devoted to social reform. He was in a sense an idealist, dreamed of building the US into the best place in the world, and hoped to see a society emerge in which religion, equality, and beauty would prevail. Lindsay read his poems in public. His work, "General William Booth Enters into Heaven" (1913), reveals the poet as a dreamer. His two other well-known poems are "The Congo" and "Santa Fe Trail." Lindsay committed suicide in 1931.

Edgar Lee Masters made himself famous with the publication of his first volume of verse, *Spoon River Anthology*. It is a collection of 200-odd elegiac poems, portraying 200-odd different characters from all walks of life: workers, farmers, clergymen, clerks, prostitutes, judges, poets, philosophers, scientists, soldiers, atheists, Christians etc.—almost everyone, now dead, but once associated with Spoon River town by birth or in some other way. It is a significant censure of the small town's corruption and depravity and of the genteel tradition in general. 19 plot lines intertwine and correlate to present the workings of the society of the town. It became popular instantly. Masters was a productive writer. In addition to the 20-odd volumes of verse, he wrote 13 plays, seven novels, and nine biographies.

Carl Sandburg (1878-1967)

Carl Sandburg was the greatest of the prairie poets.[2] His most cherished ideal in life was to be "the word of the people," to articulate in song the thoughts, feelings, and aspirations of ordinary men and women. Sandburg's poetic career was long and fruitful. His works include *Chicago Poems* (1916), *Cornhuskers* (1918), *Smoke and Steel* (1920), and *Slabs of the Sunburnt West* (1922), *Good Morning, America* (1928), *The People, Yes* (1936), and *Collected Poems* (1951). He wrote also some well-known Imagist poems such as "Fog," "Lost-," "Monotone," "The Harbor," and "Nocturne in a Deserted Brickyard." His longer poems also show Imagist influence.

Sandburg also took interest in folk songs which he tried to collect and sing during his travels. These included songs of cowboys, hobos and Black spirituals, which eventually appeared in print in his well-known *The American Songbag* (1927). Sandburg also wrote a multi-volume biography of Abraham Lincoln, *The Prairie Years* (1926) and *The War Years* (1940), an autobiography, and a historical novel of some kind.

Carl Sandburg wrote in the Whitman's tradition and shared his optimism. He sees the evils of modern life, as his poem "The Harbor" shows, and is frustrated with the evils of life as recorded in his "Chicago." And he could be very despondent and desolate as he is in "Cool Tomb." But Sandburg wrote chiefly "to help the sick and give the people hope." He knew the importance of the people, "the mob," better than any of his contemporaries, and firmly believed that the people would one day rise and come into their own. His poem, "I am the People, the Mob," reveals Sandburg at one with the masses.

Sandburg was affirmative toward the American industrial and mechanical civilization. His poem, "Chicago," is a good illustration. With all its wickedness and suffering, Chicago is building and rebuilding, and the heart of the people is throbbing with life.

So he was optimistic. He saw an America of "tomorrows" and wrote about it in his poems such as "The Prairie":

> I speak of new cities and new people.
> I tell you the past is a bucket of ashes.
> I tell you yesterday is a wind gone down,
>> a sun dropped in the west.
> I tell you there is nothing in the world
>> only an ocean of tomorrows,
> a sky of tomorrows.
> I am a brother of the cornhuskers who say
>> at sundown:
> Tomorrow is a day.

Sandburg kept in step with the evolution of modern poetry. He joined the poetic revolution which Pound, Eliot and Williams were making then, and wrote in free verse and rich and spontaneous slang. His contribution to the colloquial style in American literature should be given due recognition. Although he was not happy with the critical world which he accused of being snobbish, he did win a good measure of popular acclaim. He was awarded the American Poetry Society prize in 1919 and 1920, and the Pulitzer Prize in 1950 when his *Complete Poems* was brought out. He is a great American poet.

E. E. Cummings (1894-1963)

E. E. Cummings was a very interesting experimentalist in modern American poetry. "A juggler with syntax, grammar, and diction," he wrote entirely regardless of *any* established conventions of poetry.

Cummings went to Harvard, where he came under the influences of Tennyson, Keats, Rossetti, Swinburne, and the Decadents of the 1890s. Then he discovered free verse and the modern verse revolution in Amy Lowell's Imagist anthologies and the little magazines of the time. Cummings was also a modern painter, fascinated with Post-Impressionist and Cubist paintings and sculptures and with Cézanne, Duchamp, Picasso and other modern masters. The prevailing rebellious spirit in the art and literature of the time moved his dynamic personality to challenge tradition and assert individuality in his daring experiments.

Cummings was hostile to science and technology. He hated the inhumanity of science and materialism which dehumanized man. He even refused to have radio and TV in his house. He was formally employed for just three months his whole life. Life was too valuable for him to waste on achieving material successes. As to his basic outlook on life and society, he celebrates vitality ("aliveness") and individualism, and abhors collectivism and conformity.

Cummings' Themes

Cummings' themes tend to be overlooked. He wrote poems on love and lust usually. Nature was his favorite subject as well. There is an increasing number of nature poems that reveal the poet's fascination with a world, often a child's world, born anew with its simplicity, innocence, and spontaneous joy.

The Evolution of His Style

After he left Harvard in 1916, he began writing poems that revealed a radical break from tradition. His experiments included new spatial arrangements, both horizontal and vertical, new poems based on patterns of vowel or consonant groups, linguistic constructions dealing with "un-poetic" subjects—casual conversations, banal statements, urban impressions—all presented by means of a variety of voices and a range of tones. After his return from the World War I, he composed some of his best work, some sexually intense poems and some cubist poems.

In the 1920s Cummings tried to write in the spirit of Cubism or Dadaism, using unusual diction and phrasing. Gradually a distinct Cummings style came to maturity. In the last thirty years of his life, his linguistic play was more fully developed and controlled, with "his scrambled word order in syntactic anagram, his extension of the semantic possibilities of words he chooses to stretch, squeeze, or intensify by typographical acrobatics or grammatical innovations."[3] In short, he was "juggling" with syntax, grammar, and diction, and with verbal effects. His poems, more ideogramic and pictorial than aural, with its low-case, peculiar punctuation, and jamming of words, produce often a shocking effect and reveal the author's attitude of nonconformity. In fact Cummings assaults almost everything established.

Let's take a look at the frequently anthologized "Chanson Innocenter" (often also entitled "In Just"). The poem seems simple. Spring has come "mud-luscious," children out playing, and a lame old balloon man appears on the scene:

       spring   when the world is mud-

       luscious the little

      lame balloonman

      whistles   far   and wee

       and eddieandbill come

      running from marbles and

      piracies and ifs

      spring.

when the world is puddle-wonderful

  the queer

       old balloonman whistles

       far   and   wee

       and bettyandisbel come dancing

       from hop-scotch and jump-rope and

       it's

        spring

       and

        the

       goat-footed

    balloonman   whistles

     far

     and

   wee

    The poem celebrates innocence and nature and the joy these bring—revival and rebirth. Boys and girls, Eddie, Bill, Betty and Isabel, dance in groups of twos in joy on the playground. But the old balloon man, adult, "goat-footed," suggesting the riotous followers of Dionysus, the wine-god in Greek mythology, gives the reader an ominous impression, as it foretells the fall of innocence and the growing up into dubious adulthood.

Hart Crane (1899-1932)

Hart Crane began writing poetry in his early teens, and published his first poem at 17. His early work, carried in *Little Review*, revealed the imprint of Elizabethan literature and French symbolism. Though poor and exhausted, he kept trying to perfect his poetic art. Then with the help of a financier, he was able to focus on writing. His first volume of verse, *White Buildings*, came out in 1926, his major work, *The Bridge*, was published in 1930, and the critical reception of both works was not very good. He felt dejected. Added to this, his intense emotional stress and the Depression of the 1930s, which destroyed his faith in the future, proved to be the last straw for his fragile nerve system. He jumped into the sea on his way back from Mexico to New York in April, 1932. He was 32 then.

Crane read a lot. He had his own views on poets and poetry and had his own favorite writers. Crane's *Collected Poems* was published in 1933 and reprinted in 1958. *The Complete Poems and Selected Letters and Prose*, out in print in 1966, includes all the poems of the early and late periods of his life that had been either never included anywhere or published in various magazines.[4]

The Bridge

Crane's masterwork, *The Bridge*, taking the bridge—the Brooklyn Bridge— as a symbol of life and of the ideal future of America, was meant to be a vehement response to T. S. Eliot's *The Waste Land*.

The poem consists of the proem and eight sections, totaling 15 poems. The proem, "To Brooklyn Bridge," imaging a well-poised and free seagull, contrasting it with the confining existence of a clerk, and linking it with the Bridge, puts forward the theme of the long poem—the hope for and the problems of America.

The first section, "Ave Maria" ("Hail Mary"), is a Columbus' monologue, delineates the man's thoughts on his way home after his discovery of the New World. The second section, "Powhatan's Daughter," consists of five poems in praise of Pocahontas (the famous American Indian princess of myth and legends) as the frame of reference for measuring modern life. The daughter of Powhatan, Pocahontas by name, is seen as the Goddess of North America, the Ideal, who inspired generations of Americans to move forward.

The third section of the long poem, "Cutty Shark," reproduces the conversation that the poet-speaker has with a phantom sailor, mentioning the wreck and the loss of the ship in the end.

In the next, the fourth, section, "Cape Hatteras," the poet-speaker celebrates technological advances, renews his Whitmanesque faith, rejects pessimism, and becomes spokesman for the New World.

The fifth section includes three subdivisions, "Southern Cross," "National Winter Garden," and "Virginia." It presents various perversions of Pocahontas in modern life.

The next section, the sixth, "Quaker Hill," mentions the spread of philistinism in the wake of commercialization in a tone that suddenly drops to gloom and dejection.

"The Tunnel," the seventh section, occupies a pivotal position in the whole epic. It describes the monotonous motion on the subway, portrays its overall filthy environment, and records fragments of conversations overheard. Here the mood of the speaker sinks to the lowest of the low, as if he was right down in Hell. He identifies with Poe, somehow. Then he exits to stand by the East River and sees the harbor, indicating a kind of resurrection in process.

The poem ends with its eighth section, "Atlantis," which is full of passionate praise, extolling the mythical city as symbolic of a hopeful future. Contrasting in tone with "The Tunnel," the two sections manage to keep the double keynotes— hope and despair—of the whole poem running parallel to the end.

Crane's Reputation

Crane wrote *The Bridge* as an answer to the pessimism of T. S. Eliot's *The Waste Land*. The whole of it sounds like a huge symphony, with its movements taken from the major myths of America—Pocahontas, Rip Van Winkle, Melville, Poe, Whitman, Columbus, the subway, Atlantis—and carefully interwoven together. Crane is questing for harmony, love, and beauty. Despite its weaknesses such as incoherence in certain parts of it, difficult images and symbolism, and untended loose ends, it has been seen as a great work.

Marianne Moore (1887-1972)

Marianne Moore was born in Missouri and graduated from Bryn Mawr where she had H. D. as her classmate. Moore has a unique place in the history of American poetry. She was one of the first "new" poets in the first years of the 20th century to talk with William Carlos Williams and Wallace Stevens about the function of poetry and the role and value of the artists. All of them were part of the Imagist movement. The literary magazine, *The Dial*, which Moore edited for some time, published many of the best poets of the time. Moore's poetry has won prizes like the Pulitzer Prize and the National Book Award. Late in life Marianne Moore became nationally famous also as a baseball fan.[5]

For Marianne Moore, poetry is important because it represents the essence of life and reality. Her poem, "Poetry," is a graphic statement of her views in this regard. She feels that there are things genuine and useful, and "the raw materials of poetry in/ all its rawness." The job of a poet is to discover these. For a good poet, but not half poets, it is essential to understand all the phenomena of life and discriminate against nothing including "business documents and school-books" and the sordid and ugly. Her views on poetry in relation to life are very much akin to those of William Carlos Williams'.

Moore was noted for her observation of minute details in things great or small. She was good at catching hold of the poetic in the varied manifestations of mundane reality around her. Her poem, "The Fish," is a good illustration.

Chapter 14　Fitzgerald • Hemingway

F. Scott Fitzgerald (1896-1940)

Just as Mark Twain and William Dean Howells grew up thinking that America would become the hope of the world and became very bitter old men in the end, so F. Scott Fitzgerald and Ernest Hemingway as young people were very enthusiastic and excited about this new world they were living in but lived to realize eventually that, instead of success, it was all disaster.[1]

For Fitzgerald, who lived in the midst of the "roaring twenties" and was part of it all—driving fast cars, drinking hard whisky, and taking an immense delight in it, America was, he was perceptive enough to understand, "a moon that never rose." As much as he enjoyed the "roaring" of the postwar boom years, he foresaw its doom and failure.

Even in the best years of his career, Fitzgerald was sober enough, as an artist, to feel alien to the "vanity fair" of which he was an integral part, and as a man at once infatuated with an ideal and emaciated by an unduly early awareness of its deceptive character, he had always stood mentally aloof from the spectacle which kept passing before him.

Life and Marriage

Fitzgerald was born into a St. Paul middle-class family. He went to Princeton, but had to leave, probably partly because of his poor academic record and also because of the outbreak of the First World War. He returned to Princeton only to stay for another year, in which he managed to finish the draft of his first novel, *This Side of Paradise.* Then he left for the army. Fitzgerald was never sent abroad. During his 15-month service in Montgomery, he met Zelda Sayre, the daughter of a judge, a beautiful society girl, who told him that she was too expensive for him. After his discharge from the army in 1919, Zelda broke their engagement. Fitzgerald went back to his father's home to rewrite his novel. Six months later he surfaced again, this time triumphant with the news that his novel had been accepted and promised to sell well. The two were married.

The Fitzgeralds and the 1920s

This Side of Paradise is not really very good because juvenile, but is historically interesting. It became immensely popular for the simple reason that it caught the tone of the age. Essentially autobiographical, the book describes Fitzgerald's sense of failure with his academic performance and the frustration of his dreams at Princeton. It portrays at the same time a generation, his generation, feeling frustrated with life in which all gods are dead, all wars are fought, all faith in man is shaken. The Fitzgeralds stormed into New York as the pattern of youth, wealth, and beauty and became the admiration of all who met them.

This was also a period in which short stories were very profitable; *The Saturday Evening Post* was paying $4,000 a story to its best writers. Both Fitzgerald and Hemingway were thought of in their day as short-story writers: it was the short story that made them popular. The Fitzgeralds lived in expensive style, and their need for money was tremendous. Fitzgerald wrote at a rapid speed and made a fabulous amount of money, but it went as soon as it came. Out of the great amount of his writings in the early 1920s, came two collections, *Flappers and Philosophers* (1920) which glittered with the image of the Fitzgeralds as the symbol of an American ideal (the word "flapper," used to describe the new woman of the postwar period, became widespread henceforward), and *Tales of the Jazz Age* (1922) which, like Mark Twain's *The Gilded Age*, gave its name to an important historical period in the history of the country. In 1922 Fitzgerald finished his second novel, *The Beautiful and Damned*. The Fitzgeralds were living on the proceeds of Scott's books and stories, with their crazy parties and all that. The 1920s, or "the Jazz age," was, in the words of Malcolm Cowley, became a legend of "Americans adolescence before pain set in."[2] Fitzgerald became "the angel of the twenties" and his writings those of a man inside that legendary period.

Fitzgerald's Crack-Up

Then the Fitzgeralds went to Paris and met people like Hemingway and Gertrude Stein among others. Meanwhile, Fitzgerald began to feel the decline of his powers as a writer. He managed to produce his masterpiece, *The Great Gatsby* (1925). After this he wrote one more important book, *Tender is the Night*, and some collections of short stories such as *All the Sad Young Men* and *Taps at Reveille.*

The married life of Scott and Zelda Fitzgerald was an inspiration for Fitzgerald,[3] but they were not always happy. Zelda began to have breakdowns and in the early 1930s was put in a mental institution. Fitzgerald was cracking up. He had to write harder to earn more money to send Zelda to the best mental hospital in the country and their daughter, Scottie, to the best and most fashionable school.

Between 1934 and 1937 Fitzgerald was on the brink of despair and disintegration. He was ill with tuberculosis, drank more heavily, and made two unsuccessful attempts at suicide. By 1937 he recovered well enough to accept a writing contract for Hollywood. There for a year and a half he had to work on some very embarrassing movies, but under the healthy restorative influence of Sheilah Graham, a movie columnist, he began to live a quiet productive life.[4] Late in 1938 he was dismissed from his work, and thereafter the decline was steady. He wrote some more short stories, stayed in a New York hospital for several months, and began, in the last year of his life, one very interesting novel, entitled *The Last Tycoon*, which he never finished. In 1940, at the age of 44, he died, of frustration. He had been dead and forgotten as a writer long before.

After his death, his friend, Edmund Wilson, put together some of his very interesting writings—letters, and a series of confessional articles about his feelings of frustration and failure—into a book called *The Crack-Up*. The collection reveals the intense agony of a dedicated artist living through all the ordeals of a kaleidoscopic mundane existence.

The Great Gatsby

Fitzgerald's greatness lies in the fact that he found intuitively, in his personal experience, the embodiment of that of the nation and created a myth out of American life. The story *of The Great Gatsby* is a good illustration.

Gatsby is a poor youth from the Midwest. He falls in love with Daisy, a wealthy girl, but is too poor to marry her. The girl is then married to a rich young man, Tom Buchanan. Determined to win his lost love back, Gatsby engages himself in bootlegging and other "shady" activities, thus earning enough money to buy a magnificent imitation French villa. There he spreads dazzling parties every weekend in the hope of alluring the Buchanans to come. They finally come and Gatsby meets Daisy again, only to find that the woman before him is not quite the ideal love of his dreams. A sense of loss and disillusionment comes over him. Then Daisy kills a woman in an accident, and plots with Tom to shift the blame on Gatsby. So Gatsby is shot by the dead woman's husband, and the Buchanans escape.

Now Gatsby's life follows a clear pattern: there is, at first, a dream, then a disenchantment, and finally a sense of failure and despair. In this, Gatsby's personal experience approximates the whole of the American experience up to the first few decades of the 20th century. America had been "a fresh, green breast of the new world," had "pandered to the last and greatest of all human dreams" and promised something like "the orgiastic future" for humanity. Now the virgin forests have vanished and made way for a modern civilization, the only fitting symbol of which is the "valley of ashes," the living hell. Here modern men live in sterility and meaninglessness and futility as best illustrated by Gatsby's essentially pointless parties. The "guests" hardly know their host. Many come and go without invitation. The music, the laughter, and the faces, all blurred as one confused mass, signify the purposelessness and loneliness of the party-goers beneath their masks of relaxation and joviality.

Daisy is shallow. Her voice is "full of money." Tom is restless and wicked. Both of them represent the egocentric, careless rich. As to Gatsby, he is an enigma. On the one hand, he is charming and innocent, as he believes that the past can be retrieved. But on the other hand, he believes in the power of money and tries to make it by means fair or foul.

In addition, the behavior of these and other people like the Wilsons—all clearly denote the vanishing of the great expectations which the first settlement of the North American continent had inspired. The hope is gone; despair and doom have set in. Thus Gatsby's personal life assumes a magnitude as a "cultural-historical allegory" for the nation. Here, then, lies the greatest intellectual achievement that Fitzgerald ever achieved.[5]

Fitzgerald has often been misunderstood concerns his attitude toward the rich. Hemingway once ridiculed Fitzgerald's fascination with the rich in one of his short stories. This is not quite fair. Fitzgerald has always been critical of the rich and tried to show the disintegrating effects of wealth on the emotional make-up of his characters such as Tom and Daisy in *The Great Gatsby*.

Fitzgerald's Craftsmanship

At his best Fitzgerald's craftsmanship is impeccable.[6] The choice of a dramatic narrator, through whose consciousness everything filters, ensures the compact organic wholeness of his work. In *The Great Gatsby,* Carraway's limited omniscience deals out information in such a manner that he seems to withhold it first, thus creating a superb effect of mystery and suspense. The gradual revelation of Gatsby's story is a good example. We first hear his name mentioned by Miss Jordan Baker, and it takes some four pages before Carraway discloses in a hesitant way that he is his neighbor. Gatsby remains a hidden phantom until Mrs. Wilson's sister brings him and his fantastic parties up another sixteen pages later. All the while nothing definable shows up about Gatsby. Carraway himself is in for a story, learning about Gatsby and the kinds of romantic speculation Gatsby has inspired. And he finds that Jordan has never met Gatsby. It is not until about one fourth of the book is over that the readers are led into the presence of the man, in a fashion as sudden and abrupt as it is quiet and unobtrusive:

> I was still with Jordan Baker. We were sitting at a table with a man of about my age ….
>
> At a lull in the entertainment the man looked at me and smiled.
>
> ….
>
> "Much better," I turned again to my new acquaintance. "This is an unusual party for me. I haven't even seen the host … and this man Gatsby sent over his chauffeur with an invitation."
>
> For a moment he looked at me as if he failed to understand.
>
> "I'm Gatsby," he said suddenly. (47-48)

However, this is not the end of the mystery. Far from it. The identity of the man becomes the center of interest. A lot is to come in a well-arranged sequence. The fact that Chicago is calling adds a new dimension to Gatsby's personality. He is said to be an Oxford man, but may be not. A lunch in New York reveals a darker side of the man in touch with underground figures. Then there is Jordan Baker's story about her meeting with Gatsby and about Daisy's marriage, Carraway's own summary of the life of Gatsby, his parties, and so on and so forth until the whole secret is unraveled and past and present mingle to bring the tragic drama to a pathetic, significant finish.

Fitzgerald was one of the great stylists in American literature. T. S. Eliot read *The Great Gatsby* three times and concluded that it was "the first step that American fiction has taken since Henry James."[7] Fitzgerald's prose is smooth, sensitive, and completely original in its diction and metaphors. Its simplicity and gracefulness, its skill in manipulating the relation between the general and the specific, its bold impressionistic and colorful quality, in short, its competence to convey the vision of the author—all these reveal Fitzgerald's consummate artistry.

Fitzgerald's Reputation

Fitzgerald was essentially a 1920s person. He was part of it and eventually died with it. Inside he knew it well. Outside he saw it ironically. And he continued to write about it right until his death. Even *The Last Tycoon* is not a book about anything else. He thus became the spokesman of a crucial and revealing period in the cultural history of his country. And as such he will go down in the history of American literature.

Ernest Hemingway (1899-1961)

Hemingway was born in Oak Park, Illinois. His father was a physician, fond of hunting and fishing. He took young Ernest with him on his trips. Hemingway's style of living as an adult and the fact that his books abound in sports terms are partly traceable to his early life. As a boy, Hemingway liked boxing and football and wrote light verse and humorous stories.[8] After leaving school at 17, he felt the need to experience or observe war at close quarters,[9] and tried to enlist in the army, but was rejected because of his bad eye. He went to the Kansas City *Star* and served as a reporter. Then he was recruited as an ambulance driver working with the Red Cross and went to Europe. This led to the crucial happening in his life. On July 8, 1918 he was severely wounded in the knee in Italy. 237 steel fragments were taken out of his body. This war experience proved so shattering and nightmarish that his life and writings were permanently affected. In a sense, all his life he lived with it emotionally and continued to write about it in order to relive and forget about it.

Back to the United States, he stayed for a time in North Michigan. He met Sherwood Anderson, his stylistic mentor in a sense, who wrote letters of introduction for him to carry to Pound and Gertrude Stein when he went to Paris as a foreign reporter for the Canadian *Toronto Star*. Hemingway learned a lot from Anderson and Stein.[10] His first published book, *Three Stories and Ten Poems* (1923), owes clearly both in theme and style to Anderson. As for Gertrude Stein, Hemingway acknowledged that he learned everything from her "about the abstract relationships of words," the many truths about rhythms and the uses of words in repetition.[11] As a journalist, Hemingway trained himself in the economy of expression. His use of short sentences and paragraphs and vigorous and positive language, and the deliberate avoidance of gorgeous adjectives are some of the traces of his early journalistic practices. He settled down in Paris and worked on some short impressionist stories. Gradually a distinct style of his own began to evolve, and together with it a Hemingway theme with a Hemingway hero.

Hemingway's Theme and the Hemingway Hero

In one sense Hemingway wrote all his life about one theme, which is neatly summed up in the famous phrase, "grace under pressure," and created one hero who acts that theme out.

A Hemingway hero appeared in a 1925 book, *In Our Time*. Nick Adams is, when he first shows up, the embryonic Hemingway protagonist, introduced to a world of violence, disorder, and death, and learning the hard way about what the world is like. The very title of the book is typical of Hemingway's style of irony, being a mocking reference to a well-known phrase from a Christian prayer, "Give us peace in our time, O Lord." The irony lies in the fact that all the stories reveal that there is no peace at all in Nick's life. Growing up in violent and dismal surroundings, Nick's psychological and emotional wound is followed by a physical wound in the war, which alienates him from his society—he makes "a separate peace" with the enemy, leaves for the country swamp to fish, and learns to endure as a man. Most of Hemingway's later works are a repetition of these Nick Adams stories. The image of Nick finds newer and fuller dimensions in more stories in such collections as *Men Without Women* (1927) and *Winner Take Nothing* (1933).

Hemingway's first important novel—*The Sun Also Rises* (1926) paints the image of a whole generation, the Lost Generation, and becomes a symbol for an age. These include young English and American expatriates as well as men and women caught in the war and cut off from the old values and yet unable to come to terms with the new era when civilization had gone mad. The whole lives of people like Jake Barnes, Robert Cohn, and Brett Ashley are undercut and de-feated, and become pointless, restless and impotent. They fish, swim, and watch bullfights in a crazy and meaningless world. Take Jake Barns for example. He is wounded and made sexually impotent in the war. He finds life a nightmare after it. The only strength to live on with any dignity comes from nowhere but himself. He comes to see that he has to take care of himself and be tough with grace under pressure. His physical impotence is a token of modern man's spiritual impotence.

A Farewell to Arms (1928), his next important novel, can be read as a footnote to *The Sun Also Rises*. It explains how people like Jake Barnes come to behave the way they do. Frederic Henry goes to the war and discovers the insanity of the universe in which he lives. Guns that spit out death, the Carabinieri killing the innocent in the rain at night, his own wound and the death of his beloved Catherine—all this happens in a world of complete unreason. Lieutenant Henry becomes a very embittered man. He is completely disillusioned. He has been to the war, and has seen nothing sacred and glorious about it. He realizes that "Abstract words such as glory, honor, courage, or hallow were obscene," and feels "always embarrassed by the words sacred, glorious, and sacrifice and the expression in vain."[12] *A Farewell to Arms* caught the mood of the post-war generation, and brought international fame to young Hemingway. In the 1930s, Hemingway did not produce anything significant.

In 1940, *For Whom the Bell Tolls* came out in print. Traces of Lieutenant Henry are still clearly visible in the protagonist Robert Jordan. Here is a man living all the time in the shadow of fate and doom, keenly aware all along that he is fighting a losing battle, but he keeps on striving. Robert Jordan is no longer a Lieutenant Henry who is a solitary individual at odds with the forces dominating man. Nor is he a Jake Barnes, trying to accommodate himself to a purposeless and futile existence. The most important point to note about him is the fact that he is no longer alone. He works with a group for a just cause, and he has someone to love and die for. Nowhere else in Hemingway is the theme of human brotherhood so emphasized. Hence the significant title of the book. It is an allusion to John Donne's *Meditation* (XVII): "All mankind is of one author and

is one volume," and "Any man's death diminishes me because I am involved in mankind, and therefore never send to know for whom the bell tolls; it tolls for thee."

In 1952, Hemingway's fourth, also the last, important work, *The Old Man and the Sea* came out and helped toward restoring his literary image. It is a short novel, a fable of a kind, about an old Cuban fisherman Santiago and his battle with a great marlin. For 84 days Santiago does not catch a single fish but he does not feel discouraged. He goes far out into the sea and hooks a giant marlin. A desperate struggle ensues in which Santiago manages to kill the fish and tie it to his boat, only to find that, on the way home, he has yet to fight a more desperate struggle with the giant sharks, which eat up the marlin, leaving only a skeleton. The old man brings it home and goes to bed to dream, almost dead with exhaustion.

Here Santiago bodies forth all the best qualities of the Hemingway hero: the noble and tragic courage under pressure and despair, and the feeling of fellowship for his fellow creatures. Santiago fights to assert man's dignity, even in defeat. Moreover, he feels good to be one of the human and the natural world. He begins to experience a feeling of brotherhood and love not only for his fellowmen but for his fellow creatures in nature. This is a convincing proof that Hemingway's vision of the world has undergone a significant change.[13]

Hemingway is essentially a negative writer. He takes a negative attitude toward life. He sees the world as "all a nothing" and "all nada" ("A Clean Well-Lighted Place"). A man is to him nothing, too, because he is insignificant and powerless in face of the fate he is up against. The title of his first important book, *The Sun Also Rises*, referring to the biblical "Ecclesiastes," emphasizes the nothingness of life itself. For the preacher of the "Ecclesiastes" is downright nihilistic in tone when he says, "The sun also ariseth, and the sun goes down, and hasteth to his place where he arose," and "The thing that hath been, it is that which shall be; and that which is done is that which shall be done: and there is no new thing under the sun."

Hemingway sees life in terms of battles and tension. All of his works dramatize this concept of life, that it is dangerous and always ready to defeat and destroy you, but that, if you keep calm and stand on your set of principles, you may win on your own terms, though as the winner you get nothing except, perhaps, the knowledge that you have played well. Thus the typical Hemingway situations are usually characterized by chaos and brutality and violence (as in *A Farewell to Arms, For Whom the Bell Tolls* and many sketches in *In Our Time*), by crime and death (as in *To Have and Have Not* and "The Killers"), and sport, hard drinking and sexual promiscuity (as in *The Sun Also Rises* and some of his short stories). And the typical Hemingway hero is one who, wounded but strong, more sensitive and wounded because stronger, enjoys the pleasures of life (sex, alcohol, sport) in face of ruin and death, and maintains, through some notion of a code, an ideal of himself.

Hemingway's Style

In the latter part of his life, Hemingway came to be known as "Papa Hemingway."[14] This compliment refers in the main to his contribution to the development of a new style of writing in America, that is, the colloquial style. As we noted earlier, this style may be traced first to Mark Twain's *The Adventures of Huckleberry Finn*, the book from which Hemingway once said that "all modern American literature comes." Hemingway's apprenticeship in writing was a painful one.[15] Apart from his conscientious effort in groping for a style which he could call his own, he had the schooling of Sherwood Anderson, Gertrude Stein, and Ezra Pound, to name just a few. We mentioned Anderson and Stein earlier on. As to Pound, his advice to Hemingway was particularity and concision. The whole art of writing was, in the words of Pound, concision, or saying what you mean in the fewest and clearest words. This was in fact what Hemingway tried to achieve in writing. There have been numerous comments on his style; all seem to agree on such features of his style as simplicity and apparent naturalness of his prose, and its effect of directness, clarity and freshness. This is true in view of the fact that he always manages to choose words concrete, specific, more commonly found, more Anglo-Saxon, casual and conversational, and employ them often in a syntax of short, simple sentences, which are orderly and patterned, conversational, and sometimes ungrammatical.

But it is good to note that Hemingway's style is deliberate and polished and is never natural as it seems to be, and its simplicity can be very deceptive, as it is highly suggestive and connotative and capable of offering layers of undercurrents of meaning. Hemingway's strength lies in his short sentences and very specific details. His short sentences are powerfully loaded with the tension which he sees in life. He has an exceptional abhorrence for the vague and the general in expression. He labors to get "the real thing, the sequence of motion and fact which made the emotion," as he declares in *Death in the Afternoon*. In his opinion, a writer has got to catch "the whiteness of the bone," to catch the one specific thing and bring it to life and make it vivid for the readers and leave everything else out. Thus Hemingway's world is one of particulars. Terse, effective, and no nonsense—these are the obvious effects of his prose. Hemingway's influence as a stylist was neatly expressed in the praise of the Nobel Prize Committee about "his powerful style—forming mastery of the art" of writing modern fiction.

Hemingway's Reputation

Hemingway was a myth in his own time, and a myth in American literature. He was a glamorous public hero. His style of writing and living was probably more imitated than any other writers in human memory. He was so precisely because he acted out the theme of his own books. That was why he liked sports of all kinds, going deep-sea fishing, big game hunting, going into the bullring or becoming a prize ring boxer. His public image was one of a tough guy whom even an air-crash could not kill.

During the 1930s and the 1940s, he did not do much important writing. His *Death in the Afternoon* (1932), *Green Hills of Africa* (1935) and *The Fifth Column* (1938) did not add much to his reputation. But his non-literary activities were widely publicized and did more to advance his reputation. In 1942 he began to work for the United States Navy and for two years scoured the Cuban coast to help destroy enemy ships. In 1944 he went on several flights with the British Air Force as a reporter. He took part in the landing of the Allied Forces on the French coast and fought with a small force of his own in Paris before the French entered their capital themselves. He was injured many times, suffered at least a dozen injuries to the brain, and survived three bad automobile accidents and two air crashes. In his later years he often behaved in an odd manner and looked much older than his years. He wrote one enduring memoir, *A Moveable Feast*, which was posthumously published in 1964. Possibly because he could not write any more, or because he could not act out his code, or because of both and his ill health, he shot himself on July 2, 1961. The world was shocked into the disconcerting awareness that, with his death, an era had come to an end.

Fitzgerald and Hemingway grew up out of the same period and out of the same social situation. Fitzgerald was an analyst. He stayed in the United States and wrote about the Jazz Age. Readers go to him to know what this world was like. Hemingway, on the other hand, went away to Europe and wrote about the expatriates. His world was basically rootless. It is Fitzgerald who was so broken emotionally by the failure of the American dream.

Ultimately when the dust of time settles down and a clearer outline appears visible, it may be that both will remain great, the one as the other, but for different reasons: Hemingway predominantly for his style, and Fitzgerald for the fact that he tried to understand American culture at its roots and thus had more to say to posterity.

Chapter 15 The Southern Renaissance •
William Faulkner

The Southern Renaissance

William Faulkner (1896-1962) is associated with the American southern literary tradition.

Although the south remained conservative, there appeared, since the beginning of the 20th century, a visible sign of change in literature, and an obvious effort to reassess the past and the present and do self-searching. A few generations of southern writers have emerged to try and root their works in the south and achieve universal applicability. There was Ellen Glasgow (1874-1945) who, with her series of novels set in Virginia, focused more on the future rather than casting a backward glance. She wrote novels such as *Virginia* (1913) and *Barren Ground* (1925) to extoll the builders of the future of Virginia. Ellen Glasgow made her unique contribution to the emergence of William Faulkner.

Faulkner was the most important figure in this constellation of southern writers. He wrote 19 novels and numerous short stories. All of these relate to the south, forming a profound scrutiny of the problems which had troubled the south. Faulkner struggled to add to the American renaissance of the 1920s and helped usher in a whole new group of southern authors of the 1930s such as Katherine Anne Porter, Eudora Welty, and Carson McCullers.

The 1930s also witnessed the emergence of the Fugitives and their famous statement—*I'll Take My Stand* (1930), affirming their position on the superiority of the southern, agrarian lifestyle over that of the industrialized north.

Then the postwar period has seen a number of younger writers keeping up the southern tradition: Flannery O'Connor, William Styron, and Percy Walker, to name just a few. These writers have kept the continuity of the southern theme and kept it afloat before the readers' eyes. This glittering group of writers have managed to keep reminding the world of the existence of the resilient south.

William Faulkner (1897-1962)

Faulkner was born into a Southern family with a fairly long tradition. This is perhaps the most important of all the influences that made him what he became: a major writer in American literature. The town of Oxford where he was brought up and studied briefly at the university there, became the model for his fictional Jefferson, the seat of his fictional Yoknapatawpha county. His own family history found its way into his novels; the members of his family, including his great grandfather, grandfather, and his parents and brother, proved to be valuable prototypes for his fictional characters. And his knowledge of the life of the American Deep South, with the tragic history of rise and fall in its fortunes, its ways and mores, and its language, all fused in his imagination and recreated, became the substance of a Faulknerian world strangely inspiring both nostalgia and a sense of impending doom in modern readers.[1]

Faulkner was eager to go to the First World War, but was not sent to Europe. He was still under training when the war was over. He came back home, attended the University of Mississippi for a year, and worked to support himself. In his lifetime Faulkner cultivated a literary friendship with two men which was of great value to his career. The first was Phil Stone, a lawyer widely read in classic literature and modern French and English authors, who introduced him to the world of rising American writers such as Frost, Pound, and Sherwood Anderson, and who paid, in 1924, for the publication of a book of his poems, *The Marble Faun*. Through the recommendation of Phil Stone, Faulkner became acquainted with Sherwood Anderson in New Orleans, who helped him to write and publish his first novel, *Soldier's Pay* (1926). New Orleans was then a literary center of a kind, where the little magazine, *Double Dealer*, published avant-garde poetry. There Faulkner learned about James Joyce, Joseph Conrad, and Sigmund Freud. In 1925 he went on a trip to Europe, saw Joyce, his idol from afar, and was impressed by modern painting.

Faulkner's Road to Fame

Faulkner's first two novels, *Soldier's Pay* and *Mosquitoes* (1927) were not well received. Neither was *Sartoris* (1929), his third, but this work proved significant to his career. For one thing, Faulkner began to envisage his fictional county—Yoknapatawpha—for the first time and create a world of his own. His next book, *The Sound and the Fury* (1929), was definitely the mature work of a major author. With *As I Lay Dying* (1930), Faulkner began to worry about the critical reception of his works. His next work, *Sanctuary* (1931), sexually aggressive and sensational, earned him a rather bad reputation.

During the next ten years, he continued to work on his Yoknapatawpha county. His major works such as *Light in August* (1932), *Absalom, Absalom!* (1936), and *Go Down, Moses* (1942) appeared one after another. In the early 1940s Faulkner began to get a measure of belated recognition, but some of his works were beginning to be out of print.

It was critic Malcolm Cowley who saved Faulkner from oblivion. In 1946 Malcolm Cowley edited *The Viking Portable Faulkner*. Faulkner became the center of critical attention. Valuable studies began to appear. His mythic picture of the South, his fictional world, his distinctive narrative method, and his skillful use of language were all profusely commented upon. Cowley sent him to Stockholm. Faulkner won the Nobel Prize in 1950.

Faulkner's World

Of all Faulkner's writings, three novels—*The Sound and the Fury,*

Absalom, Absalom! and *Go Down, Moses*—are masterpieces by any literary standards, and seven or eight others are very impressive. Here the Deep South is delineated in minute detail. Its people, black and white, its small farms and magnificent mansions (some of which are decaying), its small towns with their court-houses, jails, stores and statues, its soil, rivers, and change of seasons are all parts of the general picture. Indeed, Faulkner's works have been termed the Yoknapatawpha saga, "one connected story," "one mythical kingdom" (the words are Malcolm Cowley's). Faulkner writes about the histories of a number of southern aristocratic families such as the Compsons, the Sartorises, the Sutpens and the McCaslins, and traces them back to the very beginning when the Chickasaw Indians were still lawful owners of the land. In the very rise of these family fortunes, Faulkner sees their inevitable fall. They displaced the Indians and enslaved the black race, thus putting a curse upon the land.[2] When the same story of the tragic rise and fall recurs in one novel after another, it assumes symbolic proportions. It becomes clear that what Faulkner is talking about concerns not merely the American South but the human situation in general.[3] The spiritual deterioration which characterizes the modern life of the South stems directly from the loss of love and want of emotional response. That seems to be the important message of Faulkner's stories.

The Sound and the Fury

The Sound and the Fury tells "a tale/ Told by an idiot, full of sound and fury,/ Signifying nothing." There is enough despair and nihilism but not much love and emotion in this sad story of the Compsons. Mr. Compson is disenchanted with life and the society he lives in. Unable to find meaning in the moral verities he was brought up with, he escapes into alcoholism and cynicism. Mrs. Compson is spiritually effete and has little love to spare for her children. Of the four children, Caddy is the only one capable of loving, but she loses her virginity. Her youngest brother, Benjy, is an idiot, a curse on the family. Another brother, Quentin, lives in the ideal world of his youth with his dreams of love, honor, and integrity and, when he fails to keep off the intrusion of the "loud, harsh world," he destroys himself. The life of the eldest brother, Jason, is empty and meaningless. Love is alien to him, and so are other traditional humanistic values.

The Sound and the Fury tells a story of deterioration from the past to the present. The past is idealized to form a striking contrast with the loveless present. There is in the book an acute feeling of nostalgia toward the happy past. Quentin's section offers a good illustration. As to his brothers, Benjy feels most keenly the loss of love and Jason's life embodies all the vices of the modern world.

Absalom, Absalom!

One important theme of *Absalom, Absalom!* is doom brought about by the denial of humanity. Thomas Sutpen is the son of a poor white family. After suffering humiliation and rejection at the gate of one of the great houses, he comes to see the importance of birth and blood and family, and is determined that he will never be poor and humble again. He will build a great house such as the one from which he has been turned away. So he goes to the West Indies, where he marries a woman who has Negro blood in her veins and has a son born by her. Disgusted with their origin, he deserts them, thus beginning to repeat the same tragic process of denial. Back in Jefferson he builds a great mansion out of the blood and labor of the Negroes, remarries, and has a son, Henry, and a daughter, Judith. Years later his West Indian son, Charles Bon, shows up on the scene, falls in love with Judith and is killed by Henry, his half-brother, who shares his father's denial of the Black race. Henry vanishes from the scene.

Then the Civil War comes and the defeat of the morally unjust south is complete. Sutpen comes back from the war to renew his effort of establishing a dynasty, but his continual denial of the humanity in others brings about his final downfall. He is shot dead, his mansion burnt down, and what is left is an idiot Negro grandson.

Go Down, Moses

Go Down, Moses tells roughly the same story of moral injustice which, in Faulkner's opinion, poisoned southern civilization at the root. The tragic drama of the McCaslins begins to enact itself when the first of the McCaslins is born in Carolina in the 1770s and arrives in the second decade of the 19th century in the Yoknapatawpha county. Old Carothers McCaslin brings with him a wife, two boys and a daughter. On a trip to New Orleans, Carothers buys a female Black slave, Eunice by name, who bears him a daughter called Tomey. Twenty years later, Carothers seduced his own daughter, Tomey, who becomes the mother of a boy, Tomey's Terrel. At this Eunice takes her own life. The house of the McCaslins is thus placed from the beginning on the basis of a moral wrong—an incestuous relationship and of injustice to a different race. Though the second generation of the McCaslins are enlightened enough to free some of their slaves and devise the share-cropping system on their plantation to help the poor, it is Ike McCaslin, Carothers McCaslin's grandson, who decides to end the terrible racial legacy and repent in hope of replacing it with a better order. He repudiates his family's heritage of guilt, refuses to assume the responsibility of the plantation, and goes back to his sources—the forest, the earth, for virtues of love, honor, and reason with which to expiate the sins of his ancestors.[4]

The telling of the *Go Down, Moses* story is interesting to explore. Several narrators tell stories which often contradict one another. This mode of narration has influence later writers such as Louise Erdrich (1954-) and Amy Tan (1952-).

A Different Way of Life

Against the nihilistic spirit of the southern "aristocratic" whites, there appears the healthy, seemingly primitive, way of life. In the Compsons' household, where life deteriorates and decays, there is one woman, the Black servant, Dilsey, whose heart brims over with love and compassion and who stands as the center of the family. We see, in *The Sound and the Fury*, she cares for the needs of the family. She takes care of the children in place of Mrs. Compson. She loves Benjy as a human being. Dilsey is all emotion and feeling. Her response to life and to people is natural and intuitive. She understands the plight of the Compsons well enough to pronounce their tragic end: "I've seed de first en de last ... I seed de beginning, en now I sees de ending." She seems to be saying that love and compassion are what man has lost and must recover to achieve revitalization.[5]

Another "primitive" is Sam Fathers in *Go Down, Moses*. He is a natural man close to his sources in the natural world. His feelings and responses stay natural. Deep in the forest, he initiates Ike McCaslin to virtues such as honor, pride, pity, justice, courage, love and compassion, virtues already missing from the life of the Compsons and the Sutpens. He saves Ike from the evils of modern civilization.

Faulkner states in his Nobel Prize speech that he writes to reassert "the old verities and truths of the heart, the old universal truths lacking which any story is ephemeral and doomed—love and honor and pity and pride and compassion and sacrifice." He believes that man may discover his true identity and retrieve his innate capacity to accept and endure if he keeps off modern intrusion upon the natural man within himself.

Faulkner's Ambivalence

Faulkner's attitude toward the southern "aristocratic" families that he wrote about is ambiguous. Alongside his censure of their injustice to the African Americans, there is some indication of pity and sympathy for their tragic fall. This can be sensed through reading his stories. One of his famous short stories, "A Rose for Emily," is a good index to the mixed feelings that his works reveal.

Emily is the last of a long line of the southern "aristocrats." Obstinate, asocial, out of step with the tenor of modern life, she lingers, when alive, as a "monument" to a glory gone with the wind, never to return. Yet the way Faulkner describes her, she appears to possess a measure of dignity, a stature of tragic dimensions, which inspires wonder and admiration in the minds of the townspeople. When she dies, she lies in state under a mass of bought flowers for people to view. The "rose" in the title indicates, as the tone of the story insinuates, a feeling not altogether unfriendly, one probably of compassion.

Faulkner's Formal Experiments

Faulkner was a daring formal experimentalist. He evolved his literary strategies so as to be better able to communicate his ideas. Not only was he a dedicated student of human nature, but he was also a conscious artist the way Henry James was.[6] One of his most important statements on the writers' job was the observation he made on one occasion, that "The writer's interested in all man's behavior with no judgment whatever."

Characterization was, to Faulkner, the essential medium to reveal the multifaceted nature of man. He possessed an amazing gift for creating "flesh-and-blood people that will stand up and cast a shadow." To him his characters are real and constant, enjoy autonomy, and he plays the role of a spectator-recorder. Faulkner was happy to create a fictional world which resembled the actual one.

Faulkner also experimented with authorial transcendence. The reader does hear, sometimes, an anonymous voice, but it is "the author, seeing himself distanced or as one more perspective on the scene, one more legitimate but not conclusive point of view."[7] Related to authorial transcendence is his use of a fallible narrator or multiple narrators as used in *Go Down, Moses*.

Faulkner is a difficult writer.[8] Readers have to deal with his original structures, his distinctive narrative methods and interior monologues, his stream of consciousness technique, his words run together, with no capitalization and no proper punctuation, sentences not always clearly indicated, many long ones pushed together in peculiar ways, one fragment running into another without proper notice, and the use of pronouns which often causes irritating perplexity, and added to these there is his handling of language—prose from colloquial, regional dialects to highly charged courtroom rhetoric, covering a variety of "registers" of the English language.

Faulkner's powers of imagination are very great. Rooting his works in the Deep South, he manages to create a literary milieu of his own through which he tries to transcend the limits of particularity to reach universality. He keeps moving his fictions toward the condition of myth and succeeds eventually in elevating a simple, true story of human life on to the plane of an elaborate mythology.[9] His major concern was always with the general human situation. He was no more a Southern novelist than Robert Frost was a New England poet.

Faulkner's Reputation

Faulkner has been considered America's greatest novelist to come out of the 20th century. The best of his fictions, which deal with basic human nature and the basic patterns of human behavior, rank among the most enduring works of world literature. In writing about his land and about "man in the ageless, eternal struggles," Faulkner speaks for both his people and humanity, and becomes as timeless as his stories.

Chapter 16   Anderson • Stein • Lewis • Cather • Wolfe

Sherwood Anderson (1876-1941)[1]

Sherwood Anderson's life was a peculiar and interesting story to talk about. At a certain point in his life, when he was about thirty-six, already a successful businessman with a happy family, he suffered a nervous breakdown. He might have been tormented by "a divided self." He had been running a paint business well but he felt he could be "servant to words" only. He wanted to become a writer. For a few years he ran his business by the day and wrote novels at night. Then the clash came to a head. One day, in the middle of a dictation, he stopped and left his office, never to return. He was found wandering about in a confused condition and was sent to a hospital. Thus he said farewell to the business world. He went to Chicago, then a cultural center in the Midwest. There he lived by writing advertisements for an agency while working on his novels, and felt thrilled that he was living as a writer.

Anderson's Works

Anderson wrote quite a few works. These include *Windy McPherson's Son* (1916), *Marching Men* (1917), *Winesburg, Ohio* (1919), collections of short stories such as *The Triumph of the Egg* (1921), *Horses and Men* (1923) and *Death in the Woods* (1933), and novels like *Poor White* (1920), *Many Marriages* (1923), *Dark Laughter* (1925) and *Kit Brandon* (1936). Anderson also left three personal narratives—*A Story-Teller's Story* (1924), *Tar: A Midwest Childhood* (1926) and *Sherwood Anderson's Memoirs* (1942).

Thematically, Anderson explored the psychological and emotional aspect of American small-town life, with emphasis chiefly on lower-class figures, the unsuccessful, the deprived, and the inarticulate. Anderson lived in a period of American history, when the country's transition from a rural to an industrial society was drawing to a close in the first years of the 20th century. This had been a painful experience for small-town people. Alienation, loneliness, and want of love and understanding made life intolerable, and turned people into "grotesques." Thwarted emotions, repressed drives, frustrated lives, and distorted natures became the distinct features of America's small-town life. The historic importance of Anderson lies in the fact that he offered in his *Winesburg, Ohio* rather a timeless record of these for posterity.

Technically, Anderson was a highly original writer. He depended on inspiration in his creative endeavor. Like the old writer in "The Book of the Grotesque," Anderson seemed to have a "young thing" active within him, directing his pen. He must have often had the same experience, again like the old writer, of falling into a half-dream in which he meets a procession of figures, some amusing, some almost beautiful, but all grotesques of one kind or another: He felt there was something, "the young indescribable thing within him" as he calls it, that was driving this long procession before him. Listening to the call from inside, Anderson wrote his stories that appeal not through careful fabrications of incidents or episodes, but by the sheer emotional force of the moments of revelation, or the Joycean epiphany, that these stories describe.

Winesburg, Ohio

It is Anderson's masterpiece. A book of twenty-five stories, it describes small-town grotesques, of people each with a ruling kind of passion which distorts their personalities. "Hands" relates the bitter story of Adolph Myers and his pair of sensitive hands which have lost their right to express the love of man. Myers has never been able to recover from his traumatic experience of being beaten out of his job as a schoolteacher because of his hands. He lived alone in the town for twenty years and looked sixty-five though he was only forty. "Paper Pills" tells of an old man, Doctor Reefy, whom "Winesburg had forgotten." The Doctor, who loves his fellow men, is portrayed as a gnarled apple which the pickers have rejected but which possesses a sweetness only a few people know. He finds it so hard to communicate with people that he scribbles his thoughts on some bits of paper and stuffs them away in his pockets. There these become round hard balls. "Mother" probes into a mother-son relationship which becomes very awkward and abnormal because neither is communicative enough to break through to understanding. Then there are other "grotesques" such as Doctor Parcival, Louise Trunnion, Jesse Bentley, David Hardy, Joe Welling, Alice Hindman, Wash Williams, Seth Richmond, Tandy Hard, Reverend Curtis Hartman, Kate Swift, Enoch Robinson, Belle Carpenter, Elmer Cowley, Ray Pearson, Tom Foster, and Helen White. All these people are seen suffocating in an environment, the dominant feature of which is want of understanding. Their stories reveal a nostalgic glance backward at "a kind of pastoral golden age" that has passed.

Anderson's Contribution to the Art of Fiction

Anderson was endowed with "a gift for pouring a lifetime into a moment."[2] He studied abnormal human behavior from a Freudian psychological point of view and tried to reveal the abnormal states of mind in a more or less accurate way. Then there is his style to consider. Anderson was probably the first writer since Mark Twain to write in the colloquial style.[3] He regarded the vernacular as an honest medium and developed a style of clarity, directness, and a deceptive simplicity. This style, though monotonous and crude with its sentimental expansiveness, was to influence such writers as Hemingway and Faulkner. He served as Hemingway's stylistic guide for some time. Faulkner regarded Anderson as "the father of my generation of American writers and the tradition of American writing which our successors will carry on." Anderson has been called "a writer's writer." In addition to Hemingway and Faulkner, there were also Hart Crane, Thomas Wolfe, and John Steinbeck, to name just a few, who owed a debt to him. Anderson made a difference to modern American literature as a seminal figure.

The works of Anderson have obvious weaknesses as well. For one thing, their quality is very uneven. Then there is his style: its deficiency is ruthlessly parodied in Hemingway's *The Torrents of Spring*. Anderson is not much read today. But his *Winesburg, Ohio* alone is already good enough for him to stay in the American literary pantheon.

Gertrude Stein (1874-1946)

Gertrude Stein came from a well-to-do American family and was able to live comfortably on her inheritance in Paris most of her adult life. All her life she kept writing, and was a well-known writer of over fifty books. These include *Three Lives* (1909), *Tender Buttons* (1914), *The Making of Americans* (1925), *How to Write* (1931), and *Four Saints in Three Acts*. She lectured on her theories at Cambridge and Oxford Universities, and did a lecture tour in America in 1934.

Gertrude Stein is remembered for a few things she did.[4] For one thing, she was very sensitive to the temper of her time and its subtleties of change, and felt that literature should develop ways to reflect its true nature. When she settled down in France, she began collecting modern experimental works of art like the paintings of Cézanne and Picasso. Her apartment in Paris became a meeting place, a salon of a kind, for artists and writers, especially those of the experimental and the avant-garde inclinations such as Anderson and Fitzgerald. Her memoir, *The Autobiography of Alice B. Toklas* (1933), records her encounters with those famous people. Around the 1920s Ernest Hemingway came to her for advice at the beginning of his career with a letter of introduction from Sherwood Anderson. Hemingway acknowledged that he learned everything from her "about the abstract relationships of words," the many truths about rhythms and the uses of words in repetition. Gertrude Stein offered him help to develop his style. Later the two disagreed on ideas about writing. Hemingway said in his *A Moveable Feast* (1964) to the effect that he learned from her, but she was not his mentor as she had been saying that she was. Gertrude Stein was a little presumptuous. She was an impressive presence in Paris and exerted some influence around her.

Another thing for which she has been noted is her literary theory and practice. Her literary theories are best expounded in her *How to Write*. She stressed "the value of the individual word" in her writings so as for her readers to see the objects rather than the mere printed text that describes them. One major feature of her writing is her repetitions of words which she felt could erase their superficial meaning and reveal their true sense. Her writing is filled with cryptic language and obscure abstractions which she believed would help to delineate essential reality. In most of her writings she deviates from conventional word order and coherence so that she is not always easy to understand. Sherwood Anderson took an immense interest in her laying word against word, relating sound to sound, feeling for the taste, the smell, the rhythm of the individual word. Her writing exhibits its unmistakable experimental daring and modernity.

It is good to read some of her writings. For her poetry, Stein's most famous and most frequently quoted line has been "Rose is a rose is a rose is a rose" from her domestic idyll, "Sacred Emily." Her poem, "Susie Asado" (1922), one of her rhythmic Spanish poems, is equally interesting, containing lines like "Sweet sweet sweet sweet sweet tea./ Susie Asado./ Sweet sweet sweet sweet sweet tea./ Susie Asado." The experimental nature of the writing is clear enough to demonstrate the limitless potential of available language resources.

The same feature of writing appears in Stein's prose works. One of these, "Picasso," begins thus:

One whom some were certainly following was one who was completely charming. One whom some were certainly following was one who was charming. One whom some were following was one who was completely charming. One whom some were following was one who was certainly completely charming.

And it goes on:

Some were certainly following and were certain that the one they were then following was one working and was one bringing out of himself then something. Some were certainly following and were certain that the one they were then following was one bringing out of himself then something that was coming to be a heavy thing, a solid thing, a complete thing.

Then read this:

This one always had something being coming out of this one. This one was working. This one always had been working. This one was always having something that was coming out of this one that was a solid thing, a charming thing, a lovely thing, a perplexing thing, a disconcerting thing, a simple thing, a clear thing, a complicated thing, an interesting thing, a disturbing thing, a repellant thing, a very pretty thing. This one was one certainly being one having something coming out of him. This one was one whom some were following. This one was one who was working.

Stein is not much read today. Her *Three Lives*, seen as one of the earliest modern works of American fiction, is considered her best work, but not a very good read for modern readers now.

Sinclair Lewis (1885-1951)

The first American author to win the Nobel Prize for literature, Sinclair Lewis has been called the worst important writer in American Literature.[5] Born into a middle-class family in Minnesota, Lewis was to place that class under ruthless satire, and at the same time to affirm its best virtues.

Lewis began writing when still in college and developed the habit of taking meticulous notes to be used in his novels. In 1920 his sixth book, *Main Street*, came out, and made him famous. For the next ten years the rise of Lewis was meteoric. With the appearance of *Babbitt* (1922), *Arrowsmith* (1925), and *Dodsworth* (1929), Lewis acquired an international reputation which led straight to the Nobel Prize in 1930. After he climbed to the summit of his career, a steady slide downhill began. Writing became now a mechanical routine for him. The ten novels that he wrote after 1930 made not much of a stir in critical circles as well as among the readers.

Lewis was a sociological writer. His novels form a segment of American social history. He never wrote anything before he acquainted himself thoroughly with his material. He would study the section of social life closely, record his observations in detail, overhear conversations and note them down carefully, and draw maps of the locality and even the house with its furniture before he began to work out an outline, a detailed draft, and prepare the final manuscripts for publication. This method of work shows him to be a genius of a lower intellectual order, very much inferior to that of, say, Dickens, but it had its own merit.

For several decades Lewis tried to study American middle-class life so that he got to know it inside out. *Main Street* deals with parochial small-town life. *Babbitt* paints a truthful picture of the middle-class business world of post-war America. *Arrowsmith* brings the operations of the medical profession to light. *Elmer Gantry* reveals the appalling religious decay in the country. And *Dodsworth* attacks the social standards of the middle class in general. Lewis had explicitly written to introduce this one class of the American society to the outside world. Moreover, he added one word to the English language, i.e. "Babbitt," a word denoting "the vulgar and philistine businessman."

Lewis never seemed to enjoy a respectable reputation. He was considered to be out of step with the more dynamic, more "revolutionary" spirit of the post-war literary scene. His affirmation of what he regarded as the best middle-class virtues made him appear rather old-fashioned. His style was "Edwardian," accurate in external description but lacking in psychological exploration. So he looked conservative and outmoded. That image has remained in the memory of critics and readers alike even today.

Willa Cather (1873-1947)

Willa Cather was one of the few "uneasy survivors of the nineteenth century."[6] Hanging onto the traditional values, she was never able to come to terms with modernity. In very much the same way Virginia Woolf said "On or about December 1910 human nature changed," Willa Cather made the grave statement that "in 1922 or thereabouts," the world "broke into two." And she lived in between the worlds, rejecting the modern and trying to escape into the refuge of the past. Her works are a fictional projection of her own crisis in life.

For Willa Cather, Old West functions in most of her novels as the center of moral reference against which modern existence is measured. The frontier rural community is always morally higher whereas the town is effete and corrupting. The immigrant folks are both simple and noble, and their life, though primitive, orderly and meaningful. Thus Antonia, the frontier village woman in *My Antonio* (1918), lives with attitudes "like the founders of early races," whereas the successful man of the city, Jim Burden, feels that the simple old ways have gone never to return.

The same vein of thought runs through all Willa Gather's work. *The Song of the Lark* (1915) is an implicit criticism of the culturally sophisticated East.

Here the East is evaluated, somehow, against the spiritually idealistic standards of the West and found wanting. This proves to be the burden of *A Lost Lady* (1923), in which the Old pioneers and their values are fast losing out to the new men and their different value system, one infested with small-town spirit and commercial standards.

Willa Cather keenly felt a desire to reject and withdraw from the modern world. *The Professor's House* (1925) is a good illustration. Professor St. Peter builds a new house and furnishes it so that all the modern utilities and gadgets are available to make life easy and comfortable, but he refuses to move from the old house where he wrote his book and won with it the prize money with which to build the new house. The professor has got to choose between the new and the old, and he prefers the latter. There he stays, retreating into the past. In her later fiction, Willa Cather withdraws into the historical past. *Death Comes for the Archbishop* (1927) and *Shadows on the Rock* (1931) both try to recapture an ideal past.

Willa Cather writes to champion old values and traditions. To her, modern life is suffocating. As a traditionalist to the end, she manages to leave a record of a thinking mind's response to modern life.

Thomas Wolfe (1900-1938)

Thomas Wolfe was from Asheville, North Carolina. He went to Harvard and taught at a New York university. He is noted for his "torrential" creative exuberance and verbal energy. Some of his works have continued to awaken response in contemporary readers.[7]

Wolfe was a personal writer. All his writings are self-revelations so that his art borders on being confessional. All his protagonists are in essence reproductions of his own personality. All the experiences related in his fictions are autobiographical down to the minutest detail. Nor did Wolfe deny the fact that he had written himself wholesale into his novels. He was convinced that serious creative work must be all autobiographical in the final analysis, and that people must quote from their own life experiences to create anything of substantial value.

Thus his first book, *Look Homeward, Angel* (1929), is a narrative of his boyhood experiences, his life with his parents and brothers, and his final departure from his native place. *Of Time and the River* (1935), his second novel, picks up the story where the first leaves off, and tells about his stay at Harvard, his brief career as an instructor of English in a New York university, and his trip to Europe and return to America. Although the hero of the two books is the same person by the name of Eugene Gant and his native town is Altamont, Catawba, we know very well that Eugene Gant is Thomas Wolfe fictionalized and Altamont, Catawba is but another name for Asheville, North Carolina, though, it is good to add, nothing was a literal transcription here.

The Web and The Rock (1939) continues the narrative of the previous book, while the last book, *You Can't Go Home Again* (1940) recapitulates the major events that occurred in the last few years of his life. In these last two novels, published after he died of tuberculosis of the brain, Wolfe managed to achieve a degree of objectivity in his narrative art: his personality as an artist changed and transfigured everything of real life in his works.

Wolfe was an ambitious man. He saw the whole life of America as the province of his fictional representation. What he set out to achieve was nothing short of defining the American experience. In talking about himself, he found the rhythm of American life. As the depression of the 1930s deepened, Wolfe awoke to the painful fact that America was not that great, after all.

Wolfe was an original artist. All the strengths and weaknesses evident in his art are his own. There is an abundance of inflated rhetoric, it is true, and he can be badly rhythmic, but he can be exquisitely lyrical. He is conscious of his unique power to recreate everything physical and sensual such as odors, sounds, colors, shapes, and feel of things vividly, and make these real to the senses of his readers. The dramatic power with which he endows his sensuous factual details is an eloquent testimony to his prodigious talent. And the power and the vitality that his body of prose generates are more than compensation for his rhetorical excesses and novelistic formlessness for which he is unjustly remembered.

Chapter 17   *The 1930s • Dos Passos • Steinbeck*

The 1930s

The 1930s was radically different from the 1920s in mood as well as in expression. To begin with, its mood was colored differently from the very beginning. The Wall Street crash of 1929 set the tone for the writing of the decade. On October 24, 1929 "the bottom dropped of the stock market" (to quote from critic Warren French), and the great Depression began. Banks failed, factories closed, and agriculture withered. Jobless millions roamed the streets, breadlines stretched long, and absolute poverty became a fact of life. As the Depression spread, life became a nightmarish experience for millions of people. Economic disaster and the wretched workless existence for the masses of the people brought home to all the unnerving realization that the system might have collapsed. It had failed to work because it had allowed possibilities like the depression to be built into its fabric. It had failed because it had not been able to resolve the paradox of life that it might itself have created: food rotted while people starved; textile mills shut down while people needed clothing; and farmers lost their farms because they produced too much. The "milk and honey" of the land went down the drain instead of nourishing its people. Everything seemed to be disintegrating all of a sudden and all at once, and an ordered, rational existence proved to be impossible. There was widespread panic and sheer despair for many in the bleak years of the 1930s.

F. D. Roosevelt's New Deal helped dispel the crisis-laden atmosphere hanging over the country. He found ways to obtain money from financiers and industrialists to support projects like those of the C. C. C. (Civilian Conservation

Corps) and the Federal Theater, all of which restored a measure of confidence to the defeatist nation. But nothing like a significant improvement occurred. It was not until the outbreak of World War II that the country felt safe again. The war saved the United States, in a sense.

Faced with the reality of want and despair, American writers, like their counterparts in England and Europe, found themselves asking the question, "What can writers do for the country?" This seemed to be the burden of a number of speeches at the 1935 American Writers' Conference, at which John Dos Passos, Langston Hughes, and Thornton Wilder were present and to which Hemingway sent a message of support. It was apparent that social concern was topmost in the minds of many authors, and that social involvement was to be the major feature of the literature of the 1930s. The impact of the crisis of the new decade brought about a revival of the naturalistic tradition, with the shadow of Dreiser and Norris moving behind the scene.

The writers of the 1930s responded to the turbulence of their times very well. Literary expression in the period was abundant and forceful. All the three major departments of literature—fiction, poetry, and drama—exerted their best efforts to rise to the challenge of the time. The number of people writing was amazingly huge; the number of works written was no less surprising. Although many of these are period pieces, too much time-bound and space-bound to make for permanence, they deserve adequate recognition and admiration.

Fiction

Let's take a look at the field of fiction. The 1930s was a great age of fiction. Dreiser's naturalistic style became some kind of model for the depression novelists. Gertrude Stein and Sherwood Anderson tried to add to the strength of the novel of the new period. Hemingway and Fitzgerald offered their *For Whom the Bells Tolls* and *The Last Tycoon* respectfully later in the decade and at the beginning of the next. William Faulkner and Thomas Wolfe both published their major novels in 1930. There were other southern writers such as Ellen Glasgow, Katherine Anne Porter, Eudora Welty, and Carson McCullers writing about the period.

The two major authors who became dominant figures in fiction were John Dos Passos and John Steinbeck. Dos Passos' *U.S.A.* and Steinbeck's *The Grapes of Wrath*, along with their works and those of other writers, offer an authentic account of the American experience in the debilitating years of the Depression. Then there was the "hard knocks" generation, tough, ironic and hard-boiled "children of the depression." These include James T. Farrell, Erskine Caldwell, James M. Cain, John O'Hara, Nelsen Algren, and Homer McCoy, all beginning to publish in the decade. Along with these people, a group of proletarian writers worked hard to record faithfully the details of common life and the desires of the low strata of society. Michael Gold, Jack Conroy, and John Reed were but a few names to pick out of what was once an eloquent literary movement.

Mention should be made of three novelists who were neglected in their time but have been "resurrected" somehow in the postwar years—Henry Miller, Henry Roth, and Nathanael West. Henry Miller wrote some scandalous works— *Tropic of Cancer* (1934) and *Tropic of Capricorn* (1939), was suppressed for quite some years but emerged in the 1960s as precursor to the Beat Generation. Henry Roth's *Call It Sleep* (1934) has been found fascinating in its use of Joycean interior monologue and its subtle handling of various dialects. And Nathanael West's four novels, now well evaluated, are said to relate to the black humor of the 1960s.

Another interesting figure of the period was the first African American novelist, Richard Wright, who increased the weight of the novel of the 1930s with his short stories in *Uncle Tom's Children* (1938) and other writings although his major work, *Native Son*, came out at the beginning of the next decade. We should mention in passing two popular novels, Margaret Mitchell's *Gone with the Wind* (1936) and Hervey Allen's *Anthony Adverse* (1933). These books, although not much noticed by critics, served one purpose well if nothing else:

they offered an avenue of escape from the wretched reality of the time.

The Drama

The drama of the 1930s was rich and varied. It is true that no figure comparable to O'Neill appeared, but many people of talent tried to enrich the stage with their plays. Among these were Clifford Odets, Maxwell Anderson, Lillian Hellman, and Thornton Wilder, to list just a few. O'Neill published two of his most important plays in the decade, *Mourning Becomes Electra* (1931) and *Ah, Wilderness* (1933), but neither related to the depression as they were probably carry-overs from the playwright's most creative 1920s. Clifford Odets was a major playwright of the period; his works such as *Waiting for Lefty*, *Awake and Sing*, and *Golden Boy* prove to possess some measure of enduring claim to attention. Maxwell Anderson produced a good number of plays in the 1930s, such as *Elizabeth the Great, Mary of Scotland, Valley Forge,* and *Winterset* although he did not keep up his early promise of becoming another O'Neill in the American theater. Lillian Hellman wrote some plays which both related to and transcended their time period. Her *The Children's Hour* and *The Little Foxes* can still awaken echoes today. Thornton Wilder's *Our Town*, evoking as it does American small town heritage, was a remarkable addition to the richness of the American stage of the 1930s. Also deserving mention was John Steinbeck's effort to dramatize his novel, *Of Mice and Men*, which was a successful experiment. In addition to these major figures, there were many other lesser talents working to make the Depression years theatrical. William Saroyan with his *My Heart's in the Highlands*, Robert E. Sherwood with his *Reunion in Vienna* and *Idiot's Delight*, George S. Kaufman in collaboration with Moss Hart and their *The Fabulous Invalid* and *You Can't Take It With You*, Richard Rogers with his *Pal Joey*, and a good number of musical comedies—these all contributed to the rich variety of the theater of the period.

Poetry

The 1930s was not very good for poetry. Probably because of the overwhelming influence of T. S. Eliot, poetry did not flourish in the new decade as did the novel and the drama. No new major poet appeared on the scene. The older generation was still busy working. Frost won two Pulitzer Prizes though he did not find the period congenial to develop his art much. Eliot published another of his major works, *Ash Wednesday*, "Burnt Norton" (the first of *Four Quartets*), and a couple of his poetic dramas. Ezra Pound's *Cantos* continued to grow, giving his poet-propagandist's warnings to his native country. Wallace Stevens, refusing to turn poetry to propaganda, created his permanent works such as *Ideas of Order* and *The Man with the Blue Guitar*. Marianne Moore and William Carlos Williams were in between their periods of creative highlights. E. E. Cummings and Robinson Jeffers continued to write without adding significantly to their reputation. Carl Sandburg's *The People, Yes* offered a vehement sense of optimism in face of the defeatist spirit of the times. As to Hart Crane, although his major works, *The Bridge* and *Collected Poems*, were out in print in the decade, they were clearly of the 1920s in spirit. Younger poets included Kenneth Fearing whose poetry was probably the best remembered of the radical works of the time, and Archibald MacLeish, who suffered somehow from his identification with the propagandists. One thing that deserves special mention is the rise of the New Criticism as a school of poetry writing and criticism. John Crowe Ransom, Allen Tate, Robert Penn Warren, and Cleanth Brooks, along with others, did their utmost to institute its values and bring its influence into college classrooms. For some three decades it assumed the status of some orthodoxy in the writing and criticism of poetry until the 1950s and 1960s when a change in taste and values became inevitable. But its influence has extended beyond the period of its supremacy and has left its imprint on history.[1]

James T. Farrell (1904-1979)

With regard to the fiction of the period, the efforts of some young novelists such as James T. Farrell, John O'Hara, and Erskine Caldwell deserve serious attention. These left-oriented young men poured out their torrents of anger and protest in their works. James T. Farrell was a voluminous writer.[2] In addition to the Studs trilogy which include *Young Lonigan* (1932), *The Young Manhood of Studs Lonigan* (1934) and *Judgment Day* (1935), he also wrote the Danny O'Neill pentalogy, the Bernard Carr trilogy, some seven other novels, about 200 short stories, and miscellaneous writings including literary criticism.

His reputation rests chiefly on his Studs Lonigan trilogy. Here is a meticulous record of the brutalizing experience of the Depression period in Chicago. Studs Lonigan, the protagonist of the trilogy, lives in a meaningless and violent slum environment, and encounters alienation, violence, and eventual destruction. He deteriorates with the deteriorating city of Chicago. Over and above the economic crisis, there exists an acutely felt spiritual poverty. Conventional values are uprooted. Moral sanctions fail in the wake of economic disintegration. As the social ground on which he stands falls away beneath him, he meets his doom, however hard he tries to avert it. The determinism of the 19th-century naturalists reasserts itself in Farrell's work. Farrell is noted for the absolute literalness and solidity of detail in his representation. To read him is to relive the violent rawness and distemper of the 1930s.

John O'Hara (1905-1970)

The 1930s also witnessed the vogue of the hard-boiled novels, of which the best was perhaps John O'Hara's *Appointment in Samara* (1934).[3] As is usual with O'Hara, this is a study of the life of a member of an upper class family. Julian English seems to be seized with a death wish and behaves in an abnormal way.

Through the case history of Julian English, O'Hara is presenting a segment of the life of the thirties.

O'Hara records life "with complete honesty and variety." He possesses a rich fund of knowledge of and experience with the people and their lives. But his weakness is also apparent. He is not a profound writer. He records well, but he may not understand what he notes down in his works. Thus his art often degenerates into a form of pure mimicry.

O'Hara was prolific. He wrote a good number of novels and a huge number of short stories. The portrayal of the thirties would not have been as authentic and trustworthy as it is in American fiction had there not been O'Hara's contribution.

Erskine Caldwell (1903-1987)

There is then Erskine Caldwell, a left-wing naturalist, who worked hard to document "capitalist decay." Caldwell is adept at delineating a shocking scene of violence or an act of cruelty which reveals man's capacity to do evil when he drops off all pretensions, especially so in the cruel 1930s.

Though occasionally comic, Caldwell enjoys causing extreme mental misery to his readers. A sharecropper being devoured by hogs, little girls sold into prostitution for a quarter, and events of a nature which tend to push man centuries back in his evolution. All these are portrayed in detail in his works. Reading him can be a nauseating experience. Perhaps this is just the kind of effect Caldwell intends to produce on his readers.

However, man possesses dignity and the capacity to wonder and hope. A great literary artist should possess the capacity to transcend the temporal and inspire confidence and courage with which to face life squarely. If some of the prolific writers of the Depression fail to attain permanence, it is probably because they have been found inadequate on this score.

John Dos Passos (1896-1970)

John Dos Passos was one of the 1930s' major novelists. As the leading naturalist of the Depression, he started off writing for the oppressed, calling himself in 1917 a "red radical revolutionary." But his life and attitudes changed well with time and history. In the 1930s he was close to the Communists. Then he embraced Rooseelt's New Deal. The 1950s witnessed his change to conservatism when he admired business and supported US in Vietnam War.[4] His literary output was immense. His writings were Communist-oriented for a long period. He is remembered today chiefly for his masterwork, his trilogy—*U.S.A.*

U.S.A.: The Varied Depression Experience

The trilogy is an imaginative compendium of the nation in its various facets during the first three decades of the 20th century. It comprises *The 42nd Parallel* (1930), *1919* (1932), and *The Big Money* (1936). The first of these covers the period in which America emerged as an industrial giant, the "machine" which was to dominate and impede the free growth of individual lives. *1919* is a record of the First World War, a continuation of the "depersonalizing" process that had been going on as narrated in the first book, and a preparation for documenting the booming twenties in the last, *The Big Money.* The trilogy covers the years from the beginning of the 20th century through the Sacco-Vanzetti incident in 1927. During these years, the socialist movement suffered defeat, and industrialists and financiers and big businessmen emerged winners. Individuals of all classes lost out to the "machine" which tyrannically subjected them to its will and power. Dos Passos saw this and sensed the mood of despair keenly. The world of *U.S.A.* is therefore one where, as critic Edmund Wilson observes, no birds sing, no flowers bloom, and the air is virtually unbreathable.[5]

U.S.A. belongs to that category of fiction which critic Northrop Frye would call "anatomy."[6] It is a kind of narrative in which ideas dominate. Dos Passos

uses his characters to stand for ideas, so they often appear to be stereotyped.

U.S.A. has been known as a "collectivist" novel, dealing with the lives of eleven

leading characters and over 30 minor ones to body forth one pervasive idea that

the "machine" is hostile to the physical and spiritual welfare of the individual.

Dos Passos is good at depicting the classified existence that was modern life. His

characters as individuals are all of them every moment of their lives subjected to

the pressure of the "machine" and succeed or fail depending on their response to

its workings. There is, for instance, J. Ward Moorehouse, who represents in his

life and career that section of the society—big business—which manipulates and

dominates through the "machine." This section grows aware of the operations of

the "machine," complies with its demands, submits willingly to its will and

power, and becomes its spokesman. J. Ward Moorehouse's is a success story, one

of material rise but spiritual fall.

To this segment belong Richard Ellsworth Savage and Eleanor Stoddard.

The former starts out being an idealist, gets to know the nature of the system,

learns to conform to it, and take advantage of it. He manages to attain a degree

of satisfaction in his material success though at the expense of his moral integrity.

Eleanor Stoddard is a different case from both Moorehouse and Savage. Hers is

an almost instinctive quest for a parasitic kind of happiness. Inadvertently she

accepts the tyranny of the "machine," and tries to make the best of what it can

offer her. Jumping from one man's bed to another, she succeeds in obtaining a

material security after she has gone through the stages of degradation. In their

frenzied attempt to get ahead in the world, these people lose all spiritual

orientation.

Dos Passos offers a pathetic picture of the lower class such as Janey

Williams and Mac McCreary. Coming from the working class, Janey tries to get

out of it. She accepts her world as the best possible and makes ready to cash in

on any luck that comes her way. She is obsessed with the idea of caste. She turns

her back not only on the people who try to do things for her, but also on her brother. She is intended as a foil to the one-time revolutionary, Mac McCreary.

Mac is a former Mexican revolutionary. At first he was fired with a strong sense of mission to better the lot of the whole of his class. He goes to join the revolutionaries in Mexico, but becomes entangled with a woman there. He is ultimately overwhelmed with too much capital to continue his revolutionary work. Mac's life suggests that, as soon as one gets property, his social ideas get watered down, and for him the revolution is over.

Then there are people like Charley Anderson, Mary French, and Ben Compton, who all between them represent the varied painful experience of the working class.

Dos Passos: A Courageous Experimentalist

John Dos Passos was a courageous experimentalist in the art of novel-writing. He employed, in his fiction, devices which had not been known before. In between the narratives about the lives of ordinary people, devices like the "Newsreels," the "Biographies," and the "Camera Eye" are introduced. "Newsreels" consist of newspaper headlines, extracts from newspaper reports, and bits of popular songs. These give an idea of the social unrest and the mood of the times against which the fictional characters define themselves, and establish a time scheme for the readers as well. The "Biographies" are about the famous Americans who emerged as "benefactors" of mankind, and indicate what the prodigious energy of America could produce. These cover the lives of labor leaders, electricians, scientists, heroes and villains such as Eugene Debs, Carnegie, Edison, La Follette, John Reed, Theodore Roosevelt, the Wright brothers, the Morgans, and Henry Ford. The lives of these people contrast with the commonplace existence of the ordinary people and furnish a frame of reference with which to comprehend and evaluate it. The "Camera Eye" registers the responses and reflections of some presiding consciousness, moving around alone, standing aside from or over and above the kaleidoscopic experience of the human world, meditating on it, and maturing emotionally. Here are thoughts, sometimes fragmentary, always done in an impressionistic or stream-of-consciousness manner, with motifs repeated, and themes played back and forth, all intended to increase the awareness of the readers.

In addition to these devices, Dos Passos is proficient in the use of simple diction, impressive images, rhythmical sentences and parallels. He is good at creating a proper distance between his narrator and the events narrated, and connecting thought units by the word "and"—a typical feature of 20th-century colloquial style in America. John Dos Passos is a stylist in his own way. *U.S.A.* may not expect to have many imitators, its way of writing may not be much appreciated by readers in general, but it broke new ground, and showed a new way of doing things.

Dos Passos intends to be an "architect of history." He wants to place the whole of the American experience in the first thirty years of the 20th century under close scrutiny and bring into relief the mind of a generation—his generation. As he feels the mind of a generation is its speech, he wrote *U.S.A.* in the speech of the people. Reading the trilogy, one tends to be overwhelmed by the documents, facts, and the exquisite chaos of modern experience that it contains. One tends to lose sight of order in disorder, connection in dislocation, and unity in disparateness and diversity. But one manages to secure a totality of impression, the idea that the capitalist "machine" thwarts individual growth and destroys individuality in its ruthless leveling operations. Thus *U.S.A.* is an organic whole, as well organized as *The Waste Land* and the *Cantos*.[7] Dos Passos wants to tell the truth about American life. He hopes to paint a panorama of American society. It is just to note that he did both to the best of his ability in *U.S.A.* If he had not written anything else, he would still have been a major American author of the 20th century.

John Steinbeck (1902-1968)

Another significant Depression writer was John Steinbeck.[8] He was born in Salinas, California, went to Stanford University (1919-1925), but never graduated. For some time he knocked about at various jobs and learned a lot about life, which set the basis of his works. Later, he wrote some romantic books, but none of these caught much critical attention. Then in 1935, at the age of 33, Steinbeck discovered himself. He discovered both his subject and his method. The book that appeared that year, *Tortilla Flat* (1935), made him popular. It tells, in an affectionate manner, about the life of a few Spanish bums. Though not a fighting book, it is very well done, and remains one of his better works. The next year he wrote a book about a strike which began his period of concern with a very big subject of the time, namely, the class struggle in the United States. The book was entitled *In Dubious Battle*, a very articulate "proletarian" story. Then he wrote his best-known works *Of Mice and Men* (1937) and *The Grapes of Wrath* (1939). World War II furnished Steinbeck with material for some of his books like *The Moon is Down* (1942) and *East of Eden* (1952). Like Dos Passos, Steinbeck in his later years turned very conservative. He won the Nobel Prize for literature in 1962.

Of Mice and Men

Now Steinbeck found himself in a creative rush. He managed to bring out a book a year. When *Of Mice and Men* appeared in 1937, it became a bestseller. It is a story of two migrant workers, one of whom is very strong and powerful physically but mentally weak and deficient, and the other, the younger and smaller, who takes care of the big one. What they wish for is a permanent home, a very small white house with trees around it. But this is pure daydream for the helpless. Finally disaster overtakes them. The big one is accused of having killed somebody and the local people are after him to lynch him, while the small one tries to keep him from being lynched. The story was rewritten into a play and a movie and made Steinbeck's reputation.

The Grapes of Wrath

The Grapes of Wrath tells a story of the migration of agricultural workers from the dust bowl of Oklahoma to California. The novel is full of bitterness and pain but not exactly despair. There is inconceivable suffering and privation, but a ray of hope also shines. It is essentially its humanity that triumphs. *The Grapes of Wrath* helped in great measure toward increasing the nation's awareness of the seriousness of its problems, and won in time the Pulitzer Prize for fiction. However, the book caused a good deal of controversy. It was attacked and banned for a length of time on both ideological and artistic grounds: it was accused of being communist (which it is of course not) and structurally formless.

The Grapes of Wrath is one of the major American books. The title of the book comes from "The Battle Hymn of the Republic," a war song of the Civil War, in which there are the lines, "Mine eyes have seen the glory of the coming of the Lord, / He is tramping out the vintage where the grapes of wrath are stored." The implication of this is that as injustice is building up and up, something is going to explode into violence.

The Grapes of Wrath is a crisis novel. It is Steinbeck's clear expression of sympathy with the dispossessed and the wretched. The Great Depression throws the country into abject chaos and makes life intolerable for the luckless millions. One of the worst stricken areas is the central prairie lands. There the farmers become bankrupt and begin to move in a body toward California, where they hope to have a better life. The westering is a most tragic and brutalizing human experience for families like the Joads. There is unspeakable pain and suffering on the road, and death occurs frequently. Everywhere they travel, they see a universal landscape of decay and desolation. When they reach California and try to settle down, they meet with bitter resistance from the local landowners.

Iniquity is widespread and wrath is about to overwhelm patience. The prophecy of an imminent explosion is sent forth from the anger-saturated pages: "When a majority of the people are hungry and cold they will take by force what they need," Steinbeck is saying. "Burn coffee for fuel in the ships. Burn corn to keep warm, it makes a hot fire …. Slaughter the pigs and bury them, and let the putrescence drip down into the earth." But Steinbeck then says, "There is a crime here that goes beyond denunciation." The day of wrath is coming. In the souls of the people the grapes of wrath are filling and growing heavy. Something in the nature of a social revolution would be imminent, the book is in effect saying, if nothing is done to stop the detonation. This is perhaps one of the reasons why the book was for many years banned.

Structurally, *The Grapes of Wrath* consists of two blocks of material: the westward trek of the Joads and the dispossessed Oklahomans, and the general picture of the Great Depression (as drawn in the intercalary chapters). The intercalary chapters, dispersed in between others, offer the social and historical background against which the characters move.[9] These include such as the appalling description of drought at the beginning of the book, the dismal look of Highway 66, the chapters dealing with migrant life, and the last intercalary chapter describing the rain in which the action of the novel ends. These illustrate the inherent unity of the novel.

As some critics have noted, the novel consists of three sections which correspond to "The Exodus" story in the Old Testament. The 30 chapters of the novel fall neatly into three sections: the description of the drought in the first ten, the journeying in chapters 13 through 18, and the remaining 12 devoted to a narrative of the life of the migrants in California. The Exodus tells a story about the Jews. It is also a tripartite story: escaping from the slavery of the Egyptian Pharaoh, traveling through the desert toward Canaan, and meeting with bitter resistance there. *The Grapes of Wrath*, in emphasizing the fact of the Oklahomans coming from the Oklahoma desert, crossing the big Death Valley desert and into California, the land of hope for them, works out the parallel to "the Exodus" admirably well.

The structural similarity is supported by symbols such as that of the grapes. For instance, there is mention of grapes in such *Bible* books as "Deuteronomy (XXXII, 32), "Jeremiad" (XXXI, 29), and "the Revelation." And the fact that Rose of Sharon gives milk to the dying old man, that Ma Joad always says, "We are the people" (meaning "God's chosen people"), and uncle John, placing Rose of Sharon's stillborn child in an old box and setting it in a stream among the willow stems, murmurs, "Go down an' tell 'em" (a very strong reminder of the birth and the mission of Moses). All these are but some of the many details illustrating biblical influence over the novel.

The reading of *The Grapes of Wrath* can be a very odd experience. One sees the Depression spreading devastation and desolation, the dispossessed and the wretched walking the earth like so many condemned souls in Hell, and the worst of human nature in its uncontrolled and uncontrollable manifestations. One senses despair as one reads along, and sees no prospect of compensation for all this earthly suffering until one reaches the last chapter of the book. There, in the only sensible thing that the silly Rose of Sharon does, one sees a gleam of hope, and one's confidence in man and human nature, the belief that a better life will be possible, returns. Here lies, probably, the distinction which tells Steinbeck apart from the other crisis writers of the 1930s. Amid the gloom and the defeatism which pervade the writings of the decade, Steinbeck manages to keep a refreshing faith in humanity, in the future when man will come to grips with his problems and come out all right. This ability to see beyond the immediate present into a better future has proved to be one of the things that have given Steinbeck his claim to fame and permanence.

Chapter 18 Porter • Welty • McCullers • West • The New Criticism

Katherine Anne Porter (1890-1980)

Porter was basically a short story writer. Her famous short fiction includes "The Flowering Judas" and "The Jilting of Granny Weatherall," both collected in *Flowering Judas* (1930), and makes her one of the finest short story writers of her century. Her *Pale Horse, Pale Rider* (1939) and *Leaning Tower and Other Stories* (1944) reinforced her reputation.[1] She was probably not as good at a sustained creative effort. Her one novel, *Ship of Fools*, which she began in the 1930s, came out at long last in 1962 as "one of the publishing events of all time." But it has not stood the test of time well. She is today mainly remembered for her famous short stories. Her *Collected Stories* (1965) won her both a Pulitzer Prize and a National Book Award. Her short fiction has been well anthologized and offered as "standard fare" for college classroom instruction.

Her *Ship of Fools* was based on her first voyage from Mexico to Europe in 1931. She took notes of her experience on the trip and began the long process of conceiving and writing the novel. She declared that her novel was concerned with the downhill drag of western civilization. The title is a translation of the German of Sebastian Brant's *Das Narrenschiff* which Porter read in 1932 immediately after her voyage. Sebastian Brant, a 15th-century savant with deep religious convictions and highest motives, was a satirist of human follies. So was Porter in her *Ship of Fools*, with this difference that she made it clear in her prefatory note to the novel that she was a passenger on that ship herself.

The novel consists of three parts, "Embarkation," "High Sea," and "The

Harbours." The first of these introduces the passengers. Here on board the German *Vera* is a rich assortment of people, the Germans, some Spaniards, Swiss, Mexicans, Americans, Cubans, and one Swede. In age there are little kids of six to eight years old or younger, single boys and girls, the newly wed on honeymoon, the middle-aged, and the dying old. In terms of human emotions and experiences there are exhibited the whole spectrum of emotions such as love and hate, snobbery and apathy, envy and jealousy, and the whole gamut of possible occurrences like violence and murder, incest and prostitution, theft and deception, personal incompatibility, and religious bigotry. Porter sees in the *Vera* the "universal image of the ship of this world on its voyage to eternity." It is meant as a metaphor for the macrocosmic human world.

The novel is supposed to tell the truth about man and his life. And the truth as is revealed here is disconcertingly depressing. Man is portrayed with his foibles and failings that make him out as an arrant fool. Human behavior is generally so disgusting, there is so much evil in human nature, life is so sad and lonely and sickening that it is not quite worth living. They voyage toward a place waiting dark and cold for them. One reads the book and comes away with the impression that misanthropy is justifiable.

One of Porter's oft-anthologized short stories is "The Jilting of Granny Weatherall." This was written in the stream of consciousness manner. Ellen (or Granny) Weatherall, the protagonist of the story, now eighty years old, is dying. On this last day of her life, her mind is busy shuttling back and forth between now and the past, trying to look for an answer to the puzzle that has bothered her all her life. When she was young and ready to get married, her fiancé, George, did not appear at the alter. However, she moved on and got married to John. They had five fine children together, but John died young, leaving Ellen to shift for herself all alone. The strong and able Ellen did all the hard work, brought up the children well, and had a meaningful life. She has managed to weather through it all. She has proved herself a truly wonderful and admirable woman.

Now that her end has come, she is not ready to die. Something that has gnawed at her soul all along at the bottom of her being now surfaces in her last-moment reminiscences. She would find George and tell him that she has had a good life despite his jilting of her. It is evident that she has all through the decades not forgotten George; nor has she forgiven him for the havoc he has wreaked with her life. She would like to have her vengeance on him by telling him about the wonderful life she has had. As she does not forgive, she has a quarrel with her God. So, as goes with Christian teachings, she is not forgiven. The end of the story shows that she is doomed to go down to Hell.

Granny Weatherall is a tragic heroine. Her flaw may be twofold: her un-forgiveness, and the fact that she is a one-man's woman. She loves George and has never stopped doing so, which means that she has not been emotionally loyal to her husband John. It is not fair to John. This could have been a reason for her gloomy end. "The Jilting of Granny Weatherall" is a rich and complex story, and as such it is capable of more than one interpretation. It reveals the exquisiteness of Porter's artistic imagination.

Eudora Welty (1909-2001)

Welty was born and raised in Jackson, Mississippi. She was well educated and had wide contact with life and people. Since the publication of her first story, "Death of a Traveling Salesman" in 1936 (which made her immediately famous), she had been very productive up to her death, writing short stories, novellas, and novels and winning awards including the Pulitzer Prize. She has been well known for her achievement in writing short stories.[2]

Welty emphasizes the importance of place for literary creations. In her essay "Place in Fiction" (1956), she observes clearly that "place" serves as a repository for the feelings of authors, makes them pay attention to detail and portray things with clarity, and prepares them to see through things. She feels that art that speaks most clearly, explicitly, directly, and passionately from its place of origin will remain the longest understood. She is noted for her fidelity to her place, the

American south, but manages to reach out to her readers on a more universal plane.

Welty's major themes relate to traditional southern family relationships. Her focus is not so much on describing the vicissitudes of family fortunes as on the exploration of the inner world of her characters, their interactions, and the power of love. Her characters range from aristocrats to farmers, who come forth with their interior monologues and reveal the emotional tenor of their lives. These people engage in self-searching, and look for meaning in their existence. Her most famous story, "Death of a Traveling Salesman" is a good example.

"Death of a Traveling Salesman" dramatizes the importance of family. R. J. Bowman is a shoe salesman who travels all year round in order to make a living. He does not know what it feels like to have a family. Now sick and weak, he drags himself out along and seeks help from a farmer when bogged down in an accident. Here he is very moved to see a happy family scene where the farmer and his wife live happily, expecting the birth of their baby. He feels sad and sorry for himself. He is sick and lonely, craving love and warmth but having none. He dies on a long night road stretching before him.

Here Welty offers a picture of alienation through her portrait of Bowman. Cut off from the rest of the world, Bowman lives a loveless, meaningless life with no sense of belonging whatever. In contrast, the farmer and his wife enjoy mutual love and trust and make the best of what they have got. They are poor, but they think positive, and act positive, and always have something good to look forward to. They illustrate the kind of harmony absent from the bleak existence of the salesman, the harmony of the inner with the external world, and of reason with emotion.

Welty's other works such as "A Worn Path," "Why I Live at the P.O.," "Lily Draw and the Three Ladies," "The Key," "The Whistle," or "Flowers for Marjorie," and so many other good stories all show the author's obsession with family, love, and human fellowship. Welty's preoccupation with family life is well exhibited in her novel, *Delta Wedding* (1946) as well.

Carson McCullers (1917-1967) [3]

McCullers was born in Columbus, Georgia. She was well read and attended fiction-writing classes at Columbia University. When her first novel, *The Heart Is a Lonely Hunter*, came out in 1940, her successful career began. She wrote some bestsellers, became rich and famous, suffered emotional upheavals, and died at 50. She wrote many good works such as *The Ballad of the Sad Café* (1943).

McCullers has a Gothic vision of life which her friend Tennessee Williams called the "sense of the awful." Some people, she seemed to think, are meant to live lives of horror and alienation. These mostly physical and spiritual freaks exist to represent forces that can make life miserable. It was the grotesque, the freakish, and the incongruous of the human condition that caught her attention. It was the lonely and the outcast, the sense of not belonging, that became the focus of her fiction. Love is important, but it brings with it insoluble problems that cause pain or even death. McCullers' fictional world is inhabited by hunchbacks, deaf mutes, or adolescents who find it hard to love and live normal lives. Many of them are bisexual or asexual.

The Ballad of the Sad Café is one of her well-known works. The love and pain theme runs through the whole story. The owner of the small town café, Amelia Evans, a girl of nineteen, is married with a man, Marvin Macy by name, who is said to have killed a man and still carry the victim's dry salted ear around. Having found this ghastly possession on him on the wedding night, Amelia drives Marvin out, who then runs away, robs some stores and serves time in prison, and returns in the end to avenge himself. While he is away, a hunchbacked cousin, Lyman Willis by name, shows up and somehow arouses the love latent in the still virgin Amelia. The café changes, so does her life. Then Marvin resurfaces and somehow arouses the love latent in Lyman. The hunchback then follows him around like a dog and even invites him to stay with him on Amelia's premises. The stage is thus set for the showdown between Marvin and Amelia, and Marvin wins only with the help of the hunchback. The café and Amelia are both devastated, and so is the town. Marvin and Lyman vanish.

The agony and the violence would not make sense if McCullers' characters were not understood in her way. McCullers makes it clear in the middle of section two of the three-part story that love is doomed to bring pain to the two parties involved because the conflict between them is insoluble. The lover and the beloved experience the relationship differently so that hate inevitably occurs. It is this feeling that would lead to violence, suffering, and death. The love-hate complex exists here in all the three love relationships, with Lyman epitomizing the author's notion of love.

McCullers was versatile and productive. Although sick most of her adult life, she wrote novels, novellas, short stories, and a play. She was an admirable writer.

Nathanael West (1903-1940)

An important figure to appear in the 1930s was Nathanael West, who tried to adapt European avant-gardism to American writing. Born into a wealthy New York family, Nathanael West was well read in world classics. In the mid-1920s he went to Paris where he made the acquaintance with modernist writers such as Gertrude Stein, Pound, T. S. Eliot, and James Joyce. He became one of the young expatriate writers there, exposed to the influence of French symbolism, aestheticism, and surrealism. In the Depression of the 1930s, West had contact with the writers on the left and expressed support for the Spanish people in their fight against Fascism. West died in an automobile accident in 1940.

West wrote quite a few unique novels. These include *The Dream Life of Balso Snell* (1931), *Miss Lonelyhearts* (1933), *A Cool Million: The Dismantling of Lemuel Pitkin* (1934), and *The Day of the Locust* (1939). He thought he wrote "moral satires," but there are signs of visible immorality and spiritual decay there (as W. H. Auden sees it). Reading West, one gets the impression that he delights enormously in scandalizing his readers. His subjects often involve violence of a brutalizing kind, his narratives are presented in a surrealist manner, and his characters are grotesque and dehumanized. His bleak and absurd vision comes through well in his works. He is seen as a predecessor to the American novelists of the absurd in the 1960s.[4]

Whereas he was little known when alive, he has received good posthumous critical attention. His belated recognition came in the postwar years when there appeared an enormous interest in his works. *The Complete Works of Nathanael West* came out in 1951, and he was profusely commented upon. In recent decades West's avant-gardist techniques intrigued the curious younger generation. His influence on later writers has been given sufficient credit. Carson McCullers, Flannery O'Connor, Joseph Heller, Saul Bellow, Thomas Pynchon, Ralph Ellison, and Ishmael Reed are all found to be in one way or another indebted to him.

West has been regarded as one of the best writers to come out of the 1930s and the first important postwar novelist.

The New Criticism

The New Criticism as a school of poetry and criticism established itself in the 1940s as an academic orthodoxy in the United States. It is still very much in evidence today as an influence in the literary world and in college classroom instruction. The school had its beginnings in the 1920s, took over 20 years to win acceptance and some dominance in poetry writing and criticism in the 1930s and 1940s, and aroused reaction and rebellion in the 1950s and 1960s when it gradually ceased to be a school.[5]

The New Criticism first emerged as a reaction against the then prevailing time-honored critical tendency to focus attention on the theme rather than the form of a work. The "old" critics often demanded a literary work, such as a poem, to be what it is not, and to do a job it may not be meant to do. For instance, with the "old" critics, a discussion of a poem often, if not always, focused on the life and times of the poet and seldom if ever got to the poem itself. There is an obvious overemphasis on the ethical, sociological, psychological or political point of view involved in the analysis of a poem. In the 1920s, some critics, later known as the New Critics, appeared to voice their ideas on the subject. These critics included people like T. S. Eliot, I. A. Richards, John Crowe Ransom, Allen Tate, Robert Penn Warren, William Empson, R. P. Blackmur, and Yvor Winters. They felt that a poem is first and foremost a poem, and that the job of the critic is to evaluate it on its own merits, and not in terms of the external factors such as its social, cultural, political background and possible biographical information. The critic should first find out the formal aspects of the poem's verbal structure, and the text should be the focus of critical reading and analysis.

The new idea caught on and something like a movement was afoot. In fact it was not a movement as organized as movements should be, but the convergence of similar voices and the echoes that it awoke in the young generation of the 1930s and 1940s made it look like one. And John Crowe Ransom's book, *The New Criticism* (1941), promoted the notion that there *was* such a movement in history and gave it its final historic name. It was, more accurately, a school of thought that dominated American literary criticism for over two decades. It is good to note here that, from the very outset, the New Criticism has exhibited one salient feature, i.e. it has tended to divorce criticism from social and moral concerns.

The New Criticism dates back to the 1920s. In the High Modernism of the 1920s, new developments on the literary scene proved conducive to the emergence of the New Criticism. T. S. Eliot's theories of "impersonality" and "objective correlative," I. A. Richards' ideas that more attention should be paid to the works than to the "periods" and the authors in literary criticism, and Samuel Taylor Coleridge's critical theories that emphasized the multiplicity and diversity of a work and the close reading of the text—all these made the New

Critical theories popular.

The new theory received further impetus in the 1930s when famous critics such as F. R. Leavis, R. P. Blackmur, Yvor Winters, and John Crowe Ransom chimed in. Robert Penn Warren and Cleanth Brooks edited and published a textbook, *Understanding Poetry* (1938), which explained the features of the New Critical poem and pushed the new theory into the college classroom. In addition, some literary magazines played a significant role in spreading the tenets of the New Criticism. These includes T. S. Eliot's *The Criterion* (1922-1939), Leavis' *Scrutiny* (1932-1953), Cleanth Brooks and Robert Penn Warren's *Southern Review* (1935-1942), John Crowe Ransom's *Kenyon Review* (1938-1959), and Allen Tate's *Sewanee Review*. "The Southern Critics," or the Fugitives, continued all through the 1930s and the 1940s to write and publish to support the new school of poetry and criticism and help build the New Critical theories into a coherent system.

To sum up, as a school of formalist criticism, the New Criticism focuses on the analysis of the text rather than pay attention to external elements such as its social background, its author's intention and political attitude, and its impact on society. It explores the artistic structure of the work rather than its author's frame of mind or its readers' responses. It also sees a literary work as an organic entity, the unity of content and form, and places emphasis on the close reading of the text.

Regarding the major features of the New Critical poem, it kept the basic Modernist values such as economy, wit, irony, impersonality, and careful with form, but abandoned or toned down other High Modernist features such as extreme fragmentation, paratactic syntax, ellipsis, symbolism and myth, cross-culturalism, and allusions. As a result it became cautious and traditional, and less revolutionary and disorienting, and was more amenable to all tastes and more popular with the rising younger generation of the 1940s. In literary creation, attention was paid to the poem as a well-wrought urn, with its coherent form, coherent images and figures, rhymes and stanzas, impersonality, and integrated attitude and vision. The new mode of writing soon caught on. It proved to be easier to compose. It is rational, witty, rigorous in meters and stanzas. In retrospect, it is necessary to mention that few masterpieces came out of it.

The New Criticism dominated literary criticism and poetry writing for well over two decades (right through the 1950s). A good number of writers, poets in particular, were brought up with the New Critical values, and their works formed an important part of the literary canon of contemporary American poetry. The New Criticism helped younger poets learn discreetly from the Modernist tradition, and integrate it with other traditions. When the wind of change and rebellion began to blow in the 1950s and 1960s, these young New Critical poets found it hard to adjust to the new postwar milieu. Robert Lowell was a good example. It took him almost a decade to switch to the new style in which he wrote his *Life Studies*. Others like Richard Wilbur, John Berryman, and James Merrill continued writing in traditional meters and stanzas. Elizabeth Bishop wrote both in traditional forms and free verse.

The New Criticism has been one of the many phases in the history of American literary criticism. Many poets began their careers by writing in its style and then stepped into the changed postwar postmodernist scene. It is still very much in evidence today as one critical concept and one mode of writing. This is testimony to its permanence in literary history.

Chapter 19   American Drama

American drama made its appearance in the late 19th century. Some playwrights did the spadework for the rise of American drama in the 1920s. There were, for instance, William Vaughn Moody (1869-1910), who made his tentative attempt to place realistic drama on the stage, and Eugene Walter (1874-1941) and Percy Mackaye (1875-1956), who carried out experimentation around the turn of the century.

This was an exciting time for American drama. Experimental theaters sprang up, the works of European dramatists like Ibsen, Strindberg, and George Bernard Shaw appeared on the stage, and modern American dramatists began to attract attention. The Theater Guild produced Elmer Rice's *The Adding Machine*, and Eugene O'Neill's *Beyond the Horizon* was performed on Broadway. These, together with Maxwell Andersen's *What Price Glory?*, George Kelley's *The Show-Off* and Sidney Howard's *They Knew What They Wanted*, made American drama a significant part of American literature in the 1920s.

The theater of the Depression was not depressing. Like other branches of literature of the time, it was preoccupied with social concerns. In addition to O'Neill and Maxwell Anderson, Clifford Odets with his *Waiting for Lefty* and the dramatization of Steinbeck's *Of Mice and Men* captivated large audiences. All through the 1940s and the post-war period, new playwrights and new plays kept appearing. If Eugene O'Neill dominated the theater in the 1920s, then Tennessee Williams did so in the post-war years. The staging of his *The Glass Menagerie* on Broadway in 1945 was an event of unusual significance, as it marked American drama's coming of age. Also active in the theater were Williams' contemporaries, Arthur Miller and William Inge. Miller's *Death of a Salesman* and Inge's plays of the early1950s touched the heart of the American audiences. The late 1950s saw a temporary decline in dramatic productions, but in the next decade, with Edward Albee, Arthur Kopit, David Mamet and Sam Shepard active on the scene, American drama picked up a good deal of fresh energy. Edward Albee's absurdist dramas pushed American drama into a new phase. With the passage of time there has appeared the increasingly more obvious tendency to "decentralize" from Broadway, with more and more plays staged Off-Broadway and Off-Off-Broadway.

From the end of the 1960s, American theater entered a new period in its development when diversity became one of its salient features. New voices are heard. The theatrical canon called for redefining. The multiracial and multiethnic playwrights such as August Wilson, Hanay Geiogamah, David Henry Hwang, and Luis Valdez, and the feminist playwrights like Beth Hanley, Marsha Norman, and Tina Howe all tried to place their best works on the stage. Since the 1980s, many good plays by many good playwrights have appeared. These include such authors as Doug Wright, John Patrick Shanley, Margaret Edson, Rajiv Joseph, Tracy Letts, Laurence Yep, David Hwang, Tony Kushner, and Amy Herzog. The period is still in progress, and reputations are still being made. This, then, is a sketchy overview of American drama.[1]

Eugene O'Neill (1888-1953)

We begin with Eugene O'Neill, America's greatest playwright.[2] With his father, James O'Neill, being a famous actor, love of drama ran in the blood of the man. It was some years yet before he became a mature playwright, but those years of knocking about in the world prepared him well for the vocation which he was to take. O'Neill traveled around with his father's group and took a year in Princeton, from which he was expelled because of misbehavior. He went to sea and voyaged to South America and South Africa. Back in America, he was out of work. He made friends with the lowest of society and got to know life better. The experience of wandering and loafing about stood O'Neill in good stead. He drew very much from it in his creative work.

The most decisive period in his career came in the winter of 1912-13 when he developed tuberculosis and was sent to a sanitarium. For the first time in his life he had the leisure to read and meditate. He read widely in the world's dramatic literature, and became infatuated with the works of Ibsen and Strindberg. The imitativeness of the American theater of the time, with its performances at once melodramatic and divorced from reality, disgusted young O'Neill, so that he began to think seriously of breaking new ground. After he recovered from tuberculosis, he joined, some time in 1914, the famous Professor Pierce Baker's 47 Workshop at Harvard to learn to write better. After that, he lived in Greenwich Village, New York, where he began to write. The summer of 1916 proved to be significant both for O'Neill and for American drama: the Provincetown Players produced O'Neill's first performed play, the one-act *Bound East for Cardiff.* The event marked the beginning of O'Neill's long and successful dramatic career and ushered in the modern era of the American theater. Thereafter the road to Broadway was smooth for the rising star.

There he "arrived" in 1920 with his *Beyond the Horizon.* The response was universal acclaim, and for the next fourteen years he stayed on Broadway. After *Beyond the Horizon,* a series of theatrical triumphs followed in fairly quick succession: *The Emperor Jones* (1920), *Anna Christie* (1921), *The Hairy Ape* (1922), *Desire under the Elms* (1924), *All God's Chillun Got Wings* (1924), *The Great God Brown* (1926), *Lazarus Laughed* (1926), *Strange Interlude* (1928), *Marco Millions* (1928), *Dynamo* (1929), *Mourning Becomes Electra* (1931), *Ah, Wilderness* (1933), and *Days without End* (1934). Then between 1934 and 1946 a period of silence intervened in which O'Neill suffered from ill health but planned new plays. When he came back to Broadway he brought with him *The Iceman Cometh* (1946), with which he began the last and best phase of his career. Plays staged in this period included the superb *Long Day's Journey into Night* (1956), *A Moon for the Misbegotten* (1957), and *A Touch of the Poet* (1958), all of which were performed after his death in 1953. O'Neill was a prize-winning playwright. He received the Pulitzer Prize for his *Beyond the Horizon* and *Anna Christie* between 1920 and 1922, and the Nobel Prize in 1936.

O'Neill was always active and dynamic. If the reputation of other playwrights have followed the pattern of a rise and fall, that of O'Neill has remained enduring. The magic of his power lies in his never ceasing attempt to improve his art in step with the spirit of the times. We notice that O'Neill began writing in a naturalistic vein, as is evident in his plays like *The Hairy Ape, Beyond the Horizon*, and *Anna Christie*. Then, inspired by the prevailing zest for experimentation, he moved on into a phase of obsession with symbolism and expressionism. *The Emperor Jones* is a good example. During the 1940s O'Neill turned back to the naturalistic spirit in which he wrote some of his best works like *Long Day's Journey into Night.* Thus in a sense, his career came full circle.

O'Neill was a sensitive artist. He felt "the discordant, broken, faithless rhythm" of his time and tried to "get at the root" of human desires and frustrations. The tragic sense of modern man being helpless and impotent remained with O'Neill all through his career. *The Hairy Ape* is a good illustration. It is about the problem of modern man's sense of "belonging." A stoker on a luxury liner, "Yank" by name, is happy with life until the day when he is forced to realize that he does not "belong" anywhere. He is disconcerted, becomes violent, and is even rejected by the radical workers. In his quest for self-identity, he wanders to the zoo where he finds affinity with the great ape there. He goes over to it and finds its outstretched arms lovely and fascinating: "Come on, Brother," he calls out to the gorilla, holds out his hand and invites the gorilla to shake it. Then something happens and the gorilla looks enraged. It wraps its arms around Yank. A cracking snap of crushed ribs is heard with a gasping cry. Then Yank makes to the pathetic realization that he even does not quite belong among the hairy apes. Thus crushed in the embrace of the gorilla, he dies, without ever finding his place of "belonging." The general feeling is one of total despair: Man is rootless in an indifferent and impersonal universe.

By far the best works which O'Neill ever wrote are *The Iceman Cometh* and

Long Day's Journey into Night. They represent the fact that O'Neill's lifelong quest for values ended in failure. If his earlier frustrated characters manage to retain some faith in life, then the group of misfits in *The Iceman Cometh* and the Tyrone family in *Long Day's Journey into Night* have nothing but the night stretching before them. The mood of sheer despair that pervades these plays indicates that any illusion O'Neill had cherished about life had evaporated completely. *The Iceman Cometh* offers an appalling description of the inner world of a group of people who fail to come to terms with life. Despite the fact that they come from different walks of life, there is one common denominator in their lives, that by the time they meet in a riverside bar, they have all begun to live on nothing but illusion. Afraid to face the life of the moment, they cast a backward glance at the past and brag about turning over a new leaf in life tomorrow. Though tomorrow never comes, they manage to derive from the idea a kind of courage with which to keep on living, for they all know that, as soon as that illusion vanishes, they would vanish, too, into night. They have escaped into the sanctuary of illusion, and the only way out of it is death. Nowhere else is the depth of despair in O'Neill revealed so unequivocally.

Long Day's Journey into Night is somewhat autobiographical. The Tyrones of the play are in fact modeled on the O'Neill family. The four major characters include James Tyrone, the father, a famous actor, anxious to become rich at the expense of his own talent; Mary Tyrone, the mother, a drug addict; Jamie Tyrone, their older son, and Edmund Tyrone, their younger son. The mother becomes mentally ill because she is extremely unhappy with her married life. Young Jamie loses faith in life, while Edmund the wanderer comes back with tuberculosis. All the four suffer frustrations and wish to escape from the harsh reality, James and Jamie looking for solace in their cups, while Mary and Edmund seek the protection of the fog which they hope would screen them from the intrusion of the world outside. They meet in the living room of the family's summer home at 8:30 A. M. of a day in August, 1912 and torment one another and themselves until midnight. The father is angry with the mother for her drug addiction, the mother with his sons for being good for nothing, and the sons with their parents for not being good parents. All are torn in a war between love and hate, and no one is sure which is the stronger emotion. Life is too painful for them even to try and make sense of it. Edmund's desperate advice in face of the horrible burden of Time weighing on people's shoulders and crushing them to the earth is to lose feeling in their cups and stay always drunk. Thus the long day journeys into night when the tragedy of the family is finally enacted. No relief is felt, no light is seen, and all ends in the engulfing darkness. In a figurative sense, *Long Day's Journey into Night* is a metaphor for O'Neill's lifelong endeavor to find truth and the way to acceptance. The former he found, namely, the faithless, fragmentary nature of modern life, whereas the latter he did not: for him all passed into night. In despair O'Neill thought of the old God of the Catholic church on which, it is ironic to note, he had turned his back long before.[3]

O'Neill was a tireless experimentalist in dramatic art. He took drama away from the old traditions of the 19th century and rooted it deeply in life. He seemed to agree with the early T. S. Eliot who felt that "the contemplation of the horrid or sordid or disgusting, by an artist, is the necessary and negative aspect of the impulse toward the pursuit of beauty," and saw beauty inhering in the ugly. The hollow romantic stories of heroes moving against a gorgeous background disgusted O'Neill, so that he introduced the realistic or even the naturalistic aspect of life into the American theater.

The stylistic aspect of O'Neill's art merits notice for its variety and its display of consummate craftsmanship. He borrowed freely from the best traditions of European drama, be it Greek tragedies, or the realism of Ibsen, or the expressionism of Strindberg, and fused them into the organic art of his own. He borrowed freely from modern literary techniques such as the stream-of-consciousness device with the help of which he managed to reveal the emotional and psychological complexities of modern man. And he made use of setting and stage property to help in his dramatic representation. O'Neill's ceaseless experimentation enriched American drama and influenced later playwrights such as Tennessee Williams, William Inge, and Edward Albee. It is possible that he will go down in the history of American drama as "the American Shakespeare."

Elmer Rice (1892-1967)

One of the most distinguished playwrights who remained in evidence for over four decades on the American stage was Elmer Rice, author of the well-known play, *The Adding Machine*. Elmer Rice was born in New York. He studied law at night school, but was resolved to be a dramatist. His career began in 1914 when his play, *On Trial*, was produced and became an immediate success. *On Trial* is a mystery play of victimization told through expressionist flashbacks. Rice's most influential years came in the 1920s. *The Adding Machine* was performed in 1923. It was Rice's masterpiece. Thematically it is a vehement protest against the dehumanizing effect of what T. S. Eliot termed a barbaric civilization, and thus placed its author immediately among the group of modern masters of the 1920s, along with T. S. Eliot, Pound, Williams, Stevens, Hemingway, Fitzgerald, Faulkner, and O'Neill. In technical terms it employs the expressionistic devices which also characterize the best work of Eugene O'Neill and Tennessee Williams. Rice's next success came in 1929, the year in which his *Street Scene* came out. A story of slum life, murder, and frustrated love, the play was made into a musical in 1947 by Langston Hughes and Kurt Weil. During the years that intervened between the two dates, Elmer Rice produced a series of plays which demonstrate both his range of subjects and competent artistry. These include *Left Bank* (1931), *Judgment Day* (1934), and *Dream Girl* (1945), the last being the most popular work since *Street Scene*. Rice's creativity slackened in the 1950s. Only *The Grand Tour* (1951) and *The Winner* (1954) were produced but were not well received. In 1962 he published his *Autobiography* which made a stir on the literary scene. Elmer Rice was also a novelist. *A Voyage Purilia* (1931), a Utopian satire, is the best of his fictions.

The Adding Machine

Now let us take a look at *The Adding Machine.* Mr. Zero has worked in a store for twenty-five years, doing the same job—adding figures—and is expecting a raise when his boss comes one day to tell him that he has to leave because the store has bought adding machines. The machine adds automatically. Even a high school girl can operate them to improve efficiency, economy, and business. A human will change from "antiquated adding machines" to "a superb, super-hyper-adding machine."

Zero is so angry that, in a sudden fit of exasperation, he kills his boss with a bill file. He is tried, and condemned to death. Zero dies, but it is not the end of his tragic story. He is to become a new superb, super-hyper Zero in the next world. There, the job he is assigned to do is still to operate an adding machine, only a bigger one this time. Later Zero is sent back to the human world to add figures again. He is made to believe that he has been through this process countless times and will continue to do so until his soul is thoroughly crushed. This indicates how modern mechanical civilization enslaves human souls over and over again.

The scathing irony of the play is obviously spearheaded toward the modern mechanical civilization. Machines turn people into non-humans. Men become numbered, Mr. One, Mr. Two … as if they were machines or machine parts. Zero is so dehumanized that he is almost devoid of emotional response. He becomes a mechanical imbecile. In his twenty-five years work adding figures, Mr. Zero never "missed a day, an hour, a minute." Now he can no longer think except in terms of figures. Even when defending himself in the courtroom, he cannot help dragging in figures. In the midst of confessing to the first degree murder that he has committed, he starts counting numbers from one to twelve, telling a puzzled audience that six and six makes twelve, and five is seventeen, and eight is twenty-five, and three is twenty-eight, etc. Then his mind switches back to the court proceedings, curses the figures, and says pathetically that he has worked for twenty-five years all for nothing. The human mind has been mechanized so thoroughly. That is probably the saddest part of his life as a modern man. There is a touch of pathos all through the play.

The play can be called a *tour-de-force* of Elmer Rice's. In addition to the flashback technique which helps to hold the interest of the audience by first withholding and then releasing information in an unexpected fashion, Elmer Rice made the best of every offstage effect of the theater such as sound and light. The murder scene is, for instance, rendered in such a way that a good deal is left to the imagination of the audience. Here a pantomime is going on. Mr. Zero and his boss are seen facing each other, motionless, except for the silent, incessant movement of the boss' jaws, indicating that they are talking with one another. The music keeps increasing in volume; the off-stage effects of the wind, the waves, the galloping horses, the locomotive whistling, the sleigh bells ringing, the automobile siren etc.—all these add to the tension that is building up. Then a peal of thunder is heard, and a flash of red is seen. Then all is blackness. The force of this expressionistic scene of Zero becoming a murderer does not show its dazzling effect on the perplexed audience until exactly a scene later when, into the mellowness of the quiet commonplace gossip of an evening party at the Zero's, policemen come and take the expectant Zero away to the amazement of the gaping guests.

The artistry of Elmer Rice is unique in its own way. Elmer Rice's permanence is illustrated by the fact that some of his works such as this play and *Street Scene* still possess a great appeal and awaken emotional responses in the audience today.

Susan Glaspell (1882-1948)

The early 1920s saw the upsurge of the women's liberation movement. The idea of asserting women's rights continued from the previous century with greater intensity. Feminist writings appeared also on the American stage. Susan Glaspell was a well-known feminist author of the time. She was inspired and influenced by such authors as Kate Chopin who challenged society and tradition, and became a strong and opinionated feminist. Glaspell was a founding member of Heterodoxy, a radical group of women activists prominent in the feminist movement of New York in the years 1910-1920.

Glaspell grew up in Iowa, and attended Drake University. In 1915 she founded with her husband the first influential noncommercial theater troupe in America—the Provincetown Players in Massachusetts and staged the earlier works of experimentalist drama by such authors as Eugene O'Neill. Probably mainly because of this, Glaspell has been regarded by some people as "mother of American drama." Later they moved the troupe to New York and renamed it The Playwrights' Theater. Glaspell was both a playwright and a novelist. Her plays included a pioneering feminist drama, *The Verge* (1921), and the Pulitzer Prize-winning *Alison's House* (1930). She wrote ten novels such as *Fidelity* (1915) and *The Morning Is Near Us* (1930).

Glaspell's one-act play, *Trifles*, is interesting not as a kind of detective story it resembles on surface, but as an important feminist work. Here a murder is committed. John Wright is strangled in his bed, and his wife Minnie Wright is detained as a suspect. George Henderson, the county attorney, comes along to investigate the case. Accompanying him on the scene are Henry Peters, the sheriff, Mrs. Peters, and the Hales, Lewis and his wife. What is ironic is that, while the men, especially the self-important county attorney, strut upstairs and down, and cudgel their brains looking for the required evidence for prosecution, the two women, who are supposed to take care of only trifles, move quietly around, find it, and decide to be silent about it so that their imprisoned sister could regain the freedom that in their opinion is hers.

The play derives its artistic energy from the three levels of tension subtly embedded in it. These include the tension between women vs. men, woman vs. woman, and woman vs. self. The first of these, the opposition between the two genders, is obvious to notice. The second is less evident as Mrs. Hale tactfully wins the sheriff's wife over to her side of the confrontation. The third level of tension is the least tangible: the two women both do some soul-searching and come to empathize with Minnie Wright and see her act of manslaughter as self-defense. The bird is her alter ego; her husband killing the bird is just like killing her soul.

Glaspell has contributed to the development of American drama as well as the growth of feminist awareness in America.

The Depression Period

The Depression was a period completely different from the 1920s. Such new ideas and new techniques appeared that they shook things up as nothing else had done before. The literary movements in the decade were all bound up in the social movement. For the only time in American history, writers met at a writers' congress to discuss what the function of writers should be when the country was in a crisis.

American drama, along with other literary genres and very much like them, became highly social-oriented and was produced to fulfill a clear social purpose. In 1931 actors, dramatists and producers formed their own organization, the Group Theater, to produce plays of social significance. After their first success on Broadway, *The House of Connelly* by Paul Green, the association offered 23 productions in those "fervent years," which included works by pre-eminent playwrights like Maxwell Anderson, John Howard Lawson, Sidney Kingsley, and Clifford Odets. The list of dramatists of importance in the decade is simply amazing: in addition to those mentioned above, there were Lilian Hellman (with her *The Children Hour* and *The Little Foxes*), Thornton Wilder (notably with his *Our Town*), William Saroyan, Robert Sherwood, George S. Kaufman (and his *The Fabulous Invalid*), and Richard Rogers, to name just a few out of a good many names and titles. These authors may have begun their careers earlier and continued their creativity well into the postwar period, and most of them may have written pieces which were, temporally and spatially too much products of their decade to stay vital and vibrant beyond it, but they surely all did their best to help address the problems with which their crisis-ridden country was then beset.

Clifford Odets (1906-1963)

Clifford Odets may not be the best craftsman of the group (as probably Maxwell Anderson was), but his ability to impress his audience was remarkable. He joined the Group Theater in 1930 and won recognition as one of the country's leading dramatists in 1935. This was the year in which he placed four plays on Broadway: *Waiting for Lefty*, *Till the Day I Die*, *Paradise Lost*, and *Awake and Sing!*. A period of over a decade followed in which plays such as *I Can't Sleep* (1936), *Golden Boy* (1937), *Rocket to the Moon* (1938), *Night Music* (1940), and *Clash by Night* (1941) appeared on stage. His other works include *The Big Knife* (1948), a first-rate play, *The Country Girl* (1950), and *The Flowering Peach* (1954).

A great play by Odets is *Waiting for Lefty*. It is about a taxi driver's strike. A union meeting is going on. While the drivers are trying to decide whether to go on a strike, the union boss, who has already sold out to the companies, is trying to keep them from striking. All the time people come up on the stage and tell their stories, the union boss is smoking a cigar. The smoke keeps drifting in, a telling symbol of the fact that he is the one who has got all the decisions to make.

Now Lefty is a character fighting against the corrupted union boss and trying to get the people to strike for higher wages. Throughout the play people are waiting for him before they make the final decision, but he never appears. In the meantime people keep talking about their bitter lives. Finally, there comes a shout from the back of the hall which interrupts everything. Somebody runs in and says, "Wait a minute! We've found Lefty! We found him in an alley with a bullet in his head!" The suggestion is clear, that the union boss has had him killed. The people run up on the stage and shout, "What are we going to do?" Somebody at the back of the audience shouts, "Strike! Strike!" and they pick this up on stage and join the chorus.

The interesting thing to note about the play is its acting. The actors are scattered through the audience and some of these people jump up now and then to echo in shouts what is being said on stage. It is very exciting to see one person next to you, who looks just like you, working himself up in agitation and presently standing up, shouting, "Listen! Listen!" and charging onto the stage: He is, you realize, one of the actors! The point of this arrangement was to include the audience in the acting, and its effect was powerful in the social theater of the 1930s. The audience joined the "chorus" and the whole theater was boiling. Propaganda it certainly is, but as certainly it is also exquisite art: The whole performance is a most ingenious combination of the two. And from the stories of the drivers we get very authentic details of life during the Depression. *Waiting for Lefty* is altogether a very powerful play to come out of the theater of the 1930s.

Awake and Sing is another fine work of Odets' which tells the story of a poor Jewish family. *Paradise Lost* relates the process of a middle-class family going from Depression degradation to social rebellion. Quite a few Odets plays concern the loneliness of modern life and the money-success theme in American society.

Postwar American Drama

Postwar American drama has been said to begin with the staging of *The Glass Menagerie* in 1945. Its author, Tennessee Williams (1911-1983), has certainly become one of the greatest American dramatists to go down in the country's literary history.[4]

Williams won a national drama award for a group of plays called *American Blues* in1939. His first play, *Battle of Angels* (1940), was such a fiasco that he did not surface again, until *The Glass Menagerie* was staged in 1945 and won him international recognition. After that, Williams kept writing at the rate of a play every two years, and enjoyed popularity all along except, perhaps, during the 1960s when there seemed to be a decline in his powers. But he managed to recover from it in the 1970s and has retained his hold on popular imagination ever since. Now universally accepted as one of America's classic playwrights, he is in evidence practically everywhere in the theaters of the nation. Williams was also a novelist and a poet. He wrote a novel, two volumes of poetry, six volumes of prose, and three collections of short stories.

Williams was a typical product of the post-O'Neill era. It is true that O'Neill led the American theater even in the postwar period, but the courageous endeavors of his generation made it possible for the public to accept new people like Williams, daring enough to deal with themes such as violence, sex, and homosexuality on the stage. Williams was thematically rather sensational. *A Streetcar Named Desire* (1947), a Pulitzer Prize-winning play, introduces both violence and sexual abnormality. The sexual emphasis of *Summer and Smoke* (1948) is self-evident. *The Rose Tattoo* (1951) presents a picture of depravity. *Cat on a Hot Tin Roof* (1955), another Pulitzer Prize-winning play, is in a way an amalgam of the Williamsian themes, and *Suddenly Last Summer* (1958) deals rather plainly with homosexuality. Williams' other plays include *Sweet Bird of Youth* (1959), *Period of Adjustment* (1960), *Night of the Iguana* (1961), one of his best works, *The Milk Train Does Not Stop Here Anymore* (1963), *Red Battery Sign* (1975), and *Vieux Carre* (1977) .

The Glass Menagerie

When it was first produced in New York City in 1945, *The Glass Menagerie* won immediate critical acclaim and received the New York Drama Critics Circle

Prize as the best play of the year. It is a pathetic story of a family, the Wingfields, whose major problem is existential both physically and spiritually. The world in which the family tries to survive is an impossible one. The main conflict centers on the mother's anxiety to marry off her physically disabled daughter, but other problems of an equally harassing nature exist to intensify it.

Life as a Prison

First, life as depicted in the play is a prison. There are two kinds of prisons: the world is a prison, and the self is a prison, too. The world of the major characters is delineated clearly as a prison at the beginning of the play:

> The Wingfield apartment is in the rear of the building, one of those vast hive-like conglomerations of cellular living units that flower as warty growths in the overcrowded urban centers of lower-middle class population and are symptomatic of the impulse of this largest and fundamentally enslaved section of American society to avoid fluidity and differentiation and to exist and function as one interfused mass of automation.

The image of the prison is apparent here.

In addition, the self, or memory, is a prison, too. As the narrator says, this is "a memory play." Take Tom for an example. His closing speech at the end of the play is a good explanation. He travels around the world but always feels pursued by something. He discovers eventually that it is his memory of his crippled sister that keeps harassing him:

> Then all at once my sister touches my shoulder. I turn around and look into her eyes …. Oh, Laura, Laura, I tried to leave you behind me, but I am more faithful than I intended to be.

Tom cannot flee from the prison of his own mind.

The Suffering Family

None of the members of the family is free from suffering. Mother Amanda is worried about the future of her two children, Tom and Laura. She is worried that Tom, a worker in a warehouse but dabbling in poetry, might become a drunkard, might smoke too much and become a good-for-nothing, so that she might lose her bread-earner. Amanda cannot rest in peace whenever she thinks of her daughter, Laura, a girl of 24, sensitive and lovely though slightly crippled; she often envisions her as an old maid left uncared for after she is gone.

Tom's acute mental suffering is best illustrated by his restlessness and his obsession with the idea of moving on from the humdrum life of a dull warehouse.

As to Laura, she is the archetypal Williamsian heroine, lonely and vulnerable, completely withdrawn into herself and trying to live in the world which she constructs to ward off the intrusions of a painful existence.

The Escapist Family

Living in a "mysterious universe" where there is only "everlasting darkness," all three try to escape from reality (think of "the fire-escape" from the apartment!). The play offers three kinds of escape for the suffering people: space, imagination, and time.

Tom escapes into space. He first runs away into the exciting world of the movies where he enjoys a vicarious experience of adventure, and eventually runs away from home as a merchant seaman into the wide world.

Laura escapes into her imagination. She runs into the world of her collection of glass animals, all as fragile and vulnerable as herself, in which she perceives an ideal order of everyone seeming "to get along nicely together." There is peace and harmony, but no discrimination against anything different (such as the one-horned unicorn with which she identifies herself), no competition, and no painful change.

Mother Amanda escapes into time. She derives her courage to live on from her dreams of past happiness and from her uncertain expectation of a happy future for both her children. Her groans can be very pathetic and touching: "Gone,

gone, gone. All vestiges of gracious living! Gone completely!" And she finds immense consolation in reading *Gone with the Wind*.

The End of Illusions

Although escape can offer temporary relief, people have to come back and face life. That is when and where Jim O'Connor kicks in. He comes on the scene as a reality check for everybody. A man of common sense, he brings the illusory worlds of the Wingfields to an end, and helps them see the need to address their problems instead of living in illusions.

The end of the play is not unredeemed despair. Illusions are shattered and there is despair and desolation, but the courageous mother comforts a badly hurt Laura with "dignity and tragic beauty." Toward the end of the play, Amanda says goodbye to her escapist husband's picture, and Laura lifts her hidden face to smile at her mother. She has "blown out" her candles of false hope. Illusion goes. Mother and daughter straighten up to face life.

A Typical Willliams Play

The Glass Menagerie is a typical Williams play in that here is a lonely vulnerable woman living in her illusion, which is smashed to pieces by a male intruder, who is the embodiment of reality. The whole performance is pointed against modern civilization which blasts happiness out of human existence.

The circular structure of the play is interesting to note. It begins with the image of the world as prison, and it ends with the self as prison. Complete freedom is impossible. People may find different kinds of glass menageries, but escape is not the answer to their problem. They have to "participate," which is the major mode of human existence.

Arthur Miller (1915-2005)

Another great dramatist to come out of the 1940s is Arthur Miller who has, along with Tennessee Williams, led the postwar new drama.[5] Miller grew up in the Depression. He witnessed his father's business failure and worked at a variety of proletarian jobs. His first important work, *All My Sons* (1947), did a good deal in fostering his reputation as an Ibsenian playwright. The staging of *Death of a Salesman* (1947), his masterpiece, won him the Tony Award and the Pulitzer Prize, and established him once and for all as a writer of no small talent. With *The Crucible* (1953) and *A View from the Bridge* (1955) placed on Broadway, Miller became a name forever linked with Tennessee Williams and, further back, with Eugene O'Neill. In 1965 he was elected the first American president of the international P. E. N. (International Association of Poets, Playwrights, Editors, Essayists, and Novelists).

Death of a Salesman

Arthur Miller is best known as author of *Death of a Salesman.* It is a sad version of the American dream. Willy Loman, the salesman of the title, lives in a rough world, but he keeps on dreaming of success and living in illusions and lies. He dreams of establishing his own business, and of a "big" future for his children who, however, inflated with his false praises and dreams, turn out to be good for nothing. Willy's kind of success is measured only in terms of dollars. The Lomans have "never told the truth for ten minutes" in their house. Willy has "the wrong dreams" all the time, develops the habit of talking to himself, and refuses to follow other people's advice. Even his house has "an air of the dream" about it.

Willy's Sad Life

Willy's dreaminess is a sure symptom of the insanity which is fast overtaking him. Willy's mind is falling apart under a pressure too much for it to bear. As he cannot think of his life in terms other than of worldly success, he is not mentally prepared for the tragedy which is befalling him. He cannot face the fact that, after working for the firm for over three decades and devoting the best of his mature life to its success, it now takes his salary away and refuses to accommodate him for 40 dollars a week. He cannot accept the fact that he has come full circle in his career, placed back on the road, once more working for commission as he did at the beginning of his business life, and that he is marginalized and fired by his boss in the end. He feels embittered. "Funny, y'know?" he thus says to Charley, his only friend. "After all the highways, and the trains, and the appointments, and the years, you end up worth more dead than alive." For the first time he thinks of death as a means of achieving success for his sons, if not for himself any more. He plans to stage an automobile accident so that, after he dies, his family would get twenty-thousand-dollar life insurance money. Thus the greatest tragedy of this "fine, troubled," "hard-working, unappreciated prince" dreams of vainglory in death after he fails to achieve it in life. So he is resolved to see his dream happen in the lives of his sons. In the end he drives himself into an accident and dies willingly. Willy never realizes that it is the system with its social problems that has made it impossible for him to be a good achiever, and that the American obsession with financial success has ruined him and people like him.

Willy's Self-searching

Now as the story goes, Willy is at the end of his tether. He has been contemplating suicide for some time, and feels that now the time has come for him to make the fatal decision. Before he takes that step, his mind is wild and busy sorting things out for himself. His mind keeps drifting into the past and feels pain and remorse. His reminiscences focus on two questions, the answers to which may justify his suicide. One of these concerns his own failure, and the other that of his two sons, especially Biff's, for whom he has had such great expectations and in whom he has invested so much. These questions have harassed him all his life.

Regarding his own problem, he feels that his life fails because he did not follow his older brother Ben into the jungle. Ben, now ten years dead, was a kind of pioneer like his father before him. He had ventured into the jungle at 17 and came out rich at 21. His pioneering spirit represented that of early American settlers. Willy recalled a tug of war between Ben and his wife Linda concerning his future. It occurred when Ben came for a visit and asked Willy to go with him to Alaska, but Linda wanted her family to work it out in the city. Standing in between the two, Willy finally chose to take his wife's advice and stayed in the city. Now in retrospect, Willy seems to feel sorry and subconsciously shift the blame on Linda for his failure. This is a wrong judgment.

Then for Biff's bumming around at the age 34, Willy has all along been in denial of his own share of responsibility. He loves his sons and tries to help them grow up as successful people. But his has been the wrong kind of education, inculcating his wrong kind of dream in them. Although he has always denied having any responsibility for Biff's failure, the issue has bugged him all the time and given him no peace. Then when deserted by his sons in a bar restroom, he recalled his affair with a Boston woman that Biff discovered by accident. Willy did not know how it thoroughly disgusted and frustrated Biff. The boy had loved and admired his father so much. When Biff saw his idol together with the woman in a Boston hotel room, the once promising high school basketball team captain with three colleges open to him lost his faith in life totally, and gave up his plan for a higher education. Instead, for well over the next ten years, he left home and bummed around. So Willy is in part to blame for his son's failure, but only in part. A grown-up Biff should take the most part of his failure. That Willy willingly takes the whole of it and decides to die for redemption is another of his wrong judgment.

Willy is not a perceptive person. First, the decision to stay on in the city is in the final analysis his decision. Linda, a loving, caring, and protective wife, has only offered her advice, and Willy has been the decision-maker. As to Biff's life, Willy may be accountable for its bad start, and his wrong education of his false dream of success in the city does have a negative impact on Biff's life, but Biff should have been able to bring his own life back on track after he comes of age. It would be inappropriate for Willy to think that he has ruined his son's life.

Here it is good to talk about Biff a little. A poet in temperament, the young man loves nature. He is excited to talk about the spring on a farm or a calf being born. He hates the working environment in the city. But his father's dream influences him so much that he can never settle on a farm and feel happy as his father's expectations keep fighting with his own dream in his mind. He keeps coming back home and hopes to give an account of himself to his father with whom he has been long at loggerheads. That is why they expect to see each other, but as soon as they meet, they begin to fight, and why at their last meeting, Biff asks his father to let him go, which means "let him go of his kind of dream."

Technique of the Play

The technique of the play is interesting to talk about. Willy's life and career is covered by flashbacks (in the form of stream of consciousness), and its time frame is just about one day, Willy Loman's last day of life. It begins in the wee hours of one day and ends in those of the next, about 24 hours altogether.

The characterization of the play is interesting to talk about as well. Willy's personality is portrayed and projected through other characters in the play. Willy stands in the center like a sun and all the other characters rove around him like so many stars, each of them representing a different facet of Willy's personality. Willy's is basically a "split personality." He finds it hard to choose between Linda's settled city lifestyle and Ben's adventurous pioneering. Ben features as his alter ego and his conscience in addition to being his role model, and Linda representing his love of the city and its settled spirit. So part of him loves city life well enough to stay put there, and part of him adores Ben well enough to go with him into the unknown. Here lies the line where the characters "take sides." Linda and Happy are clearly the city type, Ben and Biff (who loves nature) possess the pioneering spirit, whereas Charley symbolizes his ideal of self-employed-business success. Bernard serves as a painful reminder of Biff and his failure, and the Boston woman a continuous sense of guilt. There is also Howard, Willy's boss, who incarnates the callousness, the inhumanity, and the brutality of the social system itself.

A Symbol of Newness

When *Death of a Salesman* was first produced there was a tremendous feeling of newness. What Miller did was to wipe out the old realistic stage setting and go back to the Elizabethan kind of stage where the audience saw a house which was only a frame. People could have action in the house; they could wander out of the house. Moreover, in the case of *Death of a Salesman*, the artful manipulation of light, now shining on the left and now falling on the right, helps to change the setting in a highly flexible manner. The stage setting deals not only with space but with time. As it is "wholly or, in some places, partially transparent," it can bring back any event or person from the past in an extremely fluid way. Willy's mind shuttles quickly back and forth between the present and the past. For instance, the characters such as Ben and the woman never appear except as flashbacks across the mind of the salesman. In this way, the play seems to present Willy Loman's psychological drama in a stream-of-consciousness manner.

From every conceivable point of view, *Death of a Salesman* is a modern classic of the American theater.

The 1950s

The 1950s was a decade in which America went through substantial changes. The country became increasingly prosperous. Small town life received publicity. Technical advances like the car and the refrigerator made life easier and comfortable. But at the same time there were feelings of anxiety and disquiet. In addition to such factors as the nuclear bomb, the cold war, and Viet Nam which weighed heavily on the consciousness of the nation, there was a good deal of frustration and bitterness at different levels of existence, personal, social, as well as psychological.

American playwrights responded to the complexities of the age in a competent way. William Inge (1913-1973), Robert Anderson (1917-2009), Arthur Laurents (1917-2011) and a good many others wrote to contribute to the success of American drama in the 1950s. Take William Inge for example. His famous *Bus Stop* is an adequate expression of the period spirit. Here its main character, Cherie, feeling the pull of the booming city, comes to the city only to find disappointment in store for her. She falls in love and tries to find consolation in personal relationships but meets only disillusionment. Then she tries to escape into the sanctuary of a ranch which, however, offers nothing of the kind. The promise which the American dream inspires ceases to exist. She feels stifled.

The 1960s

In the 1960s, the tradition of the Theater of the Absurd came into vogue. The theater of the absurd refers to some plays the theme of which centers on the meaninglessness of life with its pain and suffering that seems funny, even ridiculous. Edward Albee (1928-2016) has been linked with this tradition. His famous play, *Who's Afraid of Virginia Woolf?*, is a good example. Similar works include such as the English playwright Samuel Becket's *Waiting for Godot* and *Endgame*, or Eugene Ionesco's *Amedee* and *Rhinoceros*. In these works the playwrights try to force the audience to face up to the human condition as it is, instead of presenting a false picture of it and pandering to the public need for reassurance.

Edward Albee has written in this spirit. His plays seem to have dwelled on one problem only, that is, the absurdity of human life built very much on a frail illusion and spiritual emptiness.

Edward Albee (1928-2016)

Edward Albee was the best-known playwright of the period. He was likely to stay in history alongside O'Neill, Williams, and Miller.[6] Albee hinted that he alone was the heir to the great traditions of O'Neill and Williams. His first play, *The Zoo Story* (1958), was staged in Berlin in 1959, and was later produced off Broadway. A series of one-act plays such as *The Death of Bessie Smith* (1960),

The Sandbox (1961) and *The American Dream* (1961) that followed led to his first full-length play, the three-act *Who's Afraid of Virginia Woolf?* (1962). The play represented the culmination of his powers as a dramatist. It won many awards and established its young author as one of the most distinguished playwrights to appear in the postwar period. It pushed his dramatic career to a sudden, thrilling climax which his later productions never were able to reach.

Over the years Albee has written many more plays such as *The Ballad of the Sad Cafe* (an adaptation of Carson McCullers' work, 1963), *Tiny Alice* (1964), *A Delicate Balance* (1966, winning a Pulitzer Prize), *Box* and *Quotations from Chairman Mao Tse-Tung* (1968), *All Over* (1971), *Seascape* (1975, winning another Pulitzer Prize), *The Lady from Dubuque* (1978), *The Man Who Had 3 Arms* (1983), and *Three Tall Women* (1994, winning the third Pulitzer for Drama).

Who's Afraid of Virginia Woolf?

This is a three-act play. George and Martha are a middle-aged childless couple. Childlessness has been the source of a good deal of unhappiness for both. They revel, have fun and games, try to lose themselves in their cups, but deep down, the fact of childlessness keeps harassing them and fills them with a sense of loss which they cannot face with courage. Somehow, they agree to pretend that they have a son who was born some twenty years ago, and that they should keep the secret between themselves. On the night before the supposed twenty-first birthday of their son, they invite a young couple, Nick and Honey, to come and join them in their noisy, violent, and essentially absurd and murderous "games." The four meet around two o'clock in the morning. Everybody drinks and turns quickly from mellowness to semi-insanity. It seems that life has become such an absurd business that night replaces day, and the control of reason gives way to the free play of imagination with the subconscious now running wild.

George and Martha keep up a show of violent quarrels and threaten to stop at nothing short of murder. Honey gets so drunk that she sleeps on the tiled floor of the bathroom. And Nick, who seems to maintain a balance of mind, finally succumbs to the pressure of his own psychic wound and starts chasing Martha in the kitchen and bedroom. It turns out that Nick may be impotent and his wife is slim-hipped, and though they want desperately to have children, they cannot. Like the older couple they are doomed to a lonely and empty existence. By four o'clock in the morning everyone has gone practically insane.

Just as sexual impotence in Eliot and Hemingway denotes spiritual poverty, so here in Albee childlessness is only a representation of a much graver problem with which these people are beset. Take George, the history professor, for example. His life is crippled from the very beginning by patricide or a semblance of patricide. He marries Martha, the daughter of the president of the college, with the prospect of taking over when the old man leaves the scene, but is found wanting in some of the required qualities. For a while during the war he chairs the history department but is apparently a failure in that job. He suffers defeat in his career as an academic. Thus his life has been frustration, defeat and despair. He feels the encroachment of modern civilization. He finds relief in escapism and illusion.

At home George constructs the illusion of a son having been born to him and amuses himself through life with it. But he knows it is an illusion, and not a truth, and he cries deep inside. The truth of the "sad, sad, sad" life of George and Martha breaks through the illusory surface at the beginning of the third act, "the exorcism" when Martha makes a pathetic speech which she would not make when she is sane: "Do you really have red eyes? ... Yes; you do. You cry alllll the time ... I cry all the time too. Daddy. I cry alllll the time; but deep inside, so no one can see me."

The mental suffering of all the people in the play is graphically illustrated here in this "I'll-tell-you-all" kind of speech. When Nick starts mounting his hostess like a dog and Honey screams hysterically "I want a child," the spell over all is broken. What is left is sheer despair and fear to live on with: "Who's Afraid

of Virginia Woolf?" George sings at the end of the play, and Martha, now reconciled with both life and George, finally admits that she is.

The Title of the Play

The "Virginia Woolf" in the title is significant in a couple of ways. First,
Martha is well read and has a kind of respect for language. Had she been younger,
she would have identified herself with Virginia Woolf who had an incredible
amount of verbal wit. Martha is afraid of Virginia Woolf who committed suicide
in the end. She could have done the same, given the enormous amount of despair
she feels all her life, if she had not lived on her frail illusion that she has a son.
Then "Woolf" is used as a homophone for "wolf," and the title is in fact a
humorous way of repeating a line from a ballad, "Who is afraid of the big, bad
wolf?" The wolf here is a metaphor for something terrible like poverty etc., and
the wolf that has scared the four people in the play is the hopelessness that
stretches before them. At the end of the play, however, they seem to have to come
to terms with the absurd life that they are made to live, and face with courage the
darkness which it offers them.

The Technique of the Play

Who's Afraid of Virginia Woolf? is an impressive work from a formal point
of view. The three acts, "Fun and Games," "Walpurgisnacht," and "The
Exorcism," represent the typical structural pattern of Albee's plays: normal
opening, gradual building up toward emotional crack-up, and quick drop-off. The
withholding and release of information is skillfully handled so that the audience's
interest is sustained throughout the play. What touches off the waves of hysteria
is Martha's revelation to Honey that she and George have a son. George's threat
to react violently seems puzzling, until Martha discloses that George does not
like the boy because he is not sure whether the son is his own. For a moment
George's virility is in doubt. Thus humiliated, George resolves to retaliate. The
games that he introduces to the little party lead steadily to the removal of the
spell until, in the end, their illusion evaporates and they find themselves suddenly
face to face with the naked truth of life. Martha is an archetypal character in

Albee's dramas. She is the domineering woman, the tragicomic figure who is at the center of the emotional tangle and without whom Albee's plays would have lost much of their emotional appeal.

Sam Shepard (1943-2017)

The two preeminent playwrights that have impacted contemporary American theater are Sam Shepard and David Mamet. Sam Shepard tends to explore the world of the subconscious and the repressed. He feels fascinated with subjects like incest and violence. One major subject for him is failed family relationships, relationships that can be terrible and impossible. In this world people are estranged from life, and stress and pressure come primarily from within them. Shepard tends to mystify the West and create a kind of cowboy mythology, no longer the original American mythology, but still something larger than the present-day fast-food existence in America.

Over the years, Shepard wrote a good number of plays like *Buried Child*, *Fool for Love*, *A Lie of the Mind*, *Paris, Texas*, *Motel Chronicles*, *Geography of a Horse Dreamer*, and *States of Shock*. Let's take a brief look at *Buried Child*. Here Young Vince comes home with his girlfriend Shelley to visit his family. But there is no welcome, not even sufficient attention, from his grandparents and his father. All of the three elders are preoccupied with their own thoughts. The grandfather sits in front of the TV and drinks. The grandmother is dressed in black grieving over her lost child. And the father is busy bringing vegetables to the house from a back garden. Outside the house is buried the dead child. All live in their own world and behave like borderline neurotics. There is a hint that the buried child is born out of an incestuous joining between Vince's father and his grandmother. It represents a past that bears heavily on the present.

The play seems to be saying that family generates pain. Its members look like "a global race of strangers." The children (like Vince's father) leave but are drawn back only to suffer in an embroiling relationship devoid of warmth and understanding. The desert—the mythical "West"—no longer rehabilitates like the dream that it used to be. The people live in search of meaning, but fail to find it. They feel the need to believe in something but cannot believe it. Thus they enact their versions of life very much like their fathers and grandfathers before them and then dissolve in the end. Vince comes to realize that life is a purposeless repetition through generations.[7]

David Mamet (1947-)

David Mamet is the most important playwright to emerge in the 1970s. Mamet's major thematic concern relates to his pessimistic view of the dilemma with which contemporary America is faced in the areas of social, economic, and human relationships. Over the years he has written a number of plays such as *House of Games*, *Sexual Perversity in Chicago*, *American Buffalo*, *Glengarry Glen Ross*, *The Woods*, *The Shawl*, and *Speed the Plow*. All are impressive; *American Buffalo* has been seen as one of his most ambitious works.

American Buffalo is a two-act play that established its author David Mamet's reputation. It is at once a critique of American business ethics and a portrayal of failed human relationships. The story is set in a junk store in Chicago. Three thieves plan to rob a man who bought an antique buffalo-headed nickel. The characters are Don, the owner of the small resale store, Bobby, a drug addict, now a protégé of Don's, and Don's friend, Teach, and some other misfits. The crime never occurs because the three simply do not know how to do it. They know little about the man they are to rob, do not know how to get into his apartment, prize open the safe, and identify the coin. They do not have the courage, either. They suffer from paranoia and behave like psychotics.

Their conversations are significant because they reveal their views of American business ethics. The free enterprise offers, according to one of the three, a freedom for people to do whatever they think could justify their end of making a profit. What is implied here is that, just as corporate morality differs from that of the individual, and just as the slaughter of the buffalos and the displacing of the American Indians are justifiable in terms of American progress, so is crime, including this planned, unexecuted project of petty theft. The system blurs the distinction between crime and business.

In terms of helping achieve the theme of the play, the crime is not important; it is the process of the planning that matters most. The thieves pass their time together and enjoy each other's company. They stretch their imagination, create a kind of fantasy in which they have a role to play, and feel happy enough to let their lives stay at the fictive level. There is the acutely felt need for communication. Occasionally, the three function like family. Don appears to be a father figure, with Teach and Bobby, both emotionally inadequate, like two brothers. But they could never achieve that intimate sense of attachment that promotes gratifying human relationships. They remain "isolatos" in a world of alienation.[8]

Recent American Drama

In the recent history of American drama there have been a good number of playwrights trying to offer, on Broadway or off it, a variety of productions which have invigorated the theater. The generation of authors such as Jack Geiber, Jack Richardson, Arthur Kopit, and Ronald Ribman are followed by a good number of younger playwrights, and all are trying to add in their own ways to the development of American drama.

Following the heavily political theater of the 1960s, the 1970s experienced a change in taste. The theater of the absurd was no longer the dominant trend, and realism made a comeback. Realistic, even naturalistic portrayals of life, especially life of the lower social strata, are offered on the stage. Albert Innaurato's *Gemini* (1977), Beth Henley's *Crimes of the Heart* (1979), and August Wilson's *Joe Turner's Come and Gone* (1988) are all good examples of the plays of the period.

This was also the period in which feminist theater exerted its influence. Marsha Norman's *'night, Mother* (1983), Tina Howe's *Painting Churches* (1983), and Wendy Wasserstein's *The Heidi Chronicles* (1988) were among the most successful plays that portray women's lives in a realistic way. The last couple of decades since the 1980s have witnessed some change in values again. Experimental drama is back in vogue in some plays. Symbolism, fantasy, and the theater of the absurd combine with realism and naturalism in representing life in such plays as David Henry Hwang's *The Sound of a Voice* (1983), Caryl Churchill's *Top Girls* (1982), Tony Kushner's *Angels in America* (1992), and Milcha Sanchez-Scott's *The Cuban Swimmer* (1984).

Multiracial and Multiethnic Drama

The major feature of recent American drama has been the emergence of the multiracial and multiethnic plays on the stage.[9] African Americans, Native Americans, Asian Americans, and other ethnic groups have felt the need for some theatrical expressions of their own lives. After the militant works of James Baldwin, LeRoi Jones, Lorraine Hansberry, and Ed Bullins, there has emerged August Wilson, who is probably the most powerful African American playwright of recent history. A number of other African American playwrights active at work include, to name just a few, Sonia Sanchez, Alice Childress, and Adrienne Kennedy. Regarding the plays of the Native American Indians, these began receiving attention in the late 1960s when a number of their works were staged. In the 1970s the Native American Ensemble was established and became later American Indians in the Art. In the meantime some other theatrical organizations such as Four Arrows and the Indian Performing Arts Company also came into being to help Native American Drama grow. Hanay Geiogamah was the first Native American to bring out his collection of plays in 1980. For the Asian Americans, an anthology of Asian American plays, entitled *Between Worlds*, was published in 1980. Laurence Yep and David Henry Hwang have appeared well in evidence on the stage. The Chicano theater has had such playwrights as Luis Valdez, Lynne Alverez, and Milcha Sanchez-Scott (whom we mentioned a little earlier on).

Since the 1980s, American theater has been further invigorated by a good number of playwrights and their works. Mention should be made of such well-known authors as Doug Wright (1962-), John Patrick Shanley (1950-), Margaret Edson (1961-), Rajiv Joseph (1974-), Tracy Letts (1965-), and Amy Herzog (1979-). Doug Wright is noted for his plays such as *Quills* (2000) and the prize-winning *I Am My Own Wife* (2004), the prolific John Patrick Shanley won a Pulitzer for his excellent work *Doubt, A Parable* (2004). Margaret Edson is a prize-winning playwright; her one-act play, *Wit* (1991), won the Pulitzer Prize and has been made into a movie. It is obvious that American drama is going through a process of redefining. It is a process that will enrich the American theater in a significant way.

Chapter 20   *Postwar Poetry • Some Older Poets of the 1940s Generation*

The Postwar Scene

A lot happened in the postwar period that made life drastically different. In socio-political terms, the postwar years has witnessed many great changes: memories of war savageries like those of the concentration camps, Dresden, and Hiroshima, still fresh and haunting, the cold war that went on for decades, the menace of the nuclear bomb and the shadow of fear it cast, McCarthyism and the scare and harm it caused, Civil Rights and race relations, awareness of ethnic and cultural diversity and difference, the Vietnam war, the Beat generation, communal living and drugs, the impact of the TV, feminism and the fight against patriarchy, the fight for sexual freedom, the self-assertion of the gays, the computer and the information explosion that has followed in its wake, the increase in self-awareness and identity, the consciousness of environmental protection including the ozone layer, the greenhouse effect, and species preservation, the exploration of space and the new vistas of vision it has opened up for humankind, etc., and added to all these, the economic growth and the increasing affluence. With all these happening around, human perceptions could never remain the same. Neither could human sensibility and values. Experience becomes more individualized, and expression tends to be more personal, even idiosyncratic.

Postwar American poetry was amazingly different from that of T. S. Eliot and the "orthodox" New Critical paradigm. The younger generation of poets of the 1950s and 1960s believed that the heritage of the previous period was no longer adequate enough for them to address their unique problems. They decided to break away. The rumble of rebel was heard already in the early 1950s when Charles Olson, Allen Ginsberg, and Robert Lowell, among others, decided to take a new direction in their creative endeavors. The age of Postmodernism had arrived.[1]

Postmodernism

Postmodernism represents a new mode of perception and a new way of writing. In its thematic concerns, Postmodernism views the world as one that is not to be molded, but as formless and unpredictable. Postmodernism does not endeavor to impose on life and reality, but is willing to embrace it for what it is. It tends to use topics and subjects of a personal, even a forbidden, nature. In its formal aspects, Postmodernism seeks a freedom in literary expression. It prefers, for example, colloquial and informal speech, not always grammatical and coherent in syntax. All this and more offer a striking contrast with the poetics and styles of the previous period. Postmodernism thus asserts its own identity by virtue of its negation, partial in some cases, of its inheritance. It is good to note, however, that it is closely linked with that heritage as it acknowledges part of it at least—Pound and Williams and Cummings—as the sources of their inspiration, and that their reaction against Eliot and the New Criticism is also an indication of their debt to High Modernism.

It is wrong to see Postmodernism as anything monolithic. It is a loose blanket term covering a wide range of diverse experimentations that appeared since the end of World War II. Although Allen Ginsberg, Charles Olson, John Ashbery, and Robert Lowell and more all belonged among the postmodernist group, they were a heterogeneous crowd.

The poetic scene of the 1950s was uninspired. The atmosphere proved to be stifling to some dynamic spirits. They saw little room for renovation and a broader range of activity. No palpable change in style had appeared in the field of literary creation. For the younger generation, their only way out was to look for something new that they could call their own. There had to be a change. Thus eccentricity, in the sense of being off the center, came in vogue. As critic David Perkins puts it, Dada gestures, Tibetan chants, surrealist associations, Jungian archetypes, epiphanies of Mayan and Egyptian deities—all these and more became welcome in the postwar decades. The new and fashionable easily attracted notice and helped build a reputation.

And sure enough, the wind of change was blowing. Ezra Pound and William Carlos Williams became charming and great. In the late 1940s, the two poets came out with works that appealed to the imagination of the groping younger generation. Pound's *Pisan Cantos* and Williams' *Paterson* brought a fresh breeze at the time. Spontaneous, free, autobiographical, and reflective, *Pisan Cantos* broke away from the High Modernist concrete and fragmentary mode of presentation and its doctrine of impersonality, and offered a new way of writing not seen for a long time. Its emotional intensity proved exceptionally attractive because impossible for High Modernist and New Critical poetry. Williams' *Paterson* was delightfully open. It appeared to be moving, changing, forever in process, acting on the impulse of the moment rather than planned. In the long run, both the *Cantos* and *Paterson* were to be appreciated more in terms of poetic structural considerations. Charles Olson elevated both poets to the stature of father figures for contemporary poetry. T. S. Eliot began to take back stage.

The changes in taste and values that occurred in the 1950s and 1960s and the salient features of this new, contemporary poetry, had to do with the change in the very idea of art. In the 1890s and the first years of the 20th century, art and poetry were regarded as the finished products of the creative process, closed in form, with rhymes and stanzas, coherent images and figures, and completed in plot enacted. Now art and poetry are seen as open, on-going, not as the end of thought, but as the process of the mind thinking, stressing motion, created on the impulse of the moment, and not previously well-planned. And the new verse tries to reach the common people, not just for an elite readership.

Thematically, the new poetry normally portrays everyday experiences, events, and emotions. It envisions man as vulnerable and helpless and at the mercy of overwhelming odds. It accepts life for what it is, feeling resigned, painfully aware of its inability to control and contain life. It tries to represent life as it is with its strengths and weaknesses, as something inconsistent, ever changing, and never wholly knowable. The poets' job is to seize the moment and make the best of it for themselves as well as for the world at large.

Formally, the new verse embraces open form, "the perfect, easy discipline of the swallow's dip and swoop, 'without east to west'" (as Gary Snyder states it). It rejects the "stale skunky pentameters" (as Kenneth Kock puts it). It repudiates the Eliotic, New Critical values of impersonality and objectivity as these distance art from life. It refuses to use "persona" as they feel it separates the writers from their readers. In the new verse, there is usually no surrogate speaker; the poet is often speaking himself. The poem is very often autobiographical; the tone is personal and emotional; the emotions are often intense though qualified: there is ambivalence and humor amid remorse, disgust or anguish. The diction of the new verse is mostly from daily speech, its style is conversational, colloquial, discursive and meditative, and its mood generally casual and relaxed.

Postwar Poetry

 As change became inevitable, there was a tremendous interest in poetry.[2] New schools of poetry appeared on the scene such as the Black Mountain poets, poets of the Beat Generation and the San Francisco Renaissance, poets of the New York school, and other poets who have developed their own styles and ideas of poetry like the Confessional poets.[3] And the attention that the poets of multiethnic origins began to receive was simply amazing. These included such as African American, Native American (or American Indian), Asian American, Hispanic American, and poetry by authors of other ethnic origins. It is good to add that, while the new verse became the dominant style, some poets chose to keep to the traditional forms in expressing the spirit of the new period. Richard Wilbur comes to mind along with some younger poets who think it apt to give those forms a new lease on life.

Before we read the poetry of the 1950s, it is necessary to take a good look at some of the poets who began their careers in the 1940s or slightly earlier. The picture of postwar poetry would not be what it was without their contributions.

As the war produced no significant verse in America (we remember Karl Shapiro [1913-2000] and his war poems), we will place emphasis on those who, though brought up with the New Critical values, came to see the need for change in the new period and changed to keep step with the spirit of the times. These include, among others, Elizabeth Bishop, John Berryman, and Randall Jarrell. Richard Wilbur and James Merrill merit our attention, too, in terms of their formal concerns. As to the still older poets such as Robinson Jeffers (1887-1962), Richard Eberhart (1904-2005), Stanley Kunitz (1905-2006), and Theodore Roethke (1908-1963), it is necessary to note that their contribution is by no means negligible even though there is not much space here to elaborate on their works.

Elizabeth Bishop (1911-1979)

Elizabeth Bishop was born in Worcester, Massachusetts. She lost her parents when little and was brought up by her grandparents. She graduated from Vassar College. As a poet, Elizabeth Bishop was never slighted by critical circles and has drawn more and more critical attention. Her second volume of poetry, *Poems* (1955), was awarded the Pulitzer Prize for poetry, and her fourth volume, *The Complete Poems* (1969), won a National Book Award. Her other works include *Questions of Travel* (1965) and *Geography III* (1969).

Bishop's poetry is basically related to her personal experiences. Occurrences such as the loss of her parents in her childhood, her travels in Europe and South America as well as in her home country, and her meetings with Marianne Moore and T. S. Eliot—all these, plus her interest in painting and the influence of contemporary art and surrealism, have all left a visible imprint on her work.[4]

First, regarding her sense of loss, vaguely felt at first but more keenly with time, it is built into the texture of her poetry. Her poems, "Sestina" and "One Art," are interesting illustrations. The two works are frequently anthologized (along with "The Fish"). Even though "Sestina" cannot be called autobiographical, the readers can feel the poet writing herself into her work. Here we see a grandmother and a child grieving over something to be deciphered only by the readers' imagination. That something is fully known to the grandmother and the readers, but only vaguely to the child. The emotional constraint, resulting from this deliberately elliptical description, empowers the readers' minds so that they feel the grief intensely as much as does the grandma (and the poet with her).

In a similar way, "One Art," on the art of losing, of accepting losses, leaves so much unsaid, so much open-ended, that we need to read the poem over and again to experience the pain, the agony, the "disaster" that the loser may have felt when the losses first occurred, losses ranging from trivial and less personal (as in the 2nd and 3rd stanzas), to those grave and galling to the soul (as in the last three). One can only understand how the poet can dismiss these so easily when we begin to embrace life for what it is the poet tries to do.

One thing to note about "Sestina" and "One Art" is Bishop's interest in traditional forms. Bishop was not partisan or doctrinaire in her literary creation. She regarded form as a means to help achieve theme. Whatever served her purpose was good for her. Thus she could enjoy writing in such tricky traditional patterns as the villanelle and sestina as shown in the two poems above, and at the same time write with equal facility in forms open and free and keep in step with the experimental spirit of her time.

Elizabeth Bishop wrote with increasing awareness that the time for the Modernist mode of literary creation, no matter how grand, was over and that something new had to take over from it. She was a Postmodernist both in her acceptance of life for what it is and in her openness as regards form. One basic feature of her poetry lies in its at once material portrayal of life and immaterial suggestion about it. The readers are offered an abundance of naked details and invited to relish a subtler taste. This feature of her art stems in a way from her catholic vision of life itself. This vision, large and all-inclusive, sees the world as one of joy and sorrow, physical and metaphoric, which the poet embraces and tries to represent so that life never becomes totally impossible. Bishop never theorizes about life. To her the physical, ephemeral setting, against which we live out our lives, is impersonal and non-judgmental, and there is nothing we humans could do about it but observe it faithfully and accept it. Poetry should be open because life is open. No art of any kind, not even Stevens' "jar," could impose an order on its natural wilderness. So she is open to life's numerous, probably unpredictable possibilities. She is open both in theme and form. Life is to her forever unfolding and relative, and she allows it to register itself on her mind as it unravels itself.

"Over 2,000 Illustrations and a Complete Concordance" is a good example here. The poet perceives order, as represented by the *Bible* concordance, in its first movement (ll.1-30). Once one opens the book, one always sees the same things arranged in the same manner, everything of "God's spreading fingerprint." These are always readily comprehensible ("when dwelt upon, they all resolve themselves"). The sense of order breeds a sense of control and a measure of assurance and certitude. But the 2nd movement of the poem (ll. 31-64) introduces the notion of disorder that seems to inhere in actual life experiences, i.e. her travels: Newfoundland, Rome, Mexico, North Africa, Southwest Ireland, a Moroccan city—all these in contrast to the silent order of things in the *Bible* concordance, everything is haphazard, chaotic, without a sense of direction. Order is confronted and disrupted by disorder. The open mind of the poet begins to think. In the third movement of the poem, the poet becomes aware, almost like an epiphany, that the idea of order or disorder is just our mind's response to experience and that anything can be seen in different ways and is relative in nature. Even the Nativity scene in the concordance can look different when viewed differently.

Bishop's openness is well illustrated in her attempts at achieving a sketchy but suggestive effect, which not only reveals the author's mind being open to all possibilities of interpretation but also leaves the readers wanting more. This we can feel in our reading of "The Fish." The poem can be divided into a few sections. These reveal the visible steps of movement on the part of the poet from a pure objective observation and concrete description (the first 20 lines), to some emotional involvement and the increasingly subjective depiction (the next 25 lines), to the display of admiration (ll. 45-65) and to the final highly emotionally charged decision to set the fish free (ll. 65 through the end). These steps represent the jumps in the growing awareness of the poet from observation to inspiration to discovery, enacting her notion of "the perpetually changing integration of what has been written with what is being written."

Now in the first movement of the poem (ll.1-20), the fish appears as a mere physical object. This is followed by a concrete, minute, matter-of-fact description of the fish without much of an emotional response—love or hate or any shades in between—on the part of the poet. In the second movement (ll. 20-45), the poet's subjectivity increases until the nonchalance of the fish, its arrogance, begins to awaken some echo of admiration in the poet. The admiration grows when she sees the five big hooks planted firmly in the mouth of the fish as if they were the fish's badge of courage (ll. 44-64). Then, in a moment of sudden revelation (ll. 65-76), the poet becomes aware of her own wisdom and courage of which the fish is the symbol. An overwhelming sense of pride and joy of self-recognition comes over her: she is the fish's equal, and perhaps more than that: "I stared and stared … until everything/ was rainbow, rainbow, rainbow!" Thus in exhilaration, and also probably out of gratitude for the epiphany the fish has induced to her, the poet sets it free as it well deserves. With the fish swimming back to the ocean, the readers' imagination, along with that of the author's, is set free for a wild run as well. The appreciation of the poem does not end with the conclusion of the work; and the process of diverse interpretations (readers' and author's alike) continues, probably indefinitely, regarding the question why "I let it go."

Bishop believes that life is open and endless, so is our process of perceiving it, and so is our portrayal of it in our works of art: "the *recognition* itself of what is being written must be kept fluid," as she put it in one context. This fluidity of the writer and his subject, the very notion of everything moving in a constant flux, is imbedded in the fabric of Bishop's poetry and bodies forth a good deal of contemporary epistemology. It is essentially Postmodernist.

It is good to add that Bishop's meeting with Marianne Moore in 1934 proved to be important to the evolution of her style. That she handled details with meticulous care is attributable to the influence of the older poet. Her meeting with T. S. Eliot was equally significant to her poetic career if not more. This occurred when she was attending Vassar College. In her interview with the poet, she heard the visiting T. S. Eliot call his epochal work, *The Waste Land*, "a piece of rhythmical grumbling," and she read his important essay, "Tradition and Individual Talent," from which she came to realize that writing is "the perpetually changing integration of what has been written and what is being written." She saw and understood the Postmodernist inclination in late T. S. Eliot, which affected her writings very much.

Elizabeth Bishop wasn't an inventor in the sense T. S. Eliot was. She was, to be more just, an eclectic in that she managed to build her own work on the best of her past, especially the artistic achievements of the great masters of her previous generation. Thus we see in her works visible imprints of Marianne Moore's observation of detail, Pound's Imagistic instant, Eliot's objective correlative and impersonal presentation, and Stevens' urge for aesthetic perfection. And there is also a glimpse of William Carlos Williams in her works like "A Cold Spring," or even "Brazil, January 1502."

Elizabeth Bishop has become a tradition of a kind for contemporary

American poets. She has impacted contemporary American poetry in visible ways. Richard Wilbur learned how to write poetry first from her works; Randall Jarrell felt an empathy of spirit with her; and Robert Lowell's famous "Skunk Hour" was written in response to her "Armadillo." Her criticism of her fellow poets' work has been always taken seriously. She has become one of the most admired poets of her generation.

Richard Wilbur (1921-2017)

Richard Wilbur was born in New York, and attended Amherst College and Harvard University. His first volume of poetry, *The Beautiful Changes and Other Poems*, was published in 1947 and proved to be an immediate success. A prolific and prize-winning author, he kept writing and publishing all his life. Wilbur also wrote some plays, did some translations, edited some books, and taught in a few universities. He was once president of the American Academy of Arts and Letters.[5]

Wilbur was the most elegant of his—the New Critical—generation. His poetry, formally exquisite and refined both in meter and rhyme regularity, left a very pleasant impression upon the minds of his readers. His works show well his fidelity to physical experience, and his tolerance of all formal possibilities. Critically, his grace and charm in form led, on occasion, to people branding him "elitist" and "reactionary."

However, there is no doubt that Wilbur was a Postmodernist poet. He tried to keep step with his generation in spirit. Both in theme and form, he shared the concerns of his contemporaries. To him the world is not always the best possible for us; life is a struggle, often doomed. A good deal of his poetry reveals the disturbing and ugly side of reality. The sucking center in "Marginalia," the falling earth in "Juggler," and the soul's reluctance to descend to its body in "Love Calls Us to Things of This World"—these are just a few of the poet's many attempts to depict the physical world the same way his contemporaries did.

Let's take a look at "Marginalia." The central idea which holds the three seemingly incongruous stanzas together is the poet's opinion that the best of our lives is marginal: Things concentrate on the surface of the pond which is one kind of margin in relation to its center deep down (1st stanza). The vision of beauty occurs in the interval between waking and sleep which is another kind of margin (2nd stanza). Life is a whirlpool (3rd stanza): we row at the edge of the circling current (marginal again for sure), trying to stay alive, in touch with our "final dreams" or "the complete music" which radiates from the center, the vortex, and we will eventually be sucked into that destructive middle.

Then there is "Love Calls Us to the Things of This World." The soul enjoys the peace and joy and beauty of the heavenly scene where angels (or an illusion of them) live and interact with one another so much so that it would rather stay "bodiless and simple" for eternity than descend into its natural habitat—its body. Man's world always encroaches upon the human soul, and it is a crude discordant medley. Reluctantly, however, the soul crawls into its "waking body" and acts differently. After all, this is where it belongs; the "bodiless and simple" state, absorbing as it is, lasts only "for a moment," giving an illusory sense of existence only.

Wilbur shares, with many of his contemporaries, the Postmodernist notion that reality is not always knowable. The poem, "Epistemology," consisting of two couplets, reveals the skepticism inherent in his sensibility: You may break your bones getting to know it, but reality remains nebulous and mysterious. For writers, to know or not to know it well is "… always a matter …/ Of life or death," since that knowledge can make or mar their writing careers.

What can art do to life? This has been a life-long concern for Wilbur. Art can offer relief from the humdrum life, but the escape it offers, no matter how joyous and uplifting, is at its best temporary. Ultimately we have to come back down and touch ground. The implication is that we have to face reality squarely, and try to live with it. Take "Juggler" for example. The world is "weighty"; it pulls us down. We struggle to do our best (we "bounce"), but are doomed to fall inevitably, by virtue of earth's gravity, into dull routine again. Then the juggler comes on the scene: his art intervenes and mediates between our earthly troubles and our aspirations. The "small heaven" of his balls completely keeps our mind off our worries and cares. So does his juggling of the table, the broom, and the plate. This "small heaven" reminds us of Eliot's Modernist idea of art giving shape and purpose to the chaos and purposelessness of life. But here Wilbur's Modernism ends. His Postmodernism begins when his juggler finishes and goes, leaving us behind to shift for survival with whatever is available: table, broom, etc. These are solidly ours; these are what we live by, however we feel about them. The advice for us here is to take what we have and make the best of it. This also indicates Wilbur's acceptance and tolerance of life, pleasant or otherwise.

Related to the point here is Wilbur's avowed fidelity to reality. To the details of life and the world, no matter how insignificant and little they may look, his devotion is unswerving. He enjoys contact with the true sights and sounds of the world. The meticulous care with which he presents the sight of a dying toad, physical and picturesque, in his "The Death of a Toad" offers a graphic illustration. Here poems such as "A Summer Morning," "A Fire Truck," and "Next Door" are also good examples.

With regard to form, Wilbur was, as mentioned earlier on, open to anything that could help do his job well. He refused to be dogmatic and extreme in formal patterns. For example, he did not think of traditional forms such as sonnets and terza rima as outdated. He felt drawn to these because of the power and effectiveness he saw in them. He never felt the need to discard these traditional forms. Open and tolerant, he wrote also beautiful free verse. In language he could be casual and relaxed. Altogether he is pleasant to read.

Now in retrospect, when all is said, Richard Wilbur has weathered well through time. He was consistent and perseverant in his way of composition and earned the recognition that he well deserved. He was appointed US Poet Laureate for 1988 and has been seen as one of the most accomplished poets of the contemporary period.

John Berryman (1914-1972)

John Berryman was born in McAlester, Oklahoma. He attended Columbia University and Cambridge University, taught at Harvard, Princeton and the University of Minnesota. He was a Confessional poet. All through his life and career, he wrestled with his self. When he was 12, his father shot himself outside his window. The event left him emotionally scarred so much so that he spent his whole life and poetic career thrashing things out for himself. He did not succeed. After enduring incredible despair and pain, he broke down and committed suicide: he jumped off into the river in Minneapolis in 1972.

So, the major theme of his poetry has to do with his father's suicide. He felt tormented over it. He had to confront the sense of guilt and the pain and anger that came along with it. He had to grapple with his own despair and death urges and the tangle of his own life: his love hunger and sexual guilt, his debilitating alcoholism, and his struggle with his art for perfection and recognition. In a word, he had to face his own psyche squarely. So his poetry is full of the stuff of his life. There in his works he "pried himself open" for the whole world to see: the detailed events of his life such as binges, hospitalizations, insurance forms, etc., all confessions of his involvement with loss, deaths, and terror, or sequences of confessions as attempts to come to terms with that fatal event in relation to his life.[6]

Thus reading his earlier poetry such as "The Ball Poem" and "Fare Well," and some collections of his poems, we see how hard he tried to discover the primary cause of his debilitation. His frenzy at self-dissection reached its maddest point in his *The Dream Songs* (1964-1968), which he wrote to find a way out of the maze of his life but, to his great disappointment, found none. In his later work, *Love and Fame* (1970), he delves repeatedly into his innermost world to confront possible deposits of horrors there in order to find God for salvation, only to witness a vast void characteristic of his life all the time. His life and struggle come full circle in his literary creations. In *Delusions, Etc.* he resigns to "an empty heart" and feels happy to sleep for good on the empty bed of his dream song number one.

The Dream Songs

The Dream Songs is the best of Berryman's poetry. He wrote this, on and off, for some fifteen years. Berryman was going through a hellish time emotionally. His life was a total mess. The past meddled in the present, and both intermingled with the future. Dream visions paraded through the responsive screen of his mind; the line between real and imaginary dimmed and faded out. The show was on, and no one—least of all, the poet—could stop it. Besides, the poet did not want to stop it because he needed it to afford him a window of opportunity to revisit his own life carefully and examine his psyche as does a surgeon in the operation theater. He needed space and time to think things over and decide upon a survival strategy. Berryman began *Dream Songs* with a clear sense of direction, went on braving a new world for a while, but somehow lost control in the end.

The Dream Songs is a sprawling collection of 385 poems, mostly of eighteen lines each (three six-line stanzas), composed in open form, thematically connected, but formally independent. They are not chronological or sequential. Seen as a whole, they are like projections of moments crossing time boundaries in a flow of the poet's consciousness. The scene is contemporary; it is strewn with occurrences current to the author's life. Seen in a different way, the songs turn out to be an examination of the human condition through the life of a single person.

The Dream Songs has a wide cast of characters, but it centers on the main character, a middle-aged white American, by the name of Henry, most possibly a surrogate for the poet himself, although Berryman denies it in a disclaimer. The poet needs Henry for a number of reasons. First of all, the character offers the poet some distance to cool down and view himself and his life with a degree of detachment. In so doing he could get a second opinion, about his predicament. Viewed from a slightly different angle, this distancing provides a breathing space for the poet to stop being himself and act as a spectator even though it is brief and delusive. The world has been too much with the poet, and nothing would be more grateful than an avenue of escape.

Besides the main character, there is another person, obviously Henry's friend. He is nameless, probably an African American, who addresses Henry as Mr. Bones or its variants. This friend can be a real person around Henry. He appears to be like that most of the time. But he can be imaginary, someone that, Henry in his wild fantasies feels, is present in his life. In this form the friend could be Henry's conscience, or his alter-ego, someone he could act out his wishes or daydreams with, his talking partner, his shrink, his punching bag, in a word, everything that could help save his sanity and help him drag on until the impossible point comes.

The world of *The Dream Songs* is one of darkness, disorder, and oddness. It is full of suffering and pain. Henry grieves over his loss, talking about himself sometimes in the first person, sometimes in the third, and sometimes even in the second. He has lived in misery. An inveterate alcoholic, he is life-weary, hungry for love and sex, stressed out, desperate and depressed, and always wanting to die. His father committed suicide, and his life is never the same again. He finds it hard to understand how the world can endure and live on (dream song 1). He finds life boring (dream song 14). He feels responsible for his bereavement (dream song 29). He feels angry enough to spit upon his father's grave and "ax the casket open" just to see how his father managed to do it and make him feel so downright miserable (dream song 384). He thirsts for love that has never been there for him (dream song 48). His African American companion diagnoses his malaise and concludes that Henry's disorder stems from want of love. Henry is fantasizing his wishes and trying to romanticize himself out of his dilemma (dream song 76). He is anxious to find a way to address his "to be or not to be" problem, but feels frustrated in the end (dream song 385). So Henry-Berryman resigns to his fate and gives up his fight.

In formal concerns, Berryman was ambitious. He struggled hard for a style of his own. His earlier works showed the imprints of the New Critical mode, Yeats, and Auden. But he tried not to be a mere follower of the masters. *The Dream Songs* embraced the new values of the postwar period. It is composed in the open form; its subject is autobiographical; its tone is personal and confessional. Its diction runs wild with a wide array of expressions, baby talk, black and beat slang, dialects, O's, ah's, linguistic eccentricities, illiteracies of diverse kinds, etc. It flouts grammar deliberately and confuses references on occasions. And there is a strong neurotic coloring peculiar to Berryman's language.

John Berryman has been neglected in recent decades. Some anthologies do not even include him. He deserves better. In terms of emotional intensity and poetic craft, he was probably one of the finest 1940s poets to survive into the postwar period.

Randall Jarrell (1914-1965)

Randall Jarrell was born in Nashville, Tennessee. His parents' divorce impacted his life and career. He studied under John Crowe Ransom at Vanderbilt University and came under the influence of the New Criticism and the Fugitives. He taught at universities most of his adult life. During the war, he served in the US Air Force. His emotional disturbance led probably to his death: he just walked to the path of a car on the highway. Jarrell wrote quite a few volumes of poetry such as *The Woman at the Washington Zoo* (1960) which won the National Book Award, and *The Lost World* (1965), about the best of all his works.[7]

Jarrell was an important poet and critic of his time. Though one of the 1940s generation, he felt, almost from the outset, acutely uneasy within the High Modernist and the New Critical boundaries. He was willing to dissociate himself from any convictions or opinions that were dogmatic in nature. He rebelled to look for a style of his own. His poetry strives to be pleasant and sympathetic in theme, and personal and honest in tone. And he can be sentimental and heartbreaking. His style tends to be plain, prosy, and verbose, but witty and deeply moving (which is his saving grace). As a critic he was perceptive and honest, and was feared by not a few. He was probably a better critic than he was a poet.

Theme of the Lost Child Psyche

Jarrell's poetic career can be split into three visible phases: the early poems of childhood desolation, the war poems (in which the motif of the child dying helpless and confined recurs), and the postwar return to the theme of his childhood life in a slightly altered focus. His poetry reveals his obsession with the childhood theme, which is probably traceable to his own childhood when a traumatic experience thwarted his happy growth as a kid. As a result of his parents' divorce, he was first left in the care of his paternal grandparents and great-grandparents in California, but then had to attend school in Tennessee and live with his mother. He was in a way "displaced" from the loving care of the old folks. That phase of his childhood was one of confusion and insecurity and emotional turmoil. It left a big hole of affection and motherly love, which he was busy the rest of his life trying to mend. Reading Jarrell, we need to remember that his "Mama" and "Pop" are reserved for his grandparents, and his mother appears always with the name of "Anna." As his wife put it, all his life Jarrell was struggling to maintain a precarious personal balance. In a sense he was so scarred by his childhood that he remained a child psychologically all his life. The best of his poetry always has to do with subjects associated in some ways with childhood or his reminiscence of childhood years.

Jarrell's early poems project a vague sense of a search for the lost mother and an awareness of the hopelessness of the undertaking. Poems such as "The

Skaters" and "The Bad Music" from his first book, *Blood for a Stranger* (1942), both portray a child gazing or dreaming in its earnest fantasy about its mother. There are so many stars in the sky of the "The Skaters" that it is impossible to locate the one the child wants.

In a number of Jarrell's war poems, such as "The Death of the Ball Turret Gunner," the womb and the birth-death motif recurs, representing the lost child psyche of the soldiers.

Jarrell's postwar poems such as those in the collections, *The Seven Leagues of Crutches* (1951) and *The Lost World* (1965), revert back to his early theme: the confusion, innocence, and betrayal by life. There are three poems in his 1951 volume that particularly showcase his child vision and mentality. In all of these death occurs in the child's life; pain chills and crushes the emotional resilience of the child, who has to endure the loneliness, the sense of being deserted, and possible mental derangement resulting from all the suffering involved. The child in "The Truth" has to face three deaths (father, sister, dog) and ends up in a mental institution. The child in "The Black Swan" has to cope with her sister's death and imagines her sister and herself turned into a swan by the swans. And "The Orient Express" reveals the adult poet looking around with a pair of child's eyes and feeling the same way a child does: in the sunlight he feels safe, but at dusk, his mind darkens with fear and insecurity as the lands darken.

The Lost World

"The Lost World" in *The Lost World* collection is an epitome of the best of Jarrell's poetry. It consists of three poems in which the poet, an adult now, tries to recap the warmth and security and joy of his childhood, lost in time and space, but captured and held sacred in memory. The first of these, "Children's Arms," lists the dear old things he did as a kid, the dear old possessions he had then, the dear old people he grew up with, the good old times he enjoyed, and tells everything in Jarrell's usual colloquial, anecdotal, plaintive tone of a child. What is particularly impressive is the picture of the child sitting in his tree house, feeling the sense of power and autonomy in his own world where he takes orders from no one but himself and follows none other than his own agenda. The last part of the poem relates his visit to the library when the child feels the coziness of "a womanish and childish/ And doggish universe." This world is appealing to the child because it is one where the weak stay shielded from possible harm. What is interesting here is the child's fascination with the world of animals.

This fascination is given fuller expression in the second poem, "A Night with Lions." He reminisces about his one-time play with a lion, named Tawny, which was kind, good-natured, and ready to oblige. Between the child and the beast, there was genuine cordiality and caring absent from "the Petrified Forest" which is a child's fairy-tale notion of the real world.

The third in the series, "A Street off Sunset," probably the most well-known of the three, records the poet's fond remembrance of the dear old folks who brought him up, the grandparents, Dandeen, a grandaunt, and the great-grandparents, the people who helped mend his child's universe. The famous scene, where "Mama" kills a chicken out of necessity to feed him and her folks, apparently took a long time for the child—and the poet— to understand properly: "It was an act of love if anything."

"Thinking of the Lost World" is the poem, another of his famous ones, that wraps up the autobiographical *The Lost World*. It pulls together all the loose threads of the whole volume and gives it a sense of closure. Here once again the poet reminisces back to his childhood, the best of his times, and tries to hold it up as a frame of reference against which to judge in the hope of coming to terms with the miserable present. Though the past is gone, nothing has vanished for him. He believes that its innocence and its primitive quality are perennial. Now that he is getting old, having come back to his present from his time travel, the poet feels a wave of nostalgia come over him, and is thrilled with this moment of sudden revelation to him: "I have found that Lost World in the Lost and Found." This is an echo to the title of the poem. The lost world of the past is not lost, or is lost but found again, resurrected in the act of the mind thinking. He is comforted in the discovery that the past is here to stay and that he has not lost it after all. It may be invisible and intangible, and he does not have to pay to get it back, but it is solid here with him now, providing him with the values he needs so badly to live his present life meaningfully. The universal applicability of his epiphany is self-evident.

More on Jarrell

One other thing about Jarrell is what he mentioned on one occasion as his semi-feminine mind. He enjoyed using female personae in some of his poems that involved looking at life from a woman's point of view. He used female narrators in his works because he had a special purpose in mind to accomplish. Jarrell was sensitive to human vulnerability and suffering. He was soft and tenderhearted toward the weak. This impersonation and masquerade helped him convey his feelings effectively and fully dramatized his sensibility. His famous poems in which women personae are employed include, among others, "A Girl in a Library."

Randall Jarrell was a very famous critic of his time. He was probably the greatest poet-critic of his generation. He wrote commentaries at a time when literary criticism was thriving in America. He had so much passion and respect for poetry that he even went as far as to compare poetry to air and food. In addition, he had the perspicacity, the catholic taste, and the acumen that characterize a great critic. He was widely read in literature and knew a lot about music and visual arts. With his native intelligence, he was well equipped for the job. Quite a few of his bold predictions actually came true. For instance, he predicted in his essay, "The End of the Line," that Modernism would die, at a time when Eliot and the New Criticism were still successful and influential, and sure enough Modernism did phase out in time. He also predicted that Elizabeth Bishop would become great, and so would Robert Lowell whose poetry people would read as long as men remember English. And sure enough he was right again.

As a critic, his praises were weighty, and his negative comments were no less so. Some of his cruel and harsh comments were compared to acid. His savage remarks about some fellow poets (such as Oscar Williams and Josephine Miles) were well founded and smart. Because his criticism was genuine and sincere, he left no hard feelings and made no unnecessary enemies. He helped shape his generation's taste in poetry in more than one way.

James Merrill (1926-1995)

James Merrill was born son of Charles Merrill, one of the founders of Merrill Lynch. He attended Amherst College, where he came under the influence of Marcel Proust, the French modern novelist and R. M. Rilke, the German poet. Wallace Stevens appealed to him enormously as well. The one emotional trauma that impacted his life and writing was his parents' divorce when he was still young. "Broken Home" (1966) comes to mind; so does one of the three plot threads in "The Book of Ephraim," the first part of his trilogy of the 1970s, entitled *Changing Light at Sandover*. As he grew up, Merrill discovered his homosexual orientation, and for a long time (over 25 years) lived with his companion, David Jackson, the "DJ" in his trilogy.

Merrill was a poet of immense imaginative powers. His themes include such as romantic love, family, recapturing and reevaluating the past, and science as potential destroyer of human life.

He was obsessed with form, believing that art is form. A brilliant versifier, he exhibited virtuosity in traditional forms of various kinds such as the sonnet, the sestina, blank verse, terza rima, and a host of other stanzaic patterns. He has also been noted for his love of puns, overtones, word games, and enormous wit. Essentially one of the 1940s' generation, he was brought up in the New Critical values and persisted in his creative career mostly in that way of writing. For him literary creation is a process of conscious deliberation and revision. He did not believe in spontaneity.

But he was sensitive enough to the wind of change of the 1950s and 1960s to accommodate it in his work. Although he never accepted the notion of open form, he wrote in free verse occasionally. It is notable that the archangels in his long poem speak in free verse. Some of his works reveal the subtle influence of the Confessional poets. He wrote autobiographical poems. His personal poems are often encased in traditional forms. Those works on his love for David Jackson, on his childhood experiences, etc. show well how he wrote his personal life into his works. Even in the long poem, the trilogy, his personal life is very much in evidence.

Merrill was a prolific writer. His volumes of poetry include *First Poems* (1950), *The Country of a Thousand Years of Peace* (1959), *Water Street* (1962), *Nights and Days* (1966), *Braving the Elements* (1972), and his trilogy, *Changing Light at Sandover*. In 1983 he collected some of his best poems and published *From the First Nine* and *The Changing Light at Sandover*. Merrill was also a novelist and playwright. He won the 1977 Pulitzer Prize for poetry and the 1979 National Book Award. At one time he was judge for the Yale Younger Poet series.[8]

The Trilogy

From 1955 Merrill began receiving messages from the Ouija board. Ouija is the trademark for a board with the alphabet and other signs on it. The board is used with a planchette to seek spiritualistic or telepathic messages. It was installed in his dining room, where he (as MJ in his long poem) and DJ managed to communicate with the dead, as the poet claims. The transmittals, we are told by the poet, became the substance of his trilogy.

The trilogy consists of three parts—"The Book of Ephraim" (1976), *Mirabell: Books of Number* (1978), *Scripts for the Pageant* (1980)—and a coda,

The Higher Keys (1982). It is 560 pages long, of which the first part, "The Book of Ephraim," makes up 92 pages, the second part, *Mirabell*, 183 pages, the third part, *Scripts for the Pageant*, 244 , and the coda, *The Higher Keys*, 41.

"The Book of Ephraim" consists of 28 sections, each beginning with a letter of the alphabet (from A to Z). It functions as a preface to the poem, mostly narrative, summarizing the teachings of the communicator, Ephraim, who was a favorite of Roman Emperor Tiberius (42 BC-37 AD; Roman emperor, 14-37 AD). As the poet tells us, Ephraim appears in the early phase of their Ouija board experience, and as a result, his teachings are narrated rather than presented in the form of its original's transcription.

In this section the poet wrote quite a bit of his own life into the poem, mainly the previous nineteen years of his experience. "The Book of Ephraim" is woven of three threads of narrative interest. The first of these focuses on the relationship between DJ and MJ, and their increasing contact with Ephraim at the board which increases their closeness: the Ouija board keeps them together, and opens up a new world of "the beyond" more sympathetic to their relationship. The second strand of interest relates to the novel MJ had had in mind to write and to the correlative interaction between it and the poem MJ has written. One significant character that features in both the novel and the poem is Ephraim who is Eros in the novel. He cements the love relationship between the two friend-lovers. The third strand of interest traces the history of the composition of the poem and the novel, which is important because it reveals some of Merrill's literary theories. One important of these is his effort to recapture the past. Merrill believes that the past should be able to become the present when it has been recalled and reconsidered, and there is always revision and modification of it in the mental process. As "The Book of Ephraim" goes on, the poem tells us, a higher power comes on the scene, demanding the poet to leave off his contact with Ephraim and starts writing "poems of science." Hence the next two parts of the long poem.

The second part of the poem, *Mirabell: Books of Number*, is made up of the major sections (0 to 9), each of these being split into subdivisions numbered as 0.1, 0.2, and so on. The communicator here is 741, a batlike creature thinking in terms only of numbers or mathematics. Later 741 seems to be transformed into or taken over by Mirabell, a peacock. This part adopts a scientific view of reality.

The third, the longest, part, *Scripts for the Pageant*, consists of three major sections, "YES," "&," and "NO." It raises the question of whether mankind will survive or if they have God on their side. The answer is indefinite, as it first says yes, and then no. The coda presents a big party at Merrill's boyhood home at Sandover, which offers the occasion for Merrill to read his poem to his guests from "the beyond" such as Jane Austen, T. S. Eliot, and Dante.

The thematic and formal concerns of the trilogy are obvious enough. The poem deals in the main with the disastrous effect of science and technology on man and his life. It is trying to say that the world is threatened, "the greenhouse" is being destroyed, so that it is in danger of becoming a void, one of nothingness in which man and his life matter no more. The world faces imminent ruin. Death, the sense of mortality, overwhelms. It is a black hole that has to be reckoned with. The poem expresses both intellectual uncertainty and emotional ambivalence that the thinking minds feel in face of overwhelming odds.

The trilogy also offers a positive outlook on the homosexual relationship: it reads like a song in praise of the love and companionship between two lover-friends, DJ and MJ. The themes of the poem are deftly interwoven with the help and in the guise of the Ouija board communications.

In formal terms the trilogy is a consummate work of art in conception, structure, and execution. The whole of it is organized with meticulous care, which indicates the workings of an exquisite mind. In versification, the trilogy is an adequate illustration of Merrill's versatile genius. The narration is done in blank verse; 741 communicates in lines of 14 syllables each; the archangels speak in free verse and the voice of God in ten-syllable syllabics; the dictation from the Ouija board is written out in capitals.

Changing Light at Sandover has provoked some controversy regarding some moot points such as reincarnation, the nine stages of life in the after-world, the continuous existence of the dead, and the authentic nature of the Ouija board messages. As it is, it is still anybody's guess whether and how these would affect the seriousness of the theme of the work.

Chapter 21   The Confessional School •
The Beat Generation

The Confessional School

One distinct group of poets appeared on the postwar scene. It has been known as the Confessional School. These people wrote to make confessions. Their primary focus was on self-exposure. The common features of their poems include some self-analysis, often ruthless and excruciating, of one's own background and heritage, one's own most private desires and fantasies, etc. The urgent "I'll-tell-it-all-to-you" impulse is apparent in these works.

In a broad way, this group of poets includes many people whose poetry seems to share some common features: Delmore Schwartz (with his emphasis on "the wound of consciousness"), Stanley Kunitz (with his "gang of personal devils" set loose), Theodore Roethke, John Berryman, W. D. Snodgrass, Allen Ginsberg, Robert Lowell, Sylvia Plath, Anne Sexton, and Adrienne Rich, to name the obvious few.

In a narrower survey of the scene, Lowell, Plath, and Sexton seem to stand closer and have been mentioned and meant often when the epithet "Confessional" is brought up in the context of a poetry discussion. The reasons for this are evident. Although Confessional poetry did not begin with Robert Lowell—there were Whitman, Pound, and Eliot, to some extent, to cite the famous examples in recent memory, no one made it such a vogue in the postwar period, as did Lowell with his harsh self-dissection. Lowell's *Life Studies* gave Confessional poetry a new life and a new level of popularity in an unprecedented manner, and his poetry lectures at Boston University showed the way to poetry and fame to at least two of his many students: Sylvia Plath and Anne Sexton. Plath went even further than her teacher in her frankness about herself. Thus in a sense Lowell created this postwar school of poetry. One interesting fact to note about the three poets is that they had one more thing in common: all of them stayed at one time of their lives at the McClean's (a mental hospital), Massachusetts.

We include Adrienne Rich in our discussion here but she is "Confessional" only tangentially.

Robert Lowell (1917-1977)

Lowell came from a distinguished New England family which included famous poets like James Russell Lowell and Amy Lowell. This background served Lowell well. It offered him a window of opportunity to scrutinize the decline of his New England tradition as an index to the overall disintegration that he felt overwhelming his nation. He was well educated at Harvard (for two years) and then at Kenyon College, Ohio under the well-known New Critical poet and critic John Crowe Ransom. During the war, he first tried to enlist and was rejected, but later was imprisoned for refusing to serve in protest against the allies' brutalities. All the time he kept writing poetry and received a Pulitzer for his second volume, *Lord Weary's Castle*, in 1946. He became a rising star on the scene and was appointed Consultant in Poetry at the Library of Congress in 1947. Lowell was silent for a while (1951-1959), felt unwell, stayed in an institution, and contemplated on poetry of his age. He experienced personal mental disturbances and was in fact advised by his doctor to write about his emotional agonies so as to relieve him of their pressure on his collapsing mind. The result was *Life Studies* (1959). When he appeared in print again with this new work, he had switched from the New Critical style to open form, and had inadvertently initiated a new school of verse, the Confessional poetry. He received the National Book Award for the new book. In the late 1960s he was arrested for his part in the march on the Pentagon against the Vietnam War.[1]

Lowell's Change in Style and Theme

Lowell began as a strict formalist of the New Critical school in the 1940s. All his poetry before the end of the 1950s was regular in form, witty, packed, and well crafted. Then change occurred both in his theme and form. It came about as part of the overall change in climate. The Beats, William Carlos Williams, John Berryman, the English Movement poets like Philip Larkin (1922-1985) and more helped to bring about Lowell's personal evolution as a poet. He became autobiographical in theme, and wrote in free verse.

Thematically, there was an obvious change, too. Lowell began by looking at the world outside. He was critical of the society, immoral with its dehumanizing materialism, or "Mammon's unbridled industry," and the spiritual decay it caused, as indicated in his *Land of Unlikeness* (1944) and *Lord Weary's Castle*. Here the poet recommends faith in Christ, union with God, and embracing the contemplative life. In his third volume, *The Mills of the Kavanaughs* (1951), Lowell turns away from his religious enthusiasm to some more secular material like society and individual life stories, and explores the possibility for people to find a secular stability, through supra-personal forms of belief, myth, or meditation. *The Mills of the Kavanaughs* constitutes a turning point in Lowell's career. From here onward, he veered in a new direction of writing. God does not appear much in his work after 1950.

At the end of the 1950s, Lowell turned inward and began a painful soul-searching within. He examined his societal and family background and the potential of art as a means to his own salvation. From there he proceeded to examine his origins and his own self and, after vilifying his parentage and himself and suffering intensely in the course of it, found hope in an otherwise desolate landscape. Of all this *Life Studies* is his poetic record.

Life Studies

A masterpiece of Confessional poetry, *Life Studies* consists of four parts. Part one, four poems, delimits the context of human behavior and offers the frame of reference for subsequent revelations and indicates the weakening or loss of the poet-speaker's faith in God. Here instead of finding where *life* belongs, he has now made up his mind to locate where *he* belongs ("Beyond the Alps"). Here he realizes that worldly matters need worldly standards of judgment and understanding ("The Banker's Daughter"). Here history repeats itself and has learned no wisdom ("Inauguration Day: January 1953"). And here man is seen at his most abject: he is no more than an animal ("A Mad Negro Solder Confined at Munich"), a point the poet keeps firmly in mind to come back to address at the end in "Skunk Hour." With these observations, the stage is set for the poet's self-scrutiny.

Part two is the book's prose section, entitled "91 Revere Street." It talks about two things: one relates to his father's impotence, and the other to the worsening of the poet's childhood social milieu. First, this strictly autobiographical segment reveals the poet's anxiety over a decaying culture as he sees it embodied in his father's personality. The father appears to be the archetypal effete New Englander, essentially an impotent man. In his forties, he leaves the Navy, and loses his sense of direction. He survives, in the following twenty-two years, only to become soulless, "a fish out of water."

Then, "91 Revere Street" also offers a startling portrait of the deterioration of the social milieu of the poet's childhood. The adulteration and the consequent degrading of the New England tradition is seen as an ominous sign of the nation's down-slope movement. The prose section also insinuates that the child's background and upbringing have somehow prepared him for some artistic endeavor, which paves the way for the next section, part three.

Here this section of four poems is designed to explore the possibility of art as an avenue of escape and survival for the poet. He examines, for his own reference, four American poets, of different dispositions and styles, in "Ford Madox Ford," "For George Santayana," "To Delmore Schwartz," and "Words for Hart Crane." Ford demonstrates the awkward groping ineptness. Santayana shows him the natural nobility of the artist. Schwartz is a poet both visionary and stalled, very much his self-portrait. Crane reveals to him the cost of achievement—the dedication of one's body and soul.

Then follows part four, entitled "Life Studies," which consists of two subsections of altogether 15 poems. Section one is a sequence of 11 poems, all about failure: the first seven about the family's failure, and the last four about his own. The first of these, "My Last Afternoon with Uncle Devereux," touches upon the dreams of the Winslow family and ends on a sad note of disappointment and death. It sets the tone for this part of the work. "Dunbarton" that follows reveals Grandfather's disappointment at Uncle Devereux's failure which is a negative reflection on the old man's own life. In "Grandparents," one of the book's strongest poems, the Winslow world of tradition falls, and in "Commander Lowell," the poet's parents' dream world is shattered. His father's failure is traced further back in time in "Terminal Days at Beverly Farms" and "Father's Bedroom": his father had a dream which did not happen. With his father dead, gone also is his cottage along with Mother's will to life ("For Sale").

The eighth poem, "Sailing Home from Rapallo," records the end of the Winslows' dream with Mother's death, and brings the poet face to face with himself. He feels the inadequacies of his past and begins to see his own failure, which is somehow suggestive of his daughter's possible failure ("During Fever"). "Waking in the Blue" reveals the poet's sense of his own incompetence to carry on the family tradition and his sense of guilt for it. There he wakes up, only to find the night attendant tired of grappling with the meaning of life, Stanley fighting with age, and Bobbie struggling to fend off aging. He discovers in them his own absurdity and impotence. He is waking, but he is in the blue: depressed and at a loss as to what to do. The last poem of the section, "Home after Three Months Away," portrays the poet cured and feebly poised for something like a new beginning.

And this finally brings the poet to section two of part four. The section contains four poems, which offer the long overdue self-examination. Here the poet talks all about himself. "Memories of West Street and Lepke" laments over his loss of hopes and dreams and of the vigor and valor that he thought he once had. "Man and Wife," one of the poet's most telling poems, pictures a man sandwiched between his resolve to leave tradition behind and his indecision to do so. This is a reflection of the poet's own dilemma in love and marriage. "To Speak of Woe That Is in Marriage," spoken as an interior monologue by the wife but overheard by the husband, suggests the poet's awareness of the evil power of tradition over humans as marriage illustrates, and also of his brutish behavior as part of that tradition. It can also indicate that the poet is becoming conscious of the extent of suffering he is bringing upon others and upon himself. He learns that he is repeating family—human—history. The poem implies that he must not only stay away from tradition, but also find his own way to survival. But he is confronted with the question, whether he has the will and the sense of direction to survive the wreckage that he has now become.

"Skunk Hour"

"Skunk Hour," the last poem of the book, probably the most famous of Lowell's poems, does not, at first sight, seem to offer a forthright answer. Here all around the poet is engulfed in an atmosphere of impotence: the hermit heiress living old and purposeless, "our summer millionaire" committing suicide probably because he is weary of life or of his bankruptcy or whatever might have happened to him, and the fairy decorator whose existence is meaningless and without any sense of direction. All these abnormalities of life, static and hopeless, are symbols of spiritual corruption and form an objective correlative for the poet's own personal disintegration. As "Beyond the Alps" indicates his loss of faith in God, "The Skunk Hour," echoing it at the end, reveals his loss of faith in man, in himself, and in life. His best route of escape is death. And sure enough, he knows that his mind is not right. He is going through hell.

It's a dark night, and he is out on "the hill's skull," looking at the lover-cars in the giant shadow of the graveyard. He feels bleak and his spirit sobs. Death becomes attractive. Then he sees a sight the portent of which is as ambiguous as ambiguous can be. A mother skunk is dauntlessly leading her kittens out hunting for food. They are having a hearty meal and are enjoying life. At the sight of vitality and fertility, the poet suddenly realizes that he has a thing or two to learn from the animals. Life flickers up again within him. The image of the skunk is interesting. The skunk is probably the most disgusting, the most despicable, of animals, and the poet realizes that he is not even as good as that. If man is reduced to such an abject animal state, there should be nothing left of his spiritual dignity. But then if there is the will to life and the courage with it, if we can forget our pettiness and stop self-deprecation, and try to pick up a lesson from our brute fellow creatures, then there should be probably still hope.

The title "Skunk Hour" is interesting, too. It is the hour for skunks to be out eating; it is the hour when humans should realize that they have become like skunks and should behave likewise. It is the hour when the poet reaches the lowest of the low in life, when he is at the lowest circle of hell, and achieves self-realization and makes a prophetic kind of call for humankind to do the same. It is a hellish hour for him and humankind, it is true, to get know one's own abjectness, but the way after that point can only be the way upward. Lowell's message is clear that we humans have been dehumanized, but we do not need to feel disheartened. There is yet light at the end of the tunnel. Thus on this positive note the poem ends, and so does the volume as a whole. It is natural that *Life Studies* concludes the way it does because it is meant to be a series of studies on life and survival. A series of studies of personal life to begin with, *Life Studies* becomes eventually a scrutiny of American life in general.

For the Union Dead

Lowell's interest in human survival continues in his later works such as *For the Union Dead* (1964), *History* (1973), and *Day by Day* (1977). The title poem of the volume *For the Union Dead* merits particular attention. It presents modern man's moral decline and his loss of heroism and idealism. The epigraph in Latin, which is the inscription on the Shaw Monument in Boston, makes the theme of the poem clear from the very beginning: "He [Colonel Shaw] leaves all to serve the state." But the heroic public spirit of the Union dead in the civil war is gone. Selfishness and cowardice take over and drive man countless centuries back in his evolution.

The scene of the poem is set in a modern Eliotic wasteland ("a Sahara of snow," a picture of all-engulfing cold and apathy). The poet, sizing up the cityscape, spots four of its scenic features, and has a hard time reconciling and relating them to modern man and his life. These include the old South Boston Aquarium now dilapidated and closed, the underground garage in full steam under construction, the Shaw Monument in memory of the Union dead, and the swashbuckling Mosler Safe advertisement.

The aquarium, the place where fish and reptiles used to live, is now all gone; the phase of evolution that it represents—life, creativity, striving to go upward, and all this involving vigor and courage with which to face challenges to survival and growth—is now all gone.

The underground garage, like the dinosaur steam-shovels building it, is relentless to anything in its way. When it is completed, it will accommodate, as we will be told later in the poem, "giant finned cars ... [of] a savage servility."

The Shaw Monument, which is being shaken along with the Statehouse by the construction of the garage, is no longer an object of veneration, but is now one causing pain and disgust ("a fishbone/ in the city [City of Man]'s throat"). To the poet, it is still a "compass-needle" to orient modern man, but who cares now! The neglected war dead take no interest whatever in the world around: for the angry and tense Colonel Shaw, it only suffocates; the soldiers "doze" and "muse" in the madding crowd. The ditch, once a revered symbol of heroic death and brotherhood of man because Colonel Shaw died together with his men there in the war, has lost its noble luster and become a mere feared place of death; it has become an apocalyptic warning to selfish, unprincipled modern man.

The advertisement of the American Mosler Company, with Hiroshima boiling on a Mosler safe, illustrates modern man's view of things graphically: they gloat over a petty material gain (the safety of the Mosler safe with its money and treasures kept intact from the nuclear blast in Hiroshima) in total disregard of the far more weighty issue of the loss of countless innocent lives in that disaster. The poet feels that no one can expect such people to commit themselves to noble causes such as the civil rights movement. Now man's conquest moves up ("Space is nearer"); but his spirit moves down. Shaw despairs. His spirit is breaking. He would have a blessed break and stop upholding the spirit of heroism and brotherhood for a nation of selfish individuals. With the aquarium is gone that life force, that originality to rise higher, all that has made evolution possible. There is left only a spiritual decline, "a savage servility of modern man." He is savage as is his act of building the underground garage, ignoring the state house (the public) and the Shaw Monument (the heroic). He is servile, more in the sense of cowardly, which echoes the earlier—modern man's—image of "the cowed compliant fish." Modern man is unable to deal well with challenges to justice and righteousness, such as the bombing of Hiroshima, the school integration, and the larger human rights issues (as suggested by the "drained [bloodless/ helpless/ scared] faces" of the African American school children on the TV). So through censuring modern man (himself included), the poem is really the poet's effort to find how to survive and, preferably, with dignity.

Lowell's Reputation

Lowell did not feel himself any better than his fellow creatures. "This age is mine, and I want very much to be a part of it," he said in 1965. In talking candidly about himself, he is examining the culture of his nation. His sense of mission gives his poetry an epic dimension. His prophetic denunciations and injunctions and the intensity of his commitment are morally uplifting.

Lowell was one of the finest poets in postwar America.

Sylvia Plath (1932-1963)

Sylvia Plath was a very sensitive person. She was frail and sensitive ever since she was a child. Her peculiar emotional makeup had to do with her parentage. She was of German descent: her father, Otto Plath, emigrated to the US in 1901. She had a hard time integrating herself into the rest of her community, especially in school during WWII. She felt guilty of being of German extraction and was made to feel more so by the intentional or casual anti-Nazi remarks of her fellow students. What made things worse was the death of her father when she was eight years old. The family was suddenly left to shift for itself: Her father left no retirement arrangement or money; her mother had to hunt for a job; and her grandfather lost his at the critical moment. This sense of forlornness and insecurity must have haunted the child.

Regarding her feelings for her father, there seems to be a love and hate paradox to be resolved. On the one hand, she might have hated her father for having left her and the family shiftless. After his death, her memories of her father must have come flooding back, including those of him acting like an autocrat within the family and to his wife, who gave up her job to accommodate his wishes for her to be a homemaker. Sylvia Plath once told one of her classmates that she had wished to have killed her father many times over and that, when he died, she wished that she had killed him.

But on the other hand, she loved her father very much and adored him. In fact, his death was the biggest incident of her life after which she was said to be never happy again. So her talk to her classmate, that outburst, was an indication of her troubled, abnormal psyche, which may well account for her repeated attempts at suicide.

For a while, the event did not seem to affect her life much. She did well in school, got married, and had children, writing and publishing poetry all the time. Then something disastrous occurred. Her husband, the English poet Ted Hughes (1930-1998), began seeing another woman in 1962. Her world, physical as well as emotional, finally suddenly collapsed. She poured out her emotional anguish in her poetry that she believed would make her name for her. The last few months of her life (the period of "creative fury" as critic J. D. McClatchy puts it) proved to be the most prolific and memorable when she produced almost one poem a day. Her books of verse include *A Winter Ship* (1960), *The Colossus and Other Poems* (1960), *Ariel* (1965), *Uncollected Poems* (1973), *Crystal Gazer and Other Poems* (1971), *Winter Trees* (1971), *Fiesta Melons* (1971), *Crossing the Water* (1971), *Lyonesse: Hitherto Uncollected Poems* (1971), and *Pursuit* (1973). She also wrote some plays and a novel, *The Bell Jar* (1961).[2]

For Sylvia Plath, writing was a process of release, of exorcising her acute sense of "existential anxiety," caused by her self-consciousness of being a German descendant, the shadow of her father's death, her intense subconscious dislike of her mother, and the hurt she received from the infidelity of her husband. As she did not succeed in alleviating the agony for herself, she was obsessed with death and suicide: "Dying is an art ... I guess I have a call" as she puts it in her poem "Lady Lazarus." And this, along with the suffering and the pain, became the major theme of her major works. Hence the most painful making a clean breast of it, the most intimate divulging of her innermost secret of life galling to her soul, the celebrated elements which made her "a supreme example of the confessional mode in modern literature." So there it is, this palpable autobiographical strain in her poetry, "the longest suicide note ever written."

But Sylvia Plath was not happy with a simple display of her personal experience. She would like her readers to connect, through her art, their experiences and feelings with hers. Thus isolated and private in nature, her life is transformed and magnified enough for people to relate to, without too much of a stretch of their imagination. "Daddy" and "Lay Lazarus" are both good illustrations.

"Daddy"

"Daddy," probably the most famous of all Plath's poems, spearheads its attack mainly at her father and in passing, but no less intensely, at her husband, and obliquely at her mother to whom the poet reveals her consistent hostility in poems such as "Medusa" and "The Disquieting Muses." The poet, by bringing out her pent-up mixed feelings—grief, rage and hate, and love—toward the three most important people in her life in this highly charged work, hopes to clear all accounts with history and turn her life around.

As is noted earlier on, her father's death, for which she was not prepared, left her emotionally scarred for life. Because he left her suddenly and left a black hole of emptiness in her heart, he became the villain, the bastard. That hole did not diminish with her mother, unappreciative of her probably because of the mother's attention on her younger brother (in her opinion), and it became larger and darker with her father's surrogate—her husband—storming into her life and then abandoning her as she felt her father had done. The betrayal that all this represented so outraged her, and her sense of victimization was so excruciating, that her revenge became a dire necessity if she was to move on with her life at all. In a sense the writing of "Daddy" is like a clearance sale of daddy's things along with those related to him: everything must go, everything from physical to psychic reminders of her connection with her past. It is an attempt to forget and begin all over again.

Let's begin briefly with the title, "Daddy." There is more to it than meets the eye. The word, mainly a child's moniker for its father, carries a good deal of closeness and love with it. To entitle her work—that has not much of a kind word to say about her father—in this way is decidedly an act of mixed significance. And the mixed feelings begin to flow right with the first stanza.

Now in the first stanza the poet compares her father's impact on her whole life to that of the black shoe for the foot. She complains that she has failed to live her life the way she should all because of him. The hate is obvious, but the love is equally visible: the shoe is protective as well as constraining.

The next stanza sells her father's body: the tall, powerfully built, religious man who suffers diabetes mellitus, with his toe swollen and then a leg amputated (which was all biographically true). The memory brims over with love as she recalls the endearing scene of joyous play with her father at the beach and with her childish attempts to bring him back from the dead through prayers (stanza 3).

When the hurt returns (stanzas 4 through 7), she remembers her ancestry and the anxiety she has felt because of it. Apparently she blames her father for bringing her into the world with a wrong identity. Her mother seems to appear in stanza 8 in which her native place—Austria—is mentioned, and her mask—of an attractive facade hiding her indifference to her (in her daughter's opinion)—is delineated. From that point onward, the poet imagines herself to be a Jew, which is a pure figment of her imagination, as her mother was not Jewish, just to intensify her sense of oppression. The image of the Jew continues when the father is made out as a Nazi in stanzas 9 and 10 (the biographical fact was that her father had nothing to do with Nazi Germany), symbolizing repressive forces of all kinds.

This transference leads to the identification of her father with her husband. The transition begins with "Every woman adores a Fascist,/ The boot in the face, the brute/ Brute heart of a brute like you." Here Ted Hughes is brought to the defense's seat. Although "You stand at the blackboard" alludes to her father who taught in a university, the cleft in the chin is a clear reference to her husband, who is "the black man who/ Bit my pretty red heart in two."

Back to her father in stanzas 11 and 12, she relates her suicide attempts which indicate how indispensable the father had been to her life: biographical information reveals that, as her father did not do enough to save himself from his diabetic death, it almost looked like a suicide; and Sylvia's suicide attempts have been deciphered by some people as efforts to emulate her father and rejoin him in death. Thus love breaks out of her lines here once more despite herself.

But hate again gets the upper hand in "I made a model of you." Now revenge, blood for blood, overwhelms her being. She is saying, "I cut off all communication with possible remonstrance (biographically, she was without a phone for the last period of her life); I am bent on this manslaughter. I have finally killed the both of you who, like vampires, have sucked my life out of me by making it a black mess, and 'Daddy, you can lie back now' because this time you are really dead for me."

"I'm through," repeated in the last stanza a couple of times, can mean a couple of things: either she is also dead, token of another suicide attempt, or she has done with her sale of him, cleared all accounts with him, and is now ready for a new—her own—life. Here the love element pops out again: there is a detectable love under-song in the poem.

In biographical terms, both interpretations are good since directly after she finished the poem, she wrote to her mother in a jubilant tone that she was beginning a new chapter of her life, but the optimism failed to stay strong enough to prevent her from her last, successful suicide a few months later. It is good to notice that the poem begins and ends with her life as it is first and foremost about her life rather than anybody else's.

"Lay Lazarus"

"Lady Lazarus" dramatizes her life in a more gruesome way. It is about her repeated attempts at suicide. "I have done it again./ One year in every ten/ I manage it—[.]" She has done it three times in her thirty years of life. There is indication of self-disgust and a morbid gloating over self-disposal. There is indication of suffocation and oppression (probably by the male gender). And there is indication of revenge, a kind of striking back, even in death. A struggle is going on at three different levels of gravity: Lady Lazarus with "Herr Doktor," the crowd of spectators, and her own desire for revenge and immortality.

Here the overriding emotion is rage and hate, and the undercurrent of "Daddy"'s love is gone. The name Lazarus indicates that she identifies herself possibly with three Lazaruses in Catholic history: the Lazarus in John 11.4, the one in Luke 16, and St. Lazarus the Confessor.

In the first instance, Jesus saves Lazarus to display his powers and win the faith of the crowd. This parallels the effort of "Herr Doktor" to save her and make her his "opus," "valuable," and "gold baby" so as to win admiration and confidence of the people around.

In the second instance, it is a parable about a rich man and Lazarus: the rich man refuses to offer help and goes down to eternal torment in hell while poor Lazarus goes up to heaven. As this poor Lazarus can be a leper ("Lazarus" as a first name can mean "leper"), one who loses his limbs if the disease is not cured, the connection between him and the poet-speaker here is apparent: in the poem, the lady loses all her body parts, which are strewn all around, foot, skin, teeth, bones, face, etc. She becomes an object of hypocritical sympathy. But she is not ready to let the crowd go at that. Now she is charging them for a fee and takes over the control of the situation. Shining as her own sun, she is beginning to taste success.

A third possible link with the name Lazarus is somewhat far-fetched, but is offered for a research reference. The poet might be thinking of St. Lazarus, the Confessor, a medieval Stylite monk who believed that self-discipline leads to a spiritually higher state. The lady of the poem believes that she is the one to come out victor eventually in the struggle: she'll win revenge and immortality ("Out of the ash/ I rise with my red hair/ And eat men like air").

It is good to note that, as "Lady Lazarus" is a very rich work, it can be interpreted differently. For example, it can be read simply as the poet's self-contempt for her repeated failure at suicide and her fury at it. It expresses her rage with outside interference with her attempt. She is angry with people who know no better than mind their own business like the doctor (explicitly), with her family (implicitly) who took her to hospital, and with the crowd who happened to be around the scene either because they did care or just out of some curiosity.

The poem can also be seen as a rebirth fantasy, a dramatizing of the notion that the dead can be brought back to a new, higher, stronger level of existence where oppression will not exist, or oppressor and oppressed will change roles to the satisfaction of the latter. This can be a feminist reading of the work—and of Plath's works as a whole.

Anne Sexton (1928-1974)

Anne Sexton lived a rather colorful life. She eloped with her lover (later her husband), gave birth to two daughters, experienced mental disturbances, attempted suicide, stayed in a mental hospital and was advised to write as part of her treatment, published amazing volumes of poetry, received awards and honorary doctorates, taught at universities including Harvard, and was a full professor at the time of her suicide. All these reveal the depth and extent of her experience with life and people, which gave her plentiful opportunities to observe life at close quarters. The range of human relationships that she touches upon in her work includes men and women, parents and children, and gods and humans. She was at her best when dealing with the subtleties of human emotions, especially those of her own.[3]

Anne Sexton was a forefront Confessional poet. She found her creative spring in her mental breakdowns and was further inspired during her stay at McClean's, MA. She came to poetry late. She did not write any until she was nearly thirty. Then a distinguished scholar-poet, I. A. Richards, talking about poetry on TV, proved inspiring to her, and her study under Robert Lowell (with Sylvia Plath) started her off on her career. From 1960 through her suicide in 1974, she published quite a few volumes of poetry and won some awards including a Pulitzer for her third book, *Live or Die* (1966). There is a direct connection between her emotionally disturbed life and her writing efforts. Her poetry demonstrates vividly her volcanic need to pour out so as to release her pent-up internal pressure. The effect was generally shocking. She felt that poetry should shock the senses and should almost hurt. She was painfully open about herself. "I tell so much truth in my poetry," she said on one occasion, "I am a fool if I say any more."

Her basic themes include such issues as madness, victimization, a sense of engulfing chaos, fascination with suicide and death, incest, adultery, illegitimacy, guilt, and addiction. Her first volume, *To Bedlam and Part Way Back* (1960), focuses on her mental problems, her stay in an institution, and her patching it up with her daughter and her husband. Her second book, *All My Pretty Ones* (1962), contains poems about her parents' death within three months of one another and her deliberations on death. Her prize-winning volume, *Live or Die*, her *Transformations* (1971), *The Death of Notebooks* (1974) and *The Awful Rowing Toward God* (1975) are mostly about suicide and about whether she would be able to receive religious absolution. Her work represents the journey of life that she went through, an emotionally eventful one, one that she took, struggling for survival, but eventually failing to find salvation.

Reading Anne Sexton, the readers often feel the same way as she did, her despair, her anger, and her sense of exigency. The sense of immediacy, of getting involved, or participating, is just overwhelming. Indeed, the readers need to imagine themselves into the scenarios of her circumstances to fully appreciate the emotional intensity of a life forever close to alluring death. What makes Anne Sexton fascinating was her irresistible desire to write. She must write to get what she calls "the rat" out of her system. Thus her poetry is always emotionally loaded, and as such always possesses a kind of contagious power. Anne Sexton committed suicide in 1974. She failed to handle her problems that might not be just her own but also those afflicting modern women in general. She was one of the most sensitive of them, the most hurt, and the most eloquent about their dilemma.

"Her Kind"

One of her famous poems, the one she liked so much that it has become her signature poem, is entitled "Her Kind." There are three stanzas here, each of which addresses one aspect of her personality. In the first stanza the "I" compares herself to a witch, possessed, secretive, malicious to her folks, lonely (because ostracized), gone mad. A witch is generally repressed by society and family and is always struggling to do right by herself. In the second stanza, the "I" likens herself to a housewife who is both hardworking and caring, but who is a little eccentric and wishes to have things her own way (which is another way of saying looking for freedom or release). The third stanza portrays a Dickinsonian passenger riding along with Death in his cart, not arriving in hell yet though already feeling its ordeal and torture, and still trying to stay on this side of the grave. So there are repression, the desire for escape, and the toying with the idea of death. A common denominator to all three images is the repression, the self-assertion, and the will to life versus the death wish. All help fantasize the desire to escape an abominable existence, but none proves good enough to offer complete release. "Her Kind" presents a painful self-analysis and the thought of death as a way out. It dramatizes the thirst for freedom on the one hand, and on the other, the confused states of readiness and reluctance to die.

Some of Anne Sexton's poems can be read as possible footnotes to "Her Kind." "Housewife," "Young," "The Farmer's Wife," and "Cinderella" come easily to mind.

"Death Baby"

The figure of death features prominent in the poem "Death Baby." This macabre song harps on the poet's fascination with death. She identifies herself with death all the way through. Images of death abound in this six-section poem. "I" was an ice baby that "my" sister dreamt of having been placed in the refrigerator or devoured at a dog's party. "I" had a doll that died twice. "I" died seven times in seven ways, "letting death give me a sign,/ letting death place his mark on my forehead,/ crossed over, crossed over." And "my mother" died of cancer. The poet fondles Death as if it were a cherub and loves it as she does "small children." But she is not ready to give up yet. In her deepest despair and at the bottom of her soul, she still wishes for absolution and salvation: her supplication sounds the most pathetic of all—"Oh Madonna, hold me./ I am a small handful." This desire for absolution from God is more apparent in her poem "Rowing."

Anne Sexton's contribution to Confessional poetry has been great. In time her poetry may transcend the restrictive boundaries of the label to reach a more universal plane of meaning.

Adrienne Rich (1929-2012)

Adrienne Rich was a confessional poet in a tangential way. First and foremost, she was a committed feminist poet. She was married and gave birth to three sons. Then in 1976, she declared herself a lesbian, and became an early feminist, outspoken lesbian, and a leading feminist poet in the United Sates in the 1970s and 1980s. She championed causes such as feminism and racial equality and was a role model for political poets and activists. She wrote a remarkable poetry of social commitment, and has won general approval and acceptance. She had a wide reading public and won numerous awards including a National Book Award, the Fellowship of American Poets, and the Poet's Prize. Rich has a very clear sense of mission as a social and political poet.[4]

Adrienne Rich wrote about many topics. Her basic theme is concerned with women, their oppression, and liberation. Her poetry is confined to female subjects such as the frailty of women, the oppressive patriarchy and its power, and women's aspirations to equality and power for themselves. Her poem like "Women" offers her analysis of women's problem and gives women a sense of orientation. "Autumn Equinox," somewhat autobiographical, is Rich's criticism of the time-honored tradition—marriage.

"Diving into the Wreck" (1973)

"Diving into the Wreck" can be read as the poet's reflections on her life as she reached middle age. The poem looks like a poetic record of the poet's diving experience. Here the readers are told that the poet-speaker is diving down alone, which may symbolize her plunging into the deeps of her memory. "I go down./ .../ I go down" indicates that she is going farther back in time. Her mask is her new face and her new identity. Now she is down at the bottom of her soul to discover what a wreck patriarchy has made of her life, what damages it has done to her mind, and what is still good and permanent left in her. She has to have the first-hand knowledge, not hearsay, of the tragedy of her life as a woman.

The diving metaphor, the sea metaphor, the wreck metaphor—all these portray a woman musing on the suffering of her sex and lamenting over its pathetic fate. Toward the end of the poem, the poet has mixed but basically good feelings about the fact that women have come to recognize their problem that they have been put down, but intend to address it.

This reading of the poem can be just one possible interpretation among many. It is in line with the poet's growing feminist awareness of the time.

The Beat Generation

In the 1950s there was a widespread discontentment among the postwar generation, whose voice was one of protest against all the mainstream culture that America had come to represent. This has come to be known as the Beat Generation. The word "beat," which Ginsberg and his friend Jack Kerouac picked up from a junkie friend of theirs, represented a non-conformist, rebellious attitude toward conventional values concerning sex, religion, the arts, and the American way of life. It was an attitude that resulted from the feeling of depression and exhaustion and the need to escape into an unconventional, sometimes communal, mode of living. "Beat" literature offered something like a fresh breath of wind both in the prose and poetry of the 1950s and 1960s. On the prose side Jack Kerouac's *On the Road* and William Burroughs' *Naked Lunch* are the representative works. In poetry, Ginsberg's *Howl* and Lawrence Ferlinghetti's *Pictures from the Gone World* have been recognized as the most enduring of the works that Ferlinghetti's City Lights Bookshop published in San Francisco during the "San Francisco Poetry Renaissance" of the 1950s.

Howling like a prophet on the city sidewalk in a period that he saw as one of the fall of America, Allen Ginsberg made his voice heard as the poet laureate of the Beat Generation. His first public reading of his poem *Howl* in 1955 helped kick off an outburst of literary activity on the west coast and became an event of historic significance.

It happened one October evening that year. Kenneth Rexroth (1905-1982) presided over it, and all the major figures of the Beat Generation were present. These included, in addition to Ginsberg and Snyder, now seen as the most important poets to come out of the Renaissance, Lawrence Ferlighetti (1919-2021) and Philip Whalen (1923-2002), and Jack Kerouac. Six Beat poets read their poetry to an audience of over one hundred people. The best performance was Ginsberg's reading of the first section of his *Howl*. The poet read and sobbed;

tears rolled down Rexroth's face; and the audience howled like mad. Kerouac called the evening "the night of San Francisco Poetry Renaissance." Soon poetry reading became popular in San Francisco, and poetry stormed into cafes, museums, and aquariums. Now known as the San Francisco Poetry Renaissance, this important literary movement has made itself felt and heard not only in the United States, but also internationally. Within the space of five years (1955-1960), poets such as Gary Snyder, Jack Spicer (1926-1965), William Everson (1912-1994), Philip Lamantia (1927-2005), Gregory Corso (1930-2001), Michael McClure, and Philip Whalen joined forces with Ginsberg, Kerouac, and Burroughs in their literary endeavors, and they traveled across the country, reading their poetry in bookstores, cafes, and public libraries, and finally managed to bring it to university classrooms. And with the help of publisher and poet Lawrence Ferlinghetti and with the success of their counterparts in the field of prose such as Kerouac and Burroughs, they broke the monopoly of academic verse and made their important contribution to contemporary literary history.

Although the Beat movement was and has been seen as one that threatened to discredit all the established values of the Eisenhower-Nixon period, Ginsberg had his own opinion of the effort of his associates. In a 1982 speech on Jack Kerouac, he said that the literary, spiritual or emotional aspect of the movement was not so much protest at all but a declaration of unconditioned mind beyond protest, beyond resentment, and beyond winner or loser. He said that it was a declaration of unconditioned mind, a visionary declaration, one of unworldly love that has no hope of the world and cannot change the world to its desire; he said that unworldly love means the basic nature of human minds, totally open, totally one with the space around, with life and death. So he said that, naturally, having that much insight, there would be obvious smart remarks that might change society, as a side issue, but the basic theme was beyond the rights and wrongs of political protest.

In the final analysis, the Beat Generation and the San Francisco Poetry Renaissance will have to be evaluated in historical perspective rather than in terms of the works of one or a few of its authors, however significant they may have been.

Allen Ginsberg (1926-1997)

Allen Ginsberg was a rebel, a trailblazer, and an explorer of the unknown.[5] For him, life was an open fair that offers goods that everyone can take according to his taste. He was born in Newark, New Jersey, went to Columbia University, and met the people there who were to represent with him the Beat generation. These included such as Lucien Carr, William Burroughs, and Jack Kerouac, and formed the nucleus of the Beat generation. These people, well read, well educated, and of respectable, well-off parentage, were rebellious in temperament, and enjoyed contradicting or revolting against established values of life being lived then. They had long nights of intense conversations about the status of the arts, about social life, about their souls, and thought they had achieved a very good understanding of their own soul. They came to the conclusion that they had to have a new vision, a new way of perceiving the world that would give it some meaning, that they had to find values that were valid to their generation, and that all this was supposed to be done through literature.

In their new vision they saw art as merely and ultimately self-expressive, and felt, to quote Ginsberg, that "the fullest art, the most individual, uninfluenced, unrepressed, uninhibited expression of art, is true expression and the true art." Kerouac and Burroughs introduced him to the world of drugs and its ways of transcending normal human consciousness. Kerouac also nudged him to action when he finished his *On the Road* in three weeks of "spontaneous outpouring." After he was suspended from Columbia for writing graffiti on classroom windows, Ginsberg had a good solid street education. He worked at various jobs for quite some time: he washed dishes, became a sailor, was arrested for sheltering a drug dealer, and went to a mental institution to avoid jail. This street education proved more generic to his career. He met William Carlos

Williams and embraced his literary doctrine of representing contemporary life in daily speech. By the beginning of the 1950s, he had basically completed his education for a poetic career with a clear vision of his literary future: he would write a kind of poetry of anti-mainstream in a natural, spontaneous diction. He was now poised for an ambitious endeavor.

Ginsberg had by now had a cozy coterie around him whom he saw as the cream of the intellect of his generation. In addition to the original four, there was also the second category and the third circle including, among others, Neal Cassady, Gregory Corso, and Robert LaVigne. A significant addition to this circle was Carl Solomon, a friend he met at the Columbia-Presbyterian Psychiatric Institute where the man had voluntarily committed himself after his arrest in the company of his underworld companions (it is good to note that Solomon later became the publisher of William Burroughs' famous or notorious *The Naked Lunch*). These people became, to Ginsberg, "the best minds" of his—the Beat—generation.

Howl

The title *Howl* ties in well with the theme of the poem. The loud cry comes from agony, despair, terror in face of death and annihilation; it is also an assertion of faith in one's destiny.

Howl is, first of all, a personal poem. It quotes freely from the poet's own experiences with life and people and ideas, and with the incidents of his own or his friends' lives. The line, "The best minds of my generation," refers, on the personal level, to his coterie of friends who met in Columbia University or the bars or shabby apartments of New York and discussed the ideas that became a kind of intellectual declaration of the Beat generation. Most of these people were literally institutionalized at one time or another: hence all "destroyed by madness" (except Kerouac and Burroughs to whom *Howl* makes only an oblique reference).

Howl is also prophetic and generally applicable. It consists of three sections. Section one, the longest, is a portrait of the poet and the Beat generation going through a nightmarish experience. They are depraved, decadent, and in despair. They are eccentric and unconventional, doing drugs, living communally with their sexual promiscuity and homosexuality. They are howling in an uncanny way. Section one paints and immortalizes the Beat generation with all that it is noted for: its anti-mainstream way of living, its vision and its power, its ambition and sense of mission, and the depth of their despair in face of the threat of failure.

It is good to note that the same tone is echoed in another notable Ginsberg poem entitled "America," which opens with the poet's fully-loaded complaint that he has given all to America but now he is nothing, conveying effectively the feeling of the postwar generation, especially its intellectual, thinking minds, that they had been badly cheated and ruined. The theme is pervasive in a number of Ginsberg poems.

The second section of *Howl* traces their trouble back to its root cause, the Moloch of American civilization. Here the feeling of doom becomes more intense. The section concentrates its attack on the mechanical civilization of America. Ginsberg's name for it is Moloch, the biblical heathen god of fire to which children were sacrificed. To the god of Modern America, not children but the best minds of the nation are sacrificed. Moloch has "bashed open their skulls and eaten up their brains and imagination." It breeds solitude, filth, and suffering. It builds "demonic industries! spectral nations! invincible madhouses! ... monstrous bombs!" It ruthlessly washes visions, dreams, miracles, illuminations, ecstasies, in a word, "the whole boatload of sensitive bullshit," down the American river. And of course, hope with it all. Hence "Mad generation" "down the rocks of Time!" Thus the whole of the second section reinforces the theme of the first and adds touches of tragic pathos to a portrait of the consciousness of a nation definitely gone mad. Here despair reaches its breaking point.

The third section of the poem is both an elegy about the possible defeat at the hands of fate and an effort to brace for the future. It is dedicated to the poet's friend, Carl Solomon, who is apparently madder than he is. It immortalizes Carl Solomon as a symbol of victimization. Though an elegy of sorts, pathetic in ethos, the repetitive "I'm with you in Rockland!" identifies the poet with all the inmates of the Rockland mental hospital and asserts an indomitable sense of solidarity in face of repeated oppression.

Carl Solomon is a man of imagination, a writer, to whom the life of the mind is everything. He loves his country but feels uneasy about it. He ends up in a mental hospital, probably to "die ungodly in this armed madhouse." But they— Solomon, Ginsberg, and their generation—are not done yet. Their Messianic mission is yet to be fulfilled. Here their faith in the justice of their fight and its immortality in history exhibits itself as something religious and invincible. Their drive for attaining the utmost freedom of the mind has offered Ginsberg and his Beat generation a place in history.

In formal terms Ginsberg has borrowed freely from the cataloging form of Whitman's prose poetry and from William Carlos Williams in tone and rhythm. Ginsberg's poetry is a little expansive and sprawling, but its sheer power comes through and conquers. In terms of language, *Howl* seems to be a bundle of obscenities, obscene ideas expressed in obscene words including such linguistic vulgarities as the four-letter word. So as soon as it came out in 1956, *Howl* incurred the wrath and condemnation of the dominant WASP opinion, and went through a trial. But this proved to be more than a blessing in disguise, for it rallied to the poet's support an important portion of the academic and critical community (including quite a few writers) and increased the sales. *Howl* went through over thirty imprints within a short span of time and became the best-selling volume of poetry since the end of the war. Since then it has become clear that *Howl* is a consummate work of carefully worded invectives, a torrent of deliberate voluble curses, spearheaded against an America that has destroyed "the best minds" of the postwar generation.

Ginsberg's Reputation

Ginsberg has won an international reputation. Beginning with *Howl* and the San Francisco Poetry Renaissance, his literary career stretched well over four decades. His life went through colorful stages, one of which was his conversion to Buddhism. His ideas evolved into a system of its own that exerted its due share of influence on postwar thinking. He wrote and published more and has stayed attractive to the critical circles.

Gary Snyder (1930-)

Gary Snyder was in spiritual consonance with the Beats. Connected with the Beats in the mid-1950s and early 1960s, he has been placed next to Ginsberg in reputation among this group of authors. Kerouac offered a portrait of him in his novel, *The Dharma Bums*.

Growing up in Oregon, he has an Emersonian love for nature. He imbibes the American West wildness and primitive myths such as those of the American Indians and weaves these into the very fabric of his system. He loves nature and sees it as restorative and healing. He has always tried to stay in direct contact with nature. In addition, he is interested in Chinese and Indian philosophy. He studied Zen Buddhism in Japan and lived for long in the foothills of the Sierra Mountain in California. He studied Chinese, read translations of Chinese literature, and translated the poems of the Chinese Zen poet, Han Shan. He did physical work like a timber scaler, a forest fire lookout, a logger, and a hand in a ship's engine-room. All these have impacted his poetry. "My poems follow the rhythms of my physical work I'm doing and the life I'm leading at any given time." He finds nature and the ancient traditions—especially those of the American Indians—a counterpoint to contemporary culture and its dominant values which his works criticize. He tries to hold history and wildness in his mind so that his poetry "may approach the true measure of things and stand against the unbalance and ignorance of our time." Some critics see some trace of anti-civilization in him.[6]

For Snyder the wildness is always a tonic to man. He feels that we humans need to sink back in nature to brace up for life even if it is for a stay as brief as one night. We leave the city, hiking up the mountains, going up a mile in the air, lost in meadows, snowfields, and mountain peaks, lying in sleeping bags, talking with no worry or care half the night, and listening to the wind and rain, and then we will get reenergized enough to face life anew. This is what Snyder tries to say in his "August on Sourdough, A Visit from Dick Brewer." Dick comes from San Francisco and is going to New York: his life begins from a city and ends in another, but it is made tolerable and good, Snyder suggests, by his visit to mother nature. Though different in more ways than one, the poem is a reminder of Frost's "Birches" or "Stopping by Woods on a Snowy Evening." Then we notice that, when Dick has left, the poet goes back to his mountain, "and far, far, west." The reason for this action is explained in his "Mid-August at Sourdough Mountain Lookout." He loves nature. He is close to it. Everything there fascinates him: a smoke haze in a valley, the heat, the rain, the glowing fir-cones, the rocks and meadows, and the swarms of fireflies. He sees them, hears them, and feels them. With them he is carefree: he forgets the things he reads and the friends in the cities. There in nature his imagination runs free, and he becomes whole as he drinks "cold snow-water from a tin cup" and looks down "for miles/ through high still air." He is a Thoreau in his own day.

The "still[ness]" is central to Snyder's poetic concern. He seeks to locate a point of stillness amid the constant change of the universe. This stillness is important because it offers a moment, a break, a breathing space for modern man and makes it easier for him to cope with life. What happens in the duration of this moment we can surmise from his poems: it is a moment of freedom and relief when the mind ceases to remember, the body loses its individuality and merges into nature, and the local place reveals the universal. It is Emerson, Frost,

Williams, and Zen Buddhism all in one. This is a moment of epiphany, one of ecstasy, when the poet "looks down for miles through high still air" to witness the sublime, the essence of the universe.

Such a moment of stillness occurs in his poem, "Straight-Creek—Great Burn." There is change everywhere in the world around. The dry grass is freed of snow. The chickadees are pecking seeds. The avalanche with the water under it "spills out/ rock lip pool," bending over, foaming, and returning to the deep-dark hole. Change comes over the creek boulders, the spring, the snow, the "grand dead burn pine," the lichen, the talus rock. What appears before us so far is the inanimate part of the world (ll. 1-34). Skipping lines 35-36 (which we'll discuss shortly), we notice the movement of the other part of the universe, the animate, "the feather garments" of Heaven, as represented by the birds swooping up and round, tilting back, flying apart while hanging on together, "never a leader,/ all of one swift/ empty/ dancing mind." The birds arc and loop and then settle down" (ll. 37-52). Sandwiched in between the inanimate and the animate, there is the human who, like the birds, achieve a point of stillness after hiking: "us resting on dry fern and/ watching" (ll. 35-36). This is when meditation begins, when the body becomes transparent and the mind is open to the eternal and the universal. The poetic reaches its zenith here: hence the last line, "end of the poem."

Snyder feels that the job of the poet is to catch sight of the poetic, which resides nowhere but in the natural world. Now what is the poetic to Snyder, and what is the eternal and the universal that he thinks we have got to learn about? One clue is offered when Snyder said on one occasion that his work has been "driven by the insight that all is connected and interdependent—nature, societies; rocks and stars." One early trace of the notion is already visible in his poem, "Riprap." This is a typical Snyder poem in its natural fusion of the physical with the metaphysical, of the real world with that of the imagination. The poem demonstrates at once a fine intermingling of the two planes of things and a clear distinction between them. A riprap is, Snyder notes, "[a] cobble of stone laid on steep slick rock to make a trail for horses in the mountains." But the poet sees more than a mere mountain trail here. The cobbles become words. The trail becomes matter for thought. Made of the things of the actual world ("Solidity of bark, leaf, or wall"), it looks like the Milky Way; the people and the lost ponies appear to fit in the grand scheme like straying planets; and all these are "poems" to the observing poet. What is seen is not just the three-dimensional world of ours; there is the extra dimension, the fourth, the mythical, the extra-sensual, the unknown. The mystery is deepened when we face not one world but "worlds" that are endless and perpetually changing. There is the eclectic Snyder well on display here. Each rock like a word—this sounds like Thoreau in one sense and Pound in another. There is poetry in life and nature—this is Williams. The world exists for meditation (ll. 1-6) and all change—Snyder's Zen Buddhism is speaking. The juxtaposition of images, their incremental effect, the meticulous attention to detail, the absence of connectives, the colloquial diction—all these and more form an exquisite chaos of various traditions contemporary as well as ancient and foreign.

Snyder's belief in nature will make, for him, an imprint on history.

"Against Civilization": Merwin, Bly, and Wright [7]

Sharing Snyder's stance on civilization and nature but different from him in varying aspects are a few poets whose works have revealed some shared quality. These include W. S. Merwin (1927-2019), Robert Bly (1926-2021), and James Wright (1927-1980). They do not seem to like the sight of the manifestations of "civilization" such as roads, wires, and the cityscape. They are worried about environmental pollution like global warming, oil spills, and the use of pesticides which threatens the survival of the humankind and the species in general. They feel the terror of war. Somehow they find value in the primitive, in nature and wildness, and believe that the humankind would be better off if they could live the way Snyder does, or like Robert Bly (who once stayed in the farm country of

Minnesota). To them nature and civilization form an inevitable antithesis, and we humans stand at the point where two roads branch out into the future. Critic David Perkins lump these poets together with the label of "Against Civilization."

W. S. Merwin

W. S. Merwin was born in New York. He studied medieval literature and romance languages, and stayed long in Europe—France, Spain, and Portugal. The theme of his poetry is generally concerned with the dilemmas of humankind and the wholesome effect of the natural world. He wrote about Vietnam war (read his "The Asians Dying"), the death of the whales (read "For a Coming Extinction"), the ecological pollution ("The Last One"), and the direction America takes, its poisoning of the earth and its hi-tech triumphs emerging as symbols of death. There is a pessimistic strain of thought in Merwin. Even when he writes about erotic love—and he has written quite a few of these, there is little or no warmth or emotional release. The lovers in his "Summer Doorway," for instance, look like static figures from a painting. He writes his moody and despairing feelings into his poetry as he believes that the future is so bleak that there is no point in writing. Take "For a Coming Extinction" for example. The first stanza tells of the coming extinction of the gray whale, and accuses humankind of inventing forgiveness but forgiving nothing. The second stanza continues the angry accusation against humans lording it over all other species ruthlessly simply because they were created on a different day and were given the dominion over others. The poet sees the death of the future for the humans along with the extinction of their fellow species. The last stanza of the poem, after surveying "the black garden" where all extinct and endangered species gather, ends on a bitter sarcastic attack on the self-importance of man.

But everything is not lost yet. Nature and solitude may offer "a pale resurrection" to man. "The Drunk in the Furnace" illustrates the point well. There is this deserted furnace in this gully, which looks like "a hulking black fossil"

people do not seem to know about any more. Then one day someone comes along, makes a fire, and homesteads there. He enjoys working there, and loves the music and rhythm that comes from "[h]ammer-and-anvilling with poker and bottle/ To his jugged bellowings." When he is done for the day, he "[sleeps] like an iron pig." He is carefree and happy. The people around do not like this trespasser of their territory and their lives, but the children, still innocent in their ways, seem to be learning something. "The Drunk" in the title of the poem, seen as a drunk by the community nearby, may not be a drunk after all. He is probably the most awake, the most lucid of them all. He stays away from the maddening crowds and takes up his abode in deserted nature. Here man can have a peace of mind and sleep like a pig. The gully with the furnace looks like a fallen garden of Eden, but wholesome nature can help resurrect the lost hope. It is significant that the children are intrigued and are learning. The poet sees hope in it.

Merwin's style has undergone some changes over the years, but there is always his emphasis on myths and emblems which he sees in the occurrences of daily lives. And there is always conscious artistry.

Robert Bly

Robert Bly grew up on a farm in Madison, Minnesota. He attended Harvard, spent three years in solitude, and attended the Writers' Workshop at the University of Iowa. He started a literary magazine, first entitled *The Fifties*, but with time changed it to *The Sixties*, *The Seventies*, and *The Eighties*. Along with other postmodern poets of his time, Bly stood against the kind of academic verse which Eliot and Ransom championed, and supported surrealist poetry. His magazine carried his translations of such poets as German poet Goerg Trakl and Chilean poet Pablo Neruda, hitherto little known in the US, and also helped struggling young writers out.

His first volume of verse, *Silence in the Snowy Fields*, came out in 1962, in which appeared some of his best "Snowy Fields" poetry. Pastoral life, the beauty of natural scenery, and the stillness and solitude, free of the intrusion of noise and crowds, are extolled as conducive to the life of the mind. Bly has been prolific with some twenty volumes of poetry to his credit, but his early "Snowy Fields" poems remain probably his most permanent work. In the 1960s, Bly was deeply involved in the anti-Vietnam War movement, and wrote and read a lot of his political poetry. When this phase of his life was over, he turned to meditation, seeking light and "interior space" from the unconscious, the primitive, and Oriental wisdom.

Regarding Bly's poetics, in addition to his views on surrealism, he feels that the poet must free himself from his rational ego and release the deeper, the less conscious levels of the mind, and that modern poetry should grasp the flowing psychic energy. His notion on imagery is known as the "deep image." To Ezra Pound the image was "petals on a wet black bough," Bly said on one occasion, but to him, it was "death on the wet deep roads of the guitar." This is associated with his stance on the deeper, unconscious aspect of the poetic mind. This "deep image" idea of his influenced quite a few contemporary writers like Robert Creeley, Gary Snyder, and James Wright. Bly's poetry is generally moody. There is exhibited an amount of obsession with death in some works. His 1979 volume, *This Tree Will be Here for a Thousand Years*, along with his "Snowy Fields" poetry, contains some of his best memorable poems.

James Wright

James Wright was born and grew up on a farm in Martins Ferry, Ohio and experienced poverty in the Depression. This exerted a visible influence on the themes of his work. Mostly he wrote in his poetry about the Midwest, the America he knew at first hand, the poverty of the river towns along the Ohio, the suffering, both physical and emotional, of the underdog, the low, the "social outsiders." His sympathies were always with the common run of mankind. He was sensitive to the seamy side of life and felt keenly about the sad aspects of the world of man where there is so much of loneliness, pain, weariness, and death. Hence the depressed mood of his poems.

Regarding the formal features of his work, Wright experienced some drastic stylistic change in his career. He began writing poems in traditional forms, such as the sonnets, the iambic pentameter, and regular rhymes. His first two volumes, *The Green Wall* (1957) and *Saint Judas* (1959), show the influence of Robert Frost, Edwin Arlington Robinson, John Crowe Ransom and Theodore Roethke. The change in his style had to do with his acquaintance with Trakl's poetry of semi-surreal leaping images and his friendship with Robert Bly. Wright visited Bly's farm, fell under the influence of the "deep image" or "emotive imagination," abandoned his previous methods of writing, and wrote a new poetry of leaping images and free verse of American colloquial speech. His third volume, *The Branch Will Not Break* (1963), contains remarkable Postmodernist lyrics.

One of his famous poems is "Lying in a Hammock at William Duffy's Farm in Pine Island, Minnesota." Lying in a hammock on a farm one evening, the poet sees a number of things around in nature and experiences an emotional awakening of a kind. The poet leans back as dusk falls. The mixture of feelings that these sights and sounds of nature combine to arouse in him result in a moment of ecstasy: he makes the painful self-discovery that he has somehow wasted his life, and that he should have come earlier to the farm and should have lived in nature longer. Wright's other volumes include *Collected Poems* (1972) which won him a number of awards including the Pulitzer Prize, *To a Blossoming Pear Tree* (1977), *This Journey* (1982), and *Above the River: The Collected Poems* (1990).

Chapter 22 The New York School • Meditative Poetry • The Black Mountain Poets

The New York School

The so-called New York School became well known with the publication of Donald Allen's 1960 anthology. The school then included Frank O'Hara (1926-1966), Kenneth Koch (1925-2002), John Ashbery (1927-2017), and James Schuyler (1923-1991). One of the things they all did, for a while in the 1960s, was their experiment with Surrealism. The surrealist works of Kenneth Koch, the collage of Ashbery's *The Tennis Court Oath*, and the surrealist verses of O'Hara—all these combined to make the impression that the New York School was a group of collagists, Dadaists, and surrealists and was not to be taken seriously.

This is a misunderstanding of the school. These young poets were no doubt eager to experiment; their contact with avant-garde artists in New York City offered food for thought and added to their enthusiasm to break new ground. But their experiment with surrealism lasted for a while only, and all dropped it to move on to their major phases of writing which have produced quite a good number of impressive poems. They were so immersed in their creative endeavors that they did not pay much attention to the political and social issues of the time as did their contemporaries such as Lowell and Ginsberg. They did not feel the religious impulse like Snyder or the fascination with myths like Olson. They had their own artistic concerns.

Although the poets of the New York School were different in their separate pursuits, their poetry reveals something they shared in common. For one thing, they were all vehemently up against the dominant New Critical values such as the impersonal presentation of images, and tried to assert their individual poetic voice. They also introduced the popular and the low features of life into their writings like popular songs, comic strip figures, and Hollywood movies. Thirdly, they exhibited a huge sense of humor, offering room as their poems did for elements like the vulgar and the sentimental. Finally, of course, they experimented with surrealism, for a while.

Frank O'Hara (1926-1966)

One central figure of this school was Frank O'Hara. He worked mostly in New York City, a center of innovative ferment in the arts, and he was very sensitive to what went on around him such as abstract expressionism. Apart from his personal friendships with the poets of the New York School, he was closely associated with many artists whose passion to "make it new" proved to be contagious to him. He was the poet of New York for his time.

The way he composed poems was interesting to note. His works were a lot of them "occasional" poems written for a birthday, a thank-you etc. His poems are full of names of people, places, and literary works without proper introduction. He wrote poetry effortlessly, often composing poems in his lunch hours. Hence one of his volumes entitled *The Lunch Poems*. He made less effort to get his works published, and his uncollected poems were found either from scraps of paper in boxes and trunks or retrieved from letters. These were put together and became the five-hundred-page *Collected Poems*.[1]

O'Hara's early poems like "Second Avenue" were mostly surrealistic, and as such were often painfully obscure though there is a good deal of wit there. Later he was noted for the "I do this I do that" type of poems, a kind of poems which he was pretty much the first to write. In these poems O'Hara tells in a flat tone the little things he did on just one or any of the days in his life. The details pile up not always connected; names of people appear often known to none but the author himself. The readers feel bored through most of the reading process, but feel well rewarded often by a surprise in wait for them, one that is not, however, always apparent. Often we need to reflect back on the whole poem to appreciate it well. "Why I Am Not a Painter" and "The Day Lady Died" are good examples for us here.

"Why I Am Not a Painter" talks about painting and poetry. The poet tells us in casual language about his visit to his painter friend, Mike Goldberg by name. Mike is starting a painting which has sardines in it. It takes days to finish. In the middle of it, the poet pays him another visit, and the painting is still going on. When he shows up again in the studio, the poet sees the finished painting but not the sardines in it. "It was too much," Mike tells him. Around the time, the poet himself is writing a poem about the color of orange. Soon he has written pages, twelve poems altogether, some even in prose, but he finds that "I haven't mentioned orange yet." Yet he entitles the work "Oranges." One day he sees his friend's painting on exhibition in a gallery; it is called "Sardines." Now the readers may be confused about this. The fact of the matter might be this, that sardines and oranges may be symbols of life. As life is "terrible," both the painter and the poet wish to evade it a little instead of coming to grips with it directly.

Thus O'Hara possesses a tragic vision. It is well illustrated also in his other poems such as "Joe's Jacket," where the poet-narrator is at a party and tells us why he drinks. He drinks to smother his sensitivity, he says. He drinks to kill the fear of boredom, the mounting panic of it. He drinks to reduce his seriousness (which may be induced by his fear of life), and to die a little. This all boils down to the point that just as "sardines" is too much for the painter and orange for the poet, so is life for the poet-narrator here. He wishes to be able to escape from it "a little," instead of confronting it right away.

O'Hara also wrote a number of love poems which touch upon his homosexual relationships in a natural and easy manner. It is also important to note about his language that it is colloquial, anecdotal, bare of ornaments, so that he was definitely well in step with the contemporary anti-literary, anti-artistic tradition.

John Ashbery (1927-2017)

Although regarded as one member of the New York School, John Ashbery's mature poetry reveals the salient features of a meditative mind. It is therefore more appropriate to see him as a meditative poet.

Ashbery grew up in Rochester, New York. He went to Harvard and met Kenneth Koch and Frank O'Hara there. The three moved to New York City and wrote poetry which shared features such as the emphasis on the individual voice, popular culture, high spirited humor, and experiments with surrealism. They became known as the New York School. After Harvard, Ashbery did graduate work at Columbia in English and French literature. In 1956 he went to France on a Fulbright fellowship and lived there for ten years, working as an art journalist (a job which he did for the next thirty years).

Over a long period of time, Ashbery tried to find a style of his own. He benefited from his acquaintance with painting and painters, experimented with structures of collage and fragmentation, and wrote expansive poems. Then his mature style, discursive and disorienting, appeared first in *The Double Dream of Spring* (1970) and reached its extreme in his masterwork, *Self-Portrait in a Convex Mirror* (1975). This obscure, meditative, idiosyncratic poem won the Pulitzer Prize, the National Book Award, and the National Book Critics Circle Award. After that, he wrote more, but none touched it as his best. Now Ashbery has become one of the most renowned meditative poets in contemporary America.[2]

Ashbery is very difficult to read. His obscurity is different from that of Pound and Eliot. Ashbery seldom quotes from antique sources and uses allusions. His language is easy to understand, but his meaning is hard to decipher. In his poem "Like a Sentence," Ashbery likens his poem to "brilliant woods": the woods are well lit and transparent, but people often get lost.

Let's take a couple of strophes from one of Ashbery's more lucid poems, "Grand Galop," and find out what hinders comprehension in his poetry. In the first two sections of the poem, we come in contact with two things juxtaposed: The physical aspect of reality as represented by today or Monday's lunch of Spanish omelet, lettuce and tomato salad, jello, milk and cookies, and tomorrow's lunch of sloppy joe on bun, scalloped corn, stewed tomatoes, rice pudding and milk. As this crosses the poet's mind, it focuses its attention on the metaphysical aspect of reality, which is the profound issue of getting to know reality. The poet says we have to wait for reality to reveal its totality, but that never will happen because we are time-bound and have to wait forever. Then the next physical triviality, like water dripping from an air conditioner on those passing underneath, catches the mind's attention. Thus his poetic mind seems all-inclusive and does not bother to select from its raw materials. What causes the hitch in comprehension here lies in the juxtaposition of these apparently unrelated elements. The readers' logical process of thinking is suddenly disrupted and disoriented. Hence the obscurity.

Let's take a look of some of his poems. "Illustration" (1956), one of his earliest works, begins to show the basic features of the typical Ashbery work: his obsession with getting to know reality, and his indirect mode of expression. First, the poem is all about the possibility of knowing reality. In its first section, the seminary student committing suicide is a symbol of reality that puzzles all around wishing to know her wants and help her through the ordeal. Everybody thinks that they know what she wants and offers whatever they have, but they still fail to save her because they do not know what she wants. The poet then wonders, in the second section, whether the student is the only reality for us all, because, at the same time of her suicide, other things are happening as well: the rockets soaring over the city, the feasting that is going on, in a word, so much is happening at that moment. Reality may have more than one single aspect and more than one single manifestation. It is not possible for us to see the whole of it. Our perception is questionable, too, because we are time-bound and space-bound. Even though we try to get beyond the limitations of space, and fly up and see her falling, then we would see her only from one attitude, and there can be so many attitudes. So the poet is saying that reality may not be knowable, and that it does not care whether we know it anyway. Our knowledge is incomplete and could never solve the riddle that is the miracle of reality.

One difficulty in reading Ashbery lies in his peculiar way of saying things. The first section of "Illustration" is still not quite the mature Ashbery style yet. The narrative is smooth; transitions are natural; words coalesce with their sense; the whole of it is lucid and meaningful. The Ashbery style *per se* begins to appear in the second section. Words begin to divorce from their normal significance ("resemble a taller/ Impression of ourselves," "indiscretions," "attitudes," "the end" etc.). Transitions are abrupt; ideas and images jump and lack surface connections. Lines leave things half said and leave ample room for speculation. There are so many linguistic resources available for the poet to smooth things out and help readers focus on the theme of the work, but Ashbery does not use them. As he matured as a poet, he discarded the mode of writing evident in the first section of "Illustration," and developed and persisted in that of the second section. Now this kind of writing is too idiosyncratic for the readers at large to share. The result is that, although he makes a plea to the readers in his "Paradoxes and Oxymorons" to read and make sense of what he says, much of his poetry seems to remain still unread, however much this is against his best wishes.

"Self-Portrait in a Convex Mirror"

Ashbery's most famous poem, "Self-Portrait in a Convex Mirror," best represents his view of reality and his poetics. It has to do with the 16th-century Italian Mannerist painter Parmigianino's self-portrait.

Long as it is— it is a 6-strophe, 552-line work, the poem is all about one thing: it is impossible to get to know reality and represent it fully in art. In his opinion, reality and art both change and keep on changing to become ever something else, or what he terms the "otherness." As nothing—reality or art or the artist for that matter—stays the same, it is difficult to get to know the "whole" of the truth, and it would be extravagant to expect anything like an authentic artistic representation of reality. So there has been distortion all along in art and literature.

Although it looks bizarre and extremist, Parmigianino's self-portrait represents actually the rule of distortion, rather than an exception to it, in the history of artistic portrayal of reality. It epitomizes the idea of distortion. This is what the Ashbery's poem talks about, over and again and from different angles. This argument is the thread that alone will lead us out of the labyrinth of the poem. The thesis of the poem is then just this one single point, that reality is not authentically knowable and representable; we only distort it in trying. Keep the point in mind, and we shall not lose track in our reading of the poem.

The first reading of the poem will prove to be a frustrating experience for many readers. This may have to do with the poet's abrupt transitions, his use of images and symbols that seem to be beside the point under discussion in the text, and his self-indulgence in perception and expression. But if we calm down and set our mind on plodding through the text with "normal nerve, normal breath," and persist with patience and care, we will find that the poet has never for a moment swerved from his line of thinking and has never said anything irrelevant in the whole of his 552 lines. Some critics think that Ashbery is good at piling up nonsense before letting any sense break through. The comment is nonsense itself.

In the 1st strophe (ll. 1-99), the poet sees a painting, the self-portrait in a convex mirror by Parmigianino (1503-1540). Historically, Parmigianino did this probably to show that there is no single "correct" reality (ll. 217-221). The poet feels uncomfortable with this kind of artistic representation. First, it is not authentic because it is twice removed from reality. In addition, the painting is inadequate for the expression of the soul of the person painted. Everything is framed, fixed ("life englobed"), no longer alive and changing ("The whole is stable within/ Instability"). The painting restrains reality, and it is superficial: it has its medium for the surfaces but none for the essence in the recesses. It is impossible to represent the "visible core"—the ultimate truth—of things. The Mannerist self-portrait embraces the belief that art can represent reality, but it warns that it can do so in different ways, the Mannerist distortion included, as there can be different versions of reality. Ultimately, the poet feels that the self-portrait offers no authentic representation.

The 2nd strophe (ll. 100-150) states that we as part of reality change with reality. External factors and our memories of these factors influence our thinking and our perception so that our mind itself is not in control. In addition, reality is a symphony of diverse elements, and there is no need to settle for just one mode of representation. We should assert our individuality and be tolerant toward others. Nothing is "extraneous." Realism is no good now and neither is Mannerism because reality keeps changing and proves too difficult for any style to represent it authentically. All this implies that the poet feels that there has to be a new vision of art in relation to reality.

The 3rd strophe (ll. 151-206) states that theories of art tend to codify the mind and kill our dream for perfect art. Though necessary as a guide, these theories are "weak" because they subsume and rigidify everything and become a routine for us to accept without even noticing or thinking of change. And we accept theories such as Mannerism also because it takes advantage of "our idea of distortion" and because we are accustomed to art selecting and generalizing. Ideal art should get beyond the limitations of all forms and theories. There are no such theories or forms now good enough to meet our needs. What these really do is to frame the mind and kill our dream for perfect artistic representation. The result is that a semblance of living (but not real living) occurs; we become codified and dead.

The 4th strophe (ll. 207-250) introduces the idea of otherness. Everything, including the self-portrait and the angel, constantly changes to become something else. What Parmigianino did was actually an example of catching the novelty that the process of becoming exhibits. The poet goes even further to declare that, even as the painter works, he undergoes a change and so does his room ("the strict/ Otherness of the painter in his/ Other room"). We feel startled by the change because we are not aware of it, not prepared for it (ll. 244-250).

The 5th strophe (ll. 251-310) paves the way for the exposition of the poet's own stance on reality and art. Authentic reality waits for our authentic representation. While Parmigianino's studio is proven to be no good, something new has appeared on the scene. This is the poet's vision of art in relation to reality. It may be hard to understand and may jostle people out of their established way of thinking. Although Parmigianino offers no answer to our question regarding reality and art, and his self-portrait is all surface with no recesses for the essence of reality, he represents one of the phases and one of the efforts in history to portray reality the best we can. There has been no right or wrong in our endeavor; there are only phases in our epistemological process. Our search for the best possible way goes on; the questioning of a particular style's strengths and weaknesses should be seen as normal and as no menace to anyone. What the poet implies is that he may have been writing to question the way art has been representing reality, and has thus amazed the public, but he means well and would like to see that this kind of questioning will become general and natural, and not bizarre as his own way of thinking has been criticized.

The 6th strophe (ll. 311-552) explains the poet's view of the relationship between reality and art. Coming back to the self-portrait, the poet says to Parmigianino: your painting is a page in history and that it is good and useful to look at it. He then goes on to assert that any attempt at pinpointing or nailing down reality in any way is in fact killing reality and art with it. Art, beautiful art, is part of a historical continuum and is created both on the basis and imbued with the recollection of the best of the past. Though any one style is meaningful for its own time, it represents not just one phase of history but all of it when considered out of its immediate context and in the long run of history. Reality, part of it being the self-portrait, changes and is elusive. The whole truth of reality cannot be known, but can be felt vaguely. The poet feels that he has seen the light and is determined to tell about it although he knows that he is a little ahead of time. In his opinion, change is ongoing and continuous. Reality, the artist, and his art all keep changing. The notion of continuous time (the present undivided from both the past and the present) is justified and should be good for us if we do not want to distort things in our artistic reflection. But distortion has been the rule rather than the exception in the history of art because of the constant change. The poet repeats that realism is no good; neither is the self-portrait's Mannerism. The search for the ideal art is hopeless. The hand of reality is not recording; each part of reality just happens haphazardly, in fragments, soon forgotten, except for individual occurrences (which may be recorded and noted down as all styles of art have been trying to do), remembered but not well remembered ("in cold pockets/ Of remembrance"), almost inaudible to us because outdated ("whispers out of time"). Thus the poet's view is that reality is not authentically representable. So "Self-Portrait in a Convex Mirror" is trying to say that from the beginning of time, art has been all inevitably distorting reality.

Although Ashbery has his point, he has told only one side of the truth. The whole truth may be that reality is unstable, but it has also its aspect of relative stability that makes life possible to live and gives it some meaningful, recognizable form. Ashbery's truth could lead to a void, a nothingness, where no effort, distortion or no distortion, would be worthwhile. Thus in the final analysis his is probably also a half-truth, in itself another kind of distortion. This may be where Ashbery's aesthetic crisis ultimately lies.

In conclusion, we can say that, both daring and self-indulgent, Ashbery impresses by his own kind of logic or want of logic, his complex mind, and his fine visual representation of the world. He leads the readers into a realm of enjoyment through art, very often on a personal and private level. This experience is possible often only to an elite group endowed with a sensibility similar to his own. Hence Ashbery's small readership. But Ashbery has been influential in his own way. He is one of the finest poets of his time.

A. R. Ammons (1926-2001)

Another major contemporary meditative poet is A. R. Ammons. Ammons was well read in Wordsworth, Emerson, Whitman, and Indian and Chinese philosophy, and wrote often in the Romantic tradition. Highly aware of the natural world and its multiple significance, he sees nature and life in their sundry forms of being that ranges from the infinitesimal to the infinite. He also tries to see and comprehend the silhouette of a larger design, a mystery probably unknown to man, and feels that his art should try to present his vision as accurately as possible.

One thing that we notice about Ammons' poetry is the walk motif recurrent in some of his works. As one walks, one observes the constant changes that occur around, the diversity and mutability that are the norm of nature and life. A meditative mind can transcend surface and perceive the built-in larger scheme. Ammons even goes as far as comparing a poem to a walk. One of Ammons' best poems that well reveal the poet's thematic and formal concerns is his "Corsons Inlet" (1965).

"Corsons Inlet" is both a description of the scenery along this tidal inlet in New Jersey that the poet sees while walking along it and a record of his meditations, his discoveries, and his poetic rendering of these all. The poem begins with "I went for a walk over the dunes again this morning/ to the sea," and he sees the world of nature around and meditates on its various manifestations of life and its kaleidoscopic changes: the sea surf, the naked headland, the muggy sunny scene, the wind from the sea, the sand, the eddies, the inlet's cutting edge, the grass, the white sandy paths, areas of primrose, bayberries, reeds, yarrow, the creek, the undercreek, black shoals of mussels, the air and the sun, the waterline, the gulls, the crabs, a ruddy turnstone, the white blacklegged egret, the black mudflats, swallows, the twittering of birds, their beaks and the wings, blue tiny flowers on a leafless weed, snail shell, minnows, etc. The long list reveals the poet's sharp eye for minute details of life and nature. Individually viewed, the things keep forever changing in shape and form; there may be fighting and killing (almost in the Darwinian sense or akin to Tennyson's nature "red in tooth and claw") with suffering and death, perpetual moving, always in the process of "becoming," as if there were no beginnings or ends. But out of these details, their chaos and disorder and confusion in plan and arrangement, their mutability, their motion, and their formlessness, the poet perceives an order of a large nature—the "Overall," something that, somehow, resembles Emerson's "Oversoul" or God's grand scheme of things. This "Overall," as the poet tells us, is permanent, changeless, with perfect form and order, a state of things absent from the temporal, spatial, phenomenal world of man: "No arranged terror: no forcing of images, plan,/ Or thought:/ No propaganda, no humbling of reality to precept[.]"

The poem demonstrates how nature and the poetic mind interact with one another. The mind sinks into nature, carries on a dialogue with it, and intuits the absolute inherent in it. To the mind that suffers the restrictions and limitations of human perception, nature is liberating: "I was released from forms,/ from the perpendiculars,/ straight lines, blocks, boxes, binds/ of thought/ into the hues, shadings, rises, flowing bends and blends/ of sight[.]" The mirroring mind observes, digests and creates spontaneously. Here the poet so skillfully juxtaposes the physical with the metaphorical that one glides into the other smoothly, soundlessly. Nature and art merge in a subtle, exquisite way. In this respect, Ammons reads, occasionally, like Gary Snyder. The liberating effect of nature is well reflected in the formal aspect of "Corsons Inlet." Here the poem runs in its free verse, with its run-on lines and its natural varying line lengths. It is William Carlos Williams both in subject and form and in mode of perception.

The Black Mountain Poets

One group of poets active on the postwar scene include, among others,

Charles Olson (1910-1970), Denise Levertov (1923-1997), Robert Duncan (1919-1988), and Robert Creeley (1926-2005). As these people were either associated with Black Mountain College, or with *Black Mountain Review* (edited by Robert Creeley), they have become known as the "Black Mountain Poets."

Black Mountain College was founded in the 1930s as a liberal educational center. It was near Asheville, North Carolina. In the 1950s it became a focus for all dissidents in art, literature, and matters of academic interest in general when Charles Olson was first instructor and then rector there (1951-1956). Teachers, painters, sculptors, writers, musicians, and film makers with unique ideas of their own came to visit or stay. Cid Corman's little magazine *Origin* and *Black Mountain Review* were ready to publish their works. Allen Ginsberg and Charles Olson were among the contributing editors of the *Review*. Williams Carlos Williams, Gary Snyder, Jack Kerouac, and Philip Whalen were some of their published authors. Although closed in 1956, the College did its best to help with the growth of postwar art and literature, and the Black Mountain poets made their significant addition to American literature.

Charles Olson

The leading figure of this school of poetry was Charles Olson, who joined the college in 1951 and was its rector until 1956 (year of its closure). He turned it into a center of arts. He wrote the well-known essay "Projective Verse" (1950), one of the most significant statements in postwar American poetry, and fought for the birth of a new poetry almost single-handedly against the New Critical hegemony of the publishing world then. He had the support of the brave little magazine, *Origin*, and was able over time to create a new poetic community. The first to call for a new verse in postwar America, he remained an influence on postwar American poetry. His poetry as in *In Cold Hell, In Thicket* (1953) and *The Distances* (1961) contains some of the most exquisite of poetic works written in the 20th century. His *The Maximus Poems* (1953-1968) is a collection of lyrical, sociological, and formal experimental poems which has, together with the works of Ezra Pound and William Carlos Williams, made up the basic poetics of a good deal of postwar American poetry. In theme Olson is critical of the American way of life; in form he borrows from the metrics of Pound and Williams.[3]

Charles Olson was born in Worcester, Massachusetts, and did the course work for the Ph.D. at Harvard. He did excellent work as a scholar in such fields of activity as archaeology, education, and anthropology. His first critical work, *Call Me Ishmael* (1945), reveals a seminal idiosyncratic mind. As a poet and a critic, he wrote and contributed very much toward moving American poetry away from the tradition of T. S. Eliot and the New Criticism and elevating the poetics of Williams and Pound. Olson had a huge sense of mission. He was one of the first, if not the first, to locate clearly the problem with American poetry in the 1950s. As his friend Robert Creeley put it, "… what confronted us in 1950 was a closed system indeed, poems patterned upon exterior and traditionally accepted models. The New Criticism of that period was dominant and would not admit the possibility of verse considered as an 'open field.'"

Olson and His "Projective Verse"

Olson lost no time addressing the problem. He began by defining art and poetry. "Art is the only twin life has," he states in his essay "Human Universe" (1950), "because it does not seek to describe but to enact." His essay "Projective Verse," when first published, exploded as it were on the consciousness of the people involved. William Carlos Williams called it an "excitement" that was widely shared, and across the Atlantic the British poet Donald Davie was impressed, too. Olson aimed at starting in poetry writing a revolution, the stature of which would be comparable to "the revolution of … 1910." He would like to "suggest a few ideas about what stance toward reality brings such verse [projective or OPEN verse] into being, what that stance does, both to the poet and to the reader." And he envisioned something of some magnitude for American poetry in the new period, "a change beyond, and larger than, the technical, and may, the way things look, lead to new poetics and to new concepts from which some sort of drama, say, or of epic, perhaps, may emerge." It already sounded like a manifesto. Sure enough he took the bold "advance-guard action" and developed a poetics that encouraged poets to depart from the "closed" form. In so doing he impacted quite a few of his contemporaries such as Robert Duncan, Robert Creeley, Paul Blackburn, and LeRoi Jones (Amiri Baraka). As Creeley put it, Olson became "the man from whom our creative impetus must spring."

Now this "projective or OPEN verse" was in fact free verse. As Olson defines it in his famous essay, "the NON-Projective" verse is "closed" verse, and by "closed" he means anything in the traditional form. Apparently he had the New Critical form in mind. Olson felt that it was time contemporary poets, or as he called them, "the sons of Pound and Williams," picked up the fruits of the experiments of the older poets. The new poet, he says, should work in the "OPEN," or engage in "FIELD COMPOSITION," or "COMPOSITION BY FIELD, as opposed to inherited line, stanza, over-all form, what is the 'old' base of the non-projective." He calls a poem "the field" where all the syllables and lines must be managed in their relations to each other. So "composition by field" is his way of saying writing projective verse or new free verse as against writing in traditional way. Olson declares that poetry is energy transferred from where the poet got it all the way to the reader through the poem; the poem must be, at all points, a high-energy construct and an energy discharge.

Olson emphasizes the role of breathing in the composing process. He places emphasis on the syllable which he calls "king and pin of versification." Poets should listen to the syllable constantly and scrupulously. The ear is close to the mind and has the mind's speed. The syllable is thus born of the union of the mind and the ear. "Let me put it baldly," he states in his essay. "The two halves are: the HEAD, by way of the EAR, to the SYLLABLE/ the HEART, by way of

BREATH, to the LINE [.]" The syllable and the line between them make a poem. The line comes from the breathing of the poet and ends where breathing terminates. Breath allows all the speech force of language back in the poem. He asserts that the poet can indicate exactly the breath, the pauses, the suspensions even of syllables, the juxtapositions even of parts of phrases which he intends.

Concerning form and content, Olson affirms Robert Creeley's idea that form is never more than an extension of content, and that right form is the only and exclusively possible extension of content. He says that the conventions which logic has forced on syntax must be broken, tenses and grammar must be stretched so that "all parts of speech suddenly, in composition by field, are fresh for both sound and percussive use, spring up like unknown, unnamed vegetables in the patch, when you work it, come spring." In actual writing, one perception must immediately and directly lead to a further perception.

Regarding reality, Olson sees it as infinite, forever in the process of becoming, and changing. Things happen and reflect only a part of the whole. And they are unpredictable. Our knowledge of reality can only be fragmentary and imperfect. So the job of the poet is not to describe reality, but to enact it, as truthfully and swiftly as he can. To do this well, poets need to watch and follow and change accordingly. To him, if people live in space, every moment or point is a new beginning. People must live always in the immediate present. The implication is that nothing, the writer included, is immune to change. This recalls in a way Ashbery's idea of "otherness."

So the poetic mind moves by leaps and bounds; it is often pulled along by its own associations which may be inspired by an idea, or a word, or a combination of these that the poet has already written down in the process of composition. The form is open and becomes no more than an extension of content; the content is, however, often disjunctive or haphazard. The poem possesses intrinsic coherence, no doubt, but its surface often appears rugged and difficult to connect. We experience fragments of ideas, a confusing syntax, a sudden jump from the physical level of discourse to the metaphysical. Grammar is not always followed and parentheses may not be always closed.

Olson's thought was unique and obscure and was expressed in his unique and obscure way. As to his poetry, he was equally unique and obscure, self-indulgent in his ways of expression, full of private references and allusions, such as bits of information like names of people or places known probably only to himself. So he is not easy to read, and is not much read.

The Maximus Poems

Olson's most famous work, *The Maximus Poems*, is a collection of poems that he wrote over a period of twenty years (from 1950 through his death). The collection is autobiographical, recording Olson's personal experiences and observations. It is his intellectual history in a poetic framework.

It consists of three volumes. The first of these depicts Maximus sizing up his hometown Gloucester, finding it wanting in good values, and moving on to take a systematic look at the history of the town and America. In the second volume, *Maximus IV, V, VI*, Maximus re-enacts certain myths and fables of the ancient world. The final volume, which was found among the author's papers, continues with Maximus' intense scrutiny of Gloucester and of himself. The central idea of the whole is to try to reinvent, with the help of ancient values, the town of Gloucester that has been degraded by the commercialism of modern life.

In formal terms Olson might have had a broad overall scheme as to how the poems would connect into a whole, but whatever it might be, it did not come through. The poems keep adding up without much of a thematic focus and with only loose connective tissues like the place—Gloucester—as the collection's locale, its history, its fishermen and their rituals and lives, its present-day commercial transactions, and Olson's poetic imprint.

Olson stresses the importance of being close to nature, values the people's direct, personal, wholesome link with it, and censures in contrast the capitalist proprietors' estranged relation to it. The Olson-Maximus figure is probably

Olson's ideal of men. The name, Maximus, sounds probably a little presumptuous, named after the 4th-century Phoenician mystic, but it fits Olson's ambitious plan well. This Olson-Maximus lives life to the fullest, discovers himself while discovering his place, observing, ruminating, keeping finding the ultimate relationship to both life and nature. The urge toward the mythical becomes increasingly evident in his deliberations as the collection grows in volume and moves toward its end.

"I, Maximus of Gloucester, to You," the first "letter" of *The Maximus Poems*, is a poem with an introduction and six sections. The "letter" begins with the introduction that reads like a jumble of words and phrases disconnected with one another. It is obvious that the speaker has something important to say. It may be some crystallized thought or truth about the poetic imagination in relation to reality, or the essential truth of things. "You," or the reader, needs to hear what "I" has to say so that "you" may see and know—and write—better. This is possible if we remember that the title of the poem, "I, Maximus of Gloucester, to You," is pompously similar to the way St. Paul addresses his followers in his letters (Colossians 1: 1-3).

After the introduction, six sections follow to further explain his poetics. Section one images a bird taking its bird's-eye view of the Gloucester harbor and the city of Gloucester. The bird is apparently building its nest. We do not know what the bird and the nest mean until we see in section two the bird carrying in its nervous beak "important substance" (feathers, minerals, curling hair etc.) to add to "the sum" of its nest. The bird-and-the nest metaphor seems to stand for the poetic imagination and the work of art. The nest building should be the symbol for the creative process that takes its "important substance" from the source of life—the harbor and the city.

Section three stresses the importance of hearing. He feels that modern life has made it impossible for people to hear anything. Olson's emphasis on the role of listening in the poetic process is self-evident here.

Section four is hard to read. Beginning with the third line, it becomes increasingly difficult to make sense of what the poet tries to get at. Olson seems to be saying that the composing process is closely related to life in its various manifestations. Then the bird, the nest, and what it carries all fall into place when tied in with the preceding sections.

Section five offers both a warning and an advice to poets. Modern life is ruled by the worst. It is distracting and degrading. Poets should keep their innocence intact, keep their imagination forever new, and improve their craft so that they could "enact" life in its diverse forms, good or bad. They should be faithful to their own perceptions and refuse to succumb to interference and temptations.

The last section of the poem is again a further elaboration of Olson's view of reality and his poetics. There is no sequence, or no logic in reality; things just happen which poets have got to move fast to catch. The poetic mind should get into the midst of reality as soon as possible. There is no time for the mind to work rationally, or grammatically. The nest, the poem, is in sight.

This first "letter" is typical of Olson's poetics in more than one way. Poetry, or the composing process, is a creative act of enactment, not describing, of reality. In his first "letter" here, we see the poet enacting, juxtaposing, adding things together to build toward sense. This being the first of the Maximus poems, the poet wishes to make things clear to his readers just so that they may be placed in perspective to expect what is to come forth later on.

Olson is critical of modern civilization. He always harks back to ancient values, inherent in the people who live close to nature. His poems such as "Maximus, to Gloucester, Sunday, July 19" and "The Kingfishers" are both good illustrations.

Although Olson's poetry can be lyrical, its quality is detracted by his rigid ideas. He always had rigid notions of what he was going to write, and the way he said it was very mannered sometimes. And there was the shadow of Pound and Williams. Olson tried to shake Pound off his back. He achieved partial success in his later phase, but Pound and Williams have always loomed large in his poetry. *The Maximus Poems* resembles the *Cantos* in its cumulative structure as an intellectual diary and *Paterson* in its belief in localism and its overall form. However, when all is said, Olson's part in the postwar revolution of poetry writing will be remembered in history.

Creeley, Levertov, and Duncan

Robert Creeley (1926-2005) was born in West Acton, Massachusetts. He attended Harvard and left it without a degree, received his B.A. from Black Mountain College, and an M.A. at the University of New Mexico. He published widely in the 1950s, became famous in the 1960s, and taught at some universities.

Creeley began his career as a staunch member of the Black Mountain group. Olson was a mentor to him. With regard to content, he fully agrees with Williams' "No ideas but in things," and with Pound's idea that "[a]ny tendency to abstract general statement is a greased slide." This is further affirmed in his preface to *Charles Olson: Selected Writings* (New York: 1966), where he states, "The most insistent concern I find in Olson's writing is the intent to gain the particular experience of any possibility in life, so that no abstraction intervenes." In matters of form, in face of the New Critical orthodoxy of the 1940s and 1950s, Creeley felt along with Olson that "formal" order could no longer be assumed as a necessary virtue, and that form is no more than an extension of content. Creeley's literary credo is clearly that of open form.

Creeley edited the *Black Mountain Review* (1954-1957), and helped promote the works of Olson's group of poets. Over the years Creeley developed his own style and made his presence felt on the literary scene of his time. His poetry takes daily life experiences as its subject matter, and his diction is colloquial and conversational. He is said to be the simplest of the group and of the new verse in general. His volumes of poems include *For Love: Poems 1950-1960* (1962), *Words* (1967), *The Charm: Early and Uncollected Poems* (1967),

Pieces (1969), *A Day Book* (1972), *Thirty Things* (1974), *Away* (1976), *Later* (1979), *The Collected Poems 1945-1975* (1982), *Mirrors* (1983), *The Memory Gardens* (1986), and *Windows* (1990). Creeley has written essays, stories, a novel, and a play.

Creeley's usual subject is love and marriage and the intricacies of relationships and human ties between individuals of the two sexes. "The Business," "The Riddle," "A Form of Women," "Sing Song," and "Ballad of the Despairing Husband" are just some of the titles that come to mind. But his theme is wider. "After Lorca" and "For My Mother" are neither quite of the "domestic" brand that he was at one time accused of writing. Creeley's style is interesting. It has been described as "minimal," in the sense that he prefers to be short and simple. This has proved to be his strength especially when reinforced by his subtle handling of metaphors. Creeley is suggestive. His poetry connotes superbly at its best. When his best poems appeared in *For Love: Poems 1950-1960* in 1962, his style was imitated actually. Since then he has published quite a few volumes.[4]

 It would be no good to take Creeley always at his surface. He can be deceptively simple. Read his "I Know a Man" or "Oh No," and we will find depth and complexity in his works.

Let's take a look at his "Oh No":

> If you wander far enough
> you will come to it
> and when you get there
> they will give you a place to sit
>
> for yourself only, in a nice chair,
> and all your friends will be there
> with smiles on their faces
> and they will likewise all have places.

The simplest reading of this is to see it as about a gathering "you" stumbles into. The meeting sounds as if it is scheduled to occur at regular intervals, and it encourages newcomers. The "you" seems to be a latecomer but has come anyway, only to find all his friends already there. Then the motif of a journey comes to mind, a journey of life, in which case, the "wandering far enough" might mean the end of the road, the "it" that "you" comes to is the terminal point, probably the place of the blest, or Heaven. The rest of the poem all ties in well with a happy ending for all except for the title, "Oh No." The logical response to the offer of a chair with smiles all around would be a "Thank you." The refusal to take a seat could mean either of the two things: you are not ready enough to do it because, to quote Robert Frost, you still have "miles to go"; or you would like a better offer. Suddenly we come to see the meeting differently. "You" have come to join the dead, but decide to leave. The irony in the "nice" and the forced "smiles" on the faces become instantly evident. The poem then assumes the significance of an indomitable spirit of perseverance in face of adversity, or self-defense and self-assertion against overwhelming odds. There is a tragic vision of a kind, along with the will to life and the affirmation of the human spirit.

Denise Levertov (1923-1997) is regarded as one of the most respected poets of her generation.[5] She was born and raised in England, and published her first book of poetry there—*The Double Image* (1946) in traditional English rimes and meters. Later she married an American writer and came to the United States in 1948. Over the years she taught at a number of universities including Vassar, M.I.T., and Stanford. She took an enormous interest in the poetry of William Carlos Williams and Ezra Pound and was one member of the Black Mountain group for quite some time.

With time her career developed in its own direction so that she did not think it proper to link herself with any particular school. With 30 books of poetry, translations, and essays, she went far beyond the Black Mountain phase of her career and is now evaluated in her own right.

Denise Levertov has a strong sense of mission as a poet. Her poetry exhibits an inclination toward some religious vision. There is some religious intensity to her work. She has written some religious poetry such as "Salvation." In her essay, "A Poet's View" (1984), she emphasizes the importance for an artist to believe in inspiration or the intuitive, to have "Imagination," to be sensitive to "the transcendent, the numinous," and "experience mystery" in the creative act. "The concept of 'inspiration' presupposes a power," she goes on to state, "that enters the individual and is not a personal attribute; and it is linked to a view of the artist's life as one of obedience to a vocation." It is evident that poetry has a mission to accomplish and that the poet is committed to helping people survive with illuminations and revelations of things which may have been unseen or forgotten. She claims that, if we focus enough, we may discover aspects not previously seen in an experience new or otherwise. However, she is not religious poet *per se*.

Levertov's poetry shows a clear social purpose. She was all along interested in humanitarian politics. Her enthusiasms ranged over a variety of subjects from concern with women's experience as a person, in marriage, and their sexual appetite (such as in "Eros at Temple Stream") to painful reflections on grave issues like the Vietnam War and the Gulf War. It is good to note that she was a political activist with 30 years' experience in the antiwar movement of the country. All these aspects of her writing career had no doubt to do with her upbringing and family heritage: both of her parents were committed people in terms of faith and social and political justice. It was an inheritance which the poet valued very much in her literary endeavor as her works such as "Dream Instruction," "Illustrious Ancestors," and "Making Peace" well attest.

A lot of her poetry focuses on subjects of a more personal and immediate nature. For example, there is the heart-warming interpersonal contact in "A Solitude," a poem which, in one interpretation, can be read as handling the interesting and intricate dialectics of solitude and community. The blind man lives at once in solitude and with his community. He envisions community in his solitude, and is a better and fuller person for that. "He knows where he is going" as a distinct individual. He is going nowhere because he stays forever with the community. His mind is filled with the people and things of the world. Another subject of Levertov's is her gloomy view of marriage as shown in "The Ache of Marriage": it is an institution that hurts physically, offers no spiritual relief (as there is no union of minds), and will devour us like a monster with the help of its lure of "joy." We are in danger of submersion in the flood of pain: "the ark of the ache" will stay as long as would its biblical counterpart—Noah's Ark.

Levertov's perception of the difference between man and woman is another interesting thing to note about her. It is not quite feminist in nature but comes close to it. Both "Abel's Bride" and "Leaving Forever" talk about human fidelity, the former directly and the latter obliquely. "Abel's Bride" features a third-person observer. First this person talks about man: when a man leaves home, he forgets who he is and to whom he is committed ("No mirror nests in his pockets"). He is led by his hopes of new involvement and attachment. So the woman is afraid whenever he ventures out. For her own part, the woman never forgets her identity ("When she goes out/ she looks in the glass"). She remembers her duty, remains her original, primitive self, deep and tolerant and receiving, and stays faithful to the "bones at the hearth" like a dog. She feels lucky that she sees marriage the way she does, but is sad about the uncertainty of her man.

"Leaving Forever" is more direct in tone but less explicit in sense. It is about a man and woman leaving home by ship. They think of their departure differently:

> He says the waves in the ship's wake
> are like stones rolling away.
> I don't see it that way.
> But I see the mountain turning,
> turning away its face as the ship
> takes us away.

The man feels a happy relief at leaving the "stones" of commitment and obligation behind and at a possible new beginning (don't the stones roll away from the Easter tomb in the bible?). But the woman is overcome with grief at the change: "the mountain" weeps as it is forsaken and forgotten. The woman sees herself identical with the mountain and feels sad that her man rejects and forgets so quickly. Levertov's stance was close to that of a feminist.

Robert Duncan (1919-1988) was an active supporter of Olson's views and became a unique poet of the "projective verse." Duncan is a love poet. There are quite a number of explicit sexual images in his poems. He holds that poetry is the soul of life, it is the means by which love is given and received, and life is love in its most perfect form. Love is holy. It involves loss and recovery. Hence in his poetry the recurring image of Atlantis as a paradise lost but regained through the effort of the poet. There is unified divine life in which the demonic is one with the divine.

In style, Duncan was ever open to the diverse influences over him such as Modernist verse and Olson's theory of "projective verse," believing that poetry projects, as do movies, words, and syllables which pour out of the bosom of the poet. In addition, Duncan knew well a great number of writers and styles and was ready and willing to merge these skillfully in his own work. These include the styles of poets such as Dante, Blake, Whitman, H. D., Gertrude Stein, Joyce, D. H. Lawrence, Pound, William Carlos Williams, and Olson.

Duncan's style changes and ranges from the obvious to the most subtle. He can be difficult and allusive as Pound sometimes. In addition, he was drawn to and immersed in the study of myths and ancient cultures, and took a great interest in mysticism, the magical, and the occult. He said somewhere in his *The Truth & Life of Myth: An Essay in Essential Autobiography* (1968) that fairy tales and myths were to remain the charged ground of his poetic reality. All through his career, Duncan believed in the truth of myth, and he used myths to define his function as a poet and the nature of poetry. Duncan is a prolific writer.

Now let's take a look at his "A Poem Beginning with a Line by Pindar."

Most of the basic features of Duncan's work are present here. His genuine interest in the enduring power of myth, his concerns as a poet, and his vision of poetry as a vehicle of improving the lot of the people constitute the recurring leitmotif of the work. The underlying myth used here is the Greek story of Cupid and Psyche. The essential part of the story is Psyche's thirst for knowledge that brings her through a series of ordeals in her search for her lost love. Love is the essence of Psyche's—and the poet's—creative undertaking. The job of the poet is, as indicated in the poem, to pick up where his predecessors have left off and continue their work. Here in the poem we notice Duncan's reference to Whitman (a poet of love as can be seen from his "When Lilacs Last in the Dooryard Bloom'd"), William Carlos Williams (a poet of love for life and for his country), and Ezra Pound (the basic theme of whose *Cantos*, and especially "the Pisan Cantos," can be construed as an effort toward building an earthly paradise for men). The theme of the poem is clear that love, love that resides in the heart, addresses human problems. If all the presidents had been as loving and caring as Lincoln, the nation might have been free of the suffering, the strife, and the problems that have existed. Thus Psyche's search, identical with the poet's own and running parallel to it, becomes its apt metaphor. The poem is difficult as it is full of allusions very much like a Pound poem. There has to be source hunting first. Otherwise, the formal features of the work keep in line well with those of postwar poetry.

Chapter 23   Postwar American Novel (I)

Postwar America has witnessed amazing changes. These have included the nation's prosperity and the sense of optimism it has produced, the "Cold War" between the two power blocks, the sense of crisis impending, the chaos that became institutionalized, the sense of life being absurd that undercut the very existence of man, the life of the 1950s being poisoned at the root by McCarthyism, and that of the 1960s enriched by the Civil Rights movement, the appearance of a counter culture, an upsurge of feminism and feminist power, the Vietnam War weighing on the consciousness of the people, the violence, political or racial, including the assassinations of John F. Kennedy and Martin Luther King, the widely felt skepticism, and the new advances in science and technology which brought about changes in popular outlook on life and the world. The representation of the multifaceted life of postwar America has remained the "reward and despair" of the writers who began to publish after the war.

This is a very interesting period in the history of American literature, invigorated as it is with robust energy and bustling with creative activity. The new generation has proved its newness and competence by a wide range of experimentation that would have dazzled even their brilliantly original predecessors like Faulkner and Hemingway. Critic Ihab Hassan has noticed the variety of postwar fiction. His categories are clear though somewhat arbitrary. He has listed the war novel, the southern novel, the Jewish novel, the Beat novel and alienation, the Black novel, and satire and the novel of manners, which came to public notice in the years from the end of the war through the 1960s. And the period after that has been one in which American fiction is noted for its fantasy and surrealism, its nonfiction, science fiction, black or absurd humor, parody and pop, and its experimental novelistic techniques, some of which have been branded as Postmodernist. Critic Tony Tanner has kept his attention on the development of original narrative techniques and the exploration of new fictional areas in contemporary literature. There have been achievements, as he observes, like Saul Bellow's social-psychological comedies, Norman Mailer's provocative experiments, and John Barth's brilliant "fun-house." (John Barth's 1967 essay, "The Literature of Exhaustion," has been said to have heralded a new phase in postwar literature, i.e. Postmodernist literature). Themes such as the tyranny of society, the subjugation of the individual, the quest for self-identity, and the self-indulgence of the writer in relation to his environment have become the concern of many contemporary authors. Some of these people have achieved a measure of recognition, others are still struggling, and all are doing their best to contribute to "the great American Novel" as Norman Mailer calls it, or "the bright book of life," to borrow from critic Alfred Kazin.

So there has been an impressive number of authors to talk about. The names that come immediately to mind would include Saul Bellow, Norman Mailer, J. D. Salinger, Joseph Heller, Kurt Vonnegut, Jr., John Barth, Thomas Pynchon, and Nabokov. We naturally think of other novelists whose works have impressed the postwar reading public such as Bernard Malamud, John Updike, John Cheever, Ken Kesey, Flannery O'Connor, Philip Roth, Donald Barthelme, Jack Kerouac, John Hawkes, William Gaddis, E. L. Doctorow, William Styron, Truman Capote, and Joyce Carol Oates. As such a short list tends to mislead, the readers' own discretion is advised.

Saul Bellow (1915-2005)

Saul Bellow was probably the best known writer of his generation.[1] Born into a Russian Jewish family in Canada, he grew up in Chicago. His writing career spanned over half a century. He wrote a good number of novels, short stories and plays, and won a good number of awards including the Pulitzer Prize and the 1976 Nobel Prize for literature. His 1964 novel, *Herzog* (1964), received four awards: the James L. Dow Award, the National Book Award, the Formenter Award, and the International Literature Prize (1965), and has been seen by many as his masterpiece. It made his reputation as a significant figure in postwar American fiction.

Saul Bellow's Basic Themes

Saul Bellow's basic themes are essentially three-fold: First, he views contemporary society as a threat to human life and human integrity. Modern civilization tends to dehumanize, making people lose their distinction and turning them into what he calls "fat goods." Material affluence distracts and produces a sense of alienation. Then, living in such an environment, people tend to become paranoid, high-strung, and impotent, and so lose their sanity. Saul Bellow's characters suffer most from a kind of psychosis. They go through a phase before they regain their mental balance and serenity. Finally, there is the quest motif, a quest for truth and values, difficult, excruciating, but successful in a way. To Saul Bellow, the human search for affirmation should end happily, and people should see light at the end of the tunnel. His fictional world is full of people both tragic and comic, but happy in the end. He is a very human writer.

Saul Bellow was keenly aware of his Jewish heritage. His works remind his readers in subtle or apparent ways that his characters are Jews. The Jewish condition offers a valid metaphor for Bellow to talk about human existence. The Jews are God's chosen people as they feel themselves, but are often rejected by the community at large. The awareness of being the chosen intensifies the agony of the rejection. Thus the sense of alienation they feel coincides with that of the general humanity in contemporary society. By dramatizing the Jewish dilemma, Saul Bellow succeeds in describing the human condition in general.

Saul Bellow's strength lies in his faith in man and man's ability to offer "a spirited resistance to the forces of our time" (as he puts it). His works are in essence affirmatively humanistic. As he sees it, modern man has lived through frustration and defeat, managed to grapple with destructive historical pressures, and striven for "certain durable human goods"—truth, freedom, and wisdom. Bellow writes with the confidence that he is acting "the culture figure," making explicit the implicit thoughts of the people, and expressing their common needs and preoccupations. Most of Saul Bellow's heroes are Jewish intellectuals or writers who, facing violence and victimization, try to discover "the queerness of existence" and overcome it. Very often a Bellovian protagonist, such as Tommy Wilhelm (*Seize the Day*), Asa Leventhal (*The Victim*), or Augie March, and Herzog, is found in a situation which involves a good deal of "suffering, feebleness, servitude," and is seen behaving in an impotent, tragicomic way. Moving in his cold and apathetic world, his impotence makes his life ignominious and absurd. The wretchedness of his existence is so overwhelming that one wonders how he can struggle through the quagmire of despair. However, Saul Bellow feels that "on nobler assumptions, man should have at least sufficient power to overcome ignominy and to complete his own life." So his novels usually end on a positive note. It is not always a happy ending, but it is an ending which calls for hope more than despair. This is essentially the situation with Asa Leventhal, Tommy Wilhelm, and Augie March.

Herzog

If Augie March is forever on the move, escaping into an ever new circumstance, Moses Herzog retreats into his intricate consciousness for peace and tranquility. Herzog is an unemployed professor of physics descended from unsuccessful Russian Jewish immigrant parents. At the age of 47 he looks old, with wrinkles and graying hair. He is going through a harrowing phase of life in which nothing is working out the way it should. His family life is frustrating, and so is his personal life, which he sees as a sheer waste. Divorced from his young wife Madeleine, and fighting for the custody of his daughter, June, he is for a while mentally disturbed. He begins to write letters which he does not intend to mail out. He writes to both the living and the dead—friends, acquaintances, celebrities, and leaders. His discussions in these letters range over a wide variety of subjects such as the intolerable social iniquity which is driving him out of his mind, poverty, unemployment, social unrest, political hysteria, industrial pollution, racial conflicts, crime, violence, and the appalling suffering that exists on all conceivable levels of life. All these seem to keep assailing his sanity and threatening to throw him off his mental balance.

He meditates very much and acts very little. He wishes for a morally higher life, but fails to define it as an ideal. For instance, he thinks of giving up all his possessions to help the poor, and of persuading others to do the same. He would like to see a new relationship between people, which would put an end to alienation. But the reality as he sees it is ruthless. To him human values are disintegrating. He is concerned about the development of man and his civiliza-tion, and is ambitious enough to plan a big book on social progress, but he finds it impossible to carry out his project because life has gone wrong. Unable to endure the mental torment any longer, Herzog despairs.

The real issue has to do, however, with his post-divorce neurosis, the bitter memory of his recent past which weighs him down every day. He feels mad at the way Madeleine has manipulated and then dumped him for his one-time friend Valentine Gersbach. He hears his little girl June crying at the back seat of their car. And he is mortified that he has treated his first wife Daisy badly. His suffers so much that he is afraid that he may go crazy. He writes letters endlessly and fanatically, and keeps moving from place to place with his valise full of papers just so that he may find some breathing space. On one occasion he goes with a gun to seek out Madeleine and Valentine, but backs down, moved at a glimpse of Valentine giving little June a bath. His heart softens. After spending a day with his little girl (which ends up in an accident) and a night in jail for carrying a gun, he begins to see his own weakness and the positive side of things. He allows himself to sink into the healthy influence of nature at his Ludeyville home, admits to his craziness, and recovers his full sanity. Hence the opening sentence of the book: "If I am out of my mind, it's all right with me, thought Moses Herzog."

Herzog undergoes a significant change in his personality and his way of perception. There is a gradual but clear movement from restlessness to tranquility, from cold and icy feelings to warm recollections of the past and joyful contact with child and nature, and from a negative outlook to an attitude of affirmation. At the beginning Herzog is intensely unhappy. He complains about everybody and about everything. He feels that Madeleine, Valentine and Madeleine's mother are all scheming against him; the lawyers and friends and the policemen are not helping; the city is impersonal and stifling; society and its pressures, or what he calls *Moha*, are encroaching upon individuality; and even Ramona, the woman who loves him dearly, is suspect of looking for a husband. He complains about all except himself. He broods a lot and is capable of genuine suffering. In face of what he sees as a disintegration of man and his culture, he feels a huge sense of responsibility and launches out as a Messiah figure. He sees himself as the man on whom the world depends to do certain intellectual work, change history, and influence the development of civilization.

However, he could not hope to save anybody before he saves himself. He has to touch ground and place himself under close scrutiny. The process of self-analysis has been going on even when he is at his most neurotic. All the time he is raving against everyone, his yearning mind harks back to a point of time in childhood when his loving parents offered him love and faith in human fellowship: the scene of his mother pulling him on a sled over crusty ice one January evening is always heart warming. And he frequently thinks of his brothers, Shura and Will, and his family as a whole. Family and love furnish the basis for his self-awakening. All the time he is cursing the rest of the world, he reminisces about Daisy, his first wife, whom he feels bad having mistreated somehow. This can be the beginning of his self-searching. Even before he regains full sanity, he begins to see the futility of his letter-writing, and begins to feel the warmth of humanity. However, all these remain in the form of undercurrents until the accident jostles him finally out of his dreamy state. Then he discovers his inadequacy as a human being. He has hurt the child, and he might have had himself killed. He is now thinking positive, seeing positive things in people, and beginning to forgive and love even his foes, Madeleine and Gersbach. He comes to realize his problem. He recognizes his ingratitude to people and to life in general. Now he is accepting life for what it is. He feels contented.

Change from Modernism to Postmodernism

It is interesting to note that Herzog's change is, in a sense, archetypal of the change in the temper of the times. The 1950s and 1960s witnessed a transformation on the literary scene from modernism to postmodernism. This manifested itself in both thematic and formal terms. Thematically, there is, between the two phases of literary creation, a difference in attitude toward life. The Modernists tend to impose shape and significance on life with which they feel at odds, while the Postmodernists accept life for what it is, chaotic and contingent as it is, and try to make sense of it for survival. In formal aspects, modernist writings tend to be ponderously retrospective, often full of interior monologues or stream of consciousness features, and relegating story interest to a secondary place. Postmodernist writings, however, while feeling free to borrow technically from modernist works, feel equally free to borrow from every other mode of writing that serves their purpose (in addition to their own unique creative features).

Herzog reflects both aspects well. It is basically a stream of consciousness work, especially in the first two thirds of the book. There is a lot of Mrs. Dalloway in Herzog, a lot of thinking without much plot interest. The circular structure, beginning at Ludeyville and ending there as well, draws a picture of a mind reminiscing and doing self-examination. Although told mostly in the third-person point of view, the narrative filters through Herzog's mind so that the readers come away with the impression that it is Herzog thinking and telling his story. The prose movement is intriguing in this section (about five of the nine chapters). It is agonizingly slow. For instance, Herzog is going to visit Ramona. From the time he decides to go in chapter one, up to the time he arrives in chapter five, he meditates or writes letters most of the time except for his visit to a friend, Libbie. He reminisces about his divorce with Madeleine, about Daisy, about the war and Paris, about his parents and his childhood, and about Sono, his Japanese mistress, before he arrives at Ramona's at long last. In the last third of the book, the narrative pace quickens, with more action, less thought, denoting Herzog's movement away from self-immersion to closer contact with reality and final acceptance of it.

Saul Bellow is highly critical of modern life in which the old value system is no longer functioning. His major characters, Herzog, for instance, or Mr. Sammler, or Humboldt, all represent Bellow's vision of disoriented modern man in an urban society where humanism is under determining pressures. They body forth Bellow's credo that art aims at achieving stillness in the midst of chaos, and that a novelist, beginning with disorder and disharmony, goes toward order by "an unknown process of the imagination."

Indeed, Saul Bellow's ambition is to be a social historian. He places emphasis on the truthful representation of life, and writes in the realistic tradition in which Flaubert, Stendhal, Tolstoy, and Dreiser wrote. He also draws from the modernist tradition in his creative work. His vision of the world as being chaotic and absurd and of modern man's impotence in face of life, the existentialist ideas which his works reveal, and his use of subtle techniques in exploring the subconscious of his characters—all this places him alongside such modern masters as James Joyce and Marcel Proust. And there is also an obvious postmodern element in his works. The bridging of the traditions of realism and modernism with postmodernism has put Saul Bellow at the center of postwar American literary experience.

Bellow was the most prominent postwar American novelist in vision as well as in volume of productivity. His significant body of work has impacted

American fiction visibly and transcended its Jewish label.

Norman Mailer (1923-2007)

Norman Mailer was perhaps one of the most ambitious writers of this period.[2] It was at Harvard that Mailer first decided to become a major American author. He joined the war against Japan in 1944 partly because he was obsessed with the idea to write a big war book. He volunteered as a rifleman with a reconnaissance platoon fighting in the Philippine Mountains. From there he wrote his wife four to five letters a week packed with voluminous notes just in case that, if he could not survive the war, his novel would. *The Naked and the Dead*, his first book, became a spectacular success in 1948. The critical world was thrilled at the prospect that a new major writer was emerging on the horizon.

However, popular enthusiasm for Mailer cooled down after a time. In fact he wrote no other book which touched *The Naked and the Dead* in power and popularity ever again. Not even his prize-winning books such as *The Armies of the Night*, and *The Executioner's Song* (1979). Mailer is renowned for one important essay he wrote in 1957, entitled "The White Negro," in which he defines his notion of "the existential hero." Although critical opinion has been divided about him, all seem to agree that he was a remarkable literary figure on the postwar scene.

The Naked and the Dead

The Naked and the Dead is Norman Mailer's first and best book. It tells the story of a fourteen-man platoon that lands on the barren beach of Anopopei, a small Japanese-held island in the South Pacific. The platoon is part of a six-thousand-man force deployed to seize control of the island and prepare the way for a larger American move into the Philippines. The characters include a Mississippi farmer, a Jew from Brooklyn, a Mexican-American, a west Texas rancher, a laborer from the coal mines of Montana, an Irishman from South Boston's working class, a Kansas salesman, a Chicago hoodlum, and a hedonist from Georgia. It is apparent that Mailer intends them to constitute a microcosmic portrait of the American populace.

General Edward Cummings assigns to his staff officer, Lieutenant Robert Hearn, the task of landing the platoon in the jungle south of Anopopei on a reconnaissance mission behind the Toyaku Line. Midway in the patrol's incursion, Private Wilson is shot in the belly, and of the four men who attempt to carry him back to safety, two give up in exhaustion and the other two take him over muddy hills, across baked fields and through the suffocating jungle, where he ultimately dies. The patrol goes forward on its slow and perilous journey, in the course of which Lieutenant Hearn and Corporal Roth meet their doom. The ruthless Sergeant Sam Croft drives the men onward up Mount Anaka. Just as they are about to attain the summit, a nest of hornets explodes upon them, and they fall down the mountain slope.

Meanwhile, in the absence of General Cummings, Major Dalleson orders a battalion to break through a breach in the Toyaku Line. The operation destroys a major Japanese supply depot and the secret Japanese headquarters that houses General Toyaku and his staff. The novel's climax is a victory for the US Army, but a personal defeat for Cummings. His masterful battle plan ends in nothing. The men of the reconnaissance group rejoin their regiment.

Mailer has been thought of as one of the American naturalist writers. This is true of his early works that appeared before the 1960s. In the naturalistic world, the individual is prey to certain forces over which he has no control. These forces are biological, social or geographical. The universe of *The Naked and the Dead* is a cold, indifferent, wanton cosmos where man labors only to die, and God takes no interest in his welfare. In opposition to this deterministic universe, three men try to define themselves: Croft, Cummings, and Hearn. Their lives are existential. General Cummings is obsessed with self-aggrandizement, Croft tries to seek power, and Hearn does his best to stay sane and assert dignity.

The experimental feature of the novel merits attention. Mailer wedges "chorus" and "the time machine" adroitly into his otherwise normal narrative. "Chorus" appears five times in the whole story, recording fragments of the soldiers' conversations. The locales of these chats vary from mess tents, trenches, lavatories, and camping sites. They reflect the soldiers' thoughts and attitudes. "Choruses" are generally short, roundabout one printed page. "The time machine" appears ten times. They offer the biographical sketches of the major characters, about ten in number, such as Cummings, Hearn, and Croft. The sketches describe their looks, personalities, environments of growing up, work experiences before the war etc., which serve to add to and annotate the main story line. These pieces are actually short stories, vivacious, exuberant, and entertaining with their separate narratives, dialogues, and characterizations. Between them the "chorus" and "the time machine" constitute a foil and a footnote to the whole narrative endeavor. On a different—the linguistic—level, these interpolations or flashbacks bring an animated novelty and help dispel any possible sense of monotony and dullness that a massive book like this might generate in the readers.

Mailer and Non-Fiction

Mailer is well known as an innovator of the nonfiction novel. His *Advertisements for Myself*, *Presidential Papers*, and his novel, *An American Dream* (1965) are all experiments with a new way of writing, which presents fantasy and fact with equal emphasis, interlocking the story of a fictional character with that of a real person. *An American Dream* deals with journalistic subjects in fictive methods. In *Why Are We in Vietnam?* fictional narrative and actual events claim equal attention and space. *The Armies of the Night* is a novelistic description of his personal experience in the 1967 anti-Vietnam War march on the Pentagon. Here Mailer becomes a character in the narrative, so it is Norman Mailer writing about Norman Mailer in the third person, presenting history in the form of a novel and creating a novel as history. Hence the subtitle of the book, "The Novel as History, History as a Novel." The sense of immediacy and straightforwardness which the book was able to engender exerted a good deal of influence on literary journalism, a style of writing later known as "the New Journalism." This quasi-journalistic way of writing develops further in his *Marilyn: A Novel Biography* and *The Executioner's Song*.

Norman Mailer talked a lot for some decades about the ultimate novel or the large social novel that he would write for his time. He said as far back as his *Advertisements for Myself* that his present and future work would have the deepest influence of any work being done by an American novelist in these years. Now seen in perspective, Mailer is a major writer, but his greatness has yet to be evaluated. The fact of the matter is that he did not seem to have a clear vision consistent enough to guide his creative writing. He was a multi-faceted talent— a novelist, a poet, a playwright, a filmmaker, a journalist, a politician, a performer, etc. He was, as he called himself, a chameleon. His ideas changed quickly, and so did his style. He was engaged in too many things, and might have felt disoriented sometimes. That is a shortcut which distances anyone from greatness.

J. D. Salinger (1919-2010)

J. D. Salinger was unique for a couple of reasons. He wrote one novel and became famous for it. Then, for the rest of his life since 1953, he remained a recluse in his New Hampshire home, refusing interviews or any other forms of contact with the press and the world outside. He wrote little, and lived well on his one book.[3]

Salinger was born into a Jewish middle class family in New York City. He entered Valley Forge Military Academy at 15 and felt out of place there. The academy became the prototype for Pencey, the high school, in *The Catcher in the Rye* (1951), and some aspects of Holden's life were to replicate some of young

Salinger's experience there: A classmate was expelled, another jumped to his death from a building, and he was the head of the fencing team at the academy. After graduation, he attended a short-story writing class at Columbia University, and published his first story "The Young Folks" in the *Story* magazine. This was the first time Salinger dealt with the subject of a boy thrown into the adult world to shift for himself. Then he placed his short story "Slight Rebellion off Madison" in *The New Yorker*. Another short story, "I'm Crazy," came out in print in the same time period. Both stories introduced Holden Caulfield, the main character in *The Catcher in the Rye*, and both were revised for later inclusion in the novel.

The Catcher in the Rye

Salinger's one novel, *The Catcher in the Rye,* has been a very influential book to come out of the postwar period. It relates the painful story of a high-school boy growing up in the world of decadent New York (which is probably meant to be a miniature of the West as a whole). Young Holden Caulfield is expelled from school because of poor academic performance. Afraid to meet his parents earlier than they should expect him, he checks himself into a New York City hotel that crawls with prostitutes and "queers." Soon he becomes aware that the world of adults is a "phony" one, and that he is surrounded by "jerks" of all kinds. His first night in New York ends in a bitter quarrel with a pimp who cheats him out of his pocket and beats him up.

The next morning proves dull and spiritless. The day moves on slowly, sad and weary. A meeting with a friend ends with another quarrel; drinking with an old acquaintance does little to improve his mood. He gets drunk and feels depressed and lonesome. Night falls. Holden sneaks back home to see his kid sister Phoebe. She is a loving kid, but her talk about their father "killing" him sickens him, and he thinks of an ex-schoolmate jumping out of the window and lying dead on the stone steps. Creeping out of home, he goes to his former teacher, Mr. Antolini, the one person who takes any interest in him and whom he feels he can trust, only to find that the man is a homosexual. His second night in New York thus ends with a hasty escape from Antolini's house.

Christmas is coming, but Holden feels himself sinking. Now he is thinking of going west and spending the rest of his life there. He goes to say good-bye to Phoebe who, to his dismay, insists on going with him. This unexpected act of love jostles him out of his dream and his nightmarish three-day adventure in New York. He goes home, falls ill, and recovers and convalesces in a psychiatric ward in California. It is there that he recounts his sad story of growing up in *The Catcher in the Rye*.

The novel depicts in eloquent language an adolescent's disgust and despair at the fallen state of the adult world around him. It is a world of jerks and perverts, a salient feature of which is its decadence. The hotel in which he stays, with its prostitution and all forms of sexual perversity, is to Holden the miniature of a larger space in which he is probably the only normal person. It is here that he begins, subconsciously, to lose his own innocence. He is assailed with an acute sense of not belonging anywhere, an intense anxiety of placelessness. This is well illustrated in his seemingly childish concern for the whereabouts of the ducks in the lagoon of New York City's Central Park.

The idea of having nowhere to go and belong haunts young Holden and generates a sense of alienation and despair in him. It is no wonder, then, that during his tramping in and out of the bars and hotels of New York City, he cries out in anguish for some thirty times that he is "damned lonesome and depressed"; about five times he either expresses a death-wish or thinks of death; and for once at least he contemplates suicide in a serious way. He hates the "phony," evil, crooked and cruel world of adults. He would not like to grow and change: The Egyptian mummies in the museum appeal to him because they remain the same. He would not like to work and live the way adults do, and he would take no interest in science, law, or anything in a world where life is wrong, and where one cannot find a nice and peaceful place.

If there are ever any moments in his stay in New York City which help in any way to light up the ambient gloom, these relate mostly to children and the thought of innocence. The innocence of children and reminiscences of childhood experiences ultimately save Holden from despair and doom. Realizing, only faintly maybe, that all kids like him are in danger of losing their innocence, he wishes to be a "catcher in the rye." Explaining this to his kid sister Phoebe, he says that he has kept envisioning thousands of little children playing in a field of rye, without any adult around except him standing on the edge of a cliff, just so as to catch anyone if they start to go over the cliff. He tells her that, when the kids are running and do not look where they are going, there is the danger of falling and he has to be there to catch them. What he really means is that he would stand there and save the unsuspecting children from losing their childhood integrity and goodness. As he knows that it is impossible to do, he calls himself crazy.

When it first came out in 1951, *The Catcher in the Rye* became an immediate success. It has been especially popular with the postwar young generation who have found in Holden an approximation of their own experience. Holden represents a social type of adolescents thrown upon themselves in a corrupt and decadent world. It is a critical look at the problems facing American youth during the 1950s. These are delineated in Holden's psychological battles, his depression, his nervous breakdown, sexual exploration, confrontation with vulgarity and other erratic behavior, his typical adolescent mood swings and denial, and the conspicuous absence of parental and social understanding and guidance.

Holden serves as a mirror for his peers. There is a lot in him with which the young can identify readily. Much of Holden's candid outlook on life is still relevant to the youth of today and contains a truth of an eternal nature. The fact that the boy is lonely, bewildered, and pitiful, his troubles, his failings, even his minor delinquencies, and his howling for help still find warm echoes among the young because these represent pretty much of their own situation. This accounts for the book's continual popularity. It has been read and reread by millions across the world.

The book's success has also to do with its superb handling of language. Salinger's rendering of teenage speech is wonderful: the unconscious humor, the repetitions, the slang and profanity, and the emphasis are all managed just right. His thoughtful and sympathetic insight into adolescence and adulthood, his unobtrusive symbolism, and his insistent avoiding of slogans and clichés—all these add considerably to the spectacular achievement of the novel.

Bernard Malamud (1914-1986)

Bernard Malamud has been regarded as a major Jewish writer in the postwar period. His writings are mostly about Jewish life. Malamud helped introduce marginal ethnic culture to mainstream America.[4]

Malamud was basically an autobiographical writer. He converted the facts of his Jewish life and immigrant background into imaginary fiction. Thus, for instance, his parents' Brooklyn grocery store is immortalized as the setting for *The Assistant*. *A New Life* reproduces his teaching experiences at Oregon State University. His life as a literary artist finds expression in *Pictures of Fidelman*.

Malamud's characters—a professor, a fixer, an aging writer, a rabbinical student, or an assistant—are all learning about life and struggling to survive with dignity. They grow as they strive for self-improvement and become morally better human beings. To Malamud, a Jew is a good person. One does not have to be one of the Jewish race and faith to be a Jew. Everyone is a Jew in the sense that the Jewish condition is universal to all mankind. Malamud wrote for a purpose. The pattern is generally that out of suffering and despair come epiphany and eventual development. People learn wisdom, accept responsibility, and become more loving and tolerant. Malamud once said, "My work, all of it, is an idea of dedication to the human. That's basic to every book …. I'm in defense of the human."

The Assistant

The Assistant is a typical Malamud narrative. It is a heart-warming story. Morris Bober, a Jewish immigrant, runs a small grocery store in Brooklyn, New York City, and lives a poor life with his wife Ida and daughter Helen. Business is slack, life is weary, and the only comfort for him is to look forward to taking his after-lunch nap. One night, two robbers rush in and hurt him on the head. Some time later, a poor young Italian, Frankie Alpine by name, comes along to beg for a job. Though most reluctant, Morris agrees to take him in as an assistant. Frankie works hard, but Ida and Helen are suspicious as they do not like the idea of a gentile living among them. One day Frankie is caught stealing from the cash register and has to leave.

The tiny grocery store is losing ground in face of the competition from a newer, bigger store, and then Morris is hospitalized. Frankie comes back in, saying that he owes to Morris Bober. Running the grocery store by day, the young man works at a coffee shop at night so as to keep the store alive. When Morris returns home, Frankie confesses that he was one of the two robbers. Morris, not surprised, says that he knows it. But as he cannot forgive Frankie for stealing in the shop, he dismisses him again. Then Morris dies of pneumonia, and Frankie comes back again to help with the business and the family. He behaves more and more like Morris. Later he becomes a Jew.

The Assistant successfully portrays a good old Jew, Morris Bober, kind, honest, compassionate, and capable of helping people regenerate with his "Jewishness." Morris embodies the notion that love is a moral responsibility. He knows he has to suffer, and knows he does so for a purpose. So he never gives up hope and faith in adversity. Morris is the archetype of the suffering Jew. Suffering is one major feature of his life. He suffers to atone for humankind. He falls in business, but rises in moral and spiritual stature to which Frankie's new birth is convincing testimony. Malamud reveals his consummate skill when he makes the best of the tension between optimism and pessimism, and between hope and despair. There is gloom, but there is also the light of humor to help alleviate it.

The Fixer

Another novel for which Malamud is noted is *The Fixer*, which won both the Pulitzer Prize and the National Book Award for him. Its protagonist, Yakov Bok, is the very image of the suffering Jew. The story is set in anti-Semite Czarist Russia. Young Yakov grew up in an orphanage: his mother died of childbirth, and his father was killed in a pogrom. He is pessimistic about life, and hides his identity as a Jew. He serves in the Russian army, and learns Russian, history, science, geography, and arithmetic. He works hard, and hopes for a better life. Living in his village, he feels miserable and imprisoned; even his wife leaves him. So he sets out for Kiev to get to know about the world. On one occasion he saves a brickwork owner from being smothered in the snow, and becomes his handyman. Somehow at the workplace he incurs the ill will of a superior, and is later falsely accused of ritual murder of a Christian boy. He receives inhuman treatment in prison: impossible food, beaten by fellow prisoners, narrowly escaping death by poisoning, and chained like an animal. He goes on a hunger strike, howls at the injustice against him, and argues in vain in self-defense. He refuses to succumb to the powers that be and makes no false confessions. He knows he is innocent; it is the Czarist government looking for anti-Semite excuses that deliberately confuses facts with religious prejudices and prosecutes him on false testimonies. One sympathetic magistrate is found dead; one attorney is determined to convict him. Yakov keeps his faith in himself. Despite the incredible suffering he experiences in prison, he reads, meditates, and communicates with the few people he knows. He begins to understand the meaning of responsibility and accept suffering as a way of identifying himself as a Jew and as a human being. He learns to see life in a different light: he learns to feel and be responsible for his fellow creatures, friend or foe. He becomes a symbol for the people, one of love for freedom and justice and for humanity.

The Fixer is good in formal terms. Essentially a realistic work, the novel glimmers with occasional flashes of romantic expression. For instance, the imaginary scene of the face-to-face argument between Yakov and the Czar is a *tour de force* that contributes well to Yakov's characterization. Furthermore, although based on the facts of history, Malamud's book places emphasis elsewhere. It is not history, but the process of revelation and growth through a nightmarish experience, that receives most of its attention.

Malamud's short story, "The Magic Barrel," from the National Book Award-winning collection of the same title, follows a similar pattern. Leo Finkle, the rabbinical student expecting ordination, finds the advice attractive that he should get married in order to help win a congregation. As he has no one immediately available, he seeks help from a matchmaker, Salzman. The man comes with several suggestions none of which is agreeable to Leo. Then Salzman tactfully leaves Leo with a manila envelope with the pictures of a few women in it.

One day Leo opens the envelope. The pictures are no good, but one snapshot catches his attention just at the moment he is about to give up hope. It is the picture of a young woman that he falls in love with at first sight. He tries to get information from Salzman who, however, snatches the picture away and refuses to reveal her identity. Pressed hard and in despair, Salzman blurts out that the girl is his daughter who is dead to him because she prefers prostitution to poverty. The violence of his emotional response sets Leo thinking and self-searching. For the first time he discovers and admits that he is unloved and loveless, and that, although conversant with the Jewish law, he is Godless. His conversion and redemption begins the moment he thinks of loving others more than himself. He is getting ready to suffer for the prostitute. Now he is not thinking of marriage for his own good; he comes to see that love is now a sacrifice for or a commitment to a larger cause. The way the story ends—Leo going to meet the fallen girl with flowers in his hand—is quietly provocative as it offers a possibility of growth rather than a mere reality.

As with *The Assistant*, humor here serves as a means of redeeming the absurdity of the scenario and alleviating the anguish of the suffering. Thematically, Salzman is both a clown and a means of leading to salvation. Formally, he is a structural necessity to enliven the dismal built-in atmosphere. Pages of seemingly useless stuff serve to build up the suspense which, when felt, is so rewarding. That is Malamud at his best.

John Updike (1932-2009)

John Updike was a prolific and prize-winning writer.[5] He is best known for his "Rabbit" pentalogy: *Rabbit, Run* (1960), *Rabbit Redux* (1971), *Rabbit Is Rich* (1981), *Rabbit at Rest* (1990), and *Licks of Love* (2000). The plot of the series is nicely sequential and coherent. Rabbit runs away from home in *Rabbit, Run*, comes back in *Rabbit Redux*, becomes rich in *Rabbit Is Rich*, is laid at rest in *Rabbit at Rest*, and is resurrected in the memories of his folks in *Licks of Love*. Having himself survived into the new millennium, Updike just could not resist the temptation of writing a sequel to his four Rabbit novels and so published a fifth, a novella.

This "Rabbit" is the nickname for the main character, Harry Angstrom, a person of no importance in American middle-class society. The series of novels relates the story of this man, a blue collar, whose peak in life was as a high school basketball star. The nickname indicates two major character traits of the man— his uncontrollable sexual desire and his place as a petty person in society. Like a Rabbit, he is always looking for something and is always running away from something. After the success of the first of the series, Updike kept the rate of publishing a Rabbit novel every ten years. So Harry keeps his presence fresh in the minds of the readers. Each book tries to size up the social landscape of America in the duration of ten years. The Rabbit has thus become a legend in the postwar period.

Rabbit, Run

Rabbit, Run is the first of the series. The story line is simple. Harry the Rabbit, a young man in his mid twenties, is already feeling empty and depressed. His wife, Janice, now pregnant, drinks and watches juvenile TV programs, leaving their car and small son Nelson at their parents'. Harry decides to run away. He starts housekeeping with Ruth. Harry now works as a gardener for a wealthy widow, and Ruth becomes pregnant. When Janice gives birth, Harry deserts Ruth, returns home, and works for his father-in-law. Then driven by his sexual urge, he leaves for Ruth, Janice gets drunk and drowns the baby girl while giving her a bath. Unable to deal with the situation, Harry runs away for good. Rabbit is on the run, from job to job, from adviser to adviser, and from woman to woman. He keeps on running and nothing can stop him.

Harry's problem is symptomatic of his age. He has energy enough, but does not have the proper outlet for it. He is not satisfied, yet he cannot define what he wants. Rabbit knows that he is a failure, and feels agonized over it. He is aware that he has a problem, but he cannot pinpoint it, less to say to address it. He is harassed by his sense of meaninglessness, but cannot figure out what to do about it. A concerned clergyman feels that Harry is not spiritual enough and that, separated from God, he is going through some religious crisis.

So Updike paints the portrait of a person left all alone to shift for himself in a society which generates so much hardness of the heart and offers so little hope for grace and salvation. Hence the epigraph of the book: "The motions of Grace, the hardness of the heart; external circumstances" (Pascal's *Pensee* 507).

The Plotlines of the Rabbit Series

The epigraph goes in fact for the whole of the series. The country, and Harry with it, continues its directionless existence. In *Rabbit Redux*, 36-year-old Harry comes back, works for his father-in-law, and lives his routine life in a spirit of resignation. After a fire, Janice comes back in reconciliation. In *Rabbit Is Rich*, Rabbit takes over his father-in-law's business, and becomes rich. His natural daughter (by Ruth) appears. His son, Nelson, begins substance abuse. In *Rabbit at Rest*, Harry, now in semi-retirement, plays basketball with a boy and dies of a heart attack. And in *Licks of Love*, Rabbit is back alive, resurrected in the memories of his family.

Updike's depiction of social landscape is authentic. He is preoccupied with characterization. He grapples with experience in order to reveal its essence and derive a sense of orientation. He was a serious literary artist.

John Cheever (1912-1982)

John Cheever was a fine short-story writer. His best stories are collected in *The Stories of John Cheever* (1978) which reveals his thematic concern in a graphic way. In addition to his short stories, Cheever also published some impressive novels, such as his National Book Award-winning *The Wapshot Chronicle* (1957), *The Wapshot Scandal* (1964), *Bullet Park* (1969), *Falconer* (1978), and *Oh What a Paradise it Seems* (1980).[6]

Cheever wrote mainly about the suburban middle class people. He was authentic in depicting their manners and morals, the surface reality of their existence, and their inner struggles with their sin and guilt. Life is gloomy, but they aspire for light. John Cheever has faith in man's inclination toward spiritual light. Critically, Cheever has suffered some neglect. He wrote in the more conservative mode of mannered realism.

Cheever's best work is his oft-anthologized "The Swimmer." This typical Cheever work tells the story of a middle-aged man leaving a friend's party to swim home from pool to pool across an 8-mile long area. As he swims through, Neddy meets with people, observes the landscape of life, and digest his experience with affluent but uncertain middle class America. Like the seasons rotate, from summer to autumn to approaching winter, Neddy undergoes a massive change in his own person in the process of swimming: he feels himself becoming gradually weak and elderly. When he arrives home, he finds that the house is in padlock and his family are gone.

Although told in a realistic manner, "The Swimmer" has assumed an unmistakable surreal air about it. The journey could mean that human effort is doomed to failure. It could also symbolize that no party will last forever. Neddy thus assumes suddenly the stature of a vigilant consciousness, floating around to warn the improvident world of middle-class America of what might be in store for them.

Southern Literature

During this period, southern literature continued to grow with the painstaking efforts of such writers as Flannery O'Connor (1925-1964) and William Styron (1925-2006). Flannery O'Connor has been described variously as southern, Catholic, and grotesque. She was all of these, but more. Born and raised in the south, she took what she knew best as her major subject matter. Her imagination, living through a time of mid-century Catholic revival, was colored by a religious vision evident in all her works. And she was good at representing the grotesque and violent aspects of human existence and magnifying them to shocking dimensions. "[F]or the almost-blind you draw large and startling figures," she said. But her works break through all the boundaries and apply to a much broader extent of life and experience.[7]

O'Connor' sensibility was a unique one. She took interest in the lives of those country people, often freaks, either physical or emotional or both, that embrace a single, ferocious belief, and of those southerners, often poor and benighted religious fanatics, who appear as sufferers of one kind or another in need of salvation. These poor souls become protagonists of her stories, and help make a statement of her views on the human condition. Flannery O'Connor shows understanding and compassion toward her characters, and tries to discover ways to salvation for them. Her stories are full of death, suffering, and violence, but always also moments of grace and redemption. Her characters are often uncouth and hideous, her plots jarringly unnerving, and her portrayal of violence and sinfulness appalling, but these serve to reveal her religious vision. There is in her writings a kind of mystery that cannot be readily unraveled in light of normal human experience. Her style is simple but suggestive, full of comic and melodramatic details that are meant to horrify the minds of the readers. She treats sudden and unexpected events with a calm detachment and tries to reveal and examine the invisible aspects of human nature with precision. There is a Gothic element and an obvious absurdist tendency in her works. These include *Wise Blood* (1952, a novel), *A Good Man Is Hard to Find* (1955, a collection of short stories), and *The Violent Bear Is Away* (1960, a novel). Other published works are collected in her posthumous *Everything That Rises Must Converge* (1965). *The Complete Stories* came out in 1971. When she was alive, O'Connor had already earned a substantial reputation for herself, and over the years she has been receiving growing critical attention. She will be remembered as one of the best known postwar short-story writers.

"A Good Man Is Hard to Find"

The notable ingredients of an O'Connor story converge in her most famous work, "A Good Man Is Hard to Find." This is a story about a family of six which, during their vacation, gets all killed by an escaped convict named the Misfit. The major character is the Grandmother. The Misfit is a cold-blooded criminal, with strong views on religion and society. He could not believe in something he has never seen, especially God. He and the Grandmother have an intellectual war, with the old woman feebly on the side of her inherited faith and the Misfit preaching from something like Satanism. The Grandmother, in a clear moment, assets her humanness and her religious piety. She reaches out to the convict in a Christian manner to forgive him. The Misfit, who has by now had all her family killed, draws back in horror, and shoots her.

O'Connor's fiction is steeped in the traditions of the American south. The Grandmother is a typical southern white, classy, condescending, believing in the value of her southern lineage, in God and the Word, no matter how superficially. When she painfully slowly realizes that she is facing death, she feels somehow that the Misfit is her responsibility to save because they share their roots in the Christian mystery. Then her head clears for an instant, and she murmurs: "Why, you are one of my babies. You are one of my own children!" She reaches out and touches the Misfit's shoulder. But she gets three shots in the chest. Readers would find the behavior of the Grandmother ridiculous, but O'Connor feels that the old lady's gesture of spiritual compassion will "grow, like the mustard seed, into a great crow-filled tree in the Misfit's heart and will be enough of a pain to him there to turn him into the prophet he was meant to become." O'Connor feels that the old woman's gesture "made contact with mystery."

O'Connor's Style

O'Connor constructs her story, as always, in such a way as to dramatize the sinfulness and the need for grace. The concept of grace figures prominently in her works. Here in "A Good Man Is Hard to Find," she is talking about the sinfulness of this world in which her characters live. Here is a godless place with godless people in it. The Grandmother's family is dysfunctional in Christian spirit. The Grandmother is not a very godly person. The rest of the family are not the best possible Catholics and need grace in their way.

The question here is O'Connor's notion of "a good man." The story indicates that O'Connor is not talking about the kind of good men that the readers normally have in mind. Her idea of a good man is heavily religiously colored. She is looking for someone who has "contact with Christian mysteries."

Grandma might be one such person in the last brief moment of her lucidity. The other, O'Connor might mean the Misfit to become.

Although the Misfit is a symbol of sin and a demonic character, O'Conner suggests that he kills because he has a quarrel with God and with the world for not treating him fair. The cold bloodiness of his violence makes the readers' blood curdle—he kills six innocent lives, three of which are children, and O'Connor uses strong language to condemn his heinous crime. But she still does not want to see him as devilish. She even believes that he has a greater capacity for grace.

O'Connor may have created such characters to voice her religious doubts. But she describes the Misfit's speech and behavior to insinuate that he may be impressed by his victim's show of humanity and thus begin to move toward spiritual transformation. O'Connor repeatedly states in her essays related to this story that the Misfit may be saved yet. Her essays indicate her anxiety that the readers may disagree with her view as it is close to that of a fanatic. And sure enough, a good many readers do find it hard to see it her way.

Then there is O'Connor's belief in the use of violence as a vehicle for awakening people to the need for grace. She says, "Violence is a force which can be used for good or evil, and among other things taken by it is the kingdom of heaven." This idea of hers is highly controversial as well.

William Styron (1925-2006)

William Styron was born in Newport News, Virginia. He was one of the leading southern writers. In his career, he won a number of awards including the Prix de Rome of the American Academy of Arts and Letters, the Pulitzer Prize, and the National Book Award. [8]

Styron is noted for his major works—*Lie Down in Darkness*, *The Confessions of Nat Turner*, and *Sophie's Choice*.

The Confessions of Nat Turner is a true story told in the form of fiction. The book presents the horror of slavery. Turner was born into slavery in 1800. He studied the *Bible* every day and became a preacher and a fanatic. He said he saw visions. Ezekiel came to him in a vision, telling him to lead a revolt against slave-masters. Turner claimed that he saw white spirits locked in battle with black spirits and the sun darkened. On August 21, 1831, he decided to fulfill his destiny as an angel of death. He had five slaves with him, and they began killing slave owners. Presently a small army of forty slaves began to form itself and within 36 hours they slaughtered fifty-nine white men, women and children. There were rumors of more slave revolts up in the air. Then government troops were sent out. They killed innocent black people, and the white militia murdered their own slaves. The rebellion was put down, and Turner was hanged. But the effects of his rebellion lasted for decades. The laws became more brutal and repressive regarding the slaves. A reporter interviewed Turner in prison and wrote a 20-page

report—"The Confessions of Nat Turner."

The Confessions of Nat Turner is told from an African American rebel's point of view. Styron calls it "a meditation on history."

Sophie's Choice

In 1979 Styron published his well-known novel, *Sophie's Choice*, which grew essentially out of his earlier encounter with a Polish survivor of the death camp at Auschwitz. The novel is a long, complex narrative that blends fact with autobiography, comedy with pathos, and history with fiction. It represents an attempt on the part of the author to universalize the Holocaust and explore the

extent of human evil. The story was made into a successful movie starring Maryl Streep and Kevin Kline, which won the 1983 Oscar Award.

Lie Down in Darkness

Styron's first novel, *Lie Down in Darkness* (1951), talks about the disintegration of a southern middle-class family.

Milton Loftis, the father, disregards traditional morality, and indulges in extramarital behavior. Helen, the mother, is a traditional and religious woman. Alienation occurs between the two, and Milton's emotional focus transfers itself to their daughter, Peyton. When the girl grows up, a sort of incestuous relationship develops, and the family begins to fall apart. Then Peyton is married off to the distant north. As she keeps missing home and father, Peyton seeks a mental balance through developing relationships with men, but this fails to save her from agony and despair. Eventually, she jumps down naked from a high-riser.

Here Styron successfully displays the loss of moral absolutes after the industrialization of the south and the loss of direction, the pain, and the despair that come as its aftermath. Infidelity is present; so is incest with its destructive passion. These, along with her beauty, finally encompasses Peyton's undoing. In the end, all die and lie down in darkness in the tomb of life.

Styron wrote about the conflict within the human soul. Here the influence of Faulkner and Freud is visible. He focuses on the delineation and analysis of the self-conflict that rages in the inner world of his characters to reveal the damaging effect of contemporary existence upon the human consciousness. Peyton in *Lie Down in Darkness* is a good example. She tries to shake off the shadow of her tragic home, the stifling tradition of the south, its history, and its culture, and tries to seek a new life for herself, but all to no avail. *The Confessions of Nat Turner* does not place so much emphasis on the misery of the African Americans and the grandeur of the scenes of their rebellion as on the confessions of Nat Turner. The same goes for *Sophie's Choice*. It turns on the fate of one individual whose soul and faith suffer against the vast backdrop of the brutalities of the war. She has tried to heal herself, and tried to respond to passionate love, but all to no avail. Her choice is still death.

Styron is regarded as one significant contemporary American writer.

Truman Capote (1924-1984)

Truman Capote, born in New York, was a southern writer by theme.[9] Most of his work is set in the Louisiana-Mississippi-Alabama area. The world he depicts in his works is a Gothic and violent one.

Capote was an autobiographical writer in the sense that some motifs basic to his works replicate his own life experience over and again. For instance, when he was a child, his parents were divorced and his mother was remarried. The child, thus "orphaned" and brought up by relatives, yearned at the bottom of his soul for love and understanding. This becomes a thematic thread running through many of his short stories and novels. In most of his stories, there is always a boy, thirsting for love, seeking it, and failing in his attempt.

Capote's best-known work is *In Cold Blood* (1966). It can be viewed differently: to see it as a symbol of violence in American life, or a symbol of the failure of the American Dream, or as a study of criminal behavior.

The major character is Perry Edward Smith who had a painful childhood. Later he commits burglary and serves time in a Kansas prison where he meets his future fellow murderer, Dick Hickok. Dick plans to rob a wealthy Kansas farmer, Herbert Clutter by name, who is said to keep forty thousand dollars at home to pay his workers. The two robbers come to the Clutters' house, ransack it, but find nothing. Despite the wheat farmer's pleadings for mercy, they kill the whole family. A special agent, Alvin Adams Dewey, is assigned to bring the murderers to justice. Together with the team he heads, Alvin succeeds in arresting them in Las Vegas and sends them back to Kansas for trial and execution.

In Cold Blood is remarkable in form. Capote calls it "a nonfiction novel" as it touches the boundaries of truthful reportage and the imaginary act of novel writing in its handling of the episodes of escape, pursuit, and capture, and the courtroom scenes. As such the novel has exerted its measure of influence on contemporary documentary novels in both America and Europe. It has been well received by readers and critics alike.

Capote enjoys both a national and an international reputation.

Philip Roth (1933-2018)

Philip Roth was a major American Jewish writer. He wrote a good deal of his personal Jewish experience into his fiction. His childhood in Newark, New Jersey, his college education, his brief military career, his marriage, his college teaching, his psychoanalysis, and his travel—all these find their way into his works. He became famous with his first book, *Goodbye, Columbus, and Five Short Stories* (1959), which won the National Book Award and is still considered by many to be his best. His best-known—and controversial—work is *Portnoy's Complaint* (1969).[10] Roth wrote over 20 volumes of work and was essentially a novelist of manners.

The stories in the collection, *Goodbye, Columbus*, are all about Jews and their confrontations. These include such as "Goodbye, Columbus," "The Conversion of the Jews," "Defender of the Faith," and "Eli, The Fanatic." The collection enraged the Jewish community who accused the author of being anti-Semite. Roth wrote profusely in self-defense, but the fury went on for a quite some time.

The frustrated writer decided then to write something different. *Portnoy's Complaint* came out in print to the angry uproar of the public. This is a confessional story, narrated by a patient, Alexander Portnoy. His mother's care and love almost smothers him and makes it impossible for him to live a normal life. He directs his most virulent language at his domineering mother. None of his lovers could help address his problem adequately. *Portnoy's Complaint* has been censured for its obscenity and its attack on the Jewish mother. It is full of vulgarities and profanities in language.

Over the years, Roth mellowed in spirit and tone, and edged toward affirmation. Technically, he was accomplished with his manipulation of narrative voices and style and his unfailing sense of humor.

Joyce Carol Oates (1938-)

Joyce Carol Oates is a prolific writer. She has published over 30 volumes, including novels, collections of short stories, poetry, plays, and essays. Some of her works have been very popular with the readers such as *them* (1969), *Wonderland* (1970), and *Do With Me What You Will* (1973), and she has won many awards. She was elected to the National Institute of Arts and Letters in 1978.[11]

Oates is a social novelist writing in the realist tradition. She chooses her characters from the common people, and writes about their lives. There are in her works students, merchants, teachers, clergymen, and workers, with their fears, anxieties, and misfortunes as well as their joys and laughter. Oates is good at representing the inner complexities and sufferings of her characters in face of overwhelming pressures, either from society, or from the interference of fate, or from their emotional inadequacies. Theirs is a dreadful, absurd, "Gothic" world of violence, murder, suicide, rape, and arson that occasionally recalls that of Flannery O'Connor and William Faulkner. Oates feels that she is offering an authentic representation of contemporary life. The gloom characteristic of her works has earned her the nomenclature of "the dark lady of American Letters."

The award-winning novel, *them*, is one of Oates' best works. Set in Detroit, it relates the tragic story of the two generations of a poor family during the three decades from 1937 through 1967. Intertwined and crisscrossed are the lives of the three major characters—Loretta, the mother, Jules, the son, and Maureen, the daughter. The book depicts the family's painful experience in the poor and violent slum world of Detroit of the late 1930s. These include Loretta's hard life, her prostitution during the war, and her family violence, Maureen becoming a child prostitute, falling ill, and falling in love with her instructor, Jules' elopement with Nadine, stealing and falling sick, returning home, meeting with and getting shot by Nadine, surviving the nightmare, raping a girl and becoming her pimp, getting involved in a riot, shooting a policeman, and going to California with a radical.

The novel tells a shocking tragic story. It depicts a world of chaos and despair. The continuous scenes of the wretched lives of the city poor, manslaughter, desertion, prostitution, riot, deceit, violence and death etc., reveal the emotional and psychological crisis present in contemporary American life. The descriptions are naturalistic, the sense of urgency is immediate, and the effect is just appalling.

Joyce Carol Oates will remain an impressive presence in contemporary American fiction.

Ann Beattie (1947-)

Ann Beattie has been active with writing in the last few decades. She has built a solid reputation for herself. She began to publish in the early 1970s in influential magazines like *The Atlantic Monthly* and *The New Yorker*, and won a degree of success with the reading public. Her works include *Chilly Scenes of Winter* (1976), some collections of short stories such as *Distortions* (1976) and *Secrets and Surprises* (1978) which, revealing Beattie at her best, established her place in contemporary American literature. She is noted for her keen insight and unique prose style. Beattie has kept writing and publishing.

Basically, Ann Beattie's works are observations of life and deliberations about it. Her characters come mostly from the middle class, well off and well educated, but diffident and impotent in face of widespread change and moral decline. They feel disoriented. Either they lament over the evanescence of human existence, or they indulge in their recollections of the past. They do not want to work, but seek to have a good time, and take delight in being cynical toward life and people. So Beattie's world is one that is dominated by desire and sexual depravity. Here confronted with defeat and adversity, the people do not know how to react, remain passive and helpless, and feel a profound sense of loss that they in the 1970s could never compare with the people of the previous decade in participation and accomplishment. Life is full of perversities and broken families; people need to contemplate and find ways to come to terms with the overwhelming anomie in their time and space.

Chilly Scenes of Winter is a good illustration. This is a story of a young man in his early twenties who craves for love but, frustrated in his attempt, feels loneliness and a sense of loss. The novel looks very realistic. It unfolds its authentic picture of the physical and spiritual features of life in the 1960s. When made into a movie, the work received popular acclaim. Ann Beattie has been seen as a chronicler of the temper of the 1960s.

Ann Beattie has been called a minimalist. She abstracts and simplifies life so that social reality appears to be a spare and even dull skeleton. Like Hemingway who she admits has been a major stylistic influence on her, Ann Beattie's language is sketchy and suggestive, all surface, but provocatively connotative. Beattie's stories are most realistic in appearance but not realistic in essence. She has already developed her own distinctive mode of writing.

 John Grisham (1955-)

Chapter 24　Postwar American Novel (II)

The Postmodern Novel

The period from the 1960s through the 1980s has been known as the Postmodernist period. It was a time of change in social, political, and artistic life. The race riots, the hippie counterculture, the mass media, pop art, mass poetry readings, street theater, vigorous avant-gardism in all the arts, predictions of the death of the novel, etc.—all these amazed and impacted the thinking minds of the time. The nature of things seemed to undergo a marked change. So did literary expression.

The novel went through some transformation. Traditional realistic narrative techniques were questioned and under fire. John Barth was the first to announce the death of the traditional novel and the exhaustion of the traditional novelistic resources. His 1967 essay "The Literature of Exhaustion" called for a whole new way of writing in order for the novel to continue as a genre. Experimental writing prospered. Postmodernism made a great stride forward.[1] There appeared, for instance, the novel of the absurd, metafiction, and avant-gardism in its divers forms.

The Novel of the Absurd

Let's take a look at "the novel of the absurd" first. During the period under discussion, the common run of mankind had come to sense absurdity existing on all conceivable levels of life. So in time the "absurd novelists" appeared to discover a new way of writing to voice that popular feeling and present a vision of absurdity in "absurdist" techniques.

"The novelists of the absurd" burlesqued traditional novelistic devices, and parodied other novels, other styles and forms and took them with highly equivocal attitudes. They would prove the artificiality of any literary art which falsifies reality and keeps people from seeing its absurdity. As these novelists had little or no faith in any absolutes, they were unable to produce tragedy. Instead, they offered a kind of comedy which makes the readers laugh in face of a tragic situation. This kind of humor has come to be known as Black Humor.

One other form of writing that appeared was metafiction. It is a kind of writing about fiction in the form of fiction. It is a style of fictive narrative that tries to tell the readers that fiction is fiction and is not an illusion of reality as the realists have tried to deceive them into believing. To metafictional writers, traditional realists tried to make their fiction look like reality. They agreed with poststructuralists that, as language is culture-bound and not value-neutral, all writing is a fabricated text. This is manipulated by the author in keeping with his own values. It is also subject to the reading of the readers heavily clattered with their backgrounds and cultures.

The Metafictional Novel and Avant-Gardism

A metaficitional novel may be self-referential, self-reflexive, or self-subversive. Such a narrative may have three beginnings instead of only one. It may get read or "edited" by a character in the text so that another text may appear within the major text. Notable metafictional strategies include such as text within text, authorial personae, burlesque and parody, and undecidability with no real story.

As to avant-gardism, it has been, along with terms like "postmodernism" and "metafiction," largely synonymous with "experimental" in the postwar period. An avant-gard novel represents a clean breakaway from normal novelistic conventions, has little or no story interest, often dull, not satisfying, even offensive to middlebrow taste, and is often not readable. Writers who exhibit this tendency include, among others, John Hawkes (with his *The Lime Twig* [1961]), John Barth, John Pynchon, Robert Coover (with his *The Universal Baseball Association, Inc.* [1968] and *The Public Burning* [1977]), Walter Abish (with his *Alphabetical Africa* [1974]), William Gass (with his *Willie Masters' Lonesome Wife* [1971]), Donald Barthelme, Guy Davenport, William Gaddis, and Steven Millhauser. Some of these writers, John Barth for instance, have become one of the most famous but the least read writers.

As the list of Postmodernist writers is long, we have to be selective. Let us, then, take a brief look at some of the works of Joseph Heller, Kurt Vonnegut, Ken Kesey, John Barth, Thomas Pynchon, Donald Barthelme, William Burroughs, and Vladimir Nabokov for an illustration. These authors all deal with the absurdity theme in their unique ways. Kurt Vonnegut's novels, especially *Slaughterhouse-Five*, focus particularly on the absurdity of life and man's modern disease of schizophrenia. Ken Kesey's masterpiece, *One Flew Over the Cuckoo's Nest*, amplifies, in its comic exaggeration, the plight of man being dehumanized. There are Donald Barthelme, with his paratactic, fractured nar-rative, and his disjunctive and staccato prose, and William Burroughs, who is noted for his absurdist technique of fantasizing and collage. And there is Nabokov's contribution here as well. There are a good many others, of course. These authors have, between them, worked out a new rhetoric to reflect the nature of their world of fear, neurosis, and absurdity.

Joseph Heller (1923-1999)

Joseph Heller was the most prominent American novelist of the absurd in the postwar period.[2] He served in the US Air Force during WWII, and wrote a book about his experience in the war. This is the famous *Catch-22* (1961), a novel, the title of which has become a new addition to the English language. Since then Heller wrote a few more works such as *Something Happened* (1974), but his reputation has so far rested mainly on his first book.

Catch-22 was the first book in America to treat the absurdist theme with absurdist techniques. It protests against the absurdity of modern America as embodied by the military power structure it describes. The story takes place in a United States Air Force base in wartime Italy. Here stands a military hierarchy, wielding its preposterous authority over the lives of its wretched bomber pilots, who fear flying and wish to be grounded and escape death. In face of the increasing number of flying missions and the increasing chances of meeting death, the pilots are hopeless and desperate. One of them, the protagonist, Yossarian, is afraid of death. He has lost faith in God, and feels no sense of security any more. Along with his fellow pilots, he is horrified by the sight of death and absurdity around him. He is disconcerted by the terrible death of his fellow pilot, Snowden, a boy of nineteen, which features perpetually as a heavy load on his mind: "Yossarian ripped open the snaps of Snowden's flak suit and heard himself scream wildly as Snowden's insides slithered down to the floor in a soggy pile and just kept dripping out …. He forced himself to look again. Here was God's plenty, all right, he thought bitterly as he stared—liver, lungs, kidneys, ribs, stomach and bits of the stewed potatoes Snowden had eaten that day for lunch."

And he is baffled at the conduct of another fellow pilot, Orr, first feigning madness (talking with crab apples and chestnuts in his mouth, experimenting with being shot down, being beaten up by a whore in Rome, etc.), and then disappearing mysteriously. It takes him a long time to realize that Orr has been planning his own escape all along. Yossarian's outlook undergoes a change. He was brave once but now has a different notion of courage and heroism. Soon he is seen receiving his decoration naked. He begins to ponder over ways to fend for himself, and finally manages to escape the clutches of death and war.

The world of Yossarian is an absurd one, and the way Heller exposes it is through burlesque, the ruthless burlesque of the military unreason, as critic Charles Harris puts it, as best represented by its three major features: the structured chaos of the military build-up, the military logic, one symbol of which is a "rule" known as "Catch-22," and the widespread absurdity on all levels of existence.

First, the chaos in the military structure is well illustrated in the novel. Here is a place where the absurd is the norm: people still very much alive like Doc Daneeka are declared dead and people long dead such as Mudd are kept "alive" on the official roster; one officer, Major Major, welcomes visitors in his office only when he is out; and only those are allowed to attend "educational sessions" who never ask questions. These are only a few from many of life's bizarre manifestations.

What the author castigates is the absurdity of not only the military bureaucracy but the whole of the capitalist world in which a traitor like Milo, who profiteers in the war and plots the German bombing of the American squadron, is set free simply because he has made money. Yossarin feels confused at the behavior of those at the top of the military machine, the generals, colonels, and especially Milo's enterprises. Milo is one of the very few characters that are fully portrayed in the book. He is a symbol of a system that lies at the bottom of all the absurdity: the capitalist free enterprise, portrayed as immoral and a menace to human survival. Milo is in a sense the personification of death, especially when Snowden is dying and his M&M Enterprises' medical kit fails to offer the badly needed medication.

Another object of ridicule is the military logic inherent in the monstrous establishment. The bureaucracy has more faith in paper work than in the stark reality of the war. For instance, when Yossarian moves, in the middle of the night, the bomb line (represented by a red ribbon on the map) up over Bologna, the headquarters really believe that they have captured that city and the commanding officer is actually awarded a medal.

Then there is this overriding "Catch-22," which does its work effectively in absurd situations. For instance, all bomber pilots are afraid of flying bombing missions. They have to fly unless they are crazy. Orr is crazy but cannot be grounded. All he has to do is to ask to be grounded, but as soon as he starts asking, he is no longer considered crazy and must fly more bombing missions. This is the simple logic of Catch-22. Everybody knows that Catch-22 does not exist, but all think that it exists and obey its absurd logic. This is itself a proof of the "power" of absurdity which rules and ruins modern existence.

The third manifestation of absurdity is its widespread existence in the war machine. The scramble between the generals, Major Major's promotion by an IBM machine, Colonel Scheisskopf's promotion to lieutenant general, Yossarian's liver condition, the joke about T. S. Eliot, the court martial of Clevinger, the assigning of an atheist as assistant to the chaplain, Major Major's father's not growing alfalfa, Mrs. Daneeka's reaping of the benefits from her husband's "death"—all these and a good deal more well reveal the absurd nature of life in the war system and the world at large.

In formal terms, there are a couple of things to take note of. For one thing, Joseph Heller uses an absurd linguistic surface to reflect the depth of the absurdity of the modern world. Devices such as "circular conversations," as critic Harris calls it, constructions with their comic, unexpected responses, the "wrenched cliché" which results from the change of "a key word in an otherwise hackneyed expression," juxtaposed incongruities, sudden tonal changes from seriousness to triviality—all these are skillfully employed to convey the illogicality and the unpredictability of a mad world. The effect that the burlesque and its absurd verbal expression produces is irrepressible laughter on the part of the readers; everyone would have a good laugh if they care to read the book through. The laughter is, however, inevitably followed by the acute awareness that it is based on the suffering and misfortunes of their fellow creatures. Think of the funny language which adumbrates the scene of Orr being beaten up by Nately's whore's sister and the readers laugh, but when they get to know the truth that Orr has paid her to do so just in order to appear crazy, they feel sad. Listen to the conversation between Yossarian and Milo concerning the pilot's liver trouble and the readers laugh, but when they stop to think that Yossarian refuses to eat fruits just to keep his liver condition because he has to choose the lesser evil that may allow him to live longer, they feel sad. The same comic and sad effect occurs with the joke relating to T. S. Eliot which is presented in such a funny manner but reveals such crass ignorance and incompetence of the generals who wield the power of life and death over their subordinates and may easily send them to a Snowden's death, the readers' laughter ends in tears when they become aware of the pathetic situation of the bomber pilots. Death and absurdity stalk their world. People either pretend to be mad or they are really mad when they revel in depravities (look at them in Rome) and violent feasting (think of their Thanksgiving celebrations) and can think of nothing positive about life and future. And most of them have really no choice in face of the deadly threat except escape and make the best of what they still have available. If they live for the moment, they are the living dead. Hence the death motif, which is, in the final analysis, the thematic basis on which the book's formal comedy plays itself out.

Another formal feature of the book is its apparent "formlessness." For quite some time after its appearance, *Catch-22* was seen as a structural failure despite the admiration it inspired for its narrative power. The novel is arranged by the names of the characters rather than follows a sequential order. Events recur; past and present mingle. Time as a frame of reference ceases to exist. Narrated in the third person but with Yossarian as the presiding consciousness, the book reads like a mind reminiscing about a nightmarish past. This mind does not only deny the relevance of time; it obliterates it altogether. Any notion of clock time centering round Milo, for example, is readily shattered by the psychological time that ticks in Yossarian's mind. As a result, time stops functioning as a coordinate system. It would be frustrating, for example, to pinpoint the time of Snowden's death: at one point the readers are told that he was killed over Avignon a week before Yossarian's decoration and before the Great Siege of Bologna, but at another Yossarian is seen taking his rest leave after Bologna when "Snowden was alive then, and Yossarian could tell it was Snowden's room …."

When time is absent, life loses its timely order, the book recording such life loses its timely structure, and the readers are thrown back, as it were, to the beginning of the universe when everything was wrapped up in chaos. From a traditional point of view, this may appear to be a failure. But Heller's book has appealed to its audience so much that its formlessness has been recognized as a technical innovation, as it indeed is. Heller deliberately confounds the notion of coherent time. In a world where life ceases to be rational and orderly, nothing like a sequential development is possible and to present it in any logical time sequence would be to cover up its absurdity and impede a public recognition of it. Through the confusion of time, the novel evolves from the beginning maze of farce to the eventual protest and horror that it reveals. Then the readers begin to see that the story is all about man's survival.

When it first appeared, *Catch-22* was a "curious" book to readers and critics who had initial mixed feelings about it. It is a war novel, but it represents a new mode of writing about wars, distinct from the realistic tradition as in works such as Stephen Crane's *The Red Badge of Courage*, Hemingway's *A Farewell to Arms*, contemporary works like Mailer's *The Naked and the Dead*, Irwin Shaw's *The Young Lions* (1948), and James Jones' *From Here to Eternity* (1951). It has no formal and structural precedent. Nor has it had any visible follower so far, although Thomas Pynchon's *V.* (1963) and Kurt Vonnegut's *Slaughterhouse-Five* (1969) both apparently share its absurdist techniques and features of black comedy. The book simply exploded on the critical consciousness in the early 1960s so that people had a hard time coming to terms with its novelty. It defied traditional definition; it made a tradition of itself. Gradually the critical world has come to see it as a milestone in the history of the American novel. It marked the beginning of a new genre in the American novel, "the novel of the absurd," and is now placed safely on the list of college textbooks. The book has now become a world classic.

Kurt Vonnegut (1922-2007)

Kurt Vonnegut was basically a science fiction writer. He wrote in obscurity until the publication of his sixth novel, *Slaughterhouse-Five* in 1969. The book brought him to general attention and established his place of prominence in contemporary American novel.[3] All through his long career, he has kept publishing novels. Over the years he has received numerous honors.

Slaughterhouse-Five

Slaughterhouse-Five is essentially autobiographical. The protagonist, Billy Pilgrim, offers an effective medium for Vonnegut to speak his own mind. Like Billy, he was born in 1922, became a prisoner of war during WWII, and survived the Allied firebombing of Dresden narrowly. Vonnegut, as an eyewitness of the tragic event, knew perfectly well that the bombing had no strategic importance except to diminish the morale of the Nazi regime and the German people. He learned later that the raid was the most deadly of any in WWII, including the atomic bombing of Hiroshima.

Dresden was the beginning of Vonnegut's life-long distrust of technology and his theme of man's inhumanity to man which is central to his novels and short stories. WWII led him to question many morals and traditions of human society. A decade after the war, Vonnegut realized that he was obligated to write about this largest massacre in human history. What Dresden was all about was the killing of about 135,000 people in the course of a night, and he saw a mountain of dead people ("tons of human bone meal in the ground," as he puts it in his famous novel). And that made him think. *Slaughterhouse-Five* was a vehicle for him to express his sadness for and indignation at the human race.

The Story of the Book

The story of *Slaughterhouse-Five: Or, The Children's Crusade, a Duty-*

Dance with Death (well known now simply as *Slaughterhouse-Five*) is told by a narrator, mostly third-person, except in the first and last chapters in which the author takes over the narration. The protagonist, Billy Pilgrim, survives the war and returns to his hometown, Illium, NY, where he becomes an optometrist, gets married, and lives well before he suffers a nervous breakdown. Then there is an air-crash, which he survives, but his loving wife does not. Then he becomes "vocal about flying saucers and traveling in time." He begins to talk on the radio and publish letters about his life on the planet Tralfamadore. He says he was kidnapped on the eve of his daughter's wedding, and the aliens from Tralfamadore taught him about the fourth dimension where all moments of time stay for review and reliving. Then he was released and came back to earth to spread the new knowledge to his fellow earthlings. So Billy, first becoming "unstuck in time" in the war, now travels back and forth frequently in time.

The book records his time travels, mostly his revisiting the scenes of his life when he "returns" to wartime Germany, sees his comrade Roland Weary die in the boxcar carrying them to Dresden (where they are kept in an underground slaughterhouse meat locker numbered five), sees one of his fellow prisoners executed for "stealing a teapot" after the bombing, and recalls the threat of another of his war buddies, Paul Lazaro, who vows to hire someone to kill him after the war to avenge Roland's death. Billy is shot and dies in a park where he is addressing a crowd about death. When he is shot, he "experiences death for a while. It is simply violet light and a hum." Billy is made crazy by his war experiences. He and his comrades behaved like a bunch of children in the war and after it, dying or suffering shellshock but knowing so little about the meaning of the war that their war effort seemed to be a children's crusade. Hence the second part of the book's title.

Slaughterhouse-Five is a war book, an antiwar novel. It is first a statement about war and man's inhumanity to man and about life and history. The war reveals man's savageness against man. It makes life miserable. Billy becomes schizophrenic even during the war and his life can never be happy again. After the war, he is well off, respectable, with a wife who adores him, but his mind stays split. It is so full of suffering and deaths that there is little or no room for happiness. His recollections of deaths stay forever in his mind. Death continues long after the war even as the author appears in his own voice speaking directly to the reader in the last chapter. Death is mentioned one hundred times in the novel and is always followed by "So it goes," a phrase that combines so many shades of emotional coloring such as anger, agony, apathy, helplessness, and cynic distaste at life and history.

　　Here the novel addresses the purpose of life and the meaning of history. Vonnegut seems to be fascinated with the phrase "if accident will" as an answer to his question about life and history. He implies that history has neither meaning nor purpose, and God is not interested in the human dilemma. Life is absurd, haphazard, embarrassing, so that the people do not seem to care about if it ends. In the novel the author sounds desperate, giving in to the senselessness and hopelessness of it all: "a bird has the last word" ends the book.

The Theme of the Book

　　The central theme of the book, the absurdity of life, is illustrated well in characterization and structure. Billy Pilgrim is all absurdity as a person. He looks awkward, behaves awkward, and speaks awkward. The way he walks, reacts with people, the things he does—all is intended to delineate a hapless, innocent, confused person, without much of a personal will, completely at the tender mercies of circumstances and fate. Just read chapter two and recall the scene in which he is kicked and knocked about behind the German lines, and we will understand what a veritable picture of human innocence and helplessness he is in life as well as in war. But he is, as such, the best equipped of all (very much like Forest Gump) to become a prophet with a new message, to tell something new in a world where, as Vonnegut complained on one occasion, people tend to "fart around and don't let anybody tell any different." Billy's—Vonnegut's— message is basically this, that humans should be kind and nonviolent to their fellow creatures. The underlying irony of all this arrangement is that the message, coming from an imbecile-like person and edited by his pessimistic creator, is not to be taken seriously. The irony points to the tragic vision that humans will not hear it and will never become any better.

The absurdity theme of the book is well corroborated by its structure. This is intriguing for more reasons than one. First, it is the way time is handled. Basically in the mode of the stream of consciousness but often following the jerky movements of Billy's schizophrenic states of mind, the novel approximates Billy's experiences of time in a fractured sequence. Billy's mind moves in leaps and bounds. It often works in an associational manner. When he experiences something that has the faintest connection with a past occurrence, his mind will fly off back in time to relive that point of his life. The result of all this is the absence of sequential connection in the structure of the book, and the novel reads like a collage of isolated fragments of life with no hint of a clear linear chronology. This applies both to the overall structuring of the ten chapters and to the contents of each and every one of them. Yet, time still exists to help chronicle events.

The absurdity feature of the book is also enhanced by the portrayal of scenes and the use of language that help generate a sad humor all the way through. The book contains countless scenarios, the description of which induces simultaneous irrepressible compassion and laughter.

Slaughterhouse-Five is an interesting specimen of experimentation. For one thing, it manifests evident features of metafiction. One metafictional strategy is to tell the readers that what they are reading is the author's fabrication. Vonnegut makes it very clear repeatedly that he is telling a story. "So it goes," or "listen," color everything the narrator says as doubtful. Furthermore, authorial presence and authorial comments help make the narrative appear fictional. Vonnegut appears directly in the first and last chapters of the book and talks about the process of its creation. There are also a number of occasions when he pops out in the middle of the narrative with a comment of his own. It is good to note that Vonnegut uses metafictional strategies well in his other works such as *Breakfast of the Champions*, *Jailbird*, and *Cat's Cradle*.

Vonnegut was a major postmodernist novelist.

Ken Kesey (1935-1990)

Another well-known novelist of the absurd was Ken Kesey. He was born in
Oregon, graduated from the University of Oregon, and studied at Stanford.

Kesey is well known for his novel, *One Flew Over the Cuckoo's Nest*.[4] The
story is set in a mental hospital near Portland, Oregon. The life of the inmates is
placid until Randle Patrick McMurphy storms into it. McMurphy comes after
feigning psychosis in order to avoid physical labor that he had to do on a farm of
correction for some minor offenses he had committed. At 35 he is jovial and
dynamic and feels soon repulsed by the absolute rule that Big Nurse exercises
over the patients. He begins to act to undermine her authority. Taking the lead in
the successive rebellious acts, he manages to awaken the patients to the need to
assert their rights as humans and to their potential for growth. One of them, Chief
Bromden, an American Indian of mixed blood, changes from a deaf mute to an
active follower of this hero. Confrontations occur, and Big Nurse is losing
ground. The scales are tilting toward McMurphy's side when, in a final
showdown, Big Nurse takes action to destroy the chief rebel. She has him seized
to undergo a forced lobotomy. Chief Bromden smothers the atrophied
McMurphy, and runs to freedom.

The Theme of the Book

The metaphorical significance of the story is self-evident. The mental
hospital ward is symbolic of a microcosm of the world at large, the world in
which people live. That is saying that crazy people live in a crazy world. The
world crazily dehumanizes individuals and turns them crazy.

The cold ruler of the control system, or "the Combine," is Nurse Ratched, or Big Nurse. She makes the rules and forces people to follow them. She violates human worth and human rights. The inmates feel the way Big Nurse wants them to feel; they live the way her system tells them how to live. As for room for cure and growth, there is none, and there is little enjoyment. The patients smile little, laugh less, and behave mechanically as parts of a machine. Dehumanization has gone on in full swing unchecked for a long time.

The fight between McMurphy and his followers on the one hand and Big Nurse and her jackals on the other represents the opposing forces at each other's throat in western social life. On the one hand there is Big Nurse, who represents total control. Her system is well devised. She divides her patients into neat categories. She has them spy on one another, and takes advantage of their emotional inadequacies such as fear. She tolerates no relaxation like music and laughter, and crushes any hint of disobedience. She trains her black boys and her stuff in such a way that all tune in with her in everything. She rules with absolute power, and enjoys it with full relish. She is all self-control, herself a paragon of automation of her own making. Big Nurse embodies the extremity of total control in life.

In contrast, McMurphy represents the desire for total freedom. He hates to see one person lording it over all and making all wretched. He hates the stifling atmosphere of the ward. He hates the kind of living death that the inmates are experiencing. Now that he is here, he tries to initiate a change. He introduces smiles and laughter into the lives of the miserable people. He introduces alcohol, sex, music and singing into the patients' dull, high-strung life. McMurphy's rebellion almost succeeds. The inmates all manage to recover somehow. Chief Bromden's transformation is the most noticeable. The last scene of orgy offers convincing proof that McMurphy saves them all, or almost. He has been a Jesus

Christ to them. The title of the book, although dubious, is at least meant to be a partial reference to McMurphy's redeeming action. Taken from Chief Bromden's Grandmother's song, the goose that flew over the cuckoo's nest was the one that asserted itself best.

McMurphy's Tragedy

As to McMurphy's personal tragedy, there are two basic reasons to account for it: one personal and one social. In terms of his personal conduct, there is a downside in McMurphy's character to consider, i.e, there is in him a tendency to resent and resist all rules and regulations. And McMurphy is not noted for self-control. He allows his anger to overpower him, and exposes himself as well as his buddies to unnecessary danger and death.

The social reason lies in the fact that society tries to crush any sign of individual assertion, and McMurphy gets the worst of it all. Chief Bromden acts differently. He learns to know about social repression first from his father's tragedy. Now in the ward, he sees the fight between Big Nurse and McMurphy a reenacting of the horrible drama between the government and his father. He is the only major character who grows fully in the course of the fight.

From the fight that rages between the two sides, Chief Bromden emerges the winner, with McMurphy dead and Big Nurse losing her control. As the story goes, he is both the narrator and the major character, and the novel is in a sense mainly about his spiritual progress and recovery.

The satire of the novel spearheads directly against the leveling, conforming, dehumanizing tendency of the contemporary mechanical civilization.

Chief Bromden's Father

The Absurdist Techniques of the Book

The world of *One Flew Over the Cuckoo's Nest* is an absurd one. To begin with, the fog-generating machine creates a surreal impression. It makes everything opaque and nebulous so that the real and the unreal intermingle and make for uncertainty.

Then the narrator's reliability is in question. His mental derangement throws a veil of doubt over his story. The world he sees is a cartoon world; the people he lives with are cartoon figures except they are real (as he put it) and grotesque and appear to be abstractions in a medieval morality play. Most of the time, Chief Bromden's spectrum has only two prime colors, black and white. Big Nurse is all evil; McMurphy is all good; there is nothing in between. Both are cartoons. Yet they are such people of blood and flesh. Big Nurse is so real bad, and her foe is so real good. The absurd effect thus hardly susceptibly steals into the minds of the readers.

One Flew Over the Cuckoo's Nest has become a classic.

John Barth (1930-)

John Barth was born in Maryland and became a college writing teacher in the early 1950s. Both were significant facts of his life because the first relates him to the "southern" literary tradition of Faulkner and Thomas Wolfe, and the second places him among the writers of the academia. There is a southern flavor in his writings, and many of his stories are set in a university locale. He is a prolific writer.

"The Literature of Exhaustion"

Barth was a significant writer of the period.[5] In 1967, he wrote an essay entitled "The Literature of Exhaustion," which declares the death of the traditional realist novel. Barth feels that the novel as a genre has been perfected by the great masters of the 19th century and the first part of the 20th, its possibilities as a form have been exhausted, and all the available plots have been used up. Flaubert, Tolstoy, Hemingway, and Faulkner have our respect and admiration, but possess no more appeal to writers of the last third of the 20th century. The traditional novel is dead with Joyce and Kafka. Younger writers will have to find a new way of writing. Barth did not embrace Sigmund Freud and D. H. Lawrence; he turned instead to the earliest novelists like Cervantes (1547-1616), Henry Fielding (1707-1754), Laurence Stern (1713-1768), and even *The Arabian Nights* for inspiration. He took great interest in the narrative mode of linking many stories in one framework, and found the absurdist and metafictional works of English playwright Samuel Beckett (1906-1989) and Argentine novelist Jorge Luis Borges (1899-1986) especially attractive. With the publication of his works such as *The Sot-Weed Factor* (1960) and *Lost in the Funhouse* (1968), Barth began to take the lead in the postmodern endeavor in America.

Barth's New Way of Writing

John Barth's attempt to chart out a new way of fiction writing began—if not very consciously—in his first two novels, *The Floating Opera* (1956) and *The End of the Road* (1958). Both works still follow the traditional models, but changes in theme and technique have appeared. In theme, Barth presents an absurd world with no purpose and meaning, which is to become the thematic focus of his later works as well. To the narrator of *The Floating Opera*, for instance, nothing matters in the world including the truth. He views the world as one not only absurd but also nihilistic.

Barth parodies authors like Camus on suicide in his first novel and Sartre on commitment and protean freedom in his second. He is also trying to frame exhausted literary forms within his own structures so as to reinvigorate them. Incidentally, parody and framing were to become the major features of his postmodern writing.

The world of *The End of the Road* is no less absurd and bleak to its protagonist, Jacob Horner. To him nothing is important, and he has lost interest in doing anything. He does not finish his MA degree. He does not want to go anywhere. He teaches but does not care "a damn about the job." He commits adultery with a friend's wife but feels nothing about it. Altogether he feels nothing for anything. In formal aspects, there appears a kind of playfulness similar to jazz improvisations, and to black humor then fast emerging as a trend.

The Sot-Weed Factor

The Sot-Weed Factor has been regarded by many as Barth's masterpiece. The title needs explaining. A sot-weed factor is a merchant in tobacco. *The Sot-Weed Factor* is also the title of a poem published in 1708 in London by an actual poet, Ebenezer Cooke. Now the plot of the novel follows Ebenezer Cooke through a series of adventures in 17th-century England and America. Young Englishman Ebenezer Cooke, son of a planter and trader, decides to devote himself to virginity and poetry. On one occasion he gets involved with a prostitute, Joan Toast, and gets in trouble with his father who sends him to Maryland to oversee the family plantation—Malden (a tobacco business)—there. He comes over and is plunged into the political intrigues there. Joan follows him to Maryland. The story is riddled with plots and counter-plots, coincidences, disguises, and reversals, Ebenezer's exchanges of identity, taken by pirates and thrown overboard, losing his estate and working as a servant on it, captured by the Indians, etc. Eventually he regains the plantation, marries Joan, and writes a

bitter poem, entitled *The Sot-Weed Factor*, which shows that Ebenezer has grown from an innocent fool to a worldly person.

    The Sot-Weed Factor is one of Barth's major experimental works. It is the author's deliberate attempt at the use of parody. It parodies the 18-century novel and its various conventions in general, and Henry Fielding's *Tom Jones* and the picaresque tradition in particular.

    The 18th-century world is described in such works as *Tom Jones* as one of

order and harmony. They achieve a unity of form and theme, showing an attitude of affirmation. Now John Barth sees the possibility of splitting form and theme, producing a jarring incongruity between them, in order to present the absurdity of reality. Thus *The Sot-Weed Factor* is a "formal farce," a farcical-absurd theme encased in a well-structured form.

Barth's story is outrageous. *The Sot-Weed Factor*, like *Tom Jones*, also contains a series of coincidences, but not for the same purpose. Whereas to Fielding all that happens is part of a divine design, to Barth, the unexpected occurrence is a sign of the unpredictability and absurdity of a universe capable of no design whatever. So in *The Sot-Weed Factor*, coincidences are not always credible, identities are frequently confused, and sexual encounters are tasteless at times. All these add to the improbability and absurdity of life. Instead of an ordered, meaningful world of *Tom Jones*, *The Sot-Weed Factor* presents a thoughtless world of thoughtless men and women.

In addition to parody, other postmodern strategies are also used, such as stories within the story (one prominent feature of metafiction) and black humor which permeates Ebenezer's world of cruelty, rapacity, and nightmares.

Lost in the Funhouse

The book is metafiction pure and simple. The stories in it echo the author's ideas expressed in "The Literature of Exhaustion." They are self-reflective, and self-referential. The author makes incessant comments that they are fictions, not reality.

Take the title story, "Lost in the Funhouse," for example. Every step of the way, the author is aware that he is fabricating a story, and loses no time telling his readers so. He is physically present all the time, explaining why things like italics are used, or poking fun at realist traditions and practices.

The narrative topography of the 4th paragraph may be a good illustration. The paragraph, continuing the story line of the previous three paragraphs, begins with a nine-line comment on characterization, then goes on with a 12-line description of the mother and the uncle, and then switches back to a 3-line authorial observation about James Joyce and his *Ulysses*. Then six lines of story interest follow, and another 10-line authorial comments on his use of metaphor or related narrative strategies wrap up the paragraph. If we do our sums right, authorial comments and observations account for well over 50% of the whole of the narrative. So the story is about two things at the same time: it tells a story, but also talks about how to write a story. It is fiction about fiction, or metafiction.

If we take a closer look at the structural design of the whole story, the result is even more amazing. Out of the 52-paragraphs (long and short) that make up the story, 26 are of narrative interest, 21 of both narrative interest and authorial interpolations, and 5 (i.e. paragraphs 1, 9, 34, 46, and 47) consisting wholly of the author's chat about fiction making. Even in the 26 paragraphs devoted to storytelling, authorial intrusions like addressing the readers as "you," "your," or occasionally "we" often occur so as to remind the readers that someone is manipulating behind the scene.

Such a metafictional manner of storytelling is new and offers a new way of writing. Its experimental value is significant. This is its positive side. The other side of the coin is that such a story like "Lost in the Funhouse" can put readers off because it is hardly readable. So with time, John Barth has become a least-read major author.

John Barth's Contribution

John Barth feels that the conventional novel's attempt to impose order on a disordered reality is artificial and falsifying. So he has been trying constantly to prove to his readers the artifice of his novels. Metafiction has stood the test of time and has been received as a good narrative method in literary creations. John Barth has been instrumental in helping it take root in America. Seen from a larger perspective, his effort has helped the growth of postmodernism in American novel writing. He was happy to list over 20 authors of the postmodernist tendency in his "The Literature of Replenishment" (1979), who have helped to revive the novel and injected new blood into it.

Donald Barthelme (1931-1989)

Another postmodern writer, Donald Barthelme, was a short story writer, a novelist, and a writer of children's literature. His works made him a preeminent figure in postwar experimental fiction. A trailblazer of his time, he became a postmodernist even before the nomenclature came in use. Sensitive to the change taking place in postwar life and literature, Barthelme wrote with a keen awareness that realism was outmoded for his time and that something like new modes of perception and expression truer to the spirit of the time had to appear. Influenced by the French symbolists, European surrealism of the 1920s, and writers like John Dos Passos, Barthelme has been renowned for his comic and surreal vision, his portrayal of the grotesque and the fragmented, his experimental style of montage, visual effects and graphic play, and his parody of traditional forms of storytelling, all that classified him definitely as postmodernist and avant-gardist.[6]

Barthelme was a leading figure in the renaissance of the short story as a genre, and his short stories have been collected in nine collections such as *Come Back, Dr. Caligarri* (1964), *Unspeakable Practices, Unnatural Acts* (1968), *City Life* (1971), *Sadness* (1972), *Guilty Pleasures* (1974), *Amateurs* (1976), *Great Days* (1978), and *Overnight to Many Distant Cities* (1983). His novels include *Snow White* (1967), *The Dead Father* (1977), and *The King* (1990). His children's book, *The Slightly Irregular Fire Engine: or, The Hithering Thithering Djinn* (1971) won the National Book Award for children's literature.

Snow White

The novel, *Snow White*, first brought him to national attention. It is a parody of Walt Disney's film version of the fairy tale. The Disney film follows the 19th-century German fairy-tale writer Jacob Grimm's story, "Snow White and the

Seven Dwarfs," but changes the ending somehow. Grimm's classic tale ends with Snow White marrying her Prince Charming and the stepmother's deserved death. Disney's version concludes with final reconciliation.

Barthelme's *Snow White* parodies Disney's version to show the change in values. The moral absolutes that govern the structuring of the original Walt Disney's movie are no longer valid in modern life. The homeless princess is no longer fired with her healthy urge for survival; the kind-hearted dwarfs have become capitalists driven by desires and self-interest; and evil is not necessarily punishable by death any more. Now Snow White shares an apartment with seven respectable but over-sexed small businessmen in Greenwich Village, New York.

Barthelme was a notable postmodernist. He is poking fun at the function of the storytelling form. *Snow White* consists mainly of fragmented episodes. The characters are not always distinguishable; their speeches and conversations do not always make sense. People appear strange or surreal. Snow White becomes a surreal girl. The language is intriguing in its departures from tradition like the use of headline capitals for emphasis.

Its metafictionist feature is well displayed as well. For instance, one character once remarks to the effect that they like books that have in them a lot of matter not quite relevant, but able to supply some sense of what is happening. Here he is talking, on behalf of the writer, about both his method of creation and the questionable relationship between the text and the readers' interpretations of it. In addition, the book can be irritatingly baffling. *Snow White* occasionally does not make clear sense probably because Barthelme did not think (along with modern literary theorists) language and literature can make sense of life.

Snow White has become a postmodernist classic because of its experimentalism. It is full of ironies, pastiches, and parodies of modernist fiction. And its visual effects, its incongruities, and its accurate details are both effective and entertaining. All these features show Barthelme's postmodernism adequately.

Barthelme as an Anti-Novelist

Barthelme has been dubbed as an anti-novelist. This feature of his works is evident in his short stories for which he is better known. He wrote over one hundred and fifty of them that make people see life and artistic presentations of life in a new light. His manner of writing, such as his language and its overtones, his unique sentences, his crosscutting, his collage and avant-garde techniques, and his surrealism—all these make him not always easily readable. But his pleasant black humor serves to dispel depression and gloom.

Let's take a look at the story "At the End of the Mechanical Age." The narrator, Tom, is a kind of cynic. He does not take things, institutions, and even God seriously. He is by temperament more of an idealist. The mechanical age has given the benefit of the doubt to everything including love and marriage, God's grace, and God Himself. Love is no longer what it used to be: there is no sacredness or nobility or sweetness in it any more. Marriage still carries on as a tradition, but it is already divested of divine sanction and fails. Everything is watered down, a settling for the second best. God is careless and extraneous to the human world ("Divine indifference" as one character puts it), or He is relegated to the status of a human. The mechanical age is said to be coming to an end; the new age is being sketched as in Tom's song; people seem to be still hoping.

Structurally, the story is composed of four parts, brief, abrupt in transition, and filled with strange juxtapositions of various kinds: commonsense alongside idealism, man versus man and man versus God, and real versus surreal. Life appears incoherent, tasteless, and meaningless in a Godless world of Godless people. The traditional fictional strategies and structures that reflected the values of a moral universe and made sense have ceased to do so. Parody works on several conceivable tiers. There is parody of life, of traditional narrative forms, pastiches of a few crude broad strokes, parody of the characters and their concerns, and the parody of the *Bible* and biblical figures: ridiculing the stories of creation and Noah's Ark, and of Milton's *Paradise Lost*.

However, some of his stories are more easily paraphrasable. The macabre story, "The School," is a good example.

Barthelme, by virtue of his refined tastes and exquisite powers of envisioning and execution, has become a master of the postmodern style.

Thomas Pynchon (1937-)

Thomas Pynchon was born on Long Island, studied engineering at Cornell, then majored in English, and has published quite a few novels and short stories. The publication of the *Gravity's Rainbow* in 1973 ensured Pynchon's prominence in American postmodern fiction.[7]

In his writing career Pynchon has borrowed theories from science and technology and employed them as some informing principle in his writings. These include entropy and the quantum theory. Entropy is a physics term, denoting the tendency of the universe toward uniformity. Modern physics says that the universe forever moves in a leveling or decaying process in which the distribution of energy (or heat) is becoming the same everywhere. When a state of total equilibrium is reached, the death of the universe will come. The quantum theory holds that all things contain a measure of uncertainty. That means, by extension, that man's knowledge is inaccurate. These theories well reflect Pynchon's thematic concerns. His entropic vision sees the threat of the mechanical civilization which dehumanizes humans and turns them into part of the gray mass of "inanimate automation." A reading of Pynchon's short story, "Entropy," reveals the protagonist's—and also Pynchon's—obsession with keeping his world distinct, separate and immune from the conforming forces of the actual world around him. And the quantum theory furnishes the basis for the alarming ambiguity and uncertainty that Pynchon's works generate. As a consequence, Pynchon's novels share a vague but embedded pattern that some quest or inquiry is undertaken for some truth, but the effort ends up with ambiguity if not failure, and that this outcome has to do with forces manipulating beyond man's control. Hence Pynchon's typical themes of paranoia and conspiracy.

V.

This is Pynchon's award-winning debut novel. It bodies forth his sense of the entropic breakdown of the world and his notion of life's uncertainty, and reflects the inner world of the paranoid nation after McCarthy.

The book contains two parallel narratives: Benny Profane, a perpetual wanderer whose actions, even when they are heroic, are essentially meaningless; and Herbert Stencil, obsessed with the search for the true meaning of the letter V that he found in his late father's journals. The wandering is absurd and the quest—the whole narrative—does not make sense.

Benny is a former navy man. He never stops moving around and tries to avoid entropy. Society is decaying around. Benny Profane is faced with the possibility of reaching a point of equilibrium, which means destruction or decay.

Herbert Stencil's quest constitutes the book's thematic focus. V.'s identity is multiple and uncertain, each and all of them representing a stage in the entropic evolution of man toward dehumanization and disintegration. She is Victoria, a young convent dropout, who helps to kill a British spy in Egypt, or a high-priced prostitute in Florence, or a voluptuous patroness of the theater in Paris, or the cruel Veronica Manganese in Malta, or Vera Meroving in Southwest Africa or in Valletta, Malta. She denies the humanity of others, and becomes inanimate herself. Her process toward entropy is complete. And she is not the only case of such death and inanimation: death lies at the core of earthy reality, and all seem to run to their annihilation.

The quest for the true meaning of the letter V shows that it is impossible to gain access to the truth.

The Crying of Lot 49

The same happens in *The Crying of Lot 49* in which Oedipa Maas experiences the paranoia of doubt. This attractive suburban woman of 28 becomes the executor of her lover's will, and her lover, Pierce Inverarity, has left a vast estate behind. In the process of sorting things out, she comes in contact with an old secret counter-cultural postal service known as Tristero. She investigates into the service, gets to know more about it, but feels less sure as she moves ahead in her endeavor. As all her leads double back to the Inverarity estate, she is assailed with the fear that Inverarity controlled Tristero. The character of Inverarity becomes part of the focus of her search, too. This former California real estate mogul had so many perplexing identities, one of which is The Shadow, and so many business manipulations that he becomes a demonic ambiguity haunting Oedipa. She is also overwhelmed at the entropy going on in herself and in America. One example of entropy is her husband "Muncho" Maas, a disc jockey for teenagers at a radio station. Sensitive and kind, he feels alienated from his wife and his life falls apart as he moves down slope, seducing teenage girls, doing drugs, losing his integrity and personality. With her own doubt and paranoia, Oedipa finds life empty, becomes suicidal, and awaits salvation at the auction of Inverarity's collection of stamps. This is an obvious form of entropy taking place in her. Oedipa Maas is enmeshed in a labyrinth ("Maas" in Afrikaans means "mesh"), and is doomed to look for truth like her Greek mythical namesake Oedipus does. It is necessary to add that the sense of uncertainty increases with other fictional elements such as Pynchon's language (sometimes notoriously long and convoluted), his blurring of narrator and character, and his shifting points of view.

Gravity's Rainbow

Again the same scenario occurs in *Gravity's Rainbow*, seen so far as Pynchon's masterpiece. Here we see a similar quest going on for truth. Lt. Tyrone Slothrop is assigned to find the staging areas for the rockets V-2, A4, and the mysterious of all rockets 00000. The Germans were trying to change the course of the war with their deadly missile technology. Slothrop runs all over Western Europe. He has to deal with a lot of people such as enemies, friends, and lovers. He continues his search after the war, finds traces of the rocket, but never discovers the missile itself. What is unique about Slothrop's quest is that he never gets to know fully what his quest is all about. The implication is that the world is controlled by some destructive and dehumanizing forces (which Pynchon calls "Them" in the novel), that it is progressing toward utter devastation, and that in a universe like this, nothing is certain any more.

Gravity's Rainbow offers a horrific picture of entropy on all levels of existence. One example is the disintegration of the personality of Slothrop. When he begins his search, he is vibrant and full of purpose, but as he accumulates more and more information about the Rocket, he seems to be losing steam all the time. He features less and less as a character until he fades out as one possessing no distinct integral personality. He simply falls apart and merges into the gray crowd. The quest leads inevitably, as in the case of Oedipa Maas, to dissociation.

The sense of uncertainty is enhanced by the narrative strategies employed in the storytelling. In formal respects *Gravity's Rainbow* is a landmark of postmodern fiction, acclaimed by some as the most important novel published since the end of WWII. It is famous as "historiographic metafiction." It is a mix of many genres such as science fiction, mythology, and fantasy. The world we live in is one that we do not comprehend well, so readers constantly question the nature of the reality of the world that *Gravity's Rainbow* depicts. The title itself suggests a paradox: gravity is so real and tangible here whereas the rainbow is so ethereal, dreamy, and faraway.

Furthermore, the novel's fantastic mode of narration adds an element of perplexity. First, the narrator does not seem to be reliable. We are not quite sure about the person's gender; nor are we about the individual's mental state. We deal rather with a flowing consciousness, all knowing but nebulous in nature. Then the text of *Gravity's Rainbow* is fragmented, incoherent, and often obscure. It is difficult to reconstruct a chronology and a sequence of events. Past, present, and future conflate and confuse the readers. Pynchon delights in disrupting normal modes of perception and conventional time-space expectations.

The novel is an obvious meta-narrative. Some events show that the story is just a *story*. The narrator would often hint that he is making up a story. He would address the readers as "you," and make recommendations to the readers to check out something for themselves. Also, the narrator tells his story in a way that clearly says that the timeworn method of storytelling is no longer good enough for him to describe a universe in which order and consistency, coherence, and cause and effect have ceased to be facts of life. So his book is full of disjointed bits and pieces with lengthy digressions on topics of interest to the author. Like *Moby Dick*, *Gravity's Rainbow* covers almost everything: war, military industrial complex, history, philosophy, religion, literature, mysticism, politics, feminism, psychology, cybernetics, international cartels, sex, death, etc. Each of these categories has its own multi-subdivisions. For example, literature covers such as parody, allegory, Gothicism, satire, science fiction, and poetry. The erudition that the book reveals is bewildering.

In addition, the narrative language also makes for uncertainty. Different registers of language juxtapose with or superimpose over each other and the reader's ear is tuned as it were to different frequencies in rapid succession. Lexically one sentence can sometimes cover concepts or jargons from sciences, philosophy, broad American, colloquial speech, and even the language of the pervert. The result is often that the reader's mind is being pulled in diverse directions almost at the same time and that frustration follows as expectations are not met.

Pynchon is a very talented writer. He may be difficult, but is highly rewarding to read. The picture of American postmodernism would not be complete without taking full measure of his achievements.

The "Beat" Prose Writers

Among those breaking news about the new age were two "Beat" writers who, by their sheer rebellious energy, chose the road not taken and broke new ground. They believed in their own relevance and did their best to help brush any outdated mode of writing out of the way. They have made an impact on the literature of the contemporary period. These two were William Burroughs (1914-1997) and Jack Kerouac (1922-1969). Both, regarded as literary outlaws, took it upon themselves to offer a dauntless expression of the subcultures or counterculture existing alongside the mainstream. They were ignored and dismissed as worthless for some time, but their voices were heard.

William Burroughs (1914-1997)

William Burroughs was the oldest of the "Beat" writers. He had a good education at Harvard and was widely read in literature special to his taste (such as the works by Gide and Rimbaud). He was a thinking bum for some time, bumming around but doing serious thinking. A Junkie for 15 years, he lived most of the time intellectually and psychologically on the fringes of the community. He never wrote except about such themes as drugs, perverse ways of living, violence, homosexuality, in a word, life in its most bizarre and unnatural form. His works reveal a mind thinking differently from accepted standards. Burroughs enjoyed shocking his readers out of their cozy complacency. Over the years, he put out book after book and was able to receive some critical attention. He was accepted into the American Academy and Institutes of Arts and Letters in 1983.[8]

Burroughs has been a force in postwar American literature. He exerted some influence on the "Beat" generation writers such as Ginsberg and Jack Kerouac and the San Francisco Renaissance group. He was noted for the rebellious nature of his intellectual stance toward anything established. In his opinion, the world possesses a dimension that is subterranean and thought of as ignoble and evil but is definitely part and parcel of human life and human nature. It needs a voice to assert it. The picture of life would not be whole without giving it due recognition. The voice should be radically different from the established ways of communication. Burroughs tries to explain his lifelong experimental endeavor later in his career in his book *The Third Mind* (1978, in collaboration with Brion Gysin).

Burroughs' well-known novel is *Naked Lunch*. This is a book of a peculiar kind in novel writing. It was based on his years of experience of opium addiction. Most of it was written during that period of his life. Burroughs' fictional world is peopled with schizophrenic drug addicts and sexual perverts. These people do nothing but take drugs and engage in nothing but senseless violence and sadomasochistic homosexuality.

There are characters such as William Lee, the picaro narrator and The Buyer, a narcotics agent. There are parties and groups like the Liguefactionists. There is activity such as William Lee killing men of the narcotics squad. Despite all these, there is little plot and characterization. It appears to be all confusion and chaos.

The opening episode is told in a realistic manner. It happens in a subway. The narrator, a drug addict, running away from a detective, leaps aboard a train and meets a young man. His immediate response is to prey upon and sell him some drugs. He talks about addiction, but apparently nothing happens. He then sees two acquaintances, does not speak with them, and recalls an anecdote of addiction. Disconnection occurs now and then as he leaves New York with his stock of heroin. Other cities appear and vanish, Chicago, St. Louis, New Orleans, Cuernavaca, and Tangier and so do addicts and perverts. The addict has his own way of coping. He is eager to sell his goods to the public; he is afraid of the police; and he carries casually on with his fellow addicts. His description of life and people is filled with fantasies, horrors, degradations, violence, sadism, and even cannibalism. There is brutality, rot, and death everywhere in the book.

There can be different ways to evaluate the book. One is to see it as Burroughs' self-indulgence at its worst. *Naked Lunch* makes a clear statement about Burroughs' antisocial stance. But there is also a different view of the book. For instance, the title of the book, as Burroughs puts it, "The title means exactly what the words say: NAKED Lunch—a frozen moment when everyone sees what is on the end of every fork." He meant his book to present a scenario, a moment of emotional shock, for the public to become aware of what possible dimensions life may have in addition to the one they all already know about. A third view of the book may be to read it as a document of social life. The readers may be made to see the nauseating social sordidness and become aware of a common denominator between junkie and mainstream life: in both cases there exists the control over people that degrades and dehumanizes them.

In terms of narrative techniques, Burroughs is subversively innovative. The way it was written makes *Naked Lunch* very experimental and very difficult to read. Its language is disconnected, illogical, with little or no help from regular syntax and grammar. Burroughs deliberately attempts to disrupt the commonly accepted mode of communication. So, instead of the sequential, chronological manner of storytelling, there is no sequence, no linear presentation, and nothing much of a story. There is little structure. There is montage and collage. Burroughs' own writing or other authors' works are "folded-in" or "cut-up," reshuffled so that disconnection produces a hallucinatory, surreal effect. Scenes are incomplete, chronology is disjointed, and narrators change without notice. There are no time, place, plot, and character. People generally come away with the impression that this is a different experience made known in a different manner of communication.

Largely because of its description of the experiences of junkies and sexual perverts, *Naked Lunch* was embroiled in a trial for obscenity, and was then acquitted. The lawsuit increased its fame or notoriety. William Burroughs was a genius of his own kind. A bizarre prophet with a bizarre message, he may serve a purpose of a peculiar kind, and may deserve more attention.

Jack Kerouac (1922-1969)

Jack Kerouac was born and raised in Massachusetts in a French Canadian family. He went to Columbia but did not finish there. He met the members of the Beat group, Ginsberg and Burroughs among others, and lived a stormy life. He died of alcoholism. Kerouac wrote many genres of works and was strictly autobiographical. Reading him, the readers get a peek at the behavior of a young generation, angry, depressed, directionless, but trying to make sense of life and of themselves and get somewhere eventually.

Jack Kerouac has been noted for his book, *One the Road* (1957).[9] The book celebrates one of the author's drug-fueled trips on the American highway with his friend Neal Cassady. It is a prose narrative without much of a dramatic interest, or a plot line, but there are unsettled tensions, unnerving conflicts, and unconventional subject matter that hook and hold the readers. Many characters appear in the book such as alcoholics, junkies, and jazz musicians. The two major characters, Dean Moriarty (with Neal Cassady as its prototype) and Sal Paradise (that was Jack incarnate), are both drug addicts, depraved but still groping for their truth. A first-person narrative, with a sympathetic narrator and a confessional style, *On the Road* is a story of freedom from the pressures of life.

Dean and Sal are never able to hold their job positions long because they find it difficult to keep to schedules and deadlines. They remain forever on the move. Dean Moriarty runs from place to place, enjoys experience with life and people, and tries to help his friend Sal to enjoy himself. Dean and Sal focus on the fulfillment of desire. Dean believes that life should be lived in the present or in the moment. They set out in search of truth, but always come back to square one, disillusioned and desperate. There is a lot of promiscuity and drug abuse among the characters, along with a good deal of sadness and misfortune.

Kerouac's experimental writing style is known as "spontaneous prose," which evidently enabled him to enjoy a freedom from accepted rules and limitations in writing. He claimed to have discovered this style in 1951. It was rapid writing with little or no time for meditation and less for revision. *On the Road* is a good example of writing in this style. Kerouac finished the book in three weeks of inspired typing on a 120-foot scroll of paper made continuous with scotch tape to prevent changes in his narrative thought. To Jack Kerouac writing is an undisturbed flow of action. There are no periods separating the sentences, only colons or commas or long dashes. There is no selecting, only a flowing free association of the mind into limitless thought. Obviously there are no pauses to think of the proper words to use, almost like free writing, and no time to edit and improve the writing. The author seems to write in a semi-trance, and there is an air of a stream of consciousness in which he mixes memory with dreams.

The ending of the story is unique: the story is unfinished or open, encouraging the readers to take up the tale, put their images in the same frame with his, and so pick up where he has just left off. This style, explosive, tender, reckless, and lavish, engenders a kind of cordiality and familiarity that somehow endears Kerouac to his readers. Also, the influence of jazz on the writing is obvious. Jazz constitutes an essential element of the book: there is emphasis on jazz throughout.

Vladimir Nabokov (1899-1977)

Nabokov was an American writer by adoption. He was born in St. Petersburg of Czarist Russia, and fled his country during the Russian revolution in 1919. He studied at Cambridge University. He wrote poetry and novels in Russian until 1940 when he immigrated to the United States. He taught at Wellesley and Cornell and wrote in English. The publication of *Lolita* first in

France in 1955 and then in the US three years later made him famous and financially comfortable.

Nabokov's is basically a postmodern sensibility. He is now well recognized as a great influence in postmodern literature. His literary endeavor has helped to enhance the awareness of the inadequacies of literary realism, and showed the courage to represent the new experience with new strategies.[10] His best known novels include *Lolita*, and *Pale Fire* (1962).

Lolita

By far the most sensational and influential Nabokov work is *Lolita*, an erotic story of a perverse nature, a "dirty book," as some people called it. It appealed to popular imagination, but incurred the aversion of the people with a traditional as well as a conservative taste. It was banned in France and some parts of the US immediately after its publication. The ban increased the book's popularity and its sales.

Lolita tells the story of the main character, Humbert Humbert, a middle-aged man, obsessed with a passion for little girls aged nine to fourteen. He falls for Lolita, a 12-year-old schoolgirl, which leads somehow to the death of the girl's mother. He is possessive. So the unhappy Lolita runs away with Clare Quilty, a playwright slightly younger than Humbert. When Quilty turns out to be impotent, Lolita, now sixteen, marries a poor mechanic and becomes pregnant. Sad and poor, Lolita writes to Humbert for help. Humbert comes, gives her money, and goes to find and kill Quilty. He "writes" his confession in prison and dies before the trial. His confession is edited by John Ray, Jr., a professor of psychology.

Humbert and his editor John Ray, Jr. may represent the different facets of the author's mind. John Ray, Jr. follows the conventional point of view, and thinks of Humbert's manuscript as an obscene story, one about "certain morbid states and perversions." He warns the readers that Humbert is a horrible, abject example of moral leprosy, and means to offer people a chance to learn "a general lesson." John Ray, Jr. seems to show one aspect of the author's mind—its rational side that embraces traditional values. John Ray's editing indicates that Nabokov knew that he was writing a "dirty book," and tried to forestall the forthcoming torrent of negative comments about it. The main character Humbert, on the other hand, represents a different side of the author's mind, one that follows its instinct out, consumed with passion for the nymphet idea, regardless of inhibitions and consequences.

Pale Fire

Another Nabokov novel, *Pale Fire*, has been regarded as one of the very great works of art of the 20th century. The story is intriguing in the way it is told. There is Charles Kinbote, a visiting scholar at the Wordsmith University, who claims he is the last, deposed, homosexual king, known as Charles the Beloved, of a lost kingdom, Zembla by name, in the Nordic peninsula. He fled his country because his misrule led to an anti-Royalist riot that dethroned him. He was taken captive, but managed to escape through a secret exit. The rebels sent an assassin on his scent. Now as a professor at Wordsmith University, Kinbote lives close to John Shade, a poet. Kinbote befriends Shade with information about his country and himself, hoping that the poet would immortalize both in a long poem. The assassin, Jakob Gradus, is such a dim-witted villain that he kills Shade one evening when the poet was walking with Kinbote. But Shade did write a poem, entitled *Pale Fire*, in the last twenty days of his life, which his wife now asks Kinbote to edit and publish. The Zemblan scholar is only too happy to comply with her, but the 999-line poem is, to his great dismay, not as he thought it would be; it is not a poem about his country, but is Shade's autobiographical narrative in four cantos in neo-Popean couplets. Kinbote begins to explicate the work in his own way. He sees a close correlation between each line of the poem and his lost country's history and his own lost glory. He imagines and creates what his demented mind dreams and fabricates. The critical notes and the index that result from his effort constitute a separate work in its own right, that is, an autobiographical novel that Kinbote writes for himself. There is fire in the lives of both men of which both agree that the poem and the commentary are at best its pale—inadequate—reflection. Hence the title *Pale Fire*.

Nabokov's Formal Concerns

Nabokov was a typical postmodern and metafiction writer. He tried to undermine the narrative strategies of traditional realism. He used metafictional techniques such as text within text in his writings. He told his stories in ways that often destabilize his narratives so as to confuse his readers. Both *Lolita* and *Pale Fire* are told in confusing ways. In the case of the former, Humbert is suspect as a reliable narrator, and his "book" is edited by some addle-pated professor who cannot even get Humbert's name right. And *Pale Fire* consists of a poet's long poem explicated by another person ("Foreword" and "Commentary" and "Index") so that the readers have a hard time figuring out who is talking about what.

From his postmodern point of view of artistic creation, Nabokov feels that no story could be a true story. Reality is fluid and uncertain. Nabokov theorized a lot in his novels about novel writing, and put his theories into the practice of his writing. Both his themes and narrative forms proved to be nerve-shaking in a sense, and helped usher in a new phase of novel writing in the 1960s and 1970s.

Chapter 25　Multiethnic Literature (I): African American Literature

A General Introduction: the Myth of the Exodus

African American literature has come a long way. It is a unique literature because it is all tied up with the unique experience of the African American people and the phases of their steady growth.[1] The African Americans have a history of their own. Their life in Africa before they were brought to America, the middle passage when so many of them died on the ships bringing them over, the slavery which was worse than death, the Emancipation after the Civil War, their movement to the cities where their life began to be polarized, the process of integration into the mainstream, and the Black Power movement and the Civil Rights movement—all these factors decide that the literary tradition of the African Americans is to be drastically different from the mainstream literature, which is generally Anglo-American.

For a long time the images of the African Americans in mainstream American literature had been presented in a distorted manner. Even well-wishing writers like Mark Twain were unable to overcome their prejudices. For instance, Jim in *The Adventures of Huckleberry Finn* is made out to be very funny and is important in the novel only for helping to reveal the growth of the social awareness of the white boy, Huck Finn. *Gone with the Wind*, by Margaret Mitchell (1900-1949), tells about the happy slaves happy to wait on their white masters, which is a gross distortion of African American life in the American South. Even Faulkner's *Go Down, Moses* depicts at one stage the ideal idyllic life of the past with happy African Americans as part of the picture, which tends to disgust African American readers. Neither Eugene O'Neill's *Emperor Jones* nor the famous *Uncle Tom's Cabin* is free of prejudice and condescension. These may not be intentional; the writers, dealing with an experience they do not easily share, just cannot help writing about it the way they did.

African American literature, as written by African American writers, differs in kind from all these. It centers on a myth, though also biblical, quite different from that on which mainstream American literature is based. Whereas the latter has been inspired at the outset by the myth of the Garden of Eden,[2] African American literature is patterned on that of deliverance from slavery, that of the Hebrew prophet Moses leading the Jews in their flight from bondage in Egypt. This is in a way the key to understanding this literature. The African American people often try to express their feelings and aspirations in biblical terms, possibly for want of a better medium. We have noted earlier that "Go down, Moses," one of the hundreds of African American spirituals composed in the 19th century, translates the bondage of Israel in Egypt into a parallel of their own enslavement in America. They have been oppressed so hard that they can no longer stand, and they do not want to toil in fetters any more: they want "to go," which is another way of saying "freedom" and "emancipation." This is the essential spirit running through African American literature.

The Evolution of African American Literature

African American literature has undergone a long process of evolution. Oral tradition came first in the form of songs, ballads, and spirituals, in short, folk literature in its various manifestations. Then in the 18th century, African American poets like Jupiter Hammon (1720-1800) and Phyllis Wheatley (1753-1784) appeared on the scene. The abolitionist movement and the Civil War brought a new impetus to African American literature. Paul Laurence Dunbar (1872-1906) and James Weldon Johnson (1871-1938) produced substantial works of poetry and won national recognition.

The African American novel began to make its presence felt in mid-19th century when Williams Wells Brown's *Clotel; or, The President's Daughter, a Narrative of Slave Life in the United States* (1853) appeared in print in London. Brown describes Clotel as Thomas Jefferson's daughter by his slave, and exposes the evils of slavery and the hypocrisy of public officials. This began the genre of novels on mulattoes that followed in print, such as Harriet Wilson's *Our Nig; or, Sketches from the Life of a Free Black* (1859), which was the first African American novel published in the United States, focusing, as it does, on race and class relations. Other works of the genre appeared in the later part of the 19th century and the early 20th.

Three important figures appeared around the mid-19th century and the early years of the 20th. These include Frederick Douglass (1817-1895) and his very important and influential book, *My Bondage and My Freedom* (1855),[3] Booker T. Washington (1856-1915), and W. E. B. DuBois (1868-1963). Asserting freedom and human rights for their fellow African Americans, they became leaders of African Americans in the different phases of their fight for a better existence.

The Great Migration

The next most important event after the Emancipation was the Great Migration which occurred in full swing in the years between 1890 and 1920. On the one hand the cities were developing its industrial complexes that needed labor, and on the other large numbers of sharecroppers were driven out of the country by a number of factors such as natural calamities, poor soil, and agricultural mechanization. These people moved from the south to the north and poured into the cities in large numbers. Life in the ghettos in general, visible affluence for some, and opportunities for education—all these paved the way for an inevitable literary expression.

The Harlem Renaissance

Of all the places where African Americans gathered was Harlem, New York City. Here large numbers of African Americans from all places and all walks of life made Harlem the hub of black life that drew all their artists and intellectuals over. Shortly after WWI, a black intelligentsia appeared on the scene. They rebelled against the values of their fathers and their way of life. Situated as they were within New York City, the center of artistic and literary innovations, close to avant-garde places like Greenwich Village, living in the Jazz age, the African American artists and writers were influenced by the modernist movement then developing in Europe and the United States. They took an enormous interest in their own lives and values, and tried to solicit the attention of their African American people as well as the whites. And they began a search for a distinct tradition of their own. All these characterized a great movement in the cultural and intellectual history of the African Americans. This new upsurge of African American literature in the 1920s has come to be known as the Harlem Renaissance to which African American authors like Claude McKay (1889-1948), Langston Hughes (1902-1967), Jean Toomer (1894-1967), Countee Cullen (1903-1946), and many others contributed.[4] McKay's poetry and novels, exalting the African American heritage, Langston Hughes' work exhibiting his love and knowledge of his own people, novelist-poet Jean Toomer's widely acclaimed novel, *Cane* (1923) and his other works, and the works of the talented Countee Cullen—all these played an important part in the flowering of black Harlem. African American poetry became an indispensable part of American literature. Other important works, such as Nella Larson's *Quicksand* (1928) and Zora Neale Hurston's *Their Eyes Were Watching God* (1937), appeared in the following years.

During the Harlem Renaissance, African American writers came together and wrote free of conventional restrictions, and said what they wanted to say without having to suffer any oppression by the whites and without even seeing any whites. They belonged with the African Americans, and wrote for them. As a result, they managed to build a counter culture, a battle literature, a literature which reflects the feelings, the experience, the history, and the ambitions of the African American people. Within this framework some very interesting writing developed.

Jean Toomer: *Cane*

A very interesting example is Jean Toomer, one of the leaders of the Harlem Renaissance. Toomer wrote only one novel, *Cane* (1923), but it is one of the big books in the history of African American literature. It is fascinating both in theme and in experimental techniques, showing that he was conscious of James Joyce, T. S. Eliot, and Ezra Pound, and at the same time very much in touch with his people. The novel is based on the author's experiences working in a school for African Americans in Georgia. It consists of three sections, with the first and the third set in Georgia and the second section in Chicago and Washington D.C. It is a montage of 15 poems, six prose sketches, seven stories, and a play, all about African American life in the 1920s. The novel is autobiographical as it records the personal experiences of its author as acting principal of the Sparta Agricultural and Industrial Institute, in Georgia during the summer of 1921. This was when Toomer discovered his African American heritage and renewed his faith in the folklore of his race which he thought had been lost as a result of the Great Migration.

Its subject covers a wide range of things such as black sexuality, miscegenation, and slavery. In addition to its subtle treatment of African American history and culture, it tries to address the question of identity. The book defies defining in formal terms. It is a mixture of different genres in one work, well arranged and balanced, with its unusual narrative strategies and shifting points of view. Its influence on contemporary writers is evident such as Langston

Hughes, Alice Walker, and Gloria Naylor.

Countee Cullen

Cullen was well educated at New York University and Harvard. With his poem "Shroud of Color" appearing in H. L. Mencken's *American Mercury* in 1924, and the publication of the first three volumes of poetry, *Color* (1925), *Copper Sun* (1927), and *The Ballad of the Brown Girl* (1927), he was probably the most popular African American poet and African American literary figure in America at the time. Cullen was traditional in form. He could handle "white verse"—ballads, sonnets, quatrains etc. very well. There are skill and power in his work. Thematically, he deals with the African American experience seriously, often from a religious perspective. For a long time after his death, he was ignored, but fresh interest in his poetry has appeared in recent years, and his works have been reissued. His often-anthologized poem is "Yet Do I Marvel." The poet marvels at how inscrutable God's ways are to "make a poet Black, and bid him sing!" Here is some ambiguity of feeling well portrayed: the poet is very self-conscious and probably pleased and proud that, as a black person, he could write and that he was equal with others including the whites before God. In a very vague way, the poem also reveals the poet's inferiority complex as a black person.

Langston Hughes

By far the most important person in the Harlem Renaissance was Langston Hughes, known as African Americans' poet laureate. He ultimately outgrew the movement, and developed into one of the major American authors to help make African American culture.[5]

Hughes loved literature. When still in school, he began to write and publish. Around 1925 he was working as a busboy in a hotel in Washington D.C. when he met the then well-known and influential poet, Vachel Lindsay (1879-1931). Lindsay was so struck by the poems which Hughes had submitted to him for advice that he encouraged the boy to devote himself to writing. Hughes became known as "the busboy poet." The next year with the help of novelist Carl Van Vechten (1880-1966), Hughes put his poems together in a book, entitled *The Weary Blues*. This collection marks a stage in Hughes' development as an author. The poems, like the blues songs, are sad in tone, describing the fact of having to live in a very cruel and oppressive world. But there is not much fight in them. Merely describing how things are, they read as if Hughes were trying to relieve himself and his race of a mental load and to achieve a degree of reconciliation with the wicked world. His collection of short stories, *The Ways of White Folks*, appeared in 1934.

In 1935 Hughes became one of the key speakers at the American Writers' Conference. He was one of the founders of the black theater in the Federal Theater Project during the Depression, and the editor of a good many anthologies of African American literature. And he encouraged other African American writers to write. Beginning in 1933 he wrote a column for a newspaper, the main character of which was called Jesse B. Simple, who was soon to become one of American literature's most endearing fictional figures. The sketches were later collected in books like *Simple Speaks His Mind* (1950), *The Best of Simple* (1961), and *Simple's Uncle Sam* (1965).

The year of 1951 saw the publication of *Montage of a Dream Deferred*. The very title suggests the further development of Hughes as a writer. Whereas *The Weary Blues* expresses sadness and *The Ways of White Folks* talks about Depression, *Montage of a Dream Deferred* is an angry book and shows a Hughes no longer able to contain his anger at the condition of the African Americans and the wretched poor. Langston Hughes wrote about 60 books and became a major figure not merely in African American cultural history and African American literature, but one whose contribution helped make the literary scene of modern America what it was. By virtue of his talent, his voluminous writings, and by the sheer force of his personality, he won the love of his readers, black and white alike, and enriched American culture in general and American literature in particular.

Hughes is known mainly as a poet. His poems, "The Negro Speaks of Rivers," and "As I Grew Older" are both great works to read. In the former poem, the line, "I've known rivers," is pregnant with meaning. The "I" asserts, in a quiet but touchingly deep tone, the long history, the age-old wisdom and courage, and the powerful aspiration of a race suffering mistreatment and injustice for so long. "I" does not say any more than imply, but the line, "My soul has grown deep like rivers," repeated once more at the end, is powerfully loaded and offers enough food for rumination for all.

In the poem, "As I Grew Older," the speaker has his dream when he is apparently very young, but as he grows older, he becomes painfully aware of the fact that he is black and as such he sees no light of any dream but a thick wall, which is an obvious but vivid metaphor for racial discrimination. But the poet-speaker does not feel daunted and has faith in his power.

The dream motif recurs in Hughes' poetry (such obvious titles "Dream Variations" and *Montage of a Dream Deferred* immediately come to mind). The poet's dream for light, freedom, and happiness was to generate a direct influence on the Civil Rights movement of the 1950s and 1960s. Martin Luther King, the famous Civil Rights leader, led a march of 250,000 people on Washington, D.C. and made the historic "I have a dream" speech on August 28, 1963.

Hughes' thematic concerns go far beyond racial issues. He wrote in praise of the October Revolution, sympathized with the Chinese and their revolution, and visited Spain and wrote to support the Spanish people in their fight against the Fascist regime of Franco. In form Hughes' poetry is noted for its fresh simplicity and its notable features of the free verse. His creative career has helped pave the way for the further development of African American literature.

Richard Wright and Other Famous Authors

In 1940 Richard Wright's *Native Son* came out as a watershed in the history of the African American novel. In the 1950s, African American literature flourished with preeminent authors such as Ralph Ellison (1914-1994) and James Baldwin (1924-1987), pushing it further to maturity. The 1960s proved to be a turbulent period for the United States when the African Americans awoke to the need for power, Black power, and it proved to be a period of spectacular growth in African American literature. African American writers such as Paule Marshall, Earle Conrad, John Oliver Killens, William Melvin Kelley, Jesse Hill Ford, Ishmael Reed, and John A. Williams all rose to the attention of critics and readers alike. Then in the 1960s and 1970s, notable African American writers such as Toni Morrison, Alice Walker, Maya Angelou, and Gloria Naylor produced their best works and made their presence keenly felt. African American theater was slower in developing. Nothing of importance appeared until the early 1960s when James Baldwin and Amiri Baraka (Amiri Baraka Jones) came up with their plays to arouse their African American audiences to action.

Richard Wright (1908-1960)

The major figure to appear in the 1940s was Richard Wright who became a powerful writer and a big influence over later writers.[6] Richard Wright experienced a bitter boyhood. Not happy at home with his stern mother and grandmother, he also suffered the agony of segregation in the American south of the time. Eventually he fled to Chicago, where in contact with left-wing friends and finally with the Communist Party, he began to see the Negro situation as part of the general human situation of the oppressed and wrote and published on the strength of this growing social awareness.

His first book, *Uncle Tom's Children: Four Novellas*, came out in 1938, which was followed two years later by his masterwork, *Native Son*. The book made such an impact on the consciousness of the nation that Richard Wright became a national celebrity. In 1944 he broke with the Communist Party, and the next year published his second powerful book, *Black Boy*, an autobiography relating the bitter experience of his youth. Then the racial discrimination of the country becoming increasingly intolerable to him, Wright left for Europe, where he settled down in France. Cut off to some extent from the reality of African American experience, he was seriously incapacitated in his creative work. He was to write a good deal more, novels, stories, and essays, but none of these ever touched his best work in power and critical acclaim.

Native Son is a story about an African American adolescent's growth of awareness. It consists of three sections, subtitled respectively, "Fear," "Flight," and "Fate." The opening of the novel forebodes ill for Bigger Thomas, living together with his mother and siblings in a ghetto kitchenette: he kills a big rat early in the morning. Then he goes out hunting for a job. He fights with a gang. Eventually he is hired as a chauffeur to the Daltons and drives Mary Dalton and her boyfriend, Jan, around the city. Mary and Jan drink and make love in the back seat. When Jan leaves, Bigger Thomas has to carry the drunk Mary upstairs. When the blind Mrs. Dalton enters the room, Bigger muffles Mary to keep her quiet, but inadvertently kills her. He is caught and tried, which triggers off an uproar of racist hatred and bigotry in the whole process. Bigger Thomas comes to realize before his death that he is a victim of racial fear and ghetto life.

Native Son is an extremely fascinating book. It simply exploded on the sensibility of the American reading public. Dealing with one of the thorniest problems with which America had been beleaguered, the racial question, the book pushed it into the reader's mind in a manner no one had ever done before. For the African Americans the message is clear, that they are human beings and should be treated as such, and that if nothing else can help to assert their dignity and identity, then it is legitimate to resort to violence. For the whites, the message is equally clear, that the moment has arrived when they have to come to terms with their African American fellowmen, and that, if they are not ready yet, they have got to be quick or they will have to take the consequences. Bigger Thomas, the main character of the book, embodies a new type of African American personality. Rebellious by nature, he never is able to feel at peace with the world in which he finds himself. The vehement violence which breaks out of him and which eventually leads him to the electric chair has been brewing in the bosom of his race for over three centuries, ever since the first of his ancestors were brought to the land of their enslavement. The bitterness has fermented, and the patience and humility of the African Americans are not inexhaustible. If not given the recognition that is due to them, the African Americans are perfectly ready to take the law into their own hands. Thus Bigger Thomas, more than any other African American fictional figures, represents a higher level of African American racial awareness. In him and his actions, the African Americans saw their identity, and the whites saw their folly and obligation. Richard Wright has been censured for his unabashed portrayal of violence and of a violent man as hero, but he would not have been as effective as he was had he not written the way he did in *Native Son*. Richard Wright's influence over subsequent African American writers has been great. Actually, he began the contemporary African American literary tradition of violent self-assertion. He is now seen as a classic writer in American and world literature.

Ralph Ellison: *Invisible Man*

African American literature attained to a higher degree of maturity in 1952 when Ralph Ellison's *Invisible Man* appeared in print. *Invisible Man* tells an archetypal existential story of modern times. The protagonist-narrator is nameless because he is invisible. The very opening of the book states the existentialist crisis of modern man in explicit terms:

I am an invisible man .... I am invisible, understand, simply because people refuse to see me. Like the bodiless heads you see sometimes in circus sideshows, it is as though I have been surrounded by mirrors of hard, distorting glass. When they approach me they see only my surroundings, themselves, or figments of their imagination— indeed, everything and anything except me …. You often doubt if you really exist …. You ache with the need to convince yourself that you do exist in the real world.[7]

Speaking from the hole underground which he says is "like a grave," he relates his bitter experience of having lived a death of a life for some twenty years until he discovered his invisibility. He tells us how he began life with great expectations and won the approval of the whites of his region who, pleased with his humility, sent him with a scholarship to a state college for Negroes in order to "Keep this Nigger-Boy Running." There he became the protégé of Dr. Bledsoe, the president, who, however, expelled him for having shown a white benefactor of the institution around places unfit for his eyes. Next he went to New York. What he tried to do was to be seen. In a factory on Long Island he incurred the displeasure of his fellow workers unintentionally in a disturbance and almost lost his life. Later, on the occasion of an old African American couple being driven out of a flat, he made a radical speech which subsequently put him in touch with a "brotherhood," a Communist affiliation, but he was amazed to find that the brotherhood saw the cause of the African Americans only as one of so many pawns on its chessboard. His dreams all evaporated, and he went into "hibernation" in an underground cellar. It is from there that he speaks. The book ends with the narrator's awareness that "even an invisible man has a socially responsible role to play."

The concluding section of the book, the "Epilogue," is important, particularly in view of the fact that, when the narrator thus speaks for "you"— humanity at large, he transcends the physical limits of an African American in- dividuality, becomes, all of a sudden, anyone, an Everyman, and his dilemma, thus generalized and magnified, assumes a universal magnitude. One becomes suddenly aware that what he has been talking about all along concerns the plight, not merely of an African American individual, not even of the African American race alone, but of the modern existence of man as a whole. The repeated rejection that the protagonist suffers at the hands of so many people and institutions becomes a metaphor for the rejection of the individual by society.

The question that the book ultimately raises is one of a universal nature. It is the question of the interrelationship between the self and the world. The world (or the community or society) requires that all individuals conform to its standards and values and comply with its demands. This could not be done except through the individual giving up at least part of his individuality to fit as parts into the social machine. Thus the world can be the enemy to the existence of the self. This could be one sense in which "Grandpa's injunction" can be understood. The self is placed in the enemy territory: it is in an ever on-going confrontation with the world around it. This is apparently everyone's dilemma in an age in which self-awareness and self-identity become increasingly serious considerations.

The question that the novel tries to help solve is, how people should behave in relation to society at large. Ellison's "Epilogue" addresses this beautifully well. It redefines the correlation between social responsibility and self-identity. Society may encroach upon self for role-playing, and self depends upon society for self-definition. These two, self vs. world, should not be mutually exclusive; in fact they are interdependent. There is no complete freedom or independence. Society repressing the self is not good; neither is individual's rejection of society. Life being what it is, a part of the individual has to "die" in order to live in society. The thing that matters is to strike a balance between these two. *Invisible Man* thus ends, counseling individual's participation in social life on this new, heightened level of awareness. So in the end, the protagonist is climbing out of his hole: "Here I've set out to throw my anger into the world's face, but now that I've tried to put it all down the old fascination with playing a role returns, and

I'm drawn upward again."

Invisible Man is immensely interesting as a work of art. It is more than a "protest novel." Ellison's vision is too great and his taste is too catholic to allow his book to remain merely on that level. There is, on the one hand, good reason to read the novel as one African American book on racial discrimination, black-white relationship, and the rebellious stance that the African American protagonist evinces toward an unjust and repressive society. Indeed, the book has been read that way. On the other hand, however, *Invisible Man* means much more than that. It covers a much more extensive territory of life, so that it transcends race and racial relations, and goes beyond protest to a new dimension of perception in the evolution of human awareness. In so doing, what happens to an African American becomes a metaphor, a formula, or even a paradigm for all humankind. This is ultimately the reason why *Invisible Man* has appealed to its readers so much for so long.

Another reason for its popularity is its consummate craft. The formal and technical resourcefulness that it exhibits is simply amazing. To begin with, the symbolism of the book is impressive and fascinating. It may have owed its title to H. G. Wells' *The Invisible Man*. Critics see the book's relationship to Kafka's story of *The Trial*, but it is more than that. They see Melville's *Confidence Man* in it, but it is more than that. The art of the book is ultimately Ellison's own. The notion of invisibility, the overriding symbol all through the novel, appears to be metaphysical at first because difficult to identify with immediately, but with some stretch of the imagination on the part of the readers, it becomes alarmingly physical and true as a universal fact of life. It forces all people to think and contemplate about their own situation.

Then we notice, among other things, the exquisite skill with which Ellison manipulates his prose style. This changes deliberately with the change of the narrator's environment from the South to the North and finally to his place of hibernation somewhere in New York City. As Ellison himself professes, he dreamed of a flexible and swift style, at once facing the brutal experience of modern man and expressing hope, human fraternity, and individual self-realization. It is a style which uses all the resources of the language, its riches, its idiomatic expression and the rhetorical flourishes from past periods still alive today. Thus *Invisible Man* begins with a language more or less naturalistic, moves to something like expressionistic, and ends with a surrealistic texture.[8] Ellison is trying to use a Protean style to achieve a reality no less mutable.

When asked in an interview whether the book would be remembered in twenty years, Ellison gave a modest negative answer. But its popularity has stood the test of time. With the universality of its theme and its exquisite art, the book has acquired the status of a major classic in American literature.[9]

James Baldwin (1924-1987)

James Baldwin has been seen as Richard Wright's successor in a literal as well as a figurative sense. Like Wright he went to Europe to escape the intolerable racial discrimination in the United States, and stayed there for some nine years. He did as much as did Wright (if not more) in increasing the racial awareness of the African American people. Baldwin has been regarded as the most important African American writer since Richard Wright.[10] His novel, *Go Tell It on the Mountain* (1954), is remarkable in both thematic and technical terms.

Go Tell It on the Mountain

The book consists of three sections, all about a boy, John Grimes, now 14, trying to define himself against his background—his father, his church, and all he has to face. Section one, "The Seventh Day," describes him wandering on the morning of his 14th birthday, wondering whether anyone bothers to remember it. As he moves around with the few coins his mother has given him for the occasion, he remembers how unkind his father has been to him. He feels lonely and sad. Section two, "The Prayers of the Saints," records the sad lives of John's aunt Florence and his mother, Elizabeth, and the sad but selfish behavior of his father, Gabriel. The section serves as a footnote to the wretched lives of the family and especially to the nervous relationship between John and his father. John's biological father committed suicide in prison, and Gabriel is his stepfather. The last section of the novel, "The Threshing Floor," recounts the process of John's salvation through conversion, but ends with John not feeling much better.

Thematically, Baldwin's book relates the painful reality of African American life against a historical background which shows that the African Americans as a race have been over the centuries trying to achieve self-recognition and emotional and psychological maturity. The growth of John Grimes undergoes stages which associate his earlier memories of Sunday mornings with those of other characters like Florence, Gabriel, and Elizabeth, all memories of pain and suffering peculiar to an enslaved people. What Baldwin calls in the second part of his book, "The Prayers of the Saints," reaches the height of its pathos when "Elizabeth's Prayer" begins with Elizabeth's pathetic "Lord, I wish I had of died / In Egypt Land!" Baldwin is telling his people in powerful modern language that they are suffering an age-old injustice, and that they must fight this injustice as best as they can. The power of this book lies in the fact that the reader is forever kept conscious of an oppressed race groaning and struggling for salvation.

This is evident in John's growing up experience. The boy is wretched because he feels rejected and not loved. Like all children at the threshold of their lives, John has dreams and aspirations. He does well in school and is said to have "a Great Future." He might become "a Great Leader" for his people. This inspires hope in him that he would live in a world that would be drastically different from his father's house of darkness, that he would have good food, fine clothes, expensive whisky and cigarettes, and watch movies as often as he pleases. He would look different, and people would look up to him as somebody "beautiful, tall and popular." He would be a poet, or a college president, or a movie star. This sounds all like childish vainglory, but it is all of it a dream. The fact may be that his dream would not materialize simply because he is an African American. But it indicates his determination that he would never be poor and obscure like his father and his people. He wants a different life, a life of freedom and dignity.

But as it is now, he lives in fear and uncertainty. He fears his church and his God as he feels both have let him down. He fears the white society around and the pressure of his environment. He fears his own sin and his sense of uncertainty regarding his own identity and his own destiny. And symbolic of all that he fears most is his rejecting father. He fears his father who has been unkind all along, and he fears his father's face that is terrible in anger and unutterably cruel. When his brother Roy is wounded and lies on the couch, he feels that his father hates him for not lying there instead of Roy. John feels that he is a stepson to his father although he does not know about it.

He feels it the same way when he, instead of Roy (his father's biological son), lies on the threshing floor of their storefront church, going through the process of conversion. John feels like a wanderer, one who is not seen as belonging in his father's house. The novel begins with the boy wandering around like a rootless leaf. Later, as he lies there on the church floor, seeing surreal visions, he sees his father come close and stand just above him, looking down. Then he knows that "a curse was renewed from moment to moment, from father to son," and he would carry the curse forever. The feeling of neglect and rejection has gone right down in the depth of the boy's soul. He feels he is a perpetual wanderer in "the perpetual desert."

John has had a peculiar relationship to the church. He has mixed feelings of reverence, fear, and doubt about it. He has been skeptical about salvation, and has been resisting conversion. His conversion, when it is completed, does not do much to change his status in the world and his emotional response to it. The world has not changed for him, neither has his father. He feels chilly at the sight of the saints, and feels no joy at the end of the ceremony. As he walks around, he sees the old houses still standing there as they have been for ages, the old windows still staring like so many blinded eyes, and everything that makes up the same sordid, filthy, and wretched world of his. John feels both betrayed and self-deceptive. The church and the conversion bring not much of a relief to him. A feeling of despair creeps over him.

The father, Gabriel, is another major character in the novel, next in importance to John. Gabriel is a typical stepfather, having little love for his stepson, but a lot of venom toward him. He may have faith, but he has certainly sinned against his Lord in his life. Among other things, he deserted Esther and his first son Roy (short for Royal) so that they died tragically. And he was deeply prejudiced against John, regarding him as "son of the bond woman" (an epithet that reminds people of the biblical Hagar and her son Ishmael), or "the harlot's son" whom he does not want. He is a self-styled prophet and feels that he would have an orthodox line of offspring. So his sons were both named Royal. Gabriel is not aware that it is he, either as a bum when he was young, or later as a self-styled shepherd, who makes his folks suffer, especially John.

The theme of the book is reinforced by its style and its language, which remind one constantly of the Old Testament, with the *Bible* staying in the back of the readers' mind. We notice some semblance of a stream-of-consciousness technique at work, especially in the second part of the book. Nevertheless, the bits and fragments of the lives of the Grimeses come to the reader as a whole, gradually pieced together through the church service and the prayers.

Then there is the major symbolism of the book to consider. It merits particular attention because it is powerful as it tells a truth in a forthright manner. As we noted earlier on, Gabriel calls his own son Roy. He would like to see Roy lying on the ground in the church where John lies on the night of the conversion. John is to him a kind of Ishmael, not of the royal line. All the time, Gabriel is fully aware that he is a stepfather and behaves well as one. This relationship between father and son can be seen, in a way, to signify something of a broader, more national magnitude. It can be symbolic of the place of the African Americans in the nation of the United States. It reveals the clear image of the country behaving to its black offspring like a stepfather. The African Americans have felt the way they have because of this unjust treatment.

One more thing that merits attention is the harrowing question, who makes life so painful for John? If we read the second part of the book, we will get to know that John's wretchedness is traceable back to the incident of his biological father's death in jail. His father, decent in nature and sensitive to insults and injuries, took his own life there. This proved to be a turning point for John's personal fortunes. He became a stepson. As he grows up, he becomes aware of the presence of a segment of society, the mainstream, that appears distant and oppressive to him. Thus in the final analysis, John is first and foremost victimized by the racial environment in which he lives. But this is not all of the answer to the question here. A large portion of the novel seems to suggest that the immediate cause of John's suffering is his stepfather, Gabriel. The boy lives forever in his shadow. So do the other members of his family and the other people around the man. The book probably suggests that some members of the African Americans' own community may have helped to make their world more impossible than it already is and that, somewhere along the line, the African Americans as a race may have to take some amount of responsibility for its wretchedness. The idea is more explicitly revealed in Alice Walker's *The Color Purple*.

Toni Morrison (1931-2019)

Inheriting the legacy of African American literature after Hughes, Wright, and Ellison is the preeminent contemporary novelist, Toni Morrison. She was born in Northern Ohio and was educated at Howard University and Cornell University. She began writing in the early 1960s and published her first novel, *The Bluest Eye*, in 1970. Since then she has written quite a few works of importance such as *Sula* (1973), *Song of Solomon* (1977), *Tar Baby* (1981), *Beloved* (1987), *Jazz* (1992), and *Paradise* (1998). Morrison was an award-winning writer. The many literary awards that she won included the National Book Award, the National Book Critics Circle Award, the Pulitzer Prize, and the Nobel Prize for literature in 1993. She was an international celebrity.[11]

Song of Solomon

The publication of *Song of Solomon* established Morrison's place in contemporary American literature. Winner of the National Book Critics' Circle Award, the novel is seen as another milestone in African American literature after *Native Son* and *Invisible Man*. It tells the story of an African American trying to recover his family roots. Set in a small town in Michigan, the story covers the one hundred years of African American history from the Civil War through the 1960s. The first section of the book relates the family history of the Deads. After the Civil War, emancipated slave Macon Dead I marries an American Indian girl and has two children, his son Macon Dead II and his daughter Pilate who was born without a navel. Then Macon Dead I is killed by white men and loses all his property. Macon II and his sister, pursued by the whites, are forced to kill a white man. Macon II believes that the man is hiding money but Pilate rejects material things. As they have different values, they part company.

Macon II comes to a small town in Michigan and marries Ruth, the only child of a black doctor. They have two daughters and one son, Macon Dead III or Milkman by name, who is the novel's protagonist. Macon II becomes a ruthless and greedy property owner. He cares neither for his family nor for his fellow African Americans. He is suspicious of his wife and leaves his father-in-law to die without medication. He also teaches his son to value nothing but money.

After separation from her brother, Pilate wanders around for over twenty years and also comes to the small town with her daughter Reba and granddaughter Hagar. Deserted by society, alone, without friendship and religious faith, Pilate works hard to stay alive. She thinks hard and long about the most important thing to her in life. Compassionate and full of love, she becomes a spiritually whole person. She teaches her nephew Milkman to be kind and sympathetic. Although forbidden to see his aunt, Milkman finds love and warmth in her home.

The second section of the book focuses on Milkman's search for gold which turns out to be an undertaking far more significant in nature. Believing that his father and aunt hid some gold in a cave in Virginia when they were young, Milkman sets out for the south. In Pennsylvania and Virginia he meets with many fellow African Americans who, though poor, still live their traditional lifestyle and keep their own customs and mores. The old folks tell moving folktales, and innocent children sing folk songs, all in praise of their ancestors. Of his many discoveries, Milkman finds that a song about Solomon is actually a paean to his great-grandfather Solomon. He is amazed at the rich myth and folklore about his family's history, and learns to be proud of his roots. He finds no gold, but he achieves self-knowledge and self-worth. He becomes a spiritually and morally better man. In the end he jumps off ground in face of danger from Guitar Baines, his friend, who shoots Pilate by mistake while aiming at Milkman because he thinks that Milkman has found but will not share the hidden treasure with him.

Song of Solomon is based on the myth that Africans could fly. It is unique in its treatment of racial issues. Whereas some previous African American writers offer realistic or naturalistic accounts of the tragic lives of African American people under racial discrimination and oppression and inspire and enhance African American awareness, this Morrison novel helps the African Americans discover their family history, feel proud of their roots and tradition, and look forward to a future of freedom and happiness. Milkman is brought up in the comfort of a wealthy middle class family by a selfish, greedy father. But he receives his aunt Pilate's advice and learns to face reality and think back to the past. He becomes responsible and respects and loves others. His personality undergoes a great change. Morrison manages to achieve her theme by employing folk myths and legends and magic realism to sing praise of the long history and civilization of the African Americans and expose the evils and crimes of racism. Her interlocking plotlines, varieties of language, and the tapestry of folktales, legends, magic, and fantasy—all these converge to make for the greatness of her work.

Beloved

Morrison is best known for her fifth novel, *Beloved*. It is based on the true ante-bellum story of a slave mother, Margaret Garner, killing her own children just for them to avoid slavery. "Beloved" in Morrison's novel is the word inscribed on the tombstone of the child killed by its mother. Nineteen-year-old Sethe Suggs, a runaway slave mother, is about to be captured by her pursuers. She decides to kill all her children so that they would not have to suffer the way she had as a slave. She succeeds in slashing the throat of the youngest two-year-old baby girl and is caught and serves a prison sentence. Then she gives birth to her daughter Denver, and works as a cook. Eighteen years pass, and Beloved as a baby ghost comes to haunt her mother's house at 124 Bluestone Road. She manages to drive her two brothers away, but is chased away by Paul D., her mother's former fellow slave. Beloved reappears, however, in human form, as a twenty-year-old girl, beautiful and freakish, capable of metamorphosis and of becoming invisible. She keeps following her mother around, harassing her with disturbing questions, making incessant demands for stories and for food, and accusing her of abandoning her. Sethe is on the brink of both physical and emotional collapse. Her daughter Denver asks for the help of the community, which respond and eventually drive the ghost away by singing a song of exorcism. Sethe is disintegrating. Paul D. returns to strengthen her desire for life.

The book is remarkable in its skillful fusion of its formal with its thematic concerns. The major formal feature of *Beloved* is the use of magic realism. Morrison's ghost does not make the book a ghost story. There is this obvious magic and supernatural element in the narrative: first the baby ghost causing strange voices, lights, and violent shaking, and then the ghost assuming actual human form, but behaving in uncanny ways, becoming invisible, appearing mysteriously, moving Paul D. out of Sethe's house, and exhibiting her growing psychic powers. This element shocks and jostles readers out of their normal way of living and thinking. It fits well into the larger realistic scheme to serve the author's purpose.

Talking about her book, Morrison states the importance of "dwelling on" and "coming to terms with" the truth about the past in a land where the past is either erased, absent or romanticized. The "rememory" of the past is to Morrison a very important subject to write about. Morrison feels that her people have to come to some kind of terms with their past in order to find peace and happiness. Their past is a hurdle they have to jump over in order to cope well now and in the future.

Sethe is guilt-ridden. Her physical scar is a symbol of her inner bleeding scar. The appearance of the ghost is in fact an externalization of the emotional wound in her life. The disruption of "normal" life Beloved causes forces her mother, and also Paul D., to face the fact that they need healing and renewal. Beloved makes it imperative for them to dive deep into the past when they suffered injustice and inhuman treatment and felt such despair that the only way to emancipation was death. The ghost offers Sethe a good opportunity to explain her act and subconsciously exonerate herself from the sense of "sin" and self-condemnation that cripple her life all along. Sethe is supposed to be free, but she is not. She has to address the "unspeakable," hidden deep down in her, which would weaken and humiliate her if she dare remember and speak about it. She has to face it in order to heal and live on a new basis.

Beloved thus reopens Sethe's closed emotional life (along with Paul D.) and sets her on the painful road to rebuilding self-identity. Sethe is not an isolated case. What Beloved does to her is in fact also what the African Americans need as a once enslaved race. The grandmother Baby Suggs talks about "the Misery," which indicates the harsh condition of the African American slaves. It was worse than death. It was the reason why some slaves like Sethe chose death rather than slavery: as there was nothing they could do about it, they inflicted death and pain on themselves. The sense of self-mortification afflicts and debilitates all survivors as a ghost of the past after their physical emancipation. In this sense, Beloved offers a medication and a cure for all African Americans.

Beloved is also a historical novel. It reconstructs history through black folk culture and folk tales, and brings to life the horrible experience of slavery as history. It is a powerful book: it not only makes African Americans think; it compels the white segment of the society to face history, too. They have to face the harm that racism has done to baby Suggs, Ella, Stamp, as well as Sethe and Paul D., to the countless number of African Americans dead or living, and to humanity in general. The barbaric behavior of "Schoolteacher" and his like and the horrors of the system they enforced—the Sweet Home which is a veritable hell, the slave ship, the human suffering, the indignities to which the salves were made to submit, etc.—all these should be enough of a reminder, and a shock, to all white people that history may be ignored or forgotten, but it is ever present in all lives as a point of reference.

Toni Morrison was a major contemporary American writer. She was the foremost author of contemporary black women's renaissance which includes, among others, Alice Walker, Gloria Naylor, Maya Angelou, Toni Cade Bambara, and Gayle Jones. Her works have drawn the attention of her readers to the importance of reconstructing history and interpreting the past from a racial perspective. She has blazed a new trail for her fellow writers.

Alice Walker (1944-)

Alice Walker was born into a sharecropper's family in Georgia, attended Spelman College in Atlanta, Georgia, and Sarah Lawrence College in Bronxville, New York. She began writing in college and published her first works—poems as well as stories—in 1965. Later she received fellowships in support of her writing career. She has, by virtue of the great amount of fiction, poetry, and essays she has written over the years, made herself a central figure in contemporary American literature. Her greatest achievement so far is her novel, *The Color Purple* (1982), which won for her both the American Book Award and the Pulitzer Prize.[12]

The Color Purple

The Color Purple is an epistolary novel. It consists of 90 letters, of which over two thirds (61 in number) Celie, the main character, wrote to God, 14 to her sister Nettie, and 15 Nettie wrote to Celie. The story centers on Celie's life, with Nettie's African adventure as complementary. The time frame of the novel covers over thirty years, and Celie is now in middle age, in her mid or late forties.

The story opens with Celie at 14, sexually abused by her "father" (Fonso by name) who threatened to kill her mammy if she ever told anyone but God. She gave birth to two children who were taken away from her immediately after they were born. Later her "father" "married"—sold—her off to Albert (called Mr.— for a long time in Celie's letters). The man abused her and had an evil design on her sister Nettie. So Nettie ran away and found peace working for a missionary's family and taking care of their two children, Adam and Olivia. Celie never hears from Nettie for some thirty years.

In the meantime, Celie takes care of her husband's children and endures a hard, loveless life. Her husband's lover, Shug Avery, a flashy African American singer, falls ill and is brought over for her to take care of. The two women bond well with one another, and Shug teaches Celie to love and stand up for herself. She teaches her about God. All through her progress toward emotional maturity, Celie has Shug as her spiritual guide. Invigorated with a new sense of well-being, Celie begins to assert herself. She leaves Albert and stays with Shug. Celie' self-awareness quickly grows. Then she learns that Fonso was her stepfather. Her birth father, a prosperous store owner, was lynched by the white racists who hated him because they thought he had stolen their business.

After Fonso dies, Celie comes into the property that is rightfully hers and becomes independent. She achieves rebirth. All the time she prospers, Albert goes down slope. He loses his will to life, becomes an alcoholic, and almost dies. He survives, comes to Celie, and helps her with her sewing. It turns out that he has for years kept Nettie's letters to Celie, and Celie is happy to know that Nettie has been fine all the time, married to the missionary after his wife dies. Celie reads Nettie's letters and begins writing to her. Then she learns that the missionary's two children are adopted, and are in fact Celie's blood and flesh. They come back from Africa and reunite with Celie.

The Theme of the Book

The Color Purple is essentially about African American women's growth against the backdrop of social and familial oppression. Celie, the major character, grew up in low self-esteem, knowing that she had neither good looks nor good brains. She was never self-assertive, and always suffered in agonizing silence. She subjected herself to the anguish of a loveless marriage and the drudgery of a stepmother. She saw her own children taken away and her sister run away for safety. Exposed to abuse of various kinds, she becomes callous. As she has no one to talk with—and she is too ashamed to talk with humans, she thinks of God. She writes to God but does not sign her letters. Letter writing is also her subconscious way of complaining which she dare not do in the open, of keeping track of experiences so as to understand herself in relation to her world, and learning to cope better.

Life is a learning process for Celie. Ultimately through suffering, she learns about God. She learns about man: for her black folks, she learns not to hate and reject but to understand and accept; for her white fellowmen, she learns not to hate and discriminate against them. She learns about love for others as well as for herself. And she learns about herself. She comes to see her human dignity and human worth. She is the one that eventually survives the ravages of life and gains spiritual wholeness.

From a long point of view, Celie's growth covers not only the different phases of women's liberation, i.e. from defenselessness in face of repression, to awakening and self-assertion, and to equality with men. From a feminist point of view, the book relates a story of solidarity between the oppressed women in a sexist, racist world. Along with Celie and Shug Avery, there are Sofia and Mary Agnes, among others, who fight together for survival.

The Color Purple is about black males' change and growth as well. Celie's misery is caused, immediately, by her own men folks—Fonso, her stepfather and Albert, her husband, both of whom battered her physically and mentally and made her life a hellish nightmare. These black men are violent toward their women probably because they are not happy in a society of discrimination. Albert is a classic example.

Thus *The Color Purple* marks a new phase of growth in African American consciousness. It raises questions for thought for the African Americans: they need to get to know themselves better and get ready for accountability for their own conduct and their lives. Albert learns to be humble and behave the way a respectable man should. Harpo follows his father's example and achieves reconciliation with his wife Sophia. Everybody learns about life. The new phase of African American awareness is also exhibited in Celie's keeping a white person in her employ: she learns to strike a racial balance. Love flourishes in her life. It redeems. This leads and adds to the happy ending.

The Formal Features of the Book

In formal terms the novel is impressive in more aspects than one. The first thing to note is the book's narrative scheme and the suspense with which it manages to hook and hold its readers. Their anxiety stems from the way the novel deals with the secret which lies in the heart of Celie's life and of the main plot— her biological father's death. For a long time into the novel, the readers are harassed by the incestuous violence and worried about the offspring from it. They are kept waiting until some two thirds into the story when the secret begins to trickle out and shed light on the identities of the two children.

Then, there is the language to consider. Celie's letters are written in black folk language in sharp contrast with the formal English of Nettie's letters. Celie's language is substandard, but vivacious and fresh and energetic while Nettie's is a little on the didactic side. The two registers of the language serve to reflect two levels of experience so well complementary to one another in the book.

In addition, the novel's symbolism is noticeable. The title is pregnant with meaning. The color purple indicates dignity, love, human fellowship, and surviving whole as well as suffering and pain (if we think of the color as that of an eggplant, a combination of blue and red). It represents God's creation, common humanity, significant and not to be ignored.

Altogether *The Color Purple* is a very important work in American literary history.

More African American Writers

In addition, there are a few more significant figures we need to take a look at. We mean Amiri Baraka (1934-2014), Alex Haley (1921-1992), Maya Angelou (1928-2014), and Gloria Naylor (1950-), Toni Cam Bambara (1939-1995), and Rita Dove (1952-).

Amiri Baraka was born Everett LeRoy Jones into a well-to-do middle class family in New Jersey and changed his named to Amiri Baraka ("Blessed Prince") in the 1970s when he embraced the Kawaida faith (a mixture of orthodox Islam and traditional African practices). His spiritual and artistic growth has been one of flux and change. In the 1950s he lived in the avant-garde aesthetic milieu of Greenwich Village of New York City in which Charles Olson, Frank O'Hara, and Allen Ginsberg were part of the set. He became more political in the 1960s, and left the Village for Harlem to establish the Black Arts Repertory Theater/School. Then he went back home to Newark, New Jersey to found Spirit House, and led the Black Community Development and Defense Organization, trying to enhance the racial consciousness of his fellow African Americans. In the early

1970s Baraka played key roles in some major African American conferences such as the Pan African Congress of African Peoples in Atlanta (1972) and the National Political Convention in Gary, Indiana (1974). Later he claimed he embraced a Marxist-Leninist perspective. These changes have been reflected in his works.[13]

Amiri Baraka knows what he should do as an African American artist. In one of his essays he states categorically that the mission of an African American artist is to help destroy the America as he knows it. He writes with a view to reaching and moving people, and writes so as to unite art and politics. Thus his writings, poetry, drama, and essays, especially of the more recent period, are fired with revolutionary ideology and possess a "clear revolutionary edge," so that they pierce like swords and knives into the "sinful" body of American society. Amiri Baraka was one of the masterminds of the Black Arts Movement which flourished during the whole of the 1960s and the early 1970s, and which associated Black arts with the concept of Black power. As one of the most eloquent exponents of the radical African American stance with regard to white-dominated America, Amiri Baraka has been very influential on the post-1960s African American writing. Amiri Baraka has been a prolific writer. He published his first volume of poetry, *Preface to a Twenty Volume Suicide Note*, in 1961, and has been writing drama and fiction as well as poetry. His works include *The Dead Lecturer* (1964), a volume of poems, *Dutchman and The Slave*, a book of plays (1964), *The System of Dante's Hell* (1965), his only novel, and *Tales* (1967). He also wrote studies like *Blues People: Negro Music in White America* (1963), *African American Music* (1967), *Raise Race Rays Raze: Essays Since 1965* (1971), and *The Motion of History and Other Plays* (1978).

Alex Haley was a journalist and a novelist. His major achievements were the two important books he wrote, *The Autobiography of Malcolm X* (1965), and *Roots* (1976). *Roots* is a novel of over six hundred pages, a finely wrought chronicle of an African American family from the middle of the 18th century through the time of writing. The book is based on a meticulous research which the author did for over a dozen years in the libraries and archives and on an immense amount of reading on history and anthropology.[14] The book marked a new level of self-awareness of the African American people as a race. Although Haley's influence may be more cultural than strictly literary, his *Roots* has added a new dimension to African American literature.

Maya Angelou (1928-2014) was a multi-talented genius. Hers was a spectacular African American success story. She went through a lot of adversity as a child victim of rape and a teenage mother, but she struggled upward with an amazing resilience that ultimately made her what she was. She excelled in many fields, as an actress, a dancer, a singer, a professor, a writer, a poet, an educator, a director, and a civil rights activist. Maya Angelou was most noted for her five volumes of autobiography—*I Know Why the Caged Bird Sings* (1970), *Gather Together in My Name* (1974), *Swingin' and Swingin' and Gettin' Merry Like Christmas* (1976), *The Heart of a Woman* (1981), and *All God's Children Need Traveling Shoes* (1986). Maya Angelou's poetry has inspired people all over the world. She has written some works for children. Her main theme was love and the universality of all lives. "I am human, and nothing human can be alien to me," she says. Maya Angelou is seen as one of the most phenomenal women in America today.[15]

Gloria Naylor began publishing in the early 1980s. Her first novel, *The Women of Brewster Place* (1982), won the American Book Award for the Best First Novel that year and also the National Book Award. Naylor has published novels and a collection of short stories, *Men of Brewster Place* (1998). Naylor is particularly good at depicting the lives of the African American women. Sensitive to their feelings and problems, Naylor portrays their struggles for survival with compassion and humor. Naylor's best known work is *The Women of Brewster Place*, a book of seven chapters relating the interrelated lives of seven African American women, all different in age and background but sharing the pressures of roughly the same bitter and sad existence. It was made into a successful movie. Gloria Naylor is a rising star on the contemporary American literary scene.[16]

Mention should be made of Toni Cade Bambara who fought for black America, for black women, and for the ethnic minorities in America.[17] She wrote vehemently against racial discrimination and racial stereotyping, and asserted the identity of the African Americans in face of Anglo-American culture and of some African Americans following the mainstream. Her short story collections include *Gorilla, My Love* (1971) and *The Sea Birds Are Still Alive* (1977). Her other works range from essays, poems, screenplays, and novels such as *The Salt Eaters* (1982) and *If Blessing Comes* (1987). She also edited two anthologies of African American writings.

Rita Dove is the first African American poet who was appointed to the position of Poet Laureate of the United States in 1994.[18] Dove writes mainly poetry. Her themes cover African American life and the life of other ethnic groups as well. She sees poetry in the daily lives of the people and hears poetry in their daily speech. Her poetry appeals by virtue of its lyric, often endearing tone. Dove is very often autobiographical, hoping to touch the lives of other people by first understanding and living her own to the fullest. Her collections of poems include *The Yellow House on the Corner* (1980), *Museum* (1983), *Thomas and Beulah* (1986) which won the Pulitzer Prize for her, *Grace Notes* (1989), and *Selected Poems* (1993). She has written a verse drama, some short stories, and a novel.

Chapter 26　Multiethnic Literature (II):
Other Minority Groups

 Other Minority Groups

In recent decades, diversity has been particularly prized as a strength of American culture and literature. Interest in multiculturalism has been on the increase and, along with it, the enthusiasm for the literatures of the different ethnic groups in America. This has had to do with the 1960s and 1970s when multiracial awareness grew among the various ethnic groups. The African Americans took the lead, and the other minority groups like the Hispanic Americans and the Asian Americans followed suit. This consciousness inspired instant literary expression. As a result, American literature is now no longer seen as one monolith of Anglo-American writings for which Hawthorne, Whitman, Eliot, Frost, Hemingway, Faulkner, Lowell and Bellow have been well known. It needs redefining. American literature has become more inclusive to its multi-ethnic writers. American literary history needs rewriting, which will include all of its multiracial elements.[1]

The recent literary scene has already been amazingly colorful. Following the African Americans who have in recent decades had their Ralph Ellison, Toni Morrison and Alice Walker and have received due recognition as an integral part of American literature, other minority ethnic groups such as the American Indians (or Native Americans), the Asian Americans, and the Chicano Americans have also written and received critical acclaim.

Native American Literature

Before we talk about this literature, it should be put on record that the English settlers, themselves oppressed and killed back in Europe, came to North America in early 17th century and proved to be many of them oppressors and killers the moment they set foot on the continent. Instead of showing gratitude to the native Indians, the legitimate owners of the land, who kindly helped them to settle down in their new home, these "white Europeans" (as American Indian author James Welch [1940-2003] puts it) started a horrible act of genocide which continued over a period of some two centuries. They massacred and reduced the native population from some ten million to less than one million. And these people they have placed in what they have encircled as "reservations." Human nature shows itself at its worst here.

Now the image of the American Indians in American literature has been for a long time a distorted one, presented by non-Indian authors. They appear good or bad not as the American Indians see themselves, but as some white authors conceive of them. For example, in James Fenimore Cooper's "Leatherstocking Tales," the good Indians are almost always those who stand on the side of the British against the French. As the Native American writer N. Scott Momaday puts it, "There was at one time a real danger [of the] Indian simply being frozen as an image in the American mind." Now that the Native Americans have begun telling their own stories from their own perspectives, their image has become vital and real in literature.

At the time of European settlement, well over three hundred Indian cultures existed in the North American continent. The different nations of the American Indians such as Lakota, Hopi, Chickasaw, and Mohawk all had their own separate civilizations. Now in the beginning, there was a very rich oral tradition in all Native American cultures. When the Christians came, some Christian converts began to write in English. The autobiographies of some "famous" Native

Americans began to appear. The genre remains an important part of Native American writing even today. N. Scott Momaday's *The Names* (1976) and Leslie Marmon Silko's *Storyteller* (1981) are the best samples.

Following the first Native American novel, *Life and Adventures of Joaquin Murieta* (1854), imaginative writing has improved with time. In the early 20th century John Milton Oskison's *Wild Harvest* (1925), *Black Jack Davy* (1926), and *Brother Three* (1935) were widely read. Then in the 1930s two novelists, John Joseph Matthews and D'Arcy McNickle made their impact felt and did the spade work for the outburst of Native American literary creativity of the late 1960s. Matthews' *Sundown* (1934) and McNickle's *The Surrounded* (1936) have become influential over subsequent Native American writings as works of genuine literary merit rather than of simple anthropological significance.

In 1968 N. Scott Momaday published his *House Made of Dawn* and won the Pulitzer Prize. This led to what has become known as "the Native American Renaissance" around the end of the decade. A good numer of Native American writers appeared and wrote with enthusiasm. Four major novelists achieved prominence in the last part of the 20th century. They are N. Scott Momaday, Leslie Marmon Silko, James Welch, and Gerald Vizenor. Around these literary figures revolve other writers such as Louise Erdrich, Michael Dorris, Paula Gunn Allen, Susan Power, Sherman Alexie, Linda Hogans, W. S. Penn, Gordon Henry, and Louis Owens. Today books by Native American writers fill the bookstores, and their writings have become a distinct ingredient of American literature.[2]

D'Arcy McNickle (1904-1977): *The Surrounded*

The man who initially helped set the stage for the Native American Renaissance of the 1960s was D'Arcy McNickle, the writer who devoted his life to improving the lot of his fellow American Indians.[3] McNickle was a half-breed, grew up on a reservation, and attended the University of Montana. As a young man he rejected his heritage, but later he came to embrace it and did his best to better the lives of his fellow Indians. He wrote a number of nonfiction works, and is best known for his novel, *The Surrounded* (1936), which has been seen as a milestone in the history of Native American literature.

The Surrounded tells the tragic story of a mixed-blood Indian youth. Archilde Leon feels uncomfortable on the reservation, leaves for the city, but is drawn back into the whirlpool of life in his native place. He has to take care of his trouble-making brother, is present at the scenes where two deaths occur, and becomes a scapegoat for the crimes that he witnesses happen but does not commit. He ends up surrounded, and submits to his fate in silence.

The story reveals the painful process of the disintegration of the Native American culture. It points its accusing finger directly at the intrusion of the whites into the traditional lives of the Indians. To begin with, Archilde is torn between divided allegiances to the different elements of his heritage: Indian and white, and he runs away. But the curse of being a half-breed follows him and he is destined to run into his own undoing. In the violent and deadly world, Archilde, who is too tenderhearted to kill a deer and who never kills anyone in his life, is doomed as a scapegoat for the deaths that have occurred during his stay home. The Indians start wondering about the change for the worse in their existence and about the loss of their powers. The novel records the collapse of the Indian traditional way of life as a result of outside intrusion.

N. Scott Momaday (1934-): *House Made of Dawn*

Momaday is of the most influential Native American novelist and poet. He is a Kiowa Indian, educated in the University of New Mexico and Stanford University. His first novel, *House Made of Dawn*, is a prize-winning book and his best-known novel. Momaday likes to think of himself primarily as a poet. [4]

House Made of Dawn is about the experience of a Native American in relation to his own cultural heritage as well as to the mainstream society. Abel, a Native American youth, is brought up by his grandfather. He has never known his father, and both his mother and brother died before he went to the war. He has difficulty relating both to his own Indian way of life and the life of the mainstream society. After he comes back from the war, he finds work, splitting wood for Angela, a Los Angeles woman, has an affair with her, has a fight with an albino Indian and kills him, serves a six-year sentence in prison, befriends a Navajo Indian, Ben, bullied by a corrupt policeman, Martinez, tries to seek Martinez out for revenge, is beaten almost to death, and taken to hospital. Now, Abel is convinced that the best course of action for him is to go back to his grandfather. He finds the old man dying and tries to take care of him in the last six days of his life. His grandfather devotes his last six dawns to pass necessary information for his grandson's reintegration into Indian life before he dies. Thus reeducated and reassured, Abel gets ready for the Indian ceremonial dawn running.

House Made of Dawn is a formal novelty. First, with regard to the notion of time, the novel is a chronological chaos. It consists of a prologue and four sections, "The Longhair," "The Priest of the Sun," "The Night Chanter," and "The Dawn Runner." The first and the last sections are set in the Jemez pueblo, Walatowa ("Village of the Bear"), while the other two chapters are located in Los Angeles. All the sections are dated to offer a faint notion of time for the story. This is necessary because the sections interlock, intersect, and crisscross with flashbacks and memories so that the readers tend to lose track of time. Abel's story, for instance, has to be laboriously pieced up in the course of very careful reading.

Furthermore, the book is heavily tinted in American Indian color: the race for good hunting and harvests, the fiestas, the annual eagle hunt and its sacrifice in an Indian ceremony, the Navajo night chant which offers spiritual healing (as Ben does for Abel), and the dawn running with the runner's arms and shoulders marked with burnt wood and ashes. *House Made of Dawn* is an authentic representation of the Native Americans surviving in the modern world while trying successfully to keep their traditions intact and their selfhood whole.

James Welch (1940-2003): *Fools Crow*

James Welch was born in Montana to a Blackfeet father and a Gros Ventre mother. Growing up on the reservations, Welch learned a good deal about the ways of life of both Indian nations. He was educated in the University of Minnesota and the University of Montana. The Montana plains offer the backdrop for most of his stories, and the contrast between modern and traditional lifestyles provide the basic thematic focus for his fiction. Welch's tone of storytelling is usually not optimistic. There is an element of desperation in his narratives. It may have to do with his acute awareness of "the Indian problem" (as he puts it), that once the Indians are placed on a reservation, they lose quite a bit of their traditional ways. As always, Welch presents the Indian side of the case.[5]

His third novel, *Fools Crow*, is a historical novel about the 1870 genocidal massacre of the Pikuni (Blackfeet) Indians. The focus of the tragic story is, however, on human development rather than a simple presentation of facts. The evil actions of the whites appear often in the different forms of interpolations. The protagonist is White Man's Dog (later called Fools Crow). He is not very lucky as a young man, but his childhood friend, Fast Horse, has everything. Then Yellow Kidney leads a horse-taking raid on another tribe, the Crows. Fast Horse disobeys the command so the sleeping Crow Indians get to know about the raid. The result is that Yellow Kidney is caught and tortured by the Crows beyond description.

White Man's Dog proves himself a responsible person in the fight and is honored by his people. In addition, when Yellow Kidney does not return, White Man's Dog helps his family out. He becomes a mature, respectful member. Later when his tribe and the Crows meet to have a showdown, he kills their leader and earns the name of Fools Crow. He marries Yellow Kidney's daughter and has a son born to them. On the other hand, Fast Horse leaves for where many lone people live.

The historical aspect of the novel relates to the white men's arrival, and their subjugation of the Indians through whiskey, blankets, shotguns, and massacre. The white Europeans represent the forces of darkness against which the Indians struggle for survival. What the whites try to do is to cause the physical and spiritual extinction of the Indians. In the beginning, the Indians have no immunity to the "gifts" of the white men, nor do they see through their true nature. There is the small pox ravaging the Indians, the dispensation of the northern plains, and the massacre on the Marias, which the novel reproduces from the Indian perspective. The tragic scene that Fools Crow witnesses after meeting a small group of survivors reveals the extent to which the whites have worked havoc with the Indian world.

In the camp of Heavy Runner's tribe, the houses are razed to the ground; dead bodies lie in the snow, still smoldering from the fire. Heavy Runner is killed. Though a small group escapes alive, Fools Crow shudders to realize that the tribe is extinct as there are no children left. Fools Crow's maturing occurs against this dreadful backdrop of death and annihilation. He grows to fully appreciate the traditional life of his tribe and the vital importance for him to participate in it as a responsible member. His individual fate is thus bound up with the fate of his people, and he is ready to serve his community. Given eventually the burden for healing his people, Fools Crow feels, vaguely, some hope amid the debris of devastation. Spring arrives, the son is born, and the rain comes. The world looks forward to renewal and resurrection.

As Welch states, the story is told from the Indians' point of view, "never from the white point of view." *Fools Crow* is narrated from the inside of the Indian cultural perspective. One illustration of this perspective is the dream motif that runs through the tale. There are a number of dreams that make sense in the context of the Indian lives. For instance, Eagle Ribs' dream, Fast Horse's dreams, Fools Crow's dream, etc. correlate well with the thematic concerns of the story.

Leslie Marmon Silko (1948-): *Ceremony*

Leslie Marmon Silko is of mixed blood—Laguna Indian, Mexican, and white. She was brought up in a cultural milieu in which the oral tradition was still very much valued. She listened to her great grandma's stories about a long, long time ago and felt infinitely fascinated and inspired. She attended the University of New Mexico as a law student, but quit when she saw the injustice built into the Anglo-American legal system. She turned to writing as her career in order to seek justice. When her first novel, *Ceremony*, was published in 1977, she was established as a major literary figure in the Native American Renaissance in full swing then. She became as famous as N. Scott Momaday and James Welch.[6]

Ceremony

Ceremony is a story of profound philosophical meaning. It is about the quest of its protagonist, Tayo, for the wellness of his own person, his Indian nation, and for the world in general. Tayo is a war veteran. He has been away for six years from home. During that time, he served in the US army, was in a Japanese prisoner-of-war camp, and stayed in a mental hospital in Los Angeles. Now he comes back, still sick. He keeps vomiting. His grandmother brings in the Navajo medicine man, Betonie, who restores him to some measure of health and sends him on a journey that would cure him and help the community at the same time. The Laguna land suffers drought in the meantime. This is the ceremony he has to go through for his own full recovery and the wellness of his land. He has to go and find uncle Josiah's spotted cattle. In keeping with Betonie's directions, he comes and meets Ts'eh, a half-mythic woman. With her help, he accomplishes his mission. His final test is to resist the temptation of killing Emo, a fellow Indian GI, who is a token of evil. The man has tried to hurt him earlier by cutting his stomach with a broken beer bottle, but now Tayo thinks the better of it. He tries to purge Emo of the evil in him. When he is cured, the Laguna land is blessed with rain.

Tayo is an upright and responsible man. The war taught him a lot of lies of violence and war. His vomiting is a sign that he keeps purging himself of the evil stuff. During the war he witnessed the death of his uncle Josiah and his cousin Rocky and he could do nothing to help them. So he feels responsible for their deaths and also for the ruin that is now visited on the Laguna land. Tayo sees himself connected with his fellow creatures. The spirit of fellowship proves to be the healing element for Tayo and his people.

Ceremony is a remarkable work. Its texture is woven of the Indian oral tradition of myth and legends. Silko is able to bring the greatness of her Indian heritage to the notice of the whole world which has tended to ignore the greatness of minorities like the Native Americans. Here a hero ventures out to complete a ritual for the good of the humankind. Then there is the basic story of the novel to consider. The Laguna Indians have their own myth. The woman who helps with the search, Ts'eh, turns out to be a mythic figure. When Tayo is sent away on his mission, he is told to find four things to make sure that he has reached the right place for his quest: the star overhead, the spotted cattle, a woman, and a mountain, the four things that the Navajo medicine man has seen in a vision. And

sure enough, Tayo finds all these, and fulfills the prophecy.

Leslie Marmon Silko is also noted for her short stories. These portray Native American life in its divers manifestations from an American Indian perspective.

Louise Erdrich (1954-): *Love Medicine*

Erdrich was born in Minnesota and grew up in North Dakota. She is of mixed blood. She was educated in Dartmouth College and Johns Hopkins University. Her first novel, *Love Medicine*, came out in 1984 and won a number of awards including the National Book Critics Circle Award for Best Work of

Fiction. It established her place as a major American writer. The novel was expanded in 1993 with five new stories added to the first edition. Erdrich is a prolific writer. She has also produced some volumes of poetry and works of nonfiction. In all her works, Erdrich focuses on the features of her Ojibwa Indian inheritance, but she is too sensitive to human nature to allow it to overshadow their universal significance.[7] *Love Medicine* is a good illustration.

This is a story of love and forgiveness between Native American families, which overarches half a century of four generations' history of survival. Although the larger mainstream social background looms menacing and evil, the book concentrates on the vicissitudes of Native American life working itself out within its own frame of reference. It begins with the death of June, Marie Lazarre Kashpaw's adopted daughter, in a freezing snowstorm and ends with June's son bringing her spirit home from the wilderness.

Of the first generation, Margaret Kashpaw is the one that *Love Medicine* tells some details about. One important fact from her life is that she manages to hide one of her sons, Eli Kashpaw, from being taken to school by the government at the expense of the other son, Nector Kashpaw. Consequently the two brothers grow up into two different personalities: Eli, a backwoodsman, simple and honest and celibate, while Nector, though good, is basically a city type, wily, calculating, and selfish. Margaret's part of the story forms the tapestry of life of the next generation on which the novel focuses its major narrative attention.

This generation includes three primary characters, Marie Lazarre Kashpaw, Nector Kashpaw, and Lulu Lamartine, the love triangle of the novel. Although in love with LuLu Nanapush Lamartine, Nector marries Marie. He carries on an affair with Lulu and has a son by her, Lyman Larmartine whom he never acknowledges. Marie proves to be a woman of strength, love, and understanding. She brings her children up well, and allows her adopted daughter June to go and live with her uncle, Eli, in the woods. Marie also helps Nector become the tribal chairman. Later she manages to come to terms with Lulu.

Lulu is married to Henry Lamartine Senior but none of her eight sons are his. One of them, Henry Lamartine Junior, is her brother-in-law—Beverley Lamartine's son, who later in the story, returns from Vietnam and commits suicide as he is unable to adjust to life. Nector's cigarette butt inadvertently starts the fire that burns Lulu's house. Lulu ends her relationship with Nector. In his old age, Nector suffers from loss of memory. As he is still attracted to Lulu, his grandson (Lipsha Morrissey) tries to secure his heart from wandering with a local Indian love medicine made of turkey hearts. He takes it, chokes, and dies.

Of the next generation June Morrissey Kashpaw's story stands out. When she was little, June was abandoned and lived a hard life in the woods. Her psychic wounds were such that she has to go and live with her uncle in the woods. Her marriage ends in divorce. They have a son, King Kashpaw, and she has a son, Lipsha Morrissey, by another man, Gerry Nanpush. After her death, a blue Firebird is bought with her life insurance money, and her son, Lipsha Morrissey, brings it home, which signifies her spirit's final return from the storm.

Then there is Lyman Lamartine, son of Lulu by Nector. Lyman is a young man with a good heart. He cares about his brother Henry. Henry suffers from a severe depression. Lyman tries to cheer him up but to no avail. Once the two brothers sit at the bank of a river, having a few beers together, Henry suddenly gets up and jumps into the river, never to return. Lamartine feels so guilty that he is not himself for a while before he takes a job at the Bureau of Indian Affairs (BIF). Then his mother takes him back to run a factory for her. His father, Nector, never acknowledges him, but he manages to arrive at some understanding with Marie.

With regard to still the next generation, there is Albertine Johnson, Marie's granddaughter. Albertine is not on good terms with her mother because she has not stayed on the reservation and has married a Catholic. She mourns genuinely for her aunt June's death. Albertine is a positive influence on the conflicting and wounded personalities and relationships. She has a kind of healing power with her.

Then there is Lipsha Morrissey whom we mentioned a moment earlier. He was born to but abandoned by June. He was brought up by his grandmother Marie. His quest for his identity offers a connective thematic link to the loosely knit novel. He has healing powers like his ancestors and local medicine people. He prepares a love medicine for his grandfather Nector and causes his death in a well-intentioned way. He helps his father flee to Canada and bring his mother's soul home.

In formal terms, *Love Medicine*'s point of view is fresh and provocative. With the exception of the third-person narrative of the first chapter, all the following chapters are narrated in the first person by different people. There are six narrartors, three from the older generation—Marie, Nector, and Lulu, and three from the younger—Albertine, Lipsha, and Lyman. Their stories interweave and intersect, a little like Faulkner's *Go Down Moses*, but more intricate. Told in this way, the non-chronological nature of the story is obvious. But Erdrich is skillful enough to bring all the voices well under control so that the novel is a well-wrought work of art.

Then, the circular frame of the book grabs attention, too. June serves as the connective tissue for the disparate elements of the story and encloses the whole of it within the time between her death and her spiritual return home. This is a fitting formal arrangement because June's life is a mirror for the Indian life of *Love Medicine*, with her abandonment as a child, her abuse, her unhappy marriage, her infidelity, and the love she had though in large measure unconsciously.

One more thing to note here is the fact that many of the characters appear in the author's North Dakota tetralogy. Some continue to be major characters; some become minor ones; and the later works and *Love Medicine* serve to footnote one another beautifully well in many interesting ways.

Native American Poetry

Native American poetry is amazingly rich. One unique thing about this poetry is that most of the major fiction writers are all also poets of the first intellectual order. These include, among others, N. Scott Momaday (and his "The Bear"), Paula Gunn Allen, James Welch, and Louise Erdrich. The number of modern and contemporary well-published poets is simply impressive. These include Maurice Kenny (1929-) whose *The Mama Poems* won the American Book Award in 1984; Carter Revard (1931-), well noted for his use of his native Oklahoma speech patterns; Simon Ortiz (1941-), informal in diction, and moving in mordant irony; Lance Henson (1944-), who believes that the mysterious powers of the native Americans may offer hope for America; Joy Harjo (1951-), noteworthy for her lyricism; and Diana Burns (1957-), impressive for her humor and honesty. And there are many others working in the field like Wendy Rose (1948-) and Roberta Hill Whiteman (1947-), all trying to enrich the representation of the American Indian experience. As a result of the hard work of the Native American writers, Native American works have come out of the closet and kept appearing in the bookstore today.

Asian American Literature

Now Asian American literature as a category breaks down into subdivisions such as Chinese American, Japanese American, Indian American, Korean American, and Filipino American.[8] As these Asian Americans have different cultures and historical backgrounds to fall back on in their writings, Asian American literature is variegated and highly diversified.

The origins of Asian American literature can date back to the first years of the 20th century when books on Asia or Asian Americans were written by non-Asians. Pearl Buck (1892-1973) was a good example. Her *The Good Earth* (1931) was very popular and paved the way for her Nobel Prize for literature. The first commercially successful Asian American writer was C. Y. Lee (1917-2018) whose first novel, *The Flower Drum Song* (1955) was adapted for Broadway and for a movie. Asian American literature began to make its presence felt as a category in the mid-1970s when the Civil Rights movement of the 1960s generated a spirit of ethnic nationalism among the various minority groups in the United States. "Ethnicization" of curriculum on college campuses occurred. Academic programs in Asian American studies emerged. The Immigration Reform Act of 1965, which brought in new waves of well-educated immigrants, made the cultural milieu more conducive to the further development of Asian American writing. The early 1970s witnessed the publication of some anthologies of Asian American writers.

Then in 1976 Maxine Hong Kingston made her impact with her widely acclaimed books, *The Woman Warrior*, followed by her *China Men* (1980). More Asian Americans, especially those from the Chinese, Filipino, and Japanese backgrounds who had longer history in America, kept up writing in the 1970s and 1980s. Some anthologies of their writings came out, such as Kai-yu Hsu and Helen Palumobinskas' *Asian American Authors* (1972) and Jeffrey Paul Chan's *Aiiieeeee! An Anthology of Asian American Writers* (1974). In 1982 Elaine H. Kim published her seminal study, *Asian American Literature: An Introduction to the Writings and Their Social Context*. However, it would take more time and a few more successful writers like Amy Tan, Michael Ondaatje, and Bharati Mukherjee yet for Asian American literature to receive recognition as a more distinct entity, and for mainstream publishers to take Asian American writers more seriously.

Sure enough, these writers have written since the 1970s and have become conspicuously noticeable. Amy Tan's *The Joy Luck Club* (1989) proved to be a kind of watershed. Before its publication, New York mainstream publishers released one work by an Asian American once every two or three years. After 1989 two or three Asian American works are placed on the bookstore shelves every month. In addition, more anthologies of Asian American writings have appeared in print. These include, among others, Shaw Wang's *Asian American Literature: A Brief Introduction and Anthology* (1996), Shirley Geok-lin Lim's *The Forbidden Stitch: An Asian American Women's Anthology* (1989), and Elaine

H. Kim's *Making More Waves: New Writing by Asian American Women* (1997).

Maxine Hong Kingston (1940-)

The most famous of the Asian American writers is Maxine Hong Kingston whose *The Woman Warrior: Memoirs of a Childhood among Ghosts* (1976) won the National Book Critics Circle Award for nonfiction for 1976 and established her as a preeminent contemporary American writer.[9] Kingston's parents emigrated to the US in the 1930s. She was born and raised in a bicultural milieu: there has been an obvious Chinese-American conflict and conflation in her upbringing that has made the question of identity and race and ethnicity one of her major concerns in her writing as well as in her life. *The Woman Warrior* deals with the subject; so do her other works, *China Men* and *Tripmaster Monkey: His Fake Book* (1989).

The Woman Warrior is a combination of autobiography and fiction. It consists of five sketches of both fact and fiction: "No Name Woman," "White Tigers," "Shaman," "At the Western Palace," and "A Song for a Barbarian Reed Pipe." The first chapter, "No Name Woman," is mostly factual. The No Name Woman was a housewife who gave birth to a child out of wedlock and had to commit suicide. The next chapter, "White Tigers," avenges the No Name Woman vicariously, through a woman warrior, the legendary Chinese heroine Hua Mulan. The third chapter, "Shaman," describes how the question of identity bothers the narrator and her mother. The fourth chapter, "At the Western Palace," tells about the difficulty that the narrator's aunt experiences in America. The final section, "A Song for a Barbarian Reed Pipe," is mainly about the narrator trying to deal with the painful encroachment of the world upon her selfhood in a heroic manner.

The Woman Warrior is noted for a number of things of which its symbolism and its use of language merit attention. The "ghost" in the title is symbolic all through the book. The "no name" aunt is harassed by the shrouded villagers. The woman warrior's trainers, the old-young couple, move in an atmosphere of fantasy. The narrator faces a world of apparitions all of which pose some menace to the survival of her selfhood. And the narrator has to battle the shadow of her uncertain identity. The ghosts present a backdrop of the past, of the otherness, and of the larger environment against which the narrator thrashes out the harrowing question of race and nationality for herself.

Another thing to note about *The Woman Warrior* is its use of language. Its sentences are often short and elliptical and read like Chinese translations. The prose can be beautifully idyllic and pastoral. The language of the book manages to retain the beauty of both the Chinese and the English languages to which she has been sensitive. With the succinct, imagistic element of the Chinese language subtly embedded in the English, Kingston's prose possesses an idiosyncratic feature that endears her to her readers.

Amy Tan (1952-)

Another important Asian American writer is Amy Tan, whose first novel, *The Luck Joy Club*, made quite a stir on the contemporary American literary scene. In more ways than one, the novel is a continuation of the thematic concerns of Kingston's *The Woman Warrior*.[10]

The Joy Luck Club is intriguing in both thematic and formal ways. Thematically, it is a story of eight women of two generations from four families telling their separate stories. The stories share something in common as a connective tissue between them. The way these stories are told is interesting to note. In 1949 four Chinese women form a club to play a traditional Chinese game, mah-jongg by name. They invest stocks, eat dim sum, and talk about their past. This is the club to which the title of the novel refers. About four decades later, one of them, the founder of the club, dies, and her daughter comes to take her place at the mah-jongg table. Only then does she get to know well about her mother's secret and her meaning. Her experience proves to be contagiously educational to her friends. It turns out that the younger generation has its own story to tell as well.

The Joy Luck Club consists of four parts, each of which begins with a vignette, or prologue, a brief italicized statement, narrated by one of the four mothers, which indicates the theme of the section. Each part includes four individual stories told by the four immigrant mothers or their American-born daughters. Thus in part one, and part four, the mothers speak, while the other two parts allow the daughters to talk. For each of the four families mother and daughter each tell their separate stories. These sixteen stories tell about the mothers' past and present and their daughters' rebellious growth. The talk-stories ultimately bridge the gap between the two generations and represent the efforts of the American-born daughters to understand and come to terms with their Chinese heritage.

The most important of all the stories is the leading story, that of the Woos'— Jin-mei and her mother Suyuan. The mother was the initiator of the club in San Francisco. During WWII she was forced to abandon her twin daughters in her attempt to flee for her life in face of a Japanese attack. Then she came to America and gave birth to her daughter Jin-mei. Mother and daughter see things differently. After the mother passes way, the daughter learns to understand her mother better. Reconciled with her heritage, Jin-mei visits China and reunites with her two sisters.

The formal aspect of the book is interesting to talk about, too. The sixteen stories are all narrated in the first person, two by each of the eight characters except in the case of Jin-mei, who tells four stories, two of her own, and two of her mother's, and there is little or no sense of dislocation between the different sections.

Bharati Mukherjee (1940-)

Mukherjee was born into a wealthy upper-middle class family of Calcutta,

India. She was educated in England and Switzerland before she came in 1961 to attend the University of Iowa where she received her Ph.D. Later she immigrated to the United States.

Mukherjee's fiction all explores the nature of the experience of cultural assimilation in a foreign land like North America. Assimilation means metamorphosis and self-reinvention. She approaches the issue from a woman's point of view. All her protagonists have been, so far, women, or Indian women: Tara in *The Tiger's Daughter* (1972), Dimple in *Wife* (1975), Jasmine in *Jasmine* (1989), and Hannah in *The Holder of the World* (1993). All these women try to find their new place in the new society they have come to live in. The stories are different in each case, but their message is about the same: the women like their life in the US better than in their home country.

Take *The Tiger's Daughter* for example. Tara comes to the United States at 15. Later she is married to a foreign man and comes home to India. Now she faces a cultural shock the other way round: she finds it hard to fit into the life of her native place where corruption, suffering, and poverty prove so sickening to her. Her outlook on things goes through a change. She gradually abandons her traditional view of things and embraces the new perspective she has acquired in the US. Now she is impatient to return to the States.

Mukherjee is about the most famous South Asian American writer today.

Asian American Poetry

Regarding poetry, one prolific Asian-American poet is Garrett Hongo (1951-), a Japanese American. Hongo was born and grew up in Hawaii, moved with his family to South Los Angeles, and traveled extensively in Japan. As a poet, he is motivated by his search for ethnic and familial roots, as well as cultural identity and poetic inspiration. He feels the need for a life of the mind. As his career moves on, he is increasingly fascinated with the material with which he is most acquainted: the landscapes, folkways, and societies of Japan, Hawaii, and

Southern California. Writing for him is a process of keeping his cultural and moral values intact and accommodating them in what he calls "the whirlwind" he lives in. His poetry reveals his deep attachment to the places and people he calls his own. Hongo is an award-winning poet. He has received, among other things, the Guggenheim Fellowship, the Hopwood Prize for Poetry, and the Pushcart Prize. His works include *The Buddha Bandits Down Highway 99* (1978, in collaboration with Lawson Inada and Alan Lau), *Yellow Light* (1982), and *The River of Heaven* (1988).

In the last few decades a good number of Asian American writers have written to make their voices heard. Their works include, among others, Monica Sone's *Nisei Daughter*, John Okada's *No-No Boy*, Jeanne Wakatsuki Houston and James D. Houston's *Farewell to Monzanar*, Toshio Mori's *Yokohama, California*, Diana Chang's *The Frontiers of Love*, and the shorter fiction of Frank Chin (also a playwright) and Jeffery Chan. There are, in addition, the plays of David Henry Hwang and Wakako Yamauchi, the poetry of Cathy Song, Janice Mirikitani, and Stephen Shu-ning Liu. Asian American writing is increasing in volume and is being recognized as one important component of contemporary American writing.

Chicano Literature

Another component of multiethnic American literature is Spanish-American or Chicano literature. The word "Chicano" is a derivative of "Mexicano." Chicano literature is a body of writings by Americans of Mexican extraction or Mexicans in the United States writing about the Mexican-American experience. For Chicano writers a sense of ethnicity is a critical part of their literary sensibilities, and the portrayal of the Chicanos' ethnic experience in the United States is their major concern.

This literary tradition is traceable back to the mid-19th century when the Mexicans of the Southwest were conquered and became Mexican Americans. In face of Anglo-American superiority, a Chicano consciousness began slowly taking shape. Its literary expression began to attract attention in the mid-1960s. The Civil Rights movement among the Mexican Americans brought Chicano literature to a new phase. The Chicano family, the Chicano community, and the struggle for civil rights became the thematic concerns of the Chicano writers.

Chicano literature had its renaissance from the mid-1960s through the early 1980s. This is known as the contemporary Chicano literary movement. An anthology of Chicano creative writing came out in 1970, and Chicano literature found its way into the classroom.[11]

From the very beginning, this literature has been a challenge to Anglo-American chauvinism. It has been a literary expression of the reaction to the anti-Hispanic, anti-Mexican bias present in American culture.

Chicano Fiction

Chicano fiction has developed in the last few decades. One of the major themes of the Chicano authors relates to the search for or assertion of Chicanos' identity. This involves the upholding of their cultural traditions under the pressure of mainstream values and their attempt to fight against assimilation. Jose Antonio Villarreal's novel, *Pocho*, Raymond Barrio's *Plum Plum Pickers*, and Richard Vasquez's *Chicano* are all good illustrations of the early Chicano attempt in this direction. The first of these describes the growing up of a boy with his immigrant father. *Plum Plum Pickers* is about farm workers' struggle. *Chicano* portrays the impossible demands of life for immigrant children and grandchildren. All the works exhibit the consciousness of the Chicanos as an independent ethnic entity trying to stop their values from disintegrating and getting lost.

Then there have been the Chicano Big Three, Tomas Rivera, Rudolfo Anaya, and Rolando Hinojosa, all novelists whose works continue the same preoccupation with identity. Their works, all rural in background, attempt to address the question of keeping tradition and identity intact amidst overwhelming odds.

Then there is Miguel Mendez who writes about urban Chicano life. Mendez chooses the underprivileged as his protagonists and makes a point of ending his stories with the affirmation of the Chicano heritage. His well-known novel is *Peregrinos de Aztlan*. Other well-known Chicano novelists include John Rechy, Oscar Zeta Acosta, Amado Muro (pseudonym for Chester Seltzer), Eusebio Chacon, Gary Soto and Ana Castillo, to name just a few. Some of these have won the American Book Awards for fiction.

Tomas Rivera (1935-1984)

A pioneer in the growth of modern Chicano literature is novelist Tomas Rivera. He was born in Texas, received his Ph.D. in the University of Oklahoma, and became Chancellor of the University of California at Riverside in 1969. He held the position until his death.

Rivera wrote both poems and stories to describe the lives of the Mexican-Americans. His works give his people a sense of direction. The unique tension of his writings stems from his personal experience with living in America as a Mexican-American. He knows well the dilemma and the despair that the peculiar human situation produces for his people as a minority. He is acutely conscious of the distinctiveness of his culture with its own way of life and its own traditions. At the same time he is keenly aware of the leveling, assimilating forces that the "Anglo" mainstream keeps generating. Rivera's works aim at increasing understanding among his fellow Mexican-Americans so as to help them cope better with their lives.

Chicano Poetry

Over the years Chicano poetry has experienced a spectacular growth. As with the novelists, one thematic preoccupation of the Chicano poets is with the expression of their ethnic experience and the assertion of their Chicano heritage. A lot of it is in a sense ponderously political and sociological, closely tied up with the struggle of the Chicano people for equality and recognition in a predominantly Anglo-American environment. Their poetic perspective differs from mainstream poetry, their images and metaphors are drawn from their own lives, and their language has been a mixture of English and Spanish.

What Chicano poetry tries to represent is the ghetto existence of the Chicano people, their existential dilemma of being lost in the grasp of the modern society of America, and their yearning for change. Chicano poetry strives for love, dignity, and justice for its people, and at the same time expresses the sense of pride that the Chicanos feel for being Chicano. The recent decades have witnessed a good number of Chicano poets making their presence felt. These include Luis Omar Salinas, Alurista, Richard Garcia, Abelardo Delgado, Miguel Ponce, Jose Montoya, Richard Anchez, Lorna Dee Cervantes, and Sandra Cisneros (who is also a fiction writer).

Luis Omar Salinas (1937-)

Luis Omar Salinas is a prominent Chicano poet. He began his involvement in the Chicano movement with his book of verse, *Crazy Gipsy* (1970), which contains two of his best poems, "Aztec Angel" and "Quixotic Expectations." There is a good deal of social criticism in Salinas' poetry. Highly aware of the Chicano condition in America, he possesses a tragic vision in every possible sense of the term. "Aztec Angel" is a good example. It offers a glimpse of real life in the real world of the Chicanos: alienation, derangement, and exploitation. The Aztec angel is an outsider, an outcast, who pawns his heart for truth. Alienated and marginalized, he acknowledges that he is the offspring of a tubercular woman who is, however, "beautiful." The word "beautiful" represents a firm reiteration of the poet's assertion of his ethnic values. The affirmation is noble and dignified. Salinas tends to describe the hard and humdrum reality through dreamlike images and metaphors. Surrealism functions as one major structural mechanism in his poetry.

Post-Civil Rights American Literature

The post-civil rights period began with the 1980s. Whereas the postmodernist tradition continues, it has become by and large a fact of the past. A whole new way of writing has appeared. A multi-style realism is asserting its presence.

American literature since the1980s has shown notable realistic features. Younger authors have borrowed freely from Modernism and Postmodernism in their realistic renovations, so that a new kind of realism has come into being. For want of a better term, we may call it "multi-style realism."

The period is still on-going. A good number of famous writers, essentially multicultural by nature, have appeared in all the departments of literature. A short list may include such novelists as William Vollmann (1959-), Rilla Askew (1951-), and Dan Brown (1964-) whose *The Da Vinci Code* has caught a good deal of critical attention. There are such poets as Dean Young (1955-), Philip Levine (1928-2015), Lisel Mueller (1924-), and Li-Young Lee (1957-). American theater is very active as well. There are playwrights trying to offer something new on the stage. These include such figures as Doug Wright (1962-), John Patrick Shanley (1950-), Margaret Edson (1961-), Rajiv Joseph (1974-), Tracy Letts (1965-), Tony Kushner (1956-) and Amy Herzog (1979-).

One noticeable thing about post-civil rights American literature is the inclination that some groups of writers have shown to overstep the moral bottom line that literature is written to teach people to be good. This is the time-honored principle governing literary creation which writers of successive generations from time immemorial have kept in mind in their writing careers. But some post-civil rights writers seem to have forgotten this. They have written about sex, violence, and drug addition to disorient people in their lives. These include groups such as Punk and Core, Avant-Pop, and Generation X, and authors such as Dennis Cooper (1953-), Kathy Acker (1947-1997), Donna Haraway (1944-), Mark Amerika (1960-), Kathryn Harrison (1961-) and Bret Easton Ellis (1964-).

Reconstruction of American Literary History

American literary history has been going through a process of reconstruction. The canon of American literature is being redefined to be more relevant to the reality of the nation's variegated experience. More and more writers of multiethnic origins have come to recognize the importance of their experiences and have become more vocal. As a result, an amazing assortment of writings has appeared to appeal to the imagination of the American reading public. It is true that these writings need further critical scrutiny; the country's literary awards committees need to size up the contemporary literary scene more carefully. But all these are happening. More minority writers are getting the credit they deserve. All these developments will ultimately enrich American literature as the authentic expression of the variety of experiences of all Americans. The change will impact canonizing and teaching enormously. The result will probably be a refocusing and reprioritizing of American writing in general. It will take time, but it is beginning to happen.

Notes and References

Chapter 1   Colonial America

1. See Thomas Jefferson Wertenbaker. "The Fall of the Wilderness Zion." *Puritanism in Early America*. Ed. George M. Waller (Boston, 1950; hereafter cited as *Puritanism*), 22-35.

2. Perry Miller. "The Puritan Way of Life." *Puritanism*, 9.

3. Miller. "The Puritan Way of Life," 7.

4. See Henri Petter. *The Early American Novel* (Columbus, Ohio, 1971); Cathy N. Davidson. *Revolution and the Word, The Rise of the Novel in America* (New York, 1986); Bernard Rosenthal. ed. *Critical Essays on Charles Brockden Brown* (Boston, 1981); and Steven Watts. *The Romance of Real Life, Charles Brockden Brown and the Origins of American Culture* (Baltimore, 1994).

Chapter 2   Edwards • Franklin • Crevecoeur

1. Van Wyck Brooks. *America's Coming of Age* (New York, 1915), 10-11. The influence of this statement can be felt in a number of subsequent critical works, one of which is Robert Spiller's *The Cycle of American Literature, An Essay in Historical Criticism* (New York, 1955), where Spiller says, "Diversity within unity was from start the shaping characteristic of the new people, their land, and ultimately their literature. Man's hunger, divided to serve both his physical and spiritual needs, created on the continent of North America a civilization that was similarly divided because it offered tempting satisfactions on both the higher and the lower levels. The chance to create a new order that would reflect divine goodness was made to seem possible by an infinity of

material resources which could as well feed the lowest desires. Perhaps in the beginning of American civilization can be found a clue to the incongruous mixture of naive idealism and crude materialism that produced in later years a literature of beauty, irony, affirmation, and despair. The violence of twentieth-century American literature owes much to the energy and the contrasts in its cultural origins" (16).

2. Clarence H. Faust and Thomas H. Johnson. eds. *Jonathan Edwards: Representative Selections, with Introduction, Bibliography, and Notes* (New York, 1962), 69.

3. Brooks. *America's Coming of Age*, 9.

4. See F. O. Matthiessen. *American Renaissance, Art and Expression in the Age of Emerson and Whitman* (London, 1941), 65, 66; and Marcus Cunliffe. *The Literature of the United States* (Baltimore, Maryland, 1967), 27.

5. See A. N. Kaul. *The American Vision, Actual and Ideal Society in Nineteenth-Century Fiction* (New Haven, 1963), 18-27; and Edwin S. Fussell. *Frontier. American Literature and the American West* (Princeton, New Jersey, 1965), 6-7.

Chapter 3 American Romanticism • Irving • Cooper

1. See Harry Hayden Clark. *Transitions in American Literary History* (New York, 1967; hereafter shortened as *Transitions*), 178-180; and Norman Foerster. ed. *Reinterpretations* (New York, 1982), 115-118.

2. See Clark. *Transitions*, 199-220.

3. D. H. Lawrence. *Studies in Classic American Literature* (New York, 1960), 1.

4. See also Robert Spiller. *The Cycle of American Literature*, 29-105.

5. Fred Lewis Pattee. *The Development of the American Short Story* (New York, 1966). Also see R. M. Aderman. ed. *Irving Reconsidered: A Symposium* (1969) and *Critical Essays on Washington Irving* (1990); Andrew B. Myers. ed.

A Century of Commentary on the Works of Irving (1976).

6. Arthur Hobson Quinn. *American Fiction: An Historical and Critical Survey* (New York, 1936), 45.

7. Henry Nash Smith. *Virgin Land: The American West as Symbol and Myth*, 220.

8. Edwin S. Fussell. *Frontier: American Literature and the American West*, 28.

9. See Smith. *Virgin Land*, 59-69, 212-223; and also Robert H. Zoollner. "Conceptual Ambivalence in Cooper's Leatherstooking." *American Literature* 4 (January, 1960), 397-420; A. N. Kaul. *The American Vision, Actual and Ideal Society in Nineteenth-Century Fiction*, 125-127.

10. D. H. Lawrence. *Studies in Classic American Literature*, 54.

11. Mark Twain. "Fenimore Cooper's Literary Offences." George McMichael, et al. eds. *Anthology of American Literature*. 2 Vols. 2nd Ed. (New York, 1980), II, 525. For further reading on Cooper, see William P. Kelley. *Plotting America's Past, Fenimore Cooper and the Leatherstocking Tales* (Carbondale, IL, 1983); and George Dekker. *The American Historical Romance* (Cambridge, MA, 1987).

Chapter 4　New England Transcendentalism •
Emerson • Thoreau

1. Feidelson. *Symbolism and American Literature*, 99-101; see also J. B. Moore. "Thoreau Rejects Emerson." *American Literature* IV (November, 1932), 243. See also Larzar Ziff. *Literary Democracy, The Declaration of Cultural Independence in America*. New York: Viking Press, 1981.

2. Milton R. Konvitz. ed. *Emerson, A Collection of Critical Essays* (Englewood Cliffs, NJ, 1962), 3; Myerson and Robert E. Burkholder. eds. *Critical Essays on Emerson* (1983); and Myerson Burkholder. ed. *Emerson and Thoreau: The Contemporary Reviews* (1992).

3. Konvitz. *Emerson*, 60.

4. Konvitz. *Emerson*, 4.

5. See F. O. Matthiessen. *American Renaissance*, 24; H. H. Clark. *Transitions*, 311; and Daniel Aaron. *Men of Good Hope* (New York, 1961), 8-13.

6. See R. P. Adams. "Emerson and the Organic Metaphor." In Ray Browne and Martin Light. *Critical Approaches to American Literature* (New York, 1965), 162; Everett Carter. *The American Idea* (Chapel Hill, 1977), 82; and H. H. Clark. *Transitions*, 295.

7. See Newton Arvin. "The House of Pain, Emerson and The Tragic Sense." *The Hudson Review* 12.1 (Spring, 1959), 37-53; Mildred Silver. "Emerson and the Idea of Progress." *American Literature* XII (March, 1940), 1-19; F. I. Carpenter. *Emerson Handbook*, 143-152; *Emerson, Critical Essays*, 47; and Yvor Winters. *In Defence of Reason* (New York, 1937), 262-282.

8. John Brown (1800-1859), a white fighter against slavery, who was hanged after his attempt to capture a government weapons store failed. He became an inspiration to some American authors like Thoreau and Carl Sandburg.

9. F. O. Matthiessen. *American Renaissance*, 92.

10. Marcus Cunliffe. *The Literature of the United States* (Baltimore, Maryland, 1954; rpt. 1967), 101.

11. Joseph Lawrence Basile. "Narcissus in the World of Machines." *The Southern Review* 12 (Winter 1976), 122-132.

12. In his essay, "Henry David Thoreau," in *Major American Authors*, Kenneth S. Lynn notes that throughout the book of *Walden*, Thoreau glorifies poverty. Also see Leo Stoller. "Thoreau's Doctrine of Simplicity." In *Thoreau, A Collection of Critical Essays* (Englewood Cliffs, NJ, 1963), 37-52. See also Kenneth Walter Cameron. *Thoreau's Doctrine of Simplicity* (1997); and Henry S. Salt. *Life of Henry David Thoreau* (1993).

13. Cunliffe. *The Literature of the United States*, 100.

14. See, among others, Jeffrey M. Jeske. "Walden and the Confucian *Four*

Books." *American Transcendental Quarterly* 24.1 (Fall, 1974), 29-33; and Yao-xin Chang, "Confucian Influence in Emerson, Thoreau, and Pound." Philadelphia, Temple University, 1984, 172-213.

Chapter 5   Hawthorne • Melville

1. Hubert Hoeltje. "Hawthorne, Melville, and 'Blackness.'" *American Literature* 37-1 (March, 1965), 41-51.

2. R. W. B. Lewis. *The American Adam*, 122.

3. See Harry Levin. ed. and introd. *The Scarlet Letter* (Boston, 1969), X. Also see Sacvan Bercovitch. *The Office of The Scarlet Letter* (Baltimore, 1991); Richard H. Millington. *Practicing Romance, Narrative Form and Cultural Engagement in Hawthorne's Fiction* (Princeton, NJ, 1992); Michael Dunne. *Hawthorne's Narrative Strategies* (Jackson, MS, 1995); and Charles Swann. *Nathaniel Hawthorne, Tradition and Revolution* (Cambridge, MA, 1991).

4. Arthur Hobson Quinn. *American Fiction, An Historical and Critical Survey*, 134.

5. Quinn. *American Fiction*, 139-143.

6. Henry James. *Hawthorne* (London, 1902), 183.

7. Richard Chase. *The American Novel and Its Tradition*, 92.

8. D. H. Lawrence. *Studies in Classic American Literature*, 147.

9. See James E. Miller, Jr. *A Reader's Guide to Herman Melville* (New York, 1962), 107; Howard P. Vincent. ed. *The Merrill Studies on Moby-Dick* (Columbus, 1969), 57; and James C. Wilson. ed. *The Hawthorne and Melville Friendship* (1992).

10. Richard Chase. ed. *Melville, A Collection of Critical Essays* (Englewood Cliffs, NJ, 1962), 57. See also David Reynolds. *Beneath the American Renaissance, The Subversive Imagination in the Age of Emerson and Melville* (New York, 1988); John Samson. *White Lies, Melville's Narrative of Facts* (Ithaca, NY, 1989); A. Robert Lee. *Herman Melville, Reassessments* (New

Jersey, 1984); Richard H. Brodhead. ed. *New Essays on "Moby-Dick"* (New York, 1986); John Bryant. ed. *A Companion to Melville Studies* (New York, 1986); and Clark Davis. *After the Whale: Melville in the Wake of Moby Dick* (1995).

11. Donald M. Kartiganer, and Malcolm A. Griffith. eds. *Theories of American Literature* (New York, 1972), 359.

12. Daniel Hoffman. *Form and Fable in American Fiction* (New York, 1960), 235.

13. D. H. Lawrence. *Classic American Literature*, 160.

14. Chase. ed. *Critical Essays*, 60.

Chapter 6　Whitman • Dickinson

1. See Malcolm Cowley. ed. *Walt Whitman's Leaves of Grass, The First (1855) Edition* (New York, 1959).

2. See Floyed Stovall. *The Foreground of Leaves of Grass* (Charlottesville, 1974); E. Greenspan. *Cambridge Companion to Walt Whitman* (1995); and D. Reynolds. *Walt Whiman's America, A Cultural Biography* (1995).

3. Gay Wilson Allen. *Walt Whitman Handbook* (1946). Also see his *A Reader's Guide to Walt Whitman* (New York, 1970), and *The Solitary Singer, A Critical Biography of Walt Whitman* (New York, 1967); Gay Wilson Allen and Charles T. Davis. eds. *Walt Whitman Poems* (Washington Square, New York, 1955); T. Nathanson. *Whitman's Presence, Body, Voice, and Writing in Leaves of Grass* (1992); and J. Loving. *Walt Whitman, The Song of Myself* (1999).

4. James E. Miller, Jr. *A Critical Guide to Leaves of Grass* (Chicago, 1957), 36-51; For the analysis of some Whitman poems that follows, I am indebted to this Guide of Miller's.

5. M. L. Rosenthal. *A Primer of Ezra Pound* (New York, 1960); B. Erkkila and J. Grossman. *Breaking Ground* (1996); E. Folsom and Gay Allen. eds. *Walt Whitman and the World* (1995); and R. Martin. ed. *The Continuing Presence of*

Walt Whitman (1992).

6. See George F. Whicher. *This Was a Poet, A Critical Biography of Emily Dickinson* (New York, 1939; rpt. 1957); and R. Sewall. *The Life of Emily Dickinson* (1974).

7. See Thomas E. Johnson. *Emily Dickinson, An Intepretative Biography* (Cambridge, MA, 1955); D. Porter. *Dickinson, The Modern Idiom* (1981); P. Ferlazzo. ed. *Critical Essays on Emily Dickinson* (1984); and B. Doriani. *Emily Dickinson, Daughter of Prophecy* (1996).

8. See Ruth Miller. *The Poetry of Emily Dickinson* (Connecticut, 1968).

9. See Richard Chase. *Emily Dickinson* (Toronto, 1951); J. Guthrie. *Emily Dickinson's Vision* (1998); H. Bloom. ed. *Emily Dickinson* (1999); and G. Grabber. ed. *The Emily Dickinson Handbook* (1998).

10. R. N. Linscott. ed. and introd. "Introduction." *Selected Poems and Letters of Emily Dickinson* (New York, 1959).

Chapter 7   Edgar Allan Poe

1. Robert Regan. ed. *Poe: A Collection of Critical Essays* (Englewood Cliffs, 1967), 147; M. Bonaparte. *The Life and Works of Edgar Poe, A Psychoanalytic Interpretation* (1949); J. Hammond. *An Edgar Allan Poe Companion* (1981); I. Walker. ed. *Edgar Allan Poe, The Critical Heritage* (1986); E, Carlson. ed. *Critical Essays on Poe* (1987); Kenneth Silverman. *Edgar Allan Poe* (1991); and K. Siverman. ed. *New Essays on Poe's Major Tales* (1993); *The Poe Encyclopedia* (1997).

2. See Maureen Cobb Mabbot. "Reading The Raven." *The University of Mississippi Studies in English* 3 (1982), 96-101. Poe was proud of his masterpiece which he read in public on quite a few occasions.

3. See Edward H. Davidson. *Poe, A Critical Study* (Cambridge, MA, 1957); Maurice Beebe. "The Universe of Roderick Usher." In *Poe, A Collection of Critical Essays*, 121-133; and Richard Wilbur. "The House of Poe." *Anniversary*

Lectures (Washington D.C., 1959), 24-31.

4. Shen Ning, and Donald B. Stauffer. "Poe's Influence on Modern Chinese Literature." *The University of Mississippi Studies in English* 3 (1982), 155-182.

Chapter 8   The Age of Realism • Howells • James

1. See Chapter XXII, *Virgin Land, The American West as Symbol and Myth* by Henry Nash Smith (Cambridge, MA, 1950).

2. Everett Carter. *Howells and the Age of Realism* (Hamden, Connecticut, 1966); and Michael Davitt Bell. *The Problem of American Realism, Studies in the Cultural History of a Literary Idea* (Chicago, 1993).

3. Donald Pizer. *Realism and Naturalism in Nineteenth-Century American Literature* (Carbondale and Edwardsville, 1966).

4. Donald Pizer. "The Ethical Unity of *The Rise of Silas Lapham*." In *Critics on William Dean Howells, Readings in Literary Criticism*. Ed. Paul A. Eschholz (Coral Gables, FL, 1975), 82; and also Alfred Habeggar. "The Autistic Tyrant, Howell's Self-Sacrificial Woman and Jamesian Renunciation." *Novel, A Forum on Fiction*, 10.1 (Fall, 1976), 28.

5. David L. Frazier. "Howell's Symbolic Houses, The Plutocrats and Palaces." *American Literary Realism* 10.3 (Summer, 1977), 272. Also see Donald E. Pease. ed. *New Essays on "The Rise of Silas Lapham"* (1991).

6. George McMichael, et al. eds. *Anthology of American Literature*. 2 Vols. 2nd Ed. (New York, 1980), II, 579.

7. Oscar Cargill. "Henry James' Moral Policeman, William Dean Howells." *American Literature* 29.4 (Jan., 1958), 371-398.

8. See, among other studies, William Stowe. "Intelligibility and Entertainment, Balzac and Henry James." *Comparative Literature* 35.1 (Winter, 1983), 55-69; and David Gervais. *Flaubert and Henry James* (London, 1978).

9. See Daniel Mark Fogel. *Henry James and the Structure of the Romantic Imagination* (Baton Rouge, 1981); Harold Bloom. ed. *Henry James's "The*

Ambassadors", Modern Critical Interpretations (New York, 1988); and James W. Gargano. ed. *Critical Essays on Henry James, The Late Novels* (Boston, 1987).

10. Leon Edel. *The Modern Psychological Novel* (New York, 1964), 35-52.

11. See F. O. Matthiessen. *Henry James, The Major Phase* (New York, 1964); F. W. Dupee. ed. *The Question of Henry James* (New York, 1945); Oscar Cargill. *The Novels of Henry James* (New York, 1961); Daniel Mark Fogel. ed. *A Companion to Henry James' Studies* (Connecticut, 1993); Millicent Bell. *Meaning in Henry James* (Cambridge, MA, 1991); Virginia Llewellyn Smith. *Henry James and the Real Thing, A Modern Reader's Guide* (New York, 1994); and Julie Rivkin. *False Positions, The Representational Logics of Henry James' Fictions* (Stanford, CA, 1996).

Chapter 9   Local Colorism • Mark Twain

1. See Walter Blair. *Native American Humor* (San Francisco, 1960), 124-147; and Henry B. Wonham. *Mark Twain and the Art of the Tall Tale* (New York, 1993).

2. See Howard Mumford Jones and Walter B. Rideout. eds. *Letters of Sherwood Andersen* (Boston, 1953), 32-33; Van Wyck Brooks. *The Ordeal of Mark Twain* (New York, 1920), 121-124; and Guy Cardwell. *The Man Who Was Mark Twain, Images and Ideologies* (New Haven, 1991).

3. See, among others, Susan K. Harris. *Mark Twain's Escape from Time, A Study of Patterns and Images* (Columbia, 1982); and Henry Nash Smith. *Mark Twain's Fable of Progress, Political and Economic Ideas in A Connecticut Yankee* (New Brunswick, 1964).

4. Donald M. Kartiganer and Malcolm A. Griffin. eds. *Theories of American Literature* (New York, 1972), 388.

5. Justin Kaplan. *Mr. Clemens and Mark Twain, A Biography* (New York, 1966).

6. Bernard DeVoto. *Mark Twain's America* (New York, 1932).

7. Walter Blair. *Mark Twain and Huck Finn* (Berkeley, 1962). The writer of the present lecture on Mark Twain is deeply indebted to this perceptive study of Mark Twain and his masterpiece, and also to R. C. Cosbey whose lecture on *Huck Finn* proved highly stimulating. See also Shelley Fisher Fishkin. *Was Huck Black? Mark Twain and African American Voices* (New York, 1993); and Shelley Fisher Fishkin. ed. *Lighting Out for the Territory, Reflections on Mark Twain and American Culture* (New York, 1996).

8. See note 2 above.

9. Lionel Trilling. *The Liberal Imagination* (New York, 1950), 113-117.

10. For the exposition here, see Everett Carter. *Howells and the Age of Realism*; Donald Pizer. *Realism and Naturalism in Nineteenth-Century American Literature*.

11. Richard Bridgman. *The Colloquial Style in America* (London, 1966), 195-232.

12. Philip S. Foner. *Mark Twain, Social Critic* (New York, 1958), 309.

13. Quoted in Foner. *Mark Twain*, 259.

14. Foner. 313.

Chapter 10   American Naturalism •
Crane • Norris • Dreiser • Robinson

1. For the exposition here see, among others, R. W. Horton. *Backgrounds of American Literary Thought* (Englewood Cliffs, NJ, 1974), 260-268.

2. Everett Carter. "Realism to Naturalism." In Donald M. Kartiganer and Malcolm A. Griffith. eds. *Theories of American Literature*, 394-405.

3. See Lars Ahnebrink. *The Beginnings of Naturalism in American Fiction, A Study of the Works of Hamlin Garland, Stephen Crane, and Frank Norris with Special Reference to Some European Influences* (New York, 1961).

4. See Daniel Hoffman. *Form and Fable in American Fiction* (New York,

1965).

   5. Horton. *Backgrounds*, 267-268.

   6. Joseph Conrad. "His War Book—A Preface to Stephen Crane's *The Red Badge of Courage*." In *The Idea of an American Novel*. eds. Louis D. Rubin, Jr. and John Rees Moore (New York, 1961), 276-278. See also Linda H. Davis. *Badge of Courage: Life of Stephen Crane* (1997); Lee Clerk Mitchell. *New Essays on The Red Badge of Courage* (1986); and Donald Pizer. ed. *Critical Essays on Crane* (1990).

   7. Frank Norris. *The Octopus* (New York, 1964), 405. See also Donna A. Danielewski. *A Biography of Frank Norris* (1997); and Lawrence E. Hussman. *Harbingers of a Century: The Novels of Frank Norris* (1998).

   8. See F. O. Matthiessen. *Theodore Dreiser* (William Sloane Associates, 1951), 206-207; Robert E. Spiller. *The Cycle of American Literature, An Essay in Historical Criticism*, 175; Louis J. Zanine. *Mechanism and Mysticism, The Influence of Science on the Thought and Work of Theodore Dreiser* (PA, 1993); Donald Pizer. ed. *New Essays on "Sister Carrie"* (MA, 1991); and Donald Pizer. *The Novels of Theodore Dreiser, A Critical Study* (Minneapolis, 1976).

   9. Marcus Cunliffe. *The Literature of the United States*, 211.

   10. Leslie A. Fiedler. *Love and Death in the American Novel*, 242.

   11. Charles Walcutt. "Theodore Dreiser and the Divided Stream." In A. Walton Litz. ed. *Modern American Fiction* (New York, 1963), 49.

   12. Everett Carter. "Realism to Naturalism." In *Theories of American Literature*, 402.

   13. See Donald Pizer. *Realism and Naturalism in Nineteenth-Century American Literature*.

   14. See Lionel Trilling. "Reality in America." In *The Liberal Imagination* (New York, 1940), 10-18; Donald Heiney. *Recent American Literature* (New York, 1958), 87-89; Walter Blair. *The Literature of the United States* (Glenview, 1963), 397; and Perry Miller. *Major Writers of America*. 2 Vols (New York, 1962), II, 470.

Chapter 11   The 1920s • Imagism • Pound

1. For a full treatment of the subject, see Frederick J. Hoffman. *The Twenties, American Writing in the Postwar Decade* (New York, 1949), 275-343; and George E. Mowry. ed. *The Twenties, Fords, Flappers & Fanatics* (Englewood Cliffs, NJ, 1963).

2. J. Isaacs. *The Background of Modern Poetry* (New York, 1952), 37.

3. William Pratt. *The Imagist Poem, Modern Poetry in Miniature* (New York, 1963), 24.

4. For an exhaustive treatment of the subject see Stanley Coffman. *Imagism, A Chapter/or the History of Modern Poetry* (Norman, 1951).

5. Isaacs. 45.

6. Pratt. 29.

7. Hoffman. 209.

8. *Make It New, Essays by Ezra Pound* (New Haven, 1935), 253.

9. Walter Sutton. ed. *Ezra Pound, A Collection of Critical Essays* (Englewood Cliffs, NJ, 1963), 91; see also D. Davie. *Studies in Ezra Pound* (1992); M. Kayman. *The Modernism of Ezra Pound* (1986); C. Terrell. *A Companion to the Cantos of Ezra Pound* (1980); and H. Carpenter. *A Serious Character, The Life of Ezra Pound* (1988).

10. Ezra Pound. *Selected Prose 1909-1965*. Ed. William Cookson (New York, 1970), 77.

11. Ezra Pound. *Guide to Kulchur*, 79.

12. D. D. Paige. ed. *The Letters of Ezra Pound, 1907-1941* (New York, 1950), 217.

13. See also M. L. Rosenthal. *Modern Poets, A Critical Introduction* (New York, 1960), 61-66; and R. Bush. *The Genesis of Pound's Cantos* (1976).

14. Hugh Kenner. *The Poetry of Ezra Pound* (Norfolk, 1968), 50.

15. Pound. *Selected Prose*, 77.

16. See, among others, M. B. Quinn. *Ezra Pound, An Introduction to the Poetry* (New York, 1972), 128.

17. Van Wyck Brooks. introd. *Writers at Work, The Paris Review Interviews, Second Series* (New York, 1963), 58.

18. Pound. *Critical Essays*, 91.

19. I am happy to note that Hugh Kenner holds a similar view on the subject (*The Poetry of Ezra Pound*, 286).

Chapter 12   T. S. Eliot • Stevens • Williams

1. Robert Spiller. *The Cycle of American Literature*, 211.

2. See Warren French. ed. *The Twenties, Fiction, Poetry, Drama* (Deland, Florida, 1975).

3. Grover Smith. *T. S. Eliot's Poetry and Plays, A Study in Sources and Meaning* (Chicago, 1950), 15-20; F. Pinion. *A T. S. Eliot Companion* (1988); T. Sharpe. *T. S. Eliot, A Literary Life* (1992); Anthony David Moody. *Tracing T. S. Eliot's Spirit: Essays on His Poetry and Thought* (1996); and Gareth Reeves. *T. S. Eliot's The Waste Land* (1994).

4. Donald J. Gray and G. B. Tennyson. eds. *Victorian Literature, Poetry* (New York, 1976), 212.

5. See T. S. Eliot. *Selected Essays* (New York, 1932), 117; T. S. Eliot. *The Literary and Social Criticism* (1971).

6. Smith. *T. S. Eliot's Poetry and Plays*, 69.

7. Jessie L. Western. *From Ritual to Romance* (New York, 1920), 172-174; J. Bentley. *Reading the Waste Land* (1990).

8. See William Van O'Connor. *Sense and Sensibility in Modern Poetry* (Chicago, 1948); David Perkins. *A History of Modern Poetry* (1987); H. Gardener. *The Composition of "Four Quartets"* (1977).

9. For the discussion of Wallace Stevens, see, among others, Robert Buttel. *Wallace Stevens, The Making of Harmonium* (Princeton, 1967); John J. Enck.

Wallace Stevens, Images and Judgments (New York, 1964); Marie Borroff. ed. *Wallace Stevens, A Collection of Critical Essays* (Englewood Cliffs, 1963); J. Carroll. *Wallace Stevens' Supreme Fiction, A New Romanticism* (1987); S. Axelrod and H. Deese. *Critical Essays on Wallace Stevens* (1988); A. Filreis. *Wallace Stevens and the Actual World* (1991); G. McLeod. *Wallace Stevens and Modern Art* (1993); J. McCann. *Wallace Stevens Revisited* (1995); and A. Whiting. *The Never-Resting Mind* (1996).

10. Frederick J. Hoffman. *The Twenties,* 162-165.

11. William Carlos Williams. "Authors Note." *Paterson* (New York, 1946); S. Axelrod. ed. *Critical Essays of William Carlos Williams* (1995); R. Doyle. *William Carlos Williams and the American Poem* (1982); and D. Markos. *Ideas in Things, The Poems of William Carlos Williams* (1994).

12. Daniel Hoffman et al. eds. *Harvard Guide to Contemporary American Writing* (Cambridge, MA, 1979), 453. See also C. McGowan. *William Carlos Williams' Early Poetry, The Visual Arts* (1987); and J. Mazzaro. *William Carlos Williams, The Later Poems* (1973).

Chapter 13   Frost • The Chicago Renaissance • Sandburg • Cummings • Hart Crane • Moore

1. For the discussion of Robert Frost, see, J. N, Cox. ed. *Robert Frost, A Collection of Critical Essays* (Englewood Cliffs, 963); P. Gerber. *Critical Essays on Robert Frost* (1984); Lawrence Thompson. *Robert Frost, The Early Years, 1874-1915* (New York, 1966); Lawrence Thompson and R. Wirinick. *Robert Frost, The Years of Triumph* (1970), and *Robert Frost, The Later Years* (1976); J. F. Lynen. *The Pastoral Art of Robert Frost* (New Haven, 1960); Richard Poirier. *Robert Frost. The Work of Knowing* (1977); W. Prichard. *Frost, A Literay Life Reconsidered* (1984); J. Parini. *Robert Frost, A Life* (1999); J. Meyer. *Robert Frost, A Biography* (1996); M. Marcus. *The Poems of Robert Frost* (1991); and M. Richardson. *The Ordeal of Robert Frost* (1997).

2. For Carl Sandburg, see Bruce Weirick. *From Whitman to Sandburg in American Poetry* (New York, 1928); Karl Delzer. *Curl Sandburg, A Study in Personality and Background* (New York, 1941); Richard Crowder. *Carl Sandburg* (New York, 1964); Joseph Haas. *Carl Sandburg* (New York, 1967); P. Niven. *Carl Sandburg, A Biography* (1991); N. Callahan. *Carl Sandburg, His Life and Works* (1988); and P. Yannella. *The Other Carl Sandburg* (1996).

3. For the discussion of E. E. Cummings I have followed the introductions by George James Firmage and Richard S. Kennedy in *Etcetera, The Unpublished Poems of E. E. Cummings* (New York, 1973). For further reading, see Charles Norman. *The Magic Maker, E. E. Cummings* (New York, 1964); Norman Friedman. *e. e. cummings, The Growth of a Writer* (Carbondale, 1964); Richard Kennedy. *Dreams in the Mirror, A Biography of E. E. Cummings* (1980); Richard Kennedy. *E. E. Cummings Revisited* (1993); Richard Kidder. *E. E. Cummings, An Introduction to the Poetry* (1979); N. Friedman. *(Re)Valuing Cummings* (1996).

4. See B. Weber. *Hart Crane, A Biographical and Critical Study* (1948; rpt. 1970); D. Clark. ed. *Critical Essays on Hart Crane* (1982); P. Giles. *Hart Crane, The Contexts of "The Bridge"* (1985); W. Berthoff. *Hart Crane, A Re-Introduction* (1989).

5. See C. Tomlinson. ed. *Marianne Moore, A Collection of Critical Essays* (1969); Harold Bloom. ed. *Marianne Moore* (1987); C. Molesworth. *Marianne Moore, A Literary Life* (1990); and L. Leavell. *Marianne Moore and the Visual Arts* (1995).

Chapter 14   Fitzgerald • Hemingway

1. For the discussion of Fitzgerald and Hemingway I am indebted in some sections to R. C. Cosbey's lectures.

2. Arthur Mizener. *The Far Side of Paradise, A Biography* (Boston, 1951); and J. Meyers. *Scott Fitzgerald, A Biography* (1993).

3. Andrew W. Turnbull. *Scott Fitzgerald* (New York, 1962).

4. Sheilan Graham. *The Real F. Scott Fitzgerald, Thirty Years Later* (New York); and A. Latham. *Crazy Sundays, F. Scott Fitzgerald in Hollywood* (1971).

5. Henry Dan Piper. *F. Scott Fitzgerald, A Critical Portrait* (New York,1965).

6. See James E. Miller, Jr. *F. Scott Fitzgerald, His Art and His Technique* (New York, 1964); Douglas Taylor. "*The Great Gatsby,* Style and Myth." In Max Westbrook. ed. *The Modern American Novel, Essays in Criticism* (New York, 1966), 57-67; S. Donaldson. *Fool for Love, F. Scott Fitzgerald* (1983); and R. Roulston and H. Roulston. *The Winding Road to West Egg* (1995).

7. T. S. Eliot. "Letter to Scott Fitzgerald." In Fitzgerald. *The Crack-Up*, 310.

8. For Hemingway's life see, among others, Philip Young. *Ernest Hemingway, A Reconsideration* (New York, 1967); Carlos Baker. *Ernest Hemingway, A Life Story* (New York, 1969); J. Mellow. *A Life Without Consequences* (1994); and M. Reynolds. *Hemingway, The American Homecoming* (1992).

9. J. Frederick Hoffman. *The Twenties*, 67-77.

10. Alfred Kazin. *On Native Grounds, An Interpretation of Modern American Prose Literature* (New York, 1942).

11. Bridgman. *The Colloquial Style in America*, 199.

12. Ernest Hemingway. *A Farewell to Arms* (New York, 1977), 133.

13. See Wirt Williams. *The Tragic Art of Ernest Hemingway* (Baton Rouge, 1981).

14. See Alfred Kazin. *Bright Book of Life, American Novelists and Storytellers from Hemingway to Mailer* (Boston, 1971); J. Benson. ed. *New Critical Approaches to the Short Stories of Ernesr Hemingway* (1990); F. Scafella. ed. *Hemingway, Essays of Reassessment* (1991); M. Mandel. *Reading Hemingway* (1995); S. Donaldson. ed. *The Cambridge Companion to Hemingway* (1996); A. E. Hotchner. *Papa Hemingway* (New York, 1966); and James Atlas. "Papa Lives." *The Atlantic* (October, 1983).

15. C. A. Fenton. *The Apprenticeship of Ernest Hemingway, The Early Years* (New York, 1954).

Chapter 15   The Southern Renaissance • William Faulkner

1. For a general discussion of Faulkner's works, see Michael Millgate. *The Achievement of William Faulkner* (New York, 1963); Edmund L. Volpe. *A Reader's Guide to William Faulkner* (New York, 1964); J. Blotner. *Faulkner, A Biography* (1974); H. Waggoner. *William Faulkner, From Jefferson to the World* (Lexington, 1959); Cleanth Brooks. *William Faulkner, The Yoknapatawpha County* (New Haven, 1963), and *Toward Yoknapatawpha and Beyond* (1978); Judith Wittenberg. *Faulkner, The Transfiguration of Biography* (Lincoln, 1979); D. Minter. *William Faulkner, His Life and Work* (1980/1997); and R. Gray. *The Life of William Faulkner* (1995).

2. See also Louis D. Rubin and Robert D. Jacobs. eds. *Southern Renaissance, The Literature of Modern South* (Baltimore, 1953), 206; J. Williamson. *William Faulkner and Southern History* (1993).

3. Alfred Kazin. "Faulkner in His Fury." In *Modern American Fiction, Essays in Criticism* (New York, 1963), 169-177; Frederick J. Hoffman. *William Faulkner* (New York, 1961); and David L. Minter. ed. *Twentieth-Century Interpretation of Light in August, A Collection of Critical Essays* (Englewood Cliffs, NJ, 1969).

4. Robert Penn Warren. ed. *Faulkner, A Collection of Critical Essays* (Englewood Cliffs, NJ, 1966); and Francis Lee Utley et al. eds. *Bear, Man, and God, Eight Approaches to William Faulkner's "The Bear"* (New York, 1971).

5. For Faulkner's women, see also David Williams. *Faulkner's Women, The Myth and the Muse* (Montreal, 1977); and D. Roberts. *Faulkner and Southern Womanhood* (1994).

6. For the discussion here I am indebted to Olga W. Vickery. "William Faulkner and the Figure in the Carpet." *The South Atlantic Quarterly* LXIII

(Summer, 1964), 318-335.

7. Olga W. Vickery. "William Faulkner and the Figure in the Carpet." 320-322; and P. Weinstein. ed. *Cambridge Companion to William Faulkner* (1995).

8. See also Dean Morgan Schmitter. ed. *William Faulkner* (New York, 1973), 14; and Olga W. Vickery. "Language as Theme and Technique." In *Modern American Fiction*, 192.

9. See, among others, Malcolm Cowley. "Introduction to the *Portable Faulkner.*" In Warren. ed. *Critical Essays*, 39-40; and R. Adams. *Faulkner, Myth and Motion* (1968).

Chapter 16   Anderson • Stein • Lewis • Cather • Wolfe

1. For the discussion of Sherwood Anderson, see Irving Howe. *Sherwood Anderson* (New York, 1966); Ray L. White. ed. *Achievement of Sherwood Anderson* (Chapel Hill, 1966); W. Rideout. ed. *Sherwood Anderson, A Collection of Critical Essays* (1976); D. Anderson. ed. *Critical Essays on Sherwood Anderson* (1981); and R. Papincheck. *Sherwood Anderson, A Study of the Short Stories* (1992).

2. Sherwood Anderson. *Winesburg, Ohio* (New York, 1960), 8.

3. Richard Bridgman. *The Colloquial Style in America,* 152-164.

4. Frederick J. Hoffman. *Gertrude Stein* (Minneapolis, 1961); James R. Mellow. *Charmed Circle, Gertrude Stein & Company* (New York, 1974); M. Hoffman. ed. *Critical Essays on Gertrude Stein* (1986); L. Ruddick. *Reading Gertrude Stein* (1990); J. Bowers. *Gertrude Stein* (1993); and Kirk Curnutt. ed. *The Critical Response to Gertrude Stein* (Westport, Connecticut, 2000).

5. For the discussion of Sinclair Lewis see Mark Schorer. *Sinclair Lewis, An American Life* (New York, 1961) and Mark Schorer. ed. *Sinclair Lewis, A Collection of Critical Essays* (Englewood Cliffs, 1962); D. J. Dooley. *The Art of Sinclair Lewis* (1967); and J. Lundquist. *Sinclair Lewis* (1973).

6. Robert Spiller. *The Cycle of American Literature,* 170. See also D.

Stouck. *Willa Cather's Imagination* (1975); B. Slote and V. Faulkner. eds. *The Art of Willa Cather* (1974); J. Woodress. *Willa Cather, A Literary Life* (1987); S. O'Brien. *Willa Cather, The Emerging Voice* (1987); J. March, et al. eds. *A Reader's Companion to the Fiction of Willa Cather* (1993); G. Reynolds. *Willa Cather in Context* (1996).

7. For the discussion of Thomas Wolfe see Elizabeth Nowell. *Thomas Wolfe, A Biography* (New York, 1960); Richard S. Kennedy. *The Window of Memory, The Literary Career of Thomas Wolfe* (Chapel Hill, 1962); L. Gurko. *Thomas Wolfe, Beyond the Romantic Ego* (1975); S. Philipson. ed. *Critical Essays on Thomas Wolfe* (1985); L. Field. *Thomas Wolfe and His Editors* (1987); and C. Johnson. *Of Time and the Artist* (1996).

Chapter 17   The 1930s • Dos Passos • Steinbeck

1. For the discussion of the 1930s see Warren French. ed. *The Thirties, Fiction, Poetry, Drama* (Deland, FL, 1967); Walter Blair. *American Literature, A Brief History* (Glenview, 1974); Walter Alien. *The Modern Novel in Britain and the United States* (New York, 1965); and Fon W. Boardman, Jr. *The Thirties, America and the Great Depression* (New York, 1967).

2. See, among others, W. M. Frohock. *The Novel of Violence in America* (1957), and S. J. Krause. ed. *Essays on Determinism in American Literature* (1964).

3. Edward R. Carson. *The Fiction of John O'Hara* (1961).

4. A. Hook. ed. *Dos Passos, A Collection of Critical Essays* (NJ, 1974); John D. Brantley. *The Fiction of John Dos Passos* (1968); I. Colley. *Dos Passos and the Fiction of Despair* (1978); John H. Wrenn. *John Dos Passos* (New York, 1961); M. Landsberg. *Dos Passos' Path to U. S. A., A Political Biography 1912-1936* (1972); T. Ludington. *John Dos Passos, A Twentieth-Century Odysseay* (1980); V. Carr. *Dos Passos, A Life* (1984); and B. Maine. ed. *Dos Passos, The Critical Heritage* (1988).

5. Edmund Wilson. "Dos Passos and the Social Revolution." In *The Shores of Light, A Literary Chronicle of the Twenties and the Thirties* (New York, 1952), 432-434.

6. Northrop Frye. *Anatomy of Criticism, Four Essays* (Princeton, NJ, 1957), 303-314.

7. Delmore Schwartz. "John Dos Passos and the Whole Truth." *The Southern Review* 4 (Autumn, 1938), 351-365.

8. See "John Steinbeck Number." *Modern Fiction Studies* (Spring, 1965); Warren French. *John Steinbeck* (New York, 1961); H. Levant. *The Novels of John Steinbeck* (1974); P. Lisca. *The Wide World of John Steinbeck* (1958) and *John Steinbeck, Nature and Myth* (1978); J. Parini. *John Steinbeck, A Biography* (1994); J. Timmerman. *John Steinbeck's Fiction* (1986); D. Noble. ed. *The Steinbeck Question, New Essays in Criticism* (1993). For the discussion of Steinbeck I am indebted in some sections to R. C. Cosbey's lectures.

9. For the discussion of *The Grapes of Wrath* here, see Max Westbrook. ed. *The Modern American Novel, Essays in Criticism* (New York, 1966), 170-193.

Chapter 18   Porter • Welty • McCullers • West • The New Criticism

1. R. Warren. ed. *Katherine Anne Porter, A Collection of Critical Essays* (1979); R. Binkmeyer. *Katherine Anne Porter's Artistic Development* (1993); and D. Harbour. ed. *Katherine Anne Porter* (1997).

2. H. Bloom. ed. *Eudora Welty* (1986); W. Turner and L. Harding. eds. *Critical Essays on Eudora Welty* (1989); J. Gretlund. *Eudora Welty's Aesthetics of Place* (1994).

3. V. Carr. *The Lonely Hunter, A Biography of Carson McCullers* (1975); H. Bloom. ed. *Carson McCullers* (1986); and V. Carr. *Understanding Carson McCullers* (1990).

4. Harold Bloom. ed. *Nathanael West* (New York, 1986); J. Martin. ed.

Nathanael West, A Collection of Critical Essays (New Jersey, 1971); Alistair Wisker. *The Writing of Nathanael West* (New York, 1990).

5. Gene W. Ruoff. "The New Criticism, One Child of the 30s that Grew UP." In Warren French. ed. *The Thirties, Fiction, Poetry, and Drama* (Deland, FL, 1967), 169-174; David Perkins. *A History of Modern Poetry, Modernism and After* (Cambridge, MA, 1987); and Mark Royden Winchell. *Cleanth Brooks and the Rise of Modern Criticism* (Charlottesville, VA, 1996).

Chapter 19   American Drama

1. C. W. E. Bigsby. *Recent American Drama* (Minneapolis, 1961); and C. W. E. Bigsby. *Modern American Drama, 1945-1990* (Cambridge, MA, 1990).

2. For the discussion of Eugene O'Neill, see John Gassner. ed. *O'Neill, A Collection of Critical Essays* (Englewood Cliffs, New Jersey, 1964); John Henry Raleigh. *Eugene O'Neill, The Man and His Works* (Toronto, 1969); E. Griffin. ed. *Eugene O'Neill, A Collection of Criticism* (New York, 1976); J. Martin. ed. *Critical Essays on Eugene O'Neill* (1984); Judith Barlow. *Final Acts* (1985); J. Stoupe. ed. *Critical Approaches to O'Neill* (1987); *Eugene O'Neill's Century* (1991); and J. Pfister. *Staging Depth* (1995).

3. Paul W. Gannon. *Eugene O'Neill's Long Day's Journey into Night* (New York, 1955).

4. See N. Benjamin. *Tennessee Williams, The Man and His Work* (1961); F. Donahue. *The Dramatic World of Tennessee Williams* (1964); E. Jackson. *The Broken World of Tennessee Williams* (1965); R. Hayman. *Tennessee Williams, Everyone Else Is an Audience* (1993); L. Leverich. *Tom: The Unknown Tennessee Williams* (1995); H. Bloom. ed. *Tennessee Williams' The Glass Menagerie* (1988); and M. Roudane. ed. *The Cambridge Companion to Tennessee Williams* (1997).

5. Robert A. Martin. *The Theater Essays of Arthur Miller* (New York, 1980); Dennis Welland. *Arthur Miller, A Study of His Plays* (London, 1979); Neil

Carson. *Arthur Miller* (London, 1982); J. Martine. ed. *Critical Essays on Arthur Miller* (1979); H. Koon. ed. *Death of a Salesman, A Collection of Critical Essays* (1983); S. Centola. ed. *The Achievement of Arthur Miller, New Essays* (1995); A. Griffin. *Understanding Arthur Miller* (1996); and C. W. E. Bigsby. ed. *The Cambridge Companion to Arthur Miller* (1997).

6. Christopher Bigsby. *Edward Albee* (1969); Richard E. Amacher. *Edward Albee* (1969); Christopher Bigsby. ed. *Twentieth Century Views Edward Albee* (1975); P. Kolin and J. Davis. eds. *Critical Essays on Edward Albee* (1986); H. Bloom. ed. *Edward Albee* (1987); and M. Roudane, *Understanding Edward Albee* (1987).

7. Ron Mottram. *Inner Landscape, The Theater of Sam Shepard* (Columbia, 1984); and Ellen Oumano. *Sam Shepard, The Life and Work of an American Dreamer* (New York, 1986).

8. Dennis Carroll. *David Mamet* (London, 1987).

9. See David Savron. *In Their Own Words, Contemporary American Playwrights* (New York, 1988).

Chapter 20 Postwar Poetry • Some Older Poets of the 1940s Generation

1. James Breslin. *From Modern to Contemporary, American Poetry, 1945-1965* (Chicago, 1984), and *The Psycho-Political Muse, American Poetry Since the Fifties* (Chicago, 1987); and David Parkins. *A History of Modern Poetry, Modernism and After* (Cambridge, MA, 1987).

2. Daniel Halpem. ed. *The American Poetry Anthology* (New York, 1975).

3. Donald M. Allen. ed. *The New American Poetry, 1945-1960* (New York, 1960).

4. For the discussion of Elizabeth Bishop, see James Longenbach. *Modern Poetry After Modernism* (New York, 1997), 22-48; Anne Stevenson. *Elizabeth Bishop* (New York, 1966); Harold Bloom. *Modern Critical Views, Elizabeth*

Bishop (1985); Bonnie Castello. *Elizabeth Bishop, Questions of Mastery* (1991); Lorrie Goldensohn. *Elizabeth Bishop, The Biography of a Poet* (1992); Bret Miller. *Elizabeth Bishop, Life and the Memory of It* (1993); Martin Bidney. "'Controlled Panic', Mastering the Terror of Dissolution and Isolation in Elizabeth Bishop's Epiphanies." *Style* 34.3 (Fall 2000), 487-513; and Donald E. Stanford. "The Harried Life of Elizabeth Bishop." *Sewanee Review* 102.1 (Winter 1994), 161-164.

    5. For Richard Wilbur, see Donald Hill. *Richard Wilbur* (New York, 1967); H. Stevens. *Richard Wilbur* (1977); Wendy Salinger. ed. *Richard Wilbur's Creation* (1983); Bruce Michaelson. *Wilbur's Poetry, Music in a Scattering Time* (1991); and William Butts. ed. *Conversations with Richard Wilbur* (1990).

    6. For John Berryman, see Harry Thomas. ed. *Berryman's Understanding, Reflections on the Poetry of John Berryman* (Boston, 1988), 29; J. D. McClatchy. *White Paper on Contemporary American Poetry* (New York, 1989), 146-182; H. Bloom. ed. *John Berryman* (1989); J. Haffenden. *John Berryman, A Critical Commentary* (1980); S. Matterson. *Berryman and Lowell, The Art of Living* (1987); P. Mariani. *Dream Song, The Life of John Berryman* (1990); and G. Arpin. *The Poetry of John Berryman* (1978).

    7. For Jarrell Randall, see M. L. Rosenthal. *Randall Jarrell* (Minnesota, 1972); S. Ferguson. ed. *Critical Essays on Randall Jarrell* (1983); W. Pritchard. *Randall Jarrell, A Literary Life* (1990); James Longenbach. "Randall Jarrell's Semifeminine Mind." *Southwest Review* (Summer 1996), 368; Alfred Corn. "Poetry's Ball Turret Gunner." *Nation* (August 1999), 31; Alan Williamson. "Jarrell, the Mother, the Marchen." *Twentieth Century Literature* (Fall 1994), 283; Brad Leithauser. "No Other Book, Randall Jarrell's Criticism." *New Criterion* (April 1999), 19; Jay Parini. "The Poet-Critic." *Wilson Quarterly* (Autumn 1999), 109; and Evelyn Toynton. "A Critic's Charmed Life." *American Scholar* (Autumn 1999), 134.

    8. For the discussion of James Merrill, see Judith Moffett. *Merrill: An Introduction to the Poetry* (1984); Guy L. Rotella. ed. *Critical Essays on James*

Merrill (1996); and Don Adams. *James Merrill's Poetic Quest* (1997).

Chapter 21   The Confessional School • The Beat Generation

1. For the appreciation of Lowell's works see, among others, J. Mazzaro. *The Poetic Themes of Robert Lowell* (Ann Arbor, 1965); T. Parkinson. *Robert Lowell, A Collection of Critical Essays* (New Jersey, 1968); I. Hamilton. *Robert Lowell, A Biography* (1982); P. Mariani. *Lost Puritan, A Life of Robert Lowell* (1994); Richard Tillinghast. *Robert Lowell's Life and Work* (1995); G. S. Axelrod and R. Deese. eds. *Robert Lowell, Essays on the Poetry* (1989); P. Hobsbaum. *A Reader's Guide to Robert Lowell* (1988); Helen Vendler. *The Given and the Made, Strategies of Poetic Redefinition* (Cambridge, MA, 1995); Ross Labrie, "Reassessing Robert Lowell's Catholic Poetry." *Renascence* 47.2 (Winter 1995), 117-133; Jeffrey Meyers. "The Mosler Safe in Lowell's 'For the Union Dead.'" *ANQ* 3.1 (January 1990), 23-25; and M. Walling. "Lowell's 'Skunk Hour.'" *Explicator* 49.2 (Winter, 1991),124-126.

2. For Sylvia Plath see N. Steiner. *A Closer Look at Ariel, A Memory of Sylvia Plath* (1973); P. Alexander. *Rough Magic, A Biography of Sylvia Plath* (1990); R. Hayman. *The Death and Life of Sylvia Plath* (1991); L. Wagner. ed. *Critical Views on Sylvia Plath* (1984); S. Van Dyne. *Revising Life, Sylvia Plath's Ariel Poems* (1993); and A. Strangways. *The Shaping of Shadows* (1998).

3. For Anne Sexton see Diane Wood Middlebrook. *Anne Sexton, A Biography* (Boston, 1991); Frances Bixler. ed. *Original Essays on Anne Sexton* (1988); Steven E. Colburn. ed. *Anne Sexton, Telling the Tale* (1988); Linda Wagner-Martin. *Critical Essays on Anne Sexton* (1989); Judith Nichols-Orians. "Sexton's 'The Farmer's Wife.'" *Explicator* 49.3 (1991), 190-194; Alex Beam. "The Mad Poets Society." *Atlantic Monthly* July/Aug. 2001, 96-104.

4. For Adrienne Rich see C. Werner. *Adrienne Rich, The Poet and Her Critics* (1988); J. Cooper. ed. *Reading Adrienne Rich* (1984); and M. Diaz-Diocaretz. *Transforming Poetic Discourse, Questions on Feminist Strategies in*

Adrienne Rich (1985).

5. J. Tytell. *Naked Angels, The Lives and Literature of the Beat Generation* (1976); P. Portuges. *The Visionary Poetics of Allen Ginsberg* (1978); B. Miles. *Allen Ginsberg* (1989); and Barry Miles. *Ginsberg, A Biography* (New York, 1989).

6. Bob Steuding. *Gary Snyder* (1976); Tim Dean. *Gary Snyder and the American Unconscious, Inhabiting the Ground* (1991); and John Halper. ed. *Gary Snyder, Dimensions of a Life* (1991).

7. H. Hix. *Understanding W. S. Merwin* (1991); C. Nelson and E. Folsom. eds. *W. S. Merwin, Essays on the Poetry* (1987); Dave Smith. ed. *The Pure Clear Word, Essays on the Poetry of James Wright* (1982); and Andrew Elkins. *The Poetry of James Wright* (1991).

Chapter 22   The New York School • Meditative Poetry •
The Black Mountain Poets

1. For the discussion of Frank O'Hara, see Marjory Perloff. *Frank O'Hara, Poet among Painters* (1977); and Brad Gooch. *City Poet, The Life and Times of Frank O'Hara* (1993).

2. For John Ashbery, see David Kermani. *John Ashbery, A Comprehensive Bibliography* (1976); David Lehman. ed. *Beyond Amazement, New Essays on John Ashbery* (1980); and Andrew Ross. *The Failure of Modernism, Symptoms of American Poetry* (1986).

3. Concerning Charles Olson, see G. F. Butterick. *A Guide to the Maximux Poems of Charles Olson* (1978); Thomas F. Merrill. *The Poetry of Charles Olson, A Primer* (1982); and Tom Clark. *Charles Olson, The Allegory of a Poet's Life* (1991).

4. For Robert Creeley, see Cynthia Dubin Edelberg. *Robert Creeley's Poetry* (1978); Carol F. Terrell. ed. *Robert Creeley, The Poet's Workshop* (1984); John Wilson. ed. *Robert Creeley's Life and Work, A Sense of Increment* (1987); and

Sherman Paul. *The Lost America of Love, Rereading Robert Creeley, Edward Dorn, and Robert Duncan* (1981).

5. For Denise Levertov, see I. Wagner. ed. *Denise Levertov, In Her Own Province* (1979); Harry Marten. *Understanding Denise Levertov* (1988); Linda Wagner-Martin. ed. *Critical Essays on Denise Levertov* (1991); and Audrey T. Rogers. *Denise Levertov's Poetry of Engagement* (1991).

Chapter 23   Postwar American Novel (I)

1. For the discussion of Saul Bellow, see Earl Rovit. ed. *Saul Bellow, A Collection of Critical Essays* (Englewood Cliffs, NJ, 1975); Stanley Trachtenberg. ed. *Critical Essays on Saul Bellow* (Boston, 1979); Daniel Fuchs. *Saul Bellow, Vision and Revision* (North Carolina, 1984); Peter Hyland. *Saul Bellow* (New York, 1992); Jonathan Wilson. *"Herzog", The Limit of Ideas* (Boston, 1990); and Gerhard Bach. ed. *Saul Bellow at Seventy-Five, A Collection of Critical Essays* (Tubingen, 1991).

2. For Norman Mailer, see Philip H. Bufithis. *Norman Mailer* (New York, 1978); Jennifer Bailey. *Norman Mailer, Quick-Change Artist* (New York, 1979); Donald Hilary Mills. *Mailer, A Biography* (New York, 1982); Peter Manso. ed. *Mailer, His Life and Times* (New York, 1985); Joseph Wenke. *Mailer's America* (New Hampshire, 1987); and Carl Rollyson. *The Lives of Norman Mailer* (New York, 1991).

3. For J. D. Salinger, see James Lundquist. *J. D. Salinger* (New York, 1979); William F. Belcher and James W. Lee. *J. D. Salinger and Critics* (California, 1962); and Norman Fruman and Marvin Laser. *Studies in J. D. Salinger* (New York, 1963).

4. For Malamud, see Edward Abramson. *Bernard Malamud Revisited* (New York, 1993); Joel Salzberg. ed. *Critical Essays on Bernard Malamud* (Boston, 1987); Leslie Fiedler and Joyce Field. eds. *Bernard Malamud, A Collection of Critical Essays* (New Jersey, 1975); and Lawrence Lasher. *Conversations with*

Bernard Malamud (Jackson, MS, 1991).

5. For John Updike, see P. Vaughan. *John Updike's Images of America* (1981); W. Macnaughton. ed. *Critical Essays on John Updike* (1982); and J. Schiff. *John Updike Revisited* (1998).

6. For John Cheever, see Samuel Coale. *Cheever* (1977).

7. For the discussion of Flannery O'Connor, see D. Eggenschwiler. *The Christian Humanism of Flannery O'Connor* (1972); M. Friedman, and B. Clark. eds. *Critical Essays on Flannery O'Connor* (1985); R. Brinkmeyer. *The Art and Vision of Flannery O'Connor* (1990); Gary Sloan. "O'Connor's 'A Good Man Is Hard to Find.'" *Explicator* 57.2 (Winter 1999), 118-120; Michael Clark. "Flannery O'Connor's 'A Good Man Is Hard to Find', The Moment of Grace." *English Language Notes* 29.2 (December 1991), 66-69; Stephen Brandy. "'One of My Babies', The Misfit and the Grandmother." *Studies in Short Fiction* 33.1 (Winter 1996), 107-117; and Mitchell Owens. "The Function of Signature in 'A Good Man Is Hard to Find.'" *Studies in Short Fiction* 33.1 (Winter 1996), 101-106.

8. For Styron, see M. J. Friedman and Irving Malin. eds. *Styron's "The Confessions of Nat Turner", A Critical Handbook* (1970); Irving Malin and Robert K. Morris. eds. *The Achievement of Styron* (1974); and James L. W. West III. *William Styron, A Life* (New York, 1998).

9. For Capote, see William L. Nance. *The Worlds of Capote* (1970).

10. For more on Philip Roth, see Sanford Pinsker. ed. *Critical Essays on Philip Roth* (Boston, 1982); John McDanniel. *The Fiction fo Philip Roth* (New Jersey, 1974); and Jay Halio. *Philip Roth Revisited* (1992).

11. For Oates, see Ellen Friedman. *Joyce Carol Oates* (1970); Joanne V. Creighton. *Joyce Carol Oates* (1979); Linda Wagner. *Critical Essays on Joyce Carol Oates* (1979); Harold Bloom. ed. *Joyce Carol Oates* (1986); and Joanne V. Creighton. *Joyce Carol Oates, The Middle Years* (1992).

12. C. Murphy. *Ann Beattie* (1986); and J. Montresor. *The Critical Response to Ann Beattie* (1993).

Chapter 24   Postwar American Novel (II)

1. See Elizabeth Deeds Ermarth. *Sequel to History, Postmodernism and the Crisis of Representational Time* (Princeton, NJ, 1992); David Harvey. *The Condition of Postmodernity, An Equiry into the Origins of Cultural Change* (Cambridge, MA, 1989); Linda Hutcheon. *The Politics of Postmodernism* (New York, 1989); and Stephen Tyler. *The Unspeakable, Discourse, Dialogue, and Rhetoric in the Postmodern World* (Madison, 1987).

2. Charles B. Harris. *Contemporary American Novelists of the Absurd* (New Haven, 1971); James Nagel. ed. *Critical Essays on Joseph Heller* (Boston, 1984); David Seed. *The Fiction of Joseph Heller, Against the Grain* (New York, 1989); and Sanford Pinsker. *Understanding Joseph Heller* (Columbia, SC, 1991); Robert Merrill. *Joseph Heller* (Boston, 1987).

3. Jerome Klinkowitz. *Vonnegut in Fact, The Public Spokesmanship of Personal Fiction* (Columbia, SC, 1998); Jerome Klinkowitz and John Somer. eds. *The Vonnegut Statement* (New York, 1973); Brad Stone. "Vonnegut's Last Stand." *Newsweek* 29 Sept. 1997, 78+; David Freeman and Sarah Schafer. "Vonnegut and Clancy on Technology." *Inc.* (November 1995), 63.

4. John Clark Pratt. ed. *One Flew Over the Cuckoo's Nest, Text and Criticism* (New York, 1973).

5. John Stark. *The Literature of Exhaustion* (1974); Joseph Waldmeir. ed. *Critical Essays on John Barth* (1980); Max Schulz. *The Muses of John Barth* (1990); and Patricia D. Tobin. *John Barth and the Anxiety of Continuance* (1992).

6. Wayne B. Stengel. *The Shape of Art in the Short Stories of Donald Barthelme* (1985); Lance Olsen. *Circus of the Mind in Motion, Postmodernism and the Comic Vision* (1990); Stanley Trachtenberg. *Understanding Donald Barthelme* (1990); Larry McCaffery. *The Metafictional Muse, The Works of Robert Coover, Donald Barthelme, and William H. Gass* (1982).

7. Edward Mendelson. ed. *Pynchon, A Collection of Critical Essays* (1978);

Richard Pearce. ed. *Critical Essays on Thomas Pynchon* (1981); Thomas H. Schaub. *Pynchon, The Voice of Ambiguity* (Urbana, IL, 1981); Patrick O'Donnell. ed. *New Essays on The Crying of Lot 49* (1991); J. Kerry Grant. *A Companion to "The Crying of Lot 49"* (Athens, Georgia, 1994); Charles Clerc. ed. *Approaches to Gravity's Rainbow* (Columbus, OH, 1983); and Steven Weisenburger. *A "Gravity's Rainbow" Companion, Sources and Context for Pynchon's Novel* (Athens, Georgia, 1988).

8. For William Burroughs, see Ted Morgan. *Literary Outlaw, Life and Times of William Burroughs* (New York, 1988); Jennie Skerl. *William S. Burroughs* (Boston, 1985); John Tytell. *Naked Angels, The Lives and Literature of the Beat Generation* (New York, 1976); Victor Bockris. ed. *With William Burroughs, A Report from The Bunker* (New York, 1981; rpt. 1996); Michael Goodman. *Contemporary Literary Censorship, The Case History of Burroughs' Naked Lunch* (New Jersey, 1981).

9. For Jack Kerouac, see Ann Charters. *Kerouac, A Biography* (San Francisco, 1973); Tim Hunt. *Kerouac's Crooked Road, Development of a Fiction* (Connecticut, 1981); Gerald Nicosia. *Memory Babe, A Critical Biography of Jack Kerouac* (New York, 1983); Carolyn Cassady. *Off the Road* (New York, 1990); Robert Holten. *On the Road, Kerouac's Ragged American Journey* (New York, 1999); Matt Theodo. *Understanding Jack Kerouac* (South Carolina, 2000); James Campbell. "Kerouac's Blues." *Antioch Review* 59.2 (Spring 2001), 451-459.

10. For the discussion of Vladimir Nabokov, see Alfred Appel, Jr. *Vladimir Nabokov, The Annotated Lolita* (New York, 1970); Julian Moynahan. *Vladimir Nabokov* (Minnesota, 1971); Brian Boyd. *Vladimir Nabokov, The American Years* (London, 1991); Ellen Pifer. *Nabokov and the Novel* (Cambridge, MA, 1980); Phyllis Roth. ed. *Critical Essays on Vladimir Nabokov* (Boston, 1984); Michael Wood. *The Magician's Doubts, Nabokov and the Risks of Fiction* (Princeton, NJ, 1995).

Chapter 25 Multiethnic Literature (I):
African American Literature

1. Spiller. *The Cycle of American Literature*, 15-16; M. Thomas Inge, et al. eds. *Black American Writers* (London, 1978); Ruth Miller. *Black American Literature 1760-Present* (New York, 1971); and Robert A. Bone. *The Negro Novel in America* (New Haven, 1965). In writing this chapter the present writer is indebted in some sections to R. C. Cosbey's lectures.

2. R. W. B. Lewis. *The American Adam*, 1-10.

3. For the discussion of Frederick Douglass, Booker T. Washington, and W. E. B. DuBois, see Langston Hughes and Milton Meltzer. *A Pictorial History of the Negro in America* (New York, 1956).

4. Margaret Perry. *Silence to the Drums, A Survey of the Literature of the Harlem Renaissance* (West Port, Connecticut, 1976); Bruce Kellner. ed. *The Harlem Renaissance, A Historical Dictionary of the Era* (1984); Amritjit Singh, et al. *The Harlem Renaissance, Reevaluations* (1989); and John E. Barsett. ed. *Harlem in Review, Critical Reactions to Black American Writers, 1917-1939* (1992).

5. James A. Emanuel. *Langston Hughes* (New York, 1967); Larry Neal. "Langston Hughes, Black America's Poet." In *American Writing Today* (1982), 77-89; Arnold Rampersad. *The Life of Langston Hughes* (1986-1988); R. Miller. *The Art and Imagination of Langston Hughes* (1989); and T. Dace. ed. *Langston Hughes, The Contemporary Reviews* (1997).

6. Richard Abcarian. *Richard Wright's "Native Son", A Critical Handbook* (1970); Yoshinobu Hakutani. *Critical Essays on Richard Wright* (1974); Edward Margolies. *The Art of Richard Wright* (Carbondale, 1969); Richard Macksey and Frank Moorer. eds. *Richard Wright, A Collection of Critical Essays* (1984); Robert J. Butler. *Native Son, The Emergence of A New Black Hero* (1991); and H. L. Gates, Jr., and K. A. Appiah. eds. *Richard Wright, Critical Perspectives*

Past and Present (1993).

   7. Ralph Ellison. *Invisible Man* (New York, 1952), 7.

   8. John Hersey. ed. *Ralph Ellison, A Collection of Critical Essays* (New Jersey, 1974); Valerie Bonita Gray. *Invisible Man's Literary Heritage* (1978); and Robert G. O'Malley. ed. *New Essays on Invisible Man* (1988).

   9. Kimberly Benston. ed. *Speaking for You, The Vision of Ralph Ellison* (Washington, D.C., 1987); Maryemma Graham and Amritjit Singh. eds. *Conversations with Ralph Ellison* (Jackson, MS, 1995); and Eric J. Sundquist. ed. *Cultural Contex for Ralph Ellison's "Invisible Man"* (Boston, 1995).

   10. See, among other studies, Fern Marja Eckman. *The Furious Passage of James Baldwin* (New York, 1966); Kenneth Kinnamon. ed. *James Baldwin, A Collection of Critical Essays* (New Jersey, 1974); Kenneth Kinnamon. ed. *New Essays on Native Son* (1987); Therman B. O'Daniel. ed. *James Baldwin, A Critical Evaluation* (Washington, D.C., 1975); Fred L. Standley and Nancy V. Burt. eds. *Critical Essays on James Baldwin* (1988); James Campbell. *Talking at the Gates, A Life of James Baldwin* (New York, 1991).

   11. Werner Sollors. *Amiri Baraka/LeRoi Jones, The Quest for a "Popular Modernism"* (1978); Lloyd Brown. *Amiri Baraka* (1980); and William J. Harris. *The Poetry and Poetics of Amiri Baraka, The Jazz Aesthetics* (1985).

   12. Marc C. Connor. ed. *The Aesthetics of Toni Morrison, Speaking the Unspeakable* (Jackson, MS, 2000); Karen Carmean. *Toni Morrison's World of Fiction* (Troy, NY, 1993); Trudier Harris. *Fiction and Folklore, The Novels of Toni Morrison* (Tennessee, 1991); Nellie Y. McKay. *Critical Essays on Toni Morrison* (1988); Carl D. Malmgren. "Mixed Genres and the Logic of Slavery in Toni Morrison's *Beloved*." *Critique* (Winter 1995), 96+.

   13. Henry Louise Gates, Jr., and K. A. Appiah. eds. *Alice Walker, Critical Perspectives Past and Present* (New York, 1993); Harold Bloom. ed. *Alice Walker* (1990); Charles J. Heglar. "Names and Namelessness, Alice Walker's Pattern of Surnames in *The Color Purple*." *ANQ* (Winter 2000), 13; and Stacie Lynn Hankinson. "From Monotheism to Pantheism, Liberation from Patriarchy

in Alice Walker's *The Color Purple*." *African American Review* (Spring 1992).

14. Daniel Hoffman. *Harvard Guide to Contemporary American Writing* (MA, 1979), 318-323.

15. Mary Jane Lupton. *Maya Angelou, A Critical Companion* (Connecticut, 1998); and Selwyn Cudjou. "Maya Angelou and the Autobiographical Statement." In Mari Evans. ed. *Black Women Writers (1950-1980), A Critical Evaluation* (1988).

16. Henry Louise Gates, Jr., and K. A. Appiah. eds. *Gloria Naylor, Critical Perspectives Past and Present* (New York, 1993).

17. Marie Evans. ed. *Black Women Writers 1950-1980, A Critical Evaluation* (1984), 48-72.

18. Robert McDowell. "The Assembling Vision of Rita Dove." *Callaloo* 9.1 (1986), 61-70; Arnold Rampersad. "The Poems of Rita Dove." *Callaloo* 9.1 (1986), 52-60; and Helen Vendler. "Rita Dove, Identity Markers." *Callaloo* 17.2 (1994), 381-398.

Chapter 26   Multiethnic Literature (II): Other Minority Groups

1. A. La Vonne Brown Ruoff and Jerry W. Ward, Jr. eds. *Redefining American Literary History* (New York, 1990).

2. Paula Gunn Allen. ed. *Studies in American Indian Literature, Critical Essays and Course Designs* (New York, 1983); Kathy J. Whitson. *Native American Literatures, An Encyclopedia of Works, Characters, Authors, and Themes* (California, 1999); Brian Swann and Arnold Krupat. eds. *Recovering the World, Essays on Native American Literature* (1987); Laura Coltelli. ed. *Winged Words, American Indian Writers Speak* (1990); Lori Lynn Burlingame. *Cultural Survival and the Oral Tradition in the Novels of D'Arcy McNickle and His Successors, Momaday, Silko, and Welch* (Dissertation, 1995); Harwig Isernhagen. *Conversations on American Indian Writing* (1999); and Alan R. Velie. ed. *American Indian Literature, An Anthology* (Norman, OK, 1979; rpt.

1991).

3. James Ruppert. *D'Arcy McNickle* (1988); John Purdy. *Word Ways, The Novels of D'Arcy McNickle* (1990); and Dorothy Parker. *Singing an Indian Song, A Biography of McNickle* (1992).

4. Matthias Schubnell. *N. Scott Momaday* (1985); Susan Scarberry-Garcia and Andrew Wiget. *Landmarks of Healing, A Study of "House Made of Dawn"* (1990); Tommy Joe Arrant. *"House Made of Dawn" and the Social Context of Contemporary Native American Literature* (1992).

5. Peter Wild. *James Welch* (1983).

6. P. Seyersted. *Leslie Marmon Silko* (1980); G. Salyer. *Leslie Marmon Silko* (1997); and H. Jaskowski. *Leslie Marmon Silko* (1998).

7. Lorena Laura Stookey. *Louise Erdrich, A Critical Companion* (1999); Peter G. Beidler. *A Reader's Guide to the Novels of Louise Erdrich* (1999); and Allan Chavkin and Nancy Feyl Chavkin. eds. *Conversations with Louise Erdrich and Michael Dorris* (1994).

8. Emmanuel S. Nelson. ed. *Asian American Novelsits, A Bio-Bibliographical Critical Sourcebook* (Connecticut, 2000); and Amy Ling, *Between Worlds, Women Writers of Chinese Ancestry* (1991).

9. Shirley Lim. ed. *Teaching Approaches to Maxine Hong Kingston's The Woman Warrior* (1991).

10. E. D. Huntley. *Amy Tan, A Critical Companion* (1998).

11. L. Duran and B. Russell. eds. *Introduction to Chicano Studies* (1973); and C. Tatum. *Chicano Literature* (1982).